STOLEN

Books by Daniel Palmer

DELIRIOUS

HELPLESS

STOLEN

Published by Kensington Publishing Corp.

STOLEN

DANIEL PALMER

KENSINGTON BOOKS
http://www.kensingtonbooks.com

KENSINGTON BOOKS are published by

Kensington Publishing Corp.
119 West 40th St.
New York, NY 10018

All Kensington titles, imprints, and distributed lines are available at special quantity discounts for bulk purchases for sales promotion, premiums, fundraising, educational or institutional use.

Special book excerpts or customized printings can also be created to fit specific needs. For details, write or phone the office of the Kensington Special Sales Manager: Kensington Publishing Corp., 119 West 40th St., New York, NY, 10018. Attn. Special Sales Department. Phone: 1-800-221-2647.

Kensington and the K logo Reg. U.S. Pat. & TM Off.

Library of Congress Control Number: 2013930815
ISBN-13: 978-0-7582-4666-0
ISBN-10: 0-7582-4666-8

First Hardcover Printing: May 2013
10 9 8 7 6 5 4 3 2 1

Printed in the United States of America

Dedicated with much love and gratitude to my mother,
Judy Palmer.

Prologue

You've reached twenty thousand feet above sea level. The sky is a color blue so deep, so rich, so damned infinite, it makes you want to weep. But your eyes are too frozen to form a single tear. You've got the best protective gear you can afford. Still, your body is chilled to the point where cold feels hot. Even though your hands are nested inside thick waterproof gloves—yes, the ones with QuickDry technology—your fingers feel like icicles. Your boots do their darndest to ward off the cold, but at this altitude you can ask for perfection and take whatever you get.

The sun taunts you. It's so close, seemingly an arm's reach away. You think it should melt the snow. Instead, its reflection is blinding. The wind kicks up as you inch higher, lashing your face with biting cold tendrils, just another reminder of your insignificance. You ignore the pain dulling your body, though it's persistent and relentless. You warm yourself by celebrating each small victory—another foot forward, a good purchase on the ice. You focus all your energy on one goal: summiting. You've done your homework. The weather looks good. You've been making great time. It's going to happen.

You think about all you've sacrificed to get here. The wife you left back home. You've been gone two months, with another week still to go. Tibet is a faraway place, but the Labuche Kang is like a planet unto itself.

People think you're crazy. Selfish, some have said. You ignore their criticisms. Your wife understands, and that's all that matters. You can stifle the itch to climb the same as you can will your heart to stop beating. You don't have a death wish. No, you have a life wish.

Up here, in the clouds, you feel your soul connected to God. You got a taste of that feeling when you were fifteen years old. Now, you're twenty-five, and the passion to climb has only intensified with the years.

You see your companions below. David Clegg, a Boston police officer seven years your senior, husband and father of two. The guy hasn't taken a vacation day in three years. That's how long he's been planning this trip. Behind David is Brooks Hall, a newly minted anesthesiologist from Acton, Massachusetts. Brooks is like you, a DINK, double income, no kids. You met Brooks through the New England Mountain Climbing School and went on several expeditions together. Brooks met Clegg after his wife's appendectomy. They got to talking post-op and discovered a shared passion for the mountains. You don't know the names of Clegg's kids but think Hall's wife is Amanda. Mostly what you've talked about is the mountain. Which route to take. How the snow is feeling. Gear. Weather patterns. Altitude adjustments. How amazing it feels to stand on top of the world.

You're climbing up the West Ridge. To reach the summit, you've got to cross a cornice ridgeline. The mountain face is a mixture of bare rock, solid ice, and powder snow. The cornice is nothing but a mass of snow sent down from the ridgeline, deposited there by fierce howling winds that blow from right to left. The elegant cantilevered structures leave a drop-off where no snow can accumulate, reminding you of ocean waves sitting atop a mountain.

You test the stability of the cornice. You think it'll hold. But just to be safe, you walk single file. You're in the lead, with Clegg and Hall tied to you by two climbing ropes to safeguard a fall. You've got hundreds of feet of ridgeline to cross. Each step is more exhausting than the last. You try to focus on the moment, not the summit, but it takes effort to concentrate.

Your legs are burning now. You're going too slowly. You know you could lose your one and only opportunity to summit. You decide to walk along the flattest part of the cornice to speed things up. If your muscles could talk, they'd thank you. The relief of a horizontal surface soon becomes addicting. Your mind tells you that it'll hold, because that's what you want to believe. You ignore the fact that the flattest part of the cornice is also the most dangerous.

One step . . . then another . . . and then . . .

The crack is loud, but partially concealed by rattling winds. Suddenly you remember being stranded in the middle of a frozen lake in March, the ice breaking all around you, and your father screaming, "Get back to shore!" Funny, your father's been dead for fifteen years, but the sound evokes that memory and his voice stays trapped inside your head. You're thinking about him when you hear an angry rumble like thunder just before the clap. You see Clegg and Hall standing still as statues. Sunglasses block their eyes, but you know they're wide and filled with fear. The rumble grows louder by the second, followed by another crack, this one even more threatening. The cornice gives way. One second Clegg and Hall are there, and the next, both are gone.

An avalanche of cascading snow drowns out their screams. You see the breach in the ridgeline, feel a powerful tug as the ropes securing you to the other climbers start to pull. The force of the two men in free fall drops you to the ground. Instinct takes over. You go into a self-arrest position, feet aimed at the breach, to keep from sliding forward. You're like a hooked fish being dragged toward the hole. Lying on your side, you've got the ice axe dug deep into the snow, but you still see the breach closing in fast. The climbing ropes skid along with an angry hiss, moving so quickly that the friction cuts a deep trench into the snow.

You're ten feet from the massive breach in the ridgeline, still sliding. If you fall through, Clegg and Hall will drop as well. Three hundred feet down a nearly vertical cliff face. Maybe it's willpower, but somehow you manage to stop your slide. Just your feet are dangling into the opening. You need to establish anchors before setting up a haul system. You flip onto your stomach, ready to get to work, but find the ropes are severely trenched. You hold your breath. There's no way to establish anchors now, not with the weight of two men pulling on trenched ropes. Your head pokes out over the lip of the breach, with only a well-planted ice axe to keep you from falling.

You see Hall and Clegg.

Clegg dressed in blue, Hall in yellow, dangling like helpless marionettes above infinity. An image you'll never forget. You try to shimmy backward, thinking you'll use brute force to pull the men up. They're screaming at you, begging for help. Their voices come at you as one, just like the wind. There's too much weight. Forget about going backward. They're pulling you down with them. Your breath catches, settling in your throat like frozen wind, because you realize at that very moment you're all going to die. It's a simple matter of physics: too much weight to pull against and seconds to decide what to do.

That's when you remember the Spyderco knife, ten-inch blade, ultrasharp, clipped to your parka. You slide farther into the opening as you unfold the knife with your teeth. Clegg and Hall can see your shoulders now. They're pleading with you not to do it. They can see the knife in your hand.

You've got to decide. Which rope to cut?

Whose life will you take to save your own?

Their desperate cries continue.

You begin to saw. It's not oxygen depletion making you sick. You pretend that you can't hear their pleas. You pretend it's not your hand doing the cutting. You slide another several inches into the void. You have one hand on your ice axe, the other cutting with the knife.

You think about your wife and how much you love her. Your heart aches for his wife, but *It's the only choice,* you say to yourself. *He has children. He's got kids.* Your knife slices the rope in two.

Instantly, the pull against you is halved. You know you're going to live. You hear the screams of a man falling. You watch as he goes from a person to a speck and vanishes into nothingness.

CHAPTER 1

Let me tell you how it feels to learn that your wife is going to die. It's like you've swallowed something bitter, something permanently stuck in your throat. In an instant, the future you've been planning together is gone. The sadness is all-consuming. Trust me, a heavy heart is more than an expression. You try to act strong, sound reassuring. You glom on to statistics, study the odds like a Vegas bookmaker. You say things like, "We can beat this thing. We're going to be the twenty-five percent who makes it."

At night, darker thoughts sneak past your mental defenses. You imagine your life after the inevitable. You think about all the holidays and birthdays that will come and go without your beloved. You cry and hate yourself because you're not the one who is dying.

My name is John Bodine. I'm twenty-nine years old. I'm married to the love of my life. And no matter what it takes, or how far I have to go, I'm not going to let her die.

Eight weeks earlier . . .

I'm like a dog. Soon as I heard the sound of keys jangling in the front door lock, my heartbeat kicked into overdrive. I got all excited. Five years of marriage hadn't dulled my pleasure. The sound of keys meant Ruby was home. I glanced at the electric stove, the only working clock within eyesight. Twenty minutes until midnight. Poor Ruby. Poor sweet, tired—no, make that utterly exhausted—Ruby. God, I was glad she was home.

I greeted Ruby in the cramped entranceway of our one-bedroom apartment with a mug of mint tea at the ready. Ruby's strawberry blond hair, cut stylishly and kept shoulder length, glistened from a light nighttime rain. She shivered off the cold and inhaled the sweet mint smell emanating from the steaming mug.

"My hero to the rescue," Ruby said.

Ruby cupped the mug in both hands and let the aroma warm her bones. She kissed me sweetly on the lips. Her eyes, the color of wan sapphires, flashed her desire for a more prolonged kiss with a lot less clothing. But her shoulders, sagging from the weight of her backpack stuffed with textbooks, told me otherwise. For an acupuncture and herbal medicine school that taught the healing arts, Ruby's education took an extraordinary physical and mental toll.

"Hold this," Ruby said. She handed me back the mug of tea, slung her backpack from off her shoulder, and then knelt down to unzip it on the floor. From within she pulled out a brown paper bag. The second I saw it, my eyes went wide.

"You went to Sinful Squares?" I asked, feeling my mouth already watering.

"That's why I left so early this morning. I'm sure you forgot, but it's your mom's birthday on Thursday. I mailed her a dozen of her favorite brownies, and it just so happens that I knew they were your favorite, too. Don't eat them all at once."

She gave me a soft kiss on the lips.

"Ruby, Sinful Squares is way out of your way. You didn't have to do that."

"Well, I love you, and I love your mom. So, happy birthday to us all."

We shared a brownie. Heaven.

"Want to watch TV?" Ruby asked.

"You know it."

We didn't have cable, way too expensive on our limited budget. We had cut back on most all expenses now that we had tuition to pay. But I like to please Ruby, so I rigged Hulu up to our thirty-inch television. Now she could watch her favorite shows anytime she wanted. Ruby didn't have much time for TV, but after a late-night study session, it helped her clear the brain, decompress.

As I expected, Ruby wanted to watch her favorite HGTV show, *De-*

signed to Sell. She sank deeply into the soft sofa cushions, almost vanishing between them. I always watched with Ruby, even though I'm an ESPN sort of guy, and this episode, one we'd never seen, featured a three-million-dollar Beverly Hills mansion in desperate need of a makeover before going on the market. Ruby spread her long and beautifully toned legs across my lap.

"Wait," I said, after watching a minute of the show. "The challenge is to redesign an enormous mansion with a few-thousand-dollar budget?"

"Yeah. Cool, isn't it?" Ruby said. Her voice drifted off, as if she was already in a dream.

"Well, it seems a little bit odd," I said. "I mean, they live in a mansion. You'd think they could spend a bit more, is all."

"That's not the point of the show. The point is to teach people how to do more with less."

"So if our one-bedroom got featured, they'd redesign it for what? Fifty bucks?"

Ruby dug her toes between my ribs until I cried out in mock pain. Actually, it felt pretty darn good.

"The show doesn't use a sliding scale, darling. And besides, our place doesn't need to be redesigned. I like it just the way it is."

"Small," I said.

"I prefer to think of it as conducive to closeness."

"Oh, in that case . . ."

I changed position and kissed Ruby, long and deep. Ruby responded in kind as best she could, but tonight her romantic mood had the life span of a mayfly.

"Baby, I want to," Ruby said. Her voice sounded as sweet as the mint tea tasted on her lips.

"All right, then, let's go," I whispered between gentle kisses planted on her freckled cheeks.

"But I need you to quiz me."

I sat up.

"Quiz you?" I said. "Ruby, it's after midnight."

Ruby surprised me by breaking into song. "And we're gonna let it all hang out," she sang.

The melody was to the tune of one of our favorite Eric Clapton covers. Ruby held up a finger for me to see. That was her way of marking the musical reference as being worth one point in our long-standing game. A point could be earned if either of us completed a song lyric, tune required, from something the other had said. We didn't keep a running tally, because it was obvious Ruby possessed an insurmountable lead. Let's just say if *Jeopardy* devoted an entire board to trivia about music and bands, she'd clear it without giving the other contestants a chance to buzz.

Ruby got off the sofa to grab her schoolbooks.

As I waited, I ran my hands through my hair, half expecting to feel the long locks I had chopped off after the Labuche Kang tragedy. A lot about my appearance had changed in the aftermath of that day. My face still looked young but had weathered, with newly formed creases and crevices, which Ruby thought made me ruggedly hand-some. My eyes had grown deeper set, too, and like mountain river streams, changed color with the day or my mood. Sometimes they were clear like a well-marked path, but at other times they'd cloud over, and Ruby would ask, "What are you thinking?" Ruby was the only person who could see through my haze, burrow into me, to get beyond the surface layers I allowed others to see. After the shock, the therapy sessions, the black depression, it was Ruby who brought me back from the brink. She held the map to my soul.

Ruby returned with backpack in hand.

"You can't really be serious about wanting me to quiz you," I said. "How can your brain even function?"

"Remember when I said that I loved how small our place is?" Ruby asked.

"Yeah."

"I lied."

"Oh."

"Well, not entirely. I do like being close to you."

"We could be closer," I said with a wink.

"Come on, baby. Just a quick quiz tonight."

I pretended to have fallen asleep, and Ruby needled me again in the ribs, this time with her fingers.

"I'm up! I'm up!" I said, feigning alertness.

Ruby ruffled through her backpack, looking for her notes, but something else caught her eye. "Oh, I almost forgot," she said. "I went to the computer lab and made you something today."

"Moi?"

Ruby removed a single sheet of paper from a folder in her backpack. It was a logo for my online game, *One World.* I loved the overall design she made, but it was the *O* in the word *One* that literally took away my breath.

She had created three concentric circles. The outer circle she rendered to look like wood grain, the next circle was made to look like rock, another like water, and in the center was the earth. It was astoundingly beautiful. "Professional" didn't do it justice.

"Ruby, I'm speechless. I love it."

"I'm so glad. It took me a while, but I think it came out great. What's today's number?"

"One hundred twenty-three thousand registered players."

Ruby broke into a smile. "Forget acupuncture. You're taking us to Beverly Hills, baby!"

"Last I checked, mortgage companies aren't accepting future potential as a down payment on a mansion. I really need closer to a million registered players before I can start touting my rags-to-riches story."

"I believe in you, John. I know it's going to happen."

I made a "Who knows?" shrug.

With a hundred thousand registered players, I should be rolling in the dough. Only, I didn't charge people to play. I'd basically built *FarmVille* meets *Minecraft.* It's an eco-conscious game, which takes longer to build a loyal enough following to start charging a fee. Like a lot of game designers, I make my money selling virtual items that enhance the game play. After expenses, I cleared about fifty thousand dollars, most of which got reinvested back into the business. In addition to Ruby's tuition, we have other expenses to pay as well. Rent. Food. Bills. Insurance. All the usual suspects. Hence, no cable.

"I'm glad you like the logo," Ruby said.

"I don't just like it. I love it. It goes live tomorrow."

"Good. I'm going to get something to drink before we start. Want anything?"

"No," I said.

I watched her go. Hard not to. I felt like yelling out that I was the luckiest man alive, only Ruby didn't believe in luck.

A few years back, Ruby hung a vision board on our bedroom wall.

The vision board was a three-foot-by-three-foot corkboard, covered with a purple silk cloth—for prosperity—and decorated with images and words that conveyed our shared desires. Ask and the universe will provide, at least that's what Ruby believed. I believe in relying on yourself to solve your own problems. The mountain has a cold and angry way of reinforcing that kind of thinking.

Still, Ruby pleaded with me to ask the universe to make *One World* a smash success. I thought it was silly at first, but I relented—Ruby's hard to refuse, especially when pleading—and so I tacked up the logo of a prominent gaming blog onto the vision board. A few weeks later, I got a five-star review. Did I think the universe had answered my wishes? No, not in the least. Coincidence? Sure. Now, that's something I can believe in. I have a degree in computer science from Boston University, so logic is the ruler of my world. Trusting in the universe is a heartwarming idea, but I'm a bigger believer in hard work, determination, and a sprinkle of talent.

A game designer needs to understand computers the way a general contractor must know all facets of building a house, which is why it took a team of people to put my game together, but now I manage the code and servers on my own. Anyway, the bloggers seemed to like the idea behind the game. Players are tasked with building the coolest, biggest, most awesome virtual world possible without pillaging *One World*'s limited resources. Oh, and you've got to do all this while battling marauding hordes of zombies, who come out only at night.

There was a time, not that long ago, I couldn't muster the energy to get out of bed. I just lay there, hearing Brooks's screams as he fell to his death. Dark years. Ruby plastered the vision board with every image of health and happiness she could find. Three weeks later, Ruby found a flyer for a local acupuncturist in the mail and urged me to give it a try. The results were so astounding that Ruby decided to quit her job as the in-house graphic designer for a finance company to concentrate on becoming an acupuncturist herself. I encouraged her to do it. We could squeak by on one income for a while. It's amazing how far a few judicious cuts can take you.

Ruby returned and got her study materials together, but I wasn't done trying to woo her into bed. I started rubbing the soles of her feet.

"Hmmmm," Ruby said. "That feels nice."

I removed Ruby's cotton socks and dug my thumbs gently against ten years of jogging calluses. Ruby cooed some more, and I kept on massaging. I thought about the number—one hundred twenty-three thousand registered players—and couldn't help but imagine how a million would alter our lives. I wondered if Ruby and I would start a family sooner than our current post-school thinking.

Brooks Hall would never have children, and I might. "Where's the fairness in that, dear universe?" I switched from the right foot to massage Ruby's left. My thumb traveled from the toes and finished at the heel. But my fingers brushed against something strange. A sensation that felt surprising to touch. I ran my thumb over the offending area again, and still again.

"Hey, the rest of my foot is getting jealous," Ruby said, shaking it.

I raised Ruby's leg and shifted position to get a better look at the underside of her foot.

"What is it?" Ruby asked. A touch of alarm seeped into her voice.

I went to the kitchen and grabbed the penlight flashlight I used to build or repair my computers. When I returned, Ruby was sitting on the floor cross-legged, examining the bottom of her foot. I got down on my knees and took a closer look with the penlight. Ruby's eyes were wide, dancing nervously. I knew she hated when I went silent on her.

"What's going on?" Ruby asked again.

"Have you seen this dark patchy area before?" I asked her. "Do you have any idea how long it's been there?"

"I'm not checking out the bottom of my foot every day, if that's what you're asking. John, you're scaring me."

"I don't like how this looks," I said.

I had reason to be concerned. Mountaineering exposed climbers like myself to a greater degree of ultraviolet radiation. I had studied up on the latest gear, lotions, and trends for delivering maximum sun protection. I had also learned to detect the signs and symptoms of skin cancer—asymmetrical growth, ragged edges, nonuniform coloration, and a large diameter. The oddly shaped mole on the underside of Ruby's foot, about the size of two pencil erasers, was far larger than the quarter-inch safety limit. What I didn't know, and what Ruby couldn't tell me, was if the area of concern had grown in size, and if so, how quickly it had evolved.

"John, you're really starting to freak me out," Ruby said, pulling her foot away from my lengthy and silent examination. "What are you thinking?"

I moved in close to Ruby, cupping her flushed cheeks in my hands.

"I think we need to call a doctor, just to be safe," I said. I made sure my voice sounded soothing. "But I also think that everything is going to be just fine."

Ruby looked me in the eyes and strained to smile.

We've been married five years, and we dated for an equal amount of time.

She could always tell when I was lying.

CHAPTER 2

"The cancer has spread."

The doctor's words hung in the air like an oppressively humid day, sucking up all the oxygen in the antiseptic examination room.

"The cancer has spread."

This was the culmination of a three-week journey that had begun with Ruby's first-ever visit to a dermatologist. The initial tests had come back positive for cancer—melanoma. Only we didn't know how bad it was or how much it had spread throughout her body. We were referred to a dermatological oncologist, who scheduled Ruby for a CT scan. Then we had to wait.

Ruby sleepwalked through the days following her initial diagnosis. We simply couldn't wrap our heads around what it really meant for our future. Make a checklist for a nervous breakdown, and we'd have all the symptoms. Panic? Sure. Crying easily? Of course. Upset stomach? Exhaustion? Check and check. We were trapped in a brutal, unrelenting anxiety loop.

"Shit, shit, shit!" Ruby would sometimes blurt out. "Shit, shit, shit!"

Dr. Lisa Adams, our pale-skinned dermatological oncologist, perhaps a decade older than Ruby, revealed the results of the CT scan without being overly emotional.

"I'm afraid there are some suspicious nodes in the groin," Dr. Adams said to Ruby.

In my mind "suspicious nodes" had the ring of a death sentence. Ruby gripped my hand tighter. The diagnosis threw me into a dull fog. I was too numb to process everything, and much of what Dr. Adams said next passed right through me.

"Unfortunately, the cancer has spread. . . . The melanoma appears to be stage three. . . . We have the results of the biopsy from the growth on your foot. . . . Cancer is caused by a BRAF gene mutation . . . treatment available . . ."

Her words tumbled about my head. I sensed the coming hurricane of information overload that would carry us off to a foreign country where we didn't speak the language—an alphabet soup of terms, treatments, and genetics.

"I'm twenty-eight years old," Ruby said to Dr. Adams. "I'm too young to have stage three cancer."

"I wish that were the case, Ruby," Dr. Adams said. "I really do."

The cancer has spread.

"Am I going to die?"

"This is a treatable condition," Dr. Adams replied. "We'll start the drug treatment first and gauge how well the nodes are responding. If we do get a response, then the nodes have acted as a 'marker' that will help us determine how responsive to the drug you'll be. If you don't respond to the drugs, then a surgical procedure called a node dissection becomes essential. Surgery would likely follow even if you do respond completely to the drug, as there would likely be some microscopic cancer left in the nodes. Does that make sense?"

If it did, Ruby didn't say. She clearly had other things on her mind. "What's the survival rate? Please! Am I going to die?" Ruby's last question was punctuated by a choking sob.

I embraced my wife, shuttering my eyes to hold back my own flood of gathering tears. Ruby needed me to be strong for her, present and positive.

We were talking about the vacation we going to take once we had this thing licked. Ruby was hinting at starting a family. *Now she's asking about living—survival rates! It's not fair. No, this isn't happening to us. It's not real. This is not happening!*

"I love you," I breathed into my wife's ear.

God, I love you so much.

Adams waited for the right moment before answering Ruby's questions.

"We're going to do everything we can to make sure that doesn't happen," said the doctor. "And I'm going to help you every step of the way. The tough part is that I can't beat your cancer for you. We're going to have to battle this together."

"How did it progress so fast?" Ruby asked. "Can't we just cut it all out? How did I get it on the bottom of my foot? What's the drug treatment?"

Dr. Adams listened intently to Ruby's rapid-fire questions. She studied everything about Ruby's gestures, vocal intonation, and expressions, much like a psychotherapist conducting an assessment of a new patient. I figured that in addition to answering Ruby's specific questions, Adams needed to ascertain how much information to share and what should be revealed in future discussions.

"Unfortunately, there is no curative therapy for most metastatic cancers—that is, a cancer that has spread to other parts of the body."

"What do you mean by no curative therapy?"

"We need to focus on the containment strategy I outlined for you."

"Why?" Ruby asked, pleading really. "Why is this happening now?"

"I wish I could say, Ruby," Dr. Adams said. "Most skin cancers are not hereditary, but there are certain cases where a parent with a certain type of skin cancer increases the average risk of getting a cancer yourself. Still, I would lean toward ruling out familial melanoma—"

"My mother basically lives in the sun," Ruby said. "She's never had any problems."

"But I couldn't claim that as fact," Dr. Adams said, finishing her thought.

Adams referenced Ruby's file. I suspected she was double-checking the family history—what little Ruby knew of it, anyway. In those pages, Dr. Adams would find reference to a father who died of a heart attack when Ruby was eleven, a few uncles and aunts who suffered a variety of ailments, none of which were melanoma or cancer of any kind.

"Even with further testing, I can't promise that we'll be able to figure out if a specific environmental factor is to blame for the mutation. And speaking honestly, the *why* isn't as important right now as the *what,* meaning what we are going to do to fight your cancer?"

"I want you to tell me everything about my cancer," Ruby continued. "Don't hold back. I mean it. I want to know it all."

Ruby sounded definitive. I interpreted Dr. Adams's change of expression as one of pleasant surprise. She didn't know Ruby's fighting spirit. If one thing gave me hope, it was my wife's tenacity and willpower. Both, I believed, would be as healing as the cancer was deadly. Ruby could get a Christmas present in summertime and wait six months to open it. She can keep the one-cookie promise, and I've never once heard her hit the snooze button. Yeah, she's got willpower, all right.

Dr. Adams spoke for fifteen uninterrupted minutes. She explained the gene mutation in greater detail and walked us through the recommended course of treatment. She spent some time talking about the node dissection and what Ruby should expect after her surgery. We listened with rapt attention. My head would occasionally nod my understanding, while Ruby's didn't move.

"The drug therapy I'm going to recommend has been highly effective in treating your type of cancer."

"What's the survival rate?" Ruby asked again.

Somehow, the doctor managed to skirt that question. "I really can't say definitively," Adams replied.

"Best guess," Ruby said.

"A lot of variables go into factoring survival rates."

"The number, Doctor, please," Ruby said.

I could tell Dr. Adams swallowed this part of her job like bitter medicine.

"We think of survival rates in terms of a five-year time span," Adams said. "But this doesn't mean the patient has become cancer free within that time period. It could mean they're now disease free, or it could be they're progression free. What it means is that five years after they start treatment, they're still alive."

"My number."

"Twenty-five percent," Adams said. "If we don't start treatment right away, that number could drop precipitously."

Now it was my turn to swallow that medicine.

Twenty. Five. Stinking. Percent.

"Here's where it gets a bit tricky," Adams said, speaking in a voice that suggested "a bit" meant "a lot."

I could see that Ruby was still trying to digest the 25 percent figure.

"How could it get more tricky?" she asked.

"The generic form of Verbilifide, the drug therapy you need, is currently out of stock."

"When will it be back *in* stock?" I asked the question as if the drug were some part that could be ordered and picked up at Home Depot.

"I can't tell you that."

"What the heck! Why not?" Ruby asked.

"It's just unknown," Adams said, her voice tinged with frustration. "The manufacturer sent out an alert last month. They're way behind on supply orders. To be honest, they're not the only ones. Call any oncologist and they'll tell you that we're currently in the midst of the worst shortage of generic cancer medications that we've seen in decades. It's a historic supply crisis with tremendous repercussions for both patients and their doctors."

"What do we do?" Ruby asked. "My survival hinges on starting treatment right away!"

"Verbilifide isn't in short supply, just the generic," Dr. Adams said, sounding reassuring. "We'll have to prescribe you the brand name, that's all."

"So that's not a problem, then," I said.

"The generic costs a fraction of what Verbilifide will cost for a full course of treatment."

I asked, "Meaning?"

"Meaning it will cost around three hundred thousand dollars."

Ruby and I both looked sticker shocked. It's bad enough confronting a cancer diagnosis, but to think about the financial implications conjures up the old "insult to injury" adage.

"I guess we can't just go to CVS to pick up the drugs," I said.

Ruby laughed, which almost made me cry.

"No," Adams said. "I'll need a week to order Verbilifide from a specialty pharmacy. They'd have the drug delivered to my office, and you'll need to pick it up here. Just so I'm clear, you're not worried about the cost?"

I shrugged off the number.

"Why worry about that?" I said. "That's what health insurance is for."

CHAPTER 3

From the bedroom, which doubled as a cramped home office, I opened a Safari browser on my MacBook Pro and typed the URL for my bank's Web site. Afternoon sunlight spilled into the room from two windows, which the building's superintendent kept promising to clean, while a steady breeze fluttered the curtains, casting movable shadows on the scuffed hardwood floor. Ginger, the orange tabby cat Ruby had adopted from the ASPCA last winter, perched herself on my lap and purred her pleasure. Her head darted all about, on a mouse hunt perhaps, as we'd had quite a few recent sightings. Not that we lived in a total dive, but this wasn't the Ritz, either.

Seeing nothing of interest, Ginger opted instead to stick her head inside my water glass. Reflexively, I tilted the glass, allowing Ginger a drink, because that was what I'd done a thousand times before. Ginger had grown accustomed to drinking water out of a glass, and we hadn't the time or inclination to break her of this curious habit. Meanwhile, my left hand deftly keyed in the username and password combination for my bank account. Ruby hovered close behind, scratching Ginger's orange head while her kitty drank.

"How much is in the checking account?" Ruby asked.

I clicked. Then I clicked again.

"Two thousand," I said. "Give or take a thousand."

Ruby grimaced. "What? Why are we so low?"

"Um, let's see. We're down to one income, which after business expenses, food, taxes, car payment, my school loan, your tuition, and utilities . . . leaves us with just about zero every month."

"Oh, goodness."

Ruby didn't ask me about our savings account. She knew I had drained it long ago to climb the Kang. "Live the life you want to live today," is what Ruby always preached. It's one of the reasons I loved her so much. She didn't just support my passions—she actually got me.

Today I just wanted Ruby to live. It's funny how life gets really centered, and really quickly, too, when you're forced to confront what's truly important. Each day, each moment Ruby and I had together, her health, her comfort, that's what I cared about now. That's all I cared about. I reached over my shoulder and grabbed hold of her delicate wrist. Ginger, surprised by the sudden movement, leapt from my lap and onto the floor with a soft meow.

"Don't worry," I said. "It's going to be fine."

"Do you know how much our insurance is going to cover?"

"No. But I have a call in to Atrium. They should be calling back soon. We'll figure it all out, I promise."

Ruby sighed and flopped down on the bed—technically, just a mattress and box spring on the floor. Bed frames were for grown-ups, she once said. I admired her from my desk chair, taking in every detail like a slow, calming breath. Ruby, beautiful and lithe, fit her surroundings the way a tiger blends into the jungle. I had ceded all apartment-decorating decisions to my wife. The furniture came from various consignment shops. The color scheme, turquoise and white, evoked a feeling of living in a beach cottage, because that was where she longed to be—an ocean community, replete with artsy people who valued acupuncture and holistic healing. Clutter, she kept to a minimum. Everything about our home was peaceful, like Ruby before her disease.

"You know what's weird?" Ruby said as she gazed absently up at the cracks in the ceiling, her arms bent at the elbows, hands interlocked and resting behind her head. "I don't feel sick, just tired."

"Hopefully, after that drug, we won't have to know what cancer feels like."

Ruby sat up and got cross-legged on the bed. "That drug sounded worse than the cancer."

"That drug is the most important thing in our lives."

"Liver problems. Irregular heartbeat. Skin rashes. Upset stomach. Fuck this, John. I mean it. Fuck having fucking cancer. I can't stand it."

I got up from my chair and plunked myself down on the bed beside Ruby. I put a hand on her knee but knew not to hug her. Ruby could be like Ginger that way. At times she wanted to be petted and scratched; other times she was too prickly to be touched. But I kept my hand resting on her knee, knowing she'd eventually cave in to wanting comfort. When she fell against my chest, I wrapped her in my arms and wouldn't let go.

"Are you ready to tell your mother?" I asked, brushing Ruby's hair from her face and eyes.

Ruby pulled away and sighed. "Sure," she said, "but I'm not expecting anything."

"She might surprise you," I said.

"How? By getting sober and buying a plane ticket?"

"Something like that."

Ruby shrugged off her mother the way I had the cost of her medication.

"I won't hold my breath."

The phone call from Atrium came an hour later. Ruby was fast asleep in the bedroom, cocooned within a burrow of blankets. Ginger was nestled up next to her and making that super-loud "I'm the happiest cat in the world" purr.

The agent from Atrium, a whiny-sounding man, introduced himself as Leonard Tate. "How are you doing this afternoon?" he asked.

I thought he sounded young—maybe just a few ticks past his frat party years. I told him what was going on with Ruby and how her doctor was going to prescribe her a course of treatment for Verbilifide.

"I'm sorry to hear that," Tate said, not sounding all that sorry to me.

"I wanted to make sure that everything checks out okay for my wife's treatment as far as our insurance coverage goes before we start," I said.

"Of course," Tate said.

The line went uncomfortably silent. I could hear fingers tapping away at a keyboard. He seemed to make an impossible number of keyboard clicks for the information he'd set out to retrieve. *Clickety-clack. Clickety-clack.*

Following an interminable amount of time, Tate asked for my health insurance account numbers, which I already had given to the annoying phone tree disguised as Julie, a saccharine-sounding computerized agent who couldn't have been less helpful if she spoke only Yiddish. I didn't bother asking Tate why Julie couldn't pass along my account numbers to a living, breathing person. It's been my experience that most large companies have antiquated technologies. And Atrium, both large and anonymous, trumped all other insurance companies with the lowest customer satisfaction ranking according to Ranker.com, which compiled such lists from actual customers. The Internet was a powerful equalizer that way. If you failed to meet customer expectations, you'd be sure to hear about it. Atrium knew to offset their prickly corporate culture and rankled consumer base with the lowest rates going. The bottom line was, we couldn't afford better insurance coverage.

Tate keyed in the numbers as I read them. More silence. More fingers tapping away, but this time I could hear Tate make a couple deep sighs—disconcerting, to say the least—immediately followed by yet more finger tapping. I imagined Tate was seated inside a cubicle somewhere. Maybe he had a plant on his desk. A picture of his girlfriend, perhaps. Did this stranger understand the importance of our conversation? Did he realize lives were at stake? Could he relate to me as more than just a health insurance account number on the other end of his headset?

The answer, according to Ranker.com, left little doubt.

"So, Mr. Bodine, I've pulled up your health-care policy, and I'm afraid there's a problem with the coverage."

I felt the floor drop out from underneath me. "What do you mean, a problem? My payments are automatically deducted from my bank account," I said.

"This isn't an issue with the status of your coverage. That's not in question."

"Then what is?"

A creeping sense of dread started at my toes and began to inch its way up through my body.

"Your plan will not cover the cost of Verbilifide, because there's a generic alternative available," Tate said.

My loud and relieved sigh made Ginger look, though Ruby, still buried beneath her many blankets, didn't budge.

"For a second there I thought we were going to have a real problem," I said. "The generic drug for Verbilifide isn't available," I explained. "You can check that with Ruby's doctor if you need confirmation."

"Yes, well . . ." Tate hesitated in a way I didn't like one bit.

"Yes, well, what?" I said.

"The actual availability of the medication isn't the issue as far as our policy is concerned. Technically, there is a generic alternative."

My pulse started jackhammering away, and I knew my voice would waver if I tried to speak. I felt my face flush as I attempted to swallow down a simmering rage.

"It's not available," I said, speaking the words loudly, as if maybe that would aid his comprehension. "It's out of stock."

"Yes, well, when it gets in, it will be covered—minus your deductible, of course."

"Minus my . . . when it gets in stock . . . What . . . what are you trying to say?"

Thank goodness for cordless phones. Not wanting to wake Ruby, I left the bedroom, anticipating the volcanic eruption to come.

"I'm sorry, but this is the policy. We don't cover brand-name drugs if there is a generic alternative."

"It's not available, Mr. Tate!" I shouted into the phone, squeezing the handset so hard that my fingers ached. "How can my wife take something she can't get? Tell me, how is that possible?"

"I understand that you're upset," Tate said.

"Upset? Upset? No, upset doesn't even begin to cover it. Are you telling me that my wife and I are on the hook for a three-hundred-thousand-dollar course of treatment?"

"Unless you take the generic," Tate said.

"I can't get the generic! I can't get it! What part of 'it is not available' don't you understand? How is this not getting through to you?"

A steely bolt of anger revved inside me, threatening to explode in a vitriolic tirade unless I paced the room.

"You elected to have the most inexpensive policy," Tate said. "There are a number of constraints to your drug coverage."

"I elected to have the most inexpensive coverage because that's all I could afford. The monthly premiums are already ridiculously high. For what? What in the hell am I paying you for?"

I heard footsteps behind me and whirled at the sound. Ruby ambled out of the bedroom, wrapped in a snuggly blanket. Her hair stuck out at odd angles, and she seemed unsteady on her feet. I cupped the receiver with my hand.

"What's going on?" she croaked out.

"Nothing, babe," I said. "Just talking with our insurance company. Minor hiccup. I'll get it all worked out."

"Well, keep your voice down," Ruby said, feigning an irritated tone. "You've got to let a sick girl get her rest."

"I'm sorry," I said.

"So sorry that I was such a fool," Ruby sang, soft and sweetly.

She held up a finger. Another point. I recognized the melody from a classic country tune but didn't recall the artist. I smiled weakly, giving Ruby's forehead a mollifying kiss. Meanwhile, I'm thinking, *We're screwed.*

CHAPTER 4

Standing at the base of the Wilhelm Genetics skyscraper, I tingled at the thought of riding up in the glass elevator. I was sure the view of the Boston skyline from the fortieth floor would be spectacular, but there were lots of spectacular views I could no longer stomach. I had only five minutes before my appointment with Vivian Sutcliffe, director of patient access for Wilhelm Genetics, to get my nerves on.

Train delays. Damn trains.

I did everything possible to get here early enough to take the stairs. Man plans. God laughs. Still, arranging this meeting was no simple task, and I wasn't about to let a little thing like paralyzing acrophobia keep me from making the appointment on time.

My conversation with Leonard Tate, now two days in the past, deteriorated faster than a reality star's career. Tate must have said, "I'm sorry, but that's our policy," at least a dozen times before I demanded to speak to a senior customer service representative from Atrium. Then, like tag team wrestlers, it was Carlotta Duncan's turn to say, "I'm sorry, but that's Atrium's policy."

I hung up the phone, leaving the Atrium reps with the highly ineffective parting salvo, "Thanks for nothing." I couldn't think of anything more clever to say. I was too floored, too angry, too dumbfounded to speak.

Rather than stay stuck in Atrium's maddening constraints, I turned my attention to the Web, where I found a glimmer of hope in the form of Wilhelm Genetics Access Solutions program—a service for patients and their health-care providers to assist with coverage

I arrived at Sutcliffe's office breathless, my face flushed, T-shirt soaked with sweat, and heart still hammering. I took a seat in the waiting room after giving my name to the receptionist. The demure woman seated behind a glass enclosure offered me a drink of water, along with a weary assessment of my condition. I drank in slow sips while waiting ten long minutes for Sutcliffe to show. I guess only one of us cared about being punctual.

Vivian Sutcliffe, a stocky woman dressed in a plaid skirt and black turtleneck sweater, with dark hair to match, emerged through a double set of glass doors. She gave me a congenial smile that somehow conveyed sympathy. It was certainly a practiced reaction on her part, assuming most visitors came to her under the cloud of troubled circumstance.

"Mr. Bodine," Sutcliffe said, extending her hand. "I'm so sorry I'm late. Busy morning. I hope you had an easy time getting up here. Security can be pretty arduous these days."

"It wasn't a problem," I said.

"Did you love the view coming up? I never tire of it."

"I'm sure it was beautiful," I said.

Sutcliffe paused, showed some confusion in her large brown eyes, but didn't press for an explanation. I kept pace as she led me down a carpeted corridor with low ceilings, illuminated by the artificial unpleasantness of fluorescent lights. She opened the door to a conference room, motioning me to join her inside. The room itself was small, one round table and four chairs. Thankfully, no windows.

A glossy blue folder awaited me on the conference table. It was chock-full of papers and titled *Wilhelm Genetics Access Solutions*. A photograph of a well-dressed man, maybe in his early sixties, adorned the front cover. His silver hair, neatly trimmed, accentuated deep creases on his face, giving him the distinctive look of power. I thought it peculiar that Wilhelm Genetics' marketing material didn't advertise a beaming, happy family, saved by the generosity of the Access Solutions program.

It all became clear when I read the accompanying copy. The man whose face adorned the front flap of the Access Solutions folder was Manfred von Wilhelm, CEO of Wilhelm Genetics. His message to prospective consumers was simple: "Because everyone should get the medicine they need."

Sutcliffe saw me studying Wilhelm's face.

"Mr. von Wilhelm has personally donated several million dollars to our Access Solutions fund."

"Seems like a charitable guy," I said.

"Well, our job is to help families like yours get the medication you need. We know these are tough times. Millions are uninsured, and millions more are underinsured. My office is tasked with helping families get through the financial aid process as quickly and painlessly as possible."

"To be honest, I was surprised you agreed to meet with me in person," I said. "From what I read about these programs, a lot of it is done online."

Sutcliffe seemed to take personal satisfaction from my observation. "Our office is unique in that regard. We believe, with Mr. von Wilhelm's full support, that a personal touch during what is obviously a difficult time not only builds goodwill with our customers, but sets an example for the rest of the industry to follow."

"Well, I think this industry is pretty messed up," I said. "I'm paying a lot of premiums without getting much for my money."

"Do you mind if I ask who you're insured with?"

"Atrium," I said.

Sutcliffe groaned. "Goodness, they're difficult to deal with."

I nodded my head vigorously and recounted my experience with Leonard Tate.

"So they wouldn't make a generic shortage exception?" Sutcliffe said in a voice wavering with disgust.

"What's that?" I asked.

"Some insurance companies will cover the full cost of a brand-name drug if the generic isn't available. I guess Atrium isn't one of them."

"Well, how much do you think Ruby and I will be able to get toward the cost?"

Sutcliffe already had my application. I'd sent it to her the day after I hung up on Tate. She knew how much money we made. She smiled, and I felt lighter already.

"It looks like you'll be able to get the maximum coverage."

I smiled back. My body tingled like it was full of helium.

"That's great news," I said, letting go a deep sigh. "That's incredibly generous."

"Twelve thousand dollars is the largest per patient donation of any major pharmaceutical company."

I swallowed air.

"Twelve thousand?" I said. "Ruby's course of treatment is well over three hundred thousand dollars."

Sutcliffe appeared genuinely surprised. "I'm sorry," she said. "But you don't qualify for our full access program."

"What? Why not?"

"Because you have some form of insurance. The full access program is only for the uninsured. It's also given out by lottery. We couldn't afford to give our medications out for free. I guess I should have been more clear on the phone."

I was speechless. For a while, I just stared blankly at the floor. Thinking.

This wasn't a question of going into debt. This was about not being able to get the drug at all. Twelve thousand dollars represented two weeks of treatment at most.

I buried my indignation. At least we had something—a start.

"My wife and I are truly grateful for your generosity," I said.

Vivian Sutcliffe smiled, evidently pleased. "We're glad we can help."

"One thing," I asked, my mind already racing. "If Atrium is so bad and inflexible, what are some insurance companies that would have covered us for the full course of treatment?"

"Oh, that's an easy one," Sutcliffe said. "UniSol Health is the biggest and the best. They'd cover the full cost, even if the generic were available. I should know, because that's who insures Wilhelm Genetics employees."

"Thanks," I said. I meant it, too. Because now I knew how I was going to fix our problem.

CHAPTER 5

I felt heartsick watching Ruby sleep. Was she thinner already? Had she become anemic? Her skin coloring matched the white of our bedsheets, and this was after taking Verbilifide for only two weeks. With credit cards we had enough money for another course of treatment, even though Ruby already didn't want to take it.

It was hard for me to believe the drugs were better than the cancer. Ruby would sweat off pounds she didn't have to spare while she slept. Pain would sometimes overtake her, leaving her breathless and doubled over, as though she'd been punched. Walking to the living room became a test of endurance. The drugs battling her disease kept calling up reinforcements from every vein in her body, marshaling the troops at the expense of her life spirit.

Ruby's breathing, shallow and quick, matched the rhythm of my own beating heart, as though ours were two bodies entwined as one. I sat on the edge of the bed, stroking her hair, then brushed her skin with a cool, damp cloth to soak up the sweat. Her skin felt cool to the touch, slack where it should have been pliable. I wanted to suck up her sickness, like John Coffey from *The Green Mile,* and spit it out as a vile horde of black flies. Instead, I put on her latest favorite Pandora station—Adele and music that sounded just like Adele—and settled down at my desk to get to work.

The unfairness of it all didn't matter. My wife ate organic, slept eight hours whenever she could, exercised, read up on all the supposedly dangerous products and chemicals to avoid. She embraced nature and natural living with enthusiasm, while nature kindly responded by spitting in her face. The why didn't matter anymore:

Ruby had cancer. Her life was now divided into two distinct epochs, Before Cancer (B.C.) and After Cancer (A.C.), and time would forever be measured against these markers. No, it wasn't fair at all.

I held on to this thought while I configured my phone-spoofing application.

Before Ruby's illness, I didn't know much about phone-spoofing technology. I knew it worked through either PSTN or VoIP. Yeah, tech stuff and cancer share a common alphabet soup of indecipherable terminology. Voice over Internet Protocol—that's longhand for VoIP—is a communication protocol for delivering voice and multi-media data over the Internet. Most of the phone-spoofing services I found relied on the VoIP protocol over PSTN because it was easier to use and a lot more flexible for breaking the law.

Web sites advertising this type of service tried to highlight legitimate reasons for their use. Say, for example, a business wanted to substitute the number they were calling from with a different call-back number. Well then, phone spoofing provided an excellent and reliable solution to that pretty nonexistent problem. Like I said, it was a stretch to find an application for this technology that even hinted at legitimacy. More often than not, phone spoofers were hackers, like I was about to become, and a hacker's intention is anything but legit.

Over the years, IT experts have spent countless billions beefing up their computer security infrastructure. They've brought in meatier computers, state-of-the-art virus protection software, firewalls, and various tools of the trade to keep the hackers out. What they can't upgrade are the people who work in their call centers. This weakness can't be fixed with code or by upgrading to a smarter model. People will do what people will do. When a hacker gets a customer service representative on the telephone, that's when the real magic happens; it's the moment a dedicated employee becomes the unwitting accomplice of a crime.

The technique is called social engineering, the art of manipulating people into performing actions or divulging confidential information. If social engineering is the getaway car of cybercrime, then the telephone is the gun. To commit my crime, I needed to disguise my phone number. I was about to make a bunch of calls to the customer service department at UniSol Health. Eventually, I'd rouse at least one rep's suspicion if he saw the same number popping up time and time again on his call screen. None of this could be easily done through the good old-fashioned phone network. Thankfully, the Internet makes most everything possible, especially crime.

At first I thought about using SpoofPhone. The company's tagline eliminated all doubt as to what service they provided: "The Global Leader in Caller ID Spoofing." Then I looked at the price: ten cents per minute. I figured with the number of calls I needed to make, the cost would be prohibitive. Instead, I settled on a technology called Asterisk.

Asterisk required a spare computer, which I had, and a VoIP service, which I got from VoicePulse. It didn't take much Linux knowledge to get the program installed and working. Of course, there were a few configuration files to tweak, but that was rudimentary work. Then I had to route my business phone to run through the Asterisk program. It took me three hours. Good thing I work quickly when motivated.

Before all this took place, I scanned through my database of registered *One World* game players, searching for men with a similar demographic to my own. One of these guys, unwittingly, was going to help save my wife's life.

As a matter of protocol, I don't store much customer information in my database, but I do require a credit card for buying specialty items and energy boosts for a better game-playing experience. That means I've got names and billing addresses on file. Lots of them. I also asked a bunch of voluntary questions on my registration form: phone numbers, sex, date of birth, that sort of thing. Gamers like to support the independent guy, so about half of my registered players filled out the entire form. It was enough information to get me started.

I tested out the installation by calling my cell phone from my business line. I picked a random phone number from our business card booklet, a bug exterminator in Cambridge. Mice weren't the only creatures lurking about our apartment that Ginger liked to chase.

My cell phone rang. I checked the display. Sure enough, it looked as though Ace Exterminator was calling to fix our cockroach problem once and for all.

My phone call, however, appeared to have awoken Ruby. Ginger perked up as well, first a wide yawn, paw stretch, back stretch, and shake, then a leap off the bed. I wrapped Ruby in my arms and gave her a tender kiss hello. Ginger meowed, perhaps out of jealousy, prompting me to give her head a quick scratch.

"Who called?" Ruby asked. The torpor in her voice proved contagious as I stifled a yawn of my own.

"Nobody," I said. "Wrong number."

I'm sure I looked guilty of something, but Ruby didn't seem to notice. It felt terrible to keep a secret, but then again, I knew Ruby would squash my plan during its inception stage. I was less certain how she'd react when it came time for the execution phase.

"Oh," Ruby said, a touch of disappointment in her voice. "I thought it might have been my mother calling."

A call to Ruby's mother earlier in the week had netted us a five-hundred-dollar wire transfer with a promise to visit soon.

Ruby was right not to hold her breath.

Winifred Dawes—Winnie, to her drinking buddies—hadn't left St. John once in the ten years since moving to the Caribbean retreat. Ruby had wanted to send her mother an e-mail, an impersonal update on her cancer treatment, but I insisted that we chat via Skype. Winnie talked to us from below deck. It was ten o'clock in the morning, but I knew her mug of coffee was really filled with wine. Five times in the course of our conversation, Winnie remarked on how great Ruby looked. This wasn't meant to be encouraging. It was Winnie's way of saying, "You don't really need to see me just yet." Guess the five hundred bucks bought Winnie several guilt-free weeks of getting sauced in the sun.

My mother, Pauline, a petite woman with curly gray hair and a face weathered by the weather, had flown in from Denver shortly after we gave her the news. She took a week off work from her job as a payroll clerk for Boulder, Colorado, the same city where I grew up. My mom didn't have much money to lend, but contributed what she could. I could see the heartbreak in my mother's eyes when it came time to leave. She gave Ruby a long embrace at Logan Airport, brushing aside tears as we departed. Ruby got from my mother what she never got from her own.

"I love you both," Mom had said.

She left us with a promise to return soon, which I knew would be well before Winnie ever came.

A case worker from Dr. Adams's office had been given the impossible task of finding us grants and other programs to help cover the cost of Verbilifide. The best option, Prescription Assistance, a non-profit that helped the low income and uninsured obtain unaffordable medications, did not count Verbilifide among the two thousand-some odd drugs in their program.

Strike one.

We maxed out our credit cards in procuring Ruby's next course of treatment. Strike two. Thankfully (that's sarcasm), the medication's side effects—lethargy, nausea, moodiness—were far more present and available than our limited funds. Ruby's school friends managed to raise a thousand dollars from a walkathon, while her former employer pitched in another grand. The red tape of the Wilhelm Genetics Access Solutions program didn't make life any easier. There was a rather lengthy time lag between being approved for the twelve-thousand-dollar grant and actually having the cash deposited in our bank account.

Strike three.

I kept a running tally in my head. Accounting for all funds raised, we were short a mere $270,000. Good thing I knew how to ameliorate our financial situation. The hard part would be convincing Ruby to go along with my plan.

CHAPTER 6

The UniSol Health phone tree might have been the most annoying of them all. That was probably because it felt like I'd listened to the same computerized female voice a thousand times. She sounded less pleasant to me than Freddy Krueger's nails traveling down an endless chalkboard.

Press three if you'd like to cut down this phone tree with a chain saw!

I pressed five to speak with a customer service representative—same as I'd done the last twenty-three times. Odds were good I'd get a hit eventually. Going by the numbers on the UniSol Web site, the company insured one out of every four Americans.

Ruby was out with friends from school, enjoying a little get-together, which I helped to arrange. I needed privacy to make my calls, and Ruby rarely ventured farther than our front door. The desire to socialize was just one of many things Verbilifide had extinguished, along with her appetite, ability to sleep, and a host of other activities we used to take for granted.

Ruby still had her hair—this wasn't chemo—but she looked noticeably thinner to the four girls and one guy who came over to take her out to lunch and a movie. Her friend Elisa, whose olive skin and dark hair made Ruby's sickly pallor all the more pronounced, told my wife she looked great, while her eyes betrayed the lie.

Ruby paused briefly at our apartment's threshold, giving me the same look Ginger uses whenever she wants to sleep in our bed. I gave Ruby a long hug, whispered in her ear, "You'll be fine. It's just for a little while." I actually checked the time and made a mental note of the hour. My plan already had enough pitfalls, and I sure didn't want Ruby coming home to the scene of the crime while the crime was taking place.

Social engineering exploits a weakness in one of humanity's greatest strengths: our inherent desire and ability to trust. I don't particularly enjoy lying to people, and what I was doing filled me with remorse. At least my intentions were noble, so I could justify my actions. That dollop of justification was all I needed to take those first awkward steps across the line of the law. I was a criminal as soon as I made my first call, and I did so thinking, *I'm doing this for Ruby*.

I pressed buttons so that my call would be routed to a living, breathing human being.

"Thank you for calling UniSol Health. How may I provide you with exceptional customer service?"

I wanted to say to the chipper-sounding UniSol rep, "Could you just give me the account number of a customer whose insurance will cover the full cost of Verbilifide?" But Social engineering requires a bit more subtlety, so instead I lied and said, "My name is Greg Johnson, and I'm calling to check on a prescription status."

According to my game logs, Greg Johnson is an avid player of *One World*. If he realized that he'd spent well over two hundred hours chasing away virtual zombies while building a town out of make-believe bricks, he might opt for fewer CPU cycles and more time spent with real people. But I'm not here to judge Greg. I'm trying to use him. Greg represented the latest call I made pretending to be someone I'm not. He was next on my list of potential candidates who might have UniSol health insurance that would save my wife. According to the birth date Greg entered when he registered for my game, he'll turn thirty-three this October. Assuming he didn't enter bogus data, it's close enough to my age. Good enough for my purposes.

My phone-spoofing program made the rep think Greg—aka me—was calling her from a Wisconsin area code. I had checked my log, confirming that I hadn't made any phone calls from Wisconsin yet. Heck, I'd never even been to Wisconsin. Go, Badgers!

"I'd be happy to help you with your prescription status. I just need your account number to get us started."

I groaned into the phone, feigning embarrassment at my own made-up forgetfulness.

"That's the problem," I said with another sigh. "I'm traveling on business, and I left that card at home. I've tried my wife—both the house phone and the cell. Even texted her. She's not getting back to me. But that's just like her. If she's not one place, she's another."

I didn't know what I meant by that last bit, "If she's not one place, she's another." However, the point wasn't to make a lot of sense. The point was to be chatty. Seem friendly. The guard comes down as soon as a rep thinks I'm on her side. I'm not calling to yell or harass. I'm just a regular guy with regular problems, thank you very much. I learned all this by Googling *social engineering.* The Internet is like a distance learning crime school.

"Well, that's not a problem, Mr. Johnson," the rep said. "I can look it up for you. What's your home address?"

I gave her the address Greg gave me when he registered for my game.

Fingers went tapping. A moment passed. It got real quiet when the rep became confused. Eventually, she came back on the phone and said, "I'm sorry, but we don't seem to have a customer by that name."

"Oh, my mistake," I said, sounding as chipper as she. "I must have the wrong provider. Thanks for your time."

I hung up before the rep could say good-bye. Time was running short. Ruby would be coming home, and I needed to make more calls. The next five calls yielded the same results as my attempt at being Greg Johnson. I spoofed numbers from Delaware, New Jersey, two from California, and one from Anchorage, because the Michelle Shocked song of the same name came up in my iTunes shuffle. Ruby kept such an eclectic collection of music.

I kept on calling. I got closer on my twenty-fourth call to UniSol Health. William Spader, thanks and praises, was an actual UniSol customer. Unfortunately, Spader wasn't the ideal customer.

"Could you tell me if this policy covers my wife?" I asked.

"I'm sorry," the representative said after much finger tapping. "But according to our records, you're not married."

"Oh well," I said. "Sorry about that. Thanks for your time."

I picked the next name from my list. Spoofing a Massachusetts exchange, I called again. This time, I was Elliot Uretsky. I was traveling on business and needed to look up my prescription coverage. Dang it, but go figure—I left my cards at home. So naturally, I provided my home address upon request. I verified Elliot's mother's maiden name, Askovitch, which was one of the security questions I stored in my database—oops, not encrypted—for password retrieval purposes. It was also one of the security questions UniSol asked before they'd give me any of Uretsky's account information. I found out that my policy (I mean Elliot's) covered my wife (I mean his). The rep gave me the account numbers, which I jotted down in a spiral-bound notebook.

And I picked up an interesting tidbit. It seemed that Elliot last filed a claim four months ago. He was also behind on making his payments. In my mind, that was a plus. To pull off this scam—lifesaving scam, that is—I intended to change his mailing address with UniSol so that he wouldn't be receiving any of Ruby's bills in the mail. Given that Uretsky didn't seem very interested in keeping his health insurance coverage in good standing, I suspected he was also a guy who wouldn't be looking for his bills.

Still, I decided to keep fishing, made ten more calls, got lucky twice, two names that would fulfill my purposes: Chuck Trent and Racine Romaguera. Both were in the UniSol network; both were married; both spouses were covered by hubby's insurance policy. Trent was the healthiest of the lot—he hadn't had any claims filed in the last nine months. Romaguera beat Uretsky by some, as he'd last seen a doctor six months ago.

I decided to learn a bit more about these men before I made my selection. I checked them out first on Facebook. I couldn't tell what Uretsky looked like from his profile pic, unless Uretsky and Mario from *Super Mario Bros.* were related by blood. That was because the picture Uretsky used for his Facebook profile was a screen grab from the video game.

Romaguera was a bald, good-looking, outdoorsy type.

Trent's picture showed him sunbathing on a towel. Clearly, this was a guy who thought chest hair and aviator glasses made him sexy. Their profiles were otherwise set to private, so I couldn't glean much useful data.

LinkedIn provided me with some more basic information. All three kept profiles on the world's largest professional network. Trent was in sales, which sort of explained his Facebook profile picture.

Nothing says, "Trust me," quite like a half-naked, oiled-up body. Romaguera was employed by Fidelity. Uretsky was a contract computer programmer with a passion for start-up companies. Maybe he was too busy developing software to realize that he'd fallen behind on his health insurance premiums. On the downside, Uretsky lived in Malden, and I wasn't too keen on him residing so close to my home.

But the way I saw it, Uretsky was the least likely to become suspicious. When the bills stopped coming, he wasn't going to notice. That was my thinking.

I had found my helper.

CHAPTER 7

Ruby had no idea where I was taking her. It was a sunny May afternoon, the kind of day where the warm breeze carries a sense of newness, a signal of spring. It seemed an appropriate day to kick off our new life. New beginnings—that's what this was all about. Starting today, we were no longer going to live as John Bodine and Ruby Dawes. Ruby didn't know it yet, but we were about to become Elliot and Tanya Uretsky.

Phase two of my plan went off without a hitch. Forged health insurance cards were much easier to make than credit cards, which require an image that goes on the card itself. Not to mention credit cards usually have embossed numbers and those funky holograms. I suppose I could have made a fake credit card, but I doubted it would have come with a $270,000 credit limit. For my purposes, the UniSol health insurance card I made was just as good as plastic. Even better.

Ruby walked, hands stuffed into the pockets of her well-worn gray hooded sweatshirt, moving at a brisk pace, though not so quick as to pass by her surroundings unaware. If anything, she seemed intent on taking everything in. Ruby paused as we strolled past the Coolidge Corner Theatre, a former church building converted into a classic Art Deco movie house.

"I want to go to the movies," Ruby said, reading the marquee.

"After," I said.

"After what? Where are you taking me, John?"

"I can't tell you. I have to show you."

Ruby sighed aloud and looked away.

"I'm not in the mood for surprises," I heard her mutter under her breath.

A young mother, with two young children in tow, squeezed past us on the crowded sidewalk of one of Brookline's more bustling neighborhoods. I could see Ruby take in every detail of the woman and her children as a lump found its way into my throat. I should be a father and Ruby a mother. Judging by Ruby's pained expression, I guessed she was thinking the same. I'm sure the mother passed by without giving us a second thought. To her, we were just a young couple out for a stroll on a sunny afternoon. To us, though, this mother offered a window into an experience we both longed to have.

We put off having children until my depression eased. Then it was my business that had to get off the ground. Soon after, we had Ruby's tuition to pay. It never seemed like the right time to have kids; it was something we'd put off until some future tomorrow. How could we have known that tomorrow might never come?

We walked past a bakery that smelled of cinnamon and freshly kneaded dough. With a glance, no discussion needed, I grabbed Ruby's hand and led her inside. I figured her favorite muffin, banana chocolate chip, would help her feel a little less ticked off at me. She ordered a vanilla bean Frappuccino with whipped cream. When I gave a look—Ruby never ordered such decadent drinks—her response, pre-slurp, was a straightforward, "To hell with eating healthy."

We finished our treats and then wandered another block or two, past more mothers and fathers with more kids in tow. The closer we got to our destination, the more nervous I became. It felt like the familiar ingredients of a particularly dangerous mountain climb—one part exhilaration, one part trepidation, and two parts "Holy crap."

There's no other way, I kept saying to myself. *There's no other way.*

I stopped at a four-story brownstone on Harvard Avenue. The Coolidge Corner neighborhood offered up a veritable melting pot of residents—all ages, all races, all in varying shapes and sizes. The college student population here seemed equal in proportion to the number of young professionals who called this somewhat posh city neighborhood home. Ruby looked around, didn't see anything but apartment buildings, and then looked around some more. She couldn't figure out why I had stopped walking.

"Where are we going?" she asked, perplexed.

"Here," I said, pointing to the peeling decal numbers, 457, on display in the arch window above a single glass door.

"What's here?"

I fished out a key from my front pants pocket. It was shiny brass because it was so new. The Realtor had given it to me the day before, after I signed the lease. Warily, Ruby followed me up the concrete front porch steps, still glancing around, still confused. The key felt stiff in the lock and took some twisting and pulling before I finally got the tumblers engaged. Ruby walked right past the metal bank of mailboxes, including the one that I had already labeled with the name Uretsky.

"What's going on, John? I really don't like surprises. I've had enough surprises lately."

I kissed Ruby's forehead, letting my lips linger an extra few moments to make certain my love for her sank in.

"Just give it a second, okay? I'll explain everything soon enough."

I walked ahead of Ruby, but imagined she was looking all around as we trotted up the tiled stairs in the grimy stairwell that led to the fourth-floor apartment, number twelve, the last unit in the building. Her curiosity was palpable. I felt bad for not having been more forthcoming. When I devised this plan, it seemed like a good idea. Now I worried the shock would keep Ruby from cooperating, and this endeavor would be a no-go without her.

I worked the apartment key into the lock and kept my back to Ruby so she wouldn't see my trembling hand. I reminded myself to breathe. Just relax. Like on a climbing expedition, I needed to cross this threshold feeling complete and total confidence that I'd achieve my objective. But this time, it wasn't just my life I was focused on saving.

I pushed open the door and stepped into a fully furnished apartment. Ruby followed close behind.

"Whose place is this?" she asked, taking a tentative step inside.

"Ours," I said.

Ruby put her hands on her hips. She pivoted her feet on the coated hardwood floor. From where she stood, Ruby could see into the living room, with its futon couch, two armchairs, bookshelf, a few plants, and small TV on a small TV stand. Yes, we had cable. I'd splurged. Ruby could also see the kitchen, a simple rectangular room with countertop seating. The bedroom door to her right was closed.

Because I wanted a short-term lease, it was simpler to rent a fully furnished apartment. Ruby didn't know it yet, but I'd already rented our apartment, fully furnished with our furniture, to a professor couple from a university in Barcelona, Spain, who were coming to the States for a six-month research sabbatical. Six months was a perfect length of time, since it equaled Ruby's schedule for Verbilifide treatments.

"Ours? What are you talking about?" Ruby said, her voice rising in pitch. "We have a home. I don't want to move."

"Ruby, I did something, something I probably shouldn't have done, but I did it, anyway. Come into the living room and sit down. I need to tell you everything."

CHAPTER 8

The look on Ruby's face broadcast her dismay in high definition. She knew bad news was coming and refused to take one more step into the apartment. She stood in the entranceway, arms folded, expression stern and disapproving. She couldn't imagine what I was going to say. She heard only the words, "I did something . . . something I probably shouldn't have done." If you're a fan of Lifetime movies, like Ruby is, those words, spoken by a nervous spouse, tend to be followed by revelations of infidelity, a hidden drug problem perhaps, or an admission of a felony crime. No wonder she didn't want to sit down.

"What have you done, John? If you're leaving me for another woman, I swear I'm going to kill you."

There was no jest to her threat. A heavy mood seemed to thicken the air. I took hold of her hand.

"No, baby," I said, my eyes locked firmly on hers. "There's no other woman. There can never be another woman. You're the love of my life. That's why I can't let anything happen to you."

My voice broke. A choking sob got caught somewhere in my throat, while gathering tears blurred my vision. I watched Ruby's angry expression transform into one of pure sympathy for me. How could someone vacillate between emotions that quickly? Love, that's how. But I didn't need another reminder of Ruby's genuine goodness. All I needed was for her to get better.

Ruby tugged on my hand, leading me into the living room. She sat down on the futon beside me, hand resting on my knee.

"Sweetie, talk to me. What's going on?" Ruby asked.

I swallowed hard and took several deep breaths until I felt composed enough to speak. That's when I told her everything. I explained how Atrium would cover only the cost of the generic drug, even though the generic was unavailable. And how Wilhelm Genetics could give us twelve thousand dollars toward the cost of her medication—a sliver of what we needed. I explained again how the other prescription assistance programs didn't provide coverage for Verbilifide and how some health insurance companies, such as UniSol Health, offered a generic drug exception.

"We can't just get this drug on a promise to pay the pharmaceutical company back one day," I said more than once. We needed insurance or cash, and had neither. That's when I told her about my phone-spoofing effort and how I'd found a suitable identity to steal. The Uretskys, Elliot and Tanya, had what we needed: UniSol Health.

Ruby got real quiet, as I had when I first found the cancer on the bottom of her foot. It was that kind of silence. She got up from the futon and walked around the room, inspecting every corner of the tight space like it was a crime scene—which I guess, in a way, it was. I watched her enter the bedroom and come out moments later, holding a framed picture of the two of us, taken on the top of Mount Greylock in the Berkshires. She held the picture up for me to see. She had one hand rested on her hip, body slightly tilted, as though readying to accuse me of something.

"John, what's this apartment for? Why did you fill it with our things? Explain this to me."

I expelled a heavy breath.

"Elliot Uretsky had fallen behind on his health insurance payments," I said.

"How is that helpful? Won't UniSol come after him for payment and hold his future claims?"

"It's good because he won't be wondering why he's not getting any bills from UniSol. We only need to do this for six months, and I'm counting on Uretsky being too scattered to notice his missing UniSol Health bills. Meanwhile, the bills and statements are now coming to a P.O. box I got in his name. I also made him current on his account, so there's no receivable issue, either. Still, we have to be careful. Insurance fraud is a very big problem."

"One that we're apparently contributing to," Ruby said, her arms folded across her chest.

"I figured the sudden and sustainable claims might rouse some suspicion. UniSol Health has an eight hundred number for a Special Investigations Department. The apartment is a precaution in case they sent somebody out to investigate us. If they did, they wouldn't find cause to dig very deep."

"Meaning?"

Ruby tossed the picture onto the futon like she was throwing a Frisbee.

"Meaning we have an apartment rented as Elliot and Tanya Uretsky. I made us identification cards, too."

"Made?"

"Forged."

"Goodness, John. So we don't drive?"

"Too hard to make driver's licenses. But a Mass ID is way easier to duplicate."

"Let me guess. You made it off the Internet."

I looked honestly surprised, because I was.

Now it was Ruby who looked surprised. "I was joking. You really did?"

"DocumentID.com," I said. "They sell kits. Synthetic paper. Butterfly pouches. ID laminators."

Ruby looked away.

"I think I'm going to be sick," she said.

I jumped up to grab a bucket that was tucked under the kitchen sink.

Ruby held up her hands to stop me. "I'm not really going to be sick," she said with a huff. "It's just how I feel."

At least now I was standing beside her. I reached out to touch her, but Ruby jerked away.

"We can't do this, John," she said.

"We have to."

"No. We don't."

"We don't have the money. Where are we going to get the money?"

Ruby let go an exasperated sigh. "We'll go on TV," she said. *"The Today Show."*

"You just want to go on *The Today Show* because you have a crush on Matt Lauer."

"No, John. I just don't want to be a criminal."

"And then what? What do you think they're going to talk about? Your cancer? Or the fact that I cut the rope of my climbing companion and sent him falling to his death?"

"That's not enough of a reason not to try."

I nodded my agreement. If I had to relive what I did to Brooks Hall on national television for Ruby, I'd do it in a heartbeat.

Then I said, "Even if they did pick up our story, there's no guarantee we'll raise enough money in donations. What then? We can't fall back on my plan. Not after we've exposed ourselves to the world."

"Can't you have faith in other people . . . that they'll come through for us in our time of need?"

"Climbing taught me how to rely on myself, Ruby. That's what I have faith in. Solve my own problem. I can't trust anybody more than myself."

"Oh, ye of little faith, what if we get caught?" Ruby asked.

"Who?" I said. "Who's going to catch us? Elliot Uretsky hasn't even paid his bills. He's not going to see a single statement. And we'll make our co-payments on time, every time. Like I said, this isn't permanent. In a few months' time, you'll be cured and this will all be put behind us."

"Where did you get the money for the apartment?"

"And cable," I said, making a weak attempt to lighten an increasingly tense mood. Ruby's expression conveyed a blend of disbelief and disgust. Smartly, I decided to shelve any further mood-lightening attempts. "I sold some equipment," I confessed. "But I didn't buy the furniture. I just rented a furnished apartment."

"But you need that hardware to expand your business!" Ruby exclaimed. "That's what you've been telling me."

That's Ruby for you, thinking of me when it's her life on the line.

"I don't need anything but you," I said.

"This is just like you, headstrong and impulsive."

"And it's just like you to balance me out, which is why I knew I had to ease you into this plan."

"This is how you ease?"

Time to switch tactics.

"When I was depressed, you never once gave up on me."

"Because I love you. I'd do anything for you."

"Don't you think I feel the same?"

This gave Ruby a moment's pause. "Of course."

"There's something else you should know."

"I don't think I want to," Ruby said.

"We can't leave this place for six months."

"Six months? What are you talking about?"

"Well . . . I sort of rented our apartment."

"Rented our apartment?"

"To a couple of professors from Barcelona."

"What? Why?"

"Because I couldn't sell enough equipment to afford both places."

"So what? We move here starting now? We just start living our lives as Elliot and Tanya Uretsky?"

I nodded and then said, "Hey, at least it's a short walk to the movies." Ruby shrugged that benefit off. "There's more," I said.

"More?"

"You've got to get rediagnosed. And, of course, we're going to have to find another dermatological oncologist to see."

"What do you mean? Start this whole process all over again? The MRI? PET scans? Needles? Oh God, John. You can't be serious."

"It's the only way. We'll tell them that we just moved to town. We don't have any primary care doctor, because we haven't needed one. We're young. Young people don't always go to the doctor. They'll believe us. There's no primary doctor for anybody to contact. Dr. Lisa Adams essentially no longer exists. They'll run the tests over again. They'll come to the same conclusion. Think of it as a very thorough second opinion."

Ruby scoffed and threw up her hands. "Yeah, maybe the results this time will show I'm cancer free."

"Let's hope they do."

Ruby put her hands on her hips and gazed absently out the windows directly behind the futon. Her fifty-thousand-yard stare reminded me that I needed to buy curtains for those windows. I wanted to rent a first-floor apartment because of my acrophobia but couldn't find one furnished in our price range. Light spilling inside through those very windows lit her hair, giving the appearance of an angelic glow. Ruby stood still for a long, tense moment. When she looked back at me, there were tears in her eyes.

"I don't want to do it, John," Ruby said, taking steps toward me. "I don't want to."

I opened my arms, and Ruby fell hard into me. I held on to her, rocking back and forth on my heels as Ruby wept onto my chest. Eventually, I started to cry as well. I tried to speak, but I'm sure it was hard for Ruby to understand me, as I was struggling to catch my breath.

"I can't risk it, Ruby," I said, my voice cracking and quavering. The tears were flowing freely now. I don't often cry, and I could sense my tears were bringing Ruby closer to me. "I don't want to trust our lives to the kindness of strangers. I don't want to wait for the cheaper drug to miraculously become available. I don't want to waste time chasing grants and assistance programs. I want you to take the medicine you need without having to worry about how we're going to pay for it. You have a right to live. This isn't your fault. This is just how it is. And I've got a way to fix it. Please, baby. Please let me fix this—this one thing, the only thing about your cancer that I can control. Please, don't say no. Please."

Ruby pulled away, her eyes ringed black with running mascara. She sniffled and forced a half smile. "I'm not okay with it," she said. "But if you think it's the only way, I'll do it."

CHAPTER 9

We'd been living as Elliot and Tanya Uretsky for six weeks, a milestone for sure, but tomorrow would be the biggest day of this ongoing charade. Tomorrow we were getting a progress report from Ruby's new oncologist, Dr. Anna Lee.

As far as Dr. Lee's practice was concerned, Ruby was just a new patient, Tanya Uretsky, who had no primary care physician, no past medical history to share, who appeared to be afflicted with an aggressive melanoma caused by a mutation in the BRAF gene. Dr. Lee had prescribed Ruby a course of Verbilifide, not knowing Ruby had been taking the drug for weeks. Surgery would follow once Dr. Lee saw how the nodes were responding to the treatment. We worried that traces of Verbilifide might show up in her blood work, but apparently that wasn't the case.

Ruby, dressed in spandex workout clothes, was on her yoga mat in the downward dog position, and I was on my computer, debugging code and occasionally leering at Ruby. A knock on the door startled us.

Ruby sprang to her feet with a graceful motion. She flashed me a nervous look. "What do we do?" she whispered.

"Um, we answer the door," I said, without glancing up.

Ruby came over to me and got close to my ear. She smelled like strawberries and sweat. Love it. "What if it's somebody who knows what we did?"

"Nobody knows what we did," I said. "Just answer the door."

Ruby grabbed her towel, dabbed at her skin, went over to the door, and asked, "Who is it?"

"Hi! It's Rhonda Jennings, your downstairs neighbor."

Rhonda's high-pitched voice was cheery and warm. Even so, Ruby turned to me, still looking unsure, so I motioned for her to open the door. Clearly, one of us had grown more accustomed to our new identities.

Rhonda Jennings entered our apartment with a bright smile and a fine-smelling pie. My kind of neighbor. She was sweet-faced, with shoulder-length, straight blond hair and an athletic build—not a runner's body, but maybe a onetime field hockey player's. Her cornflower-blue eyes surveyed our place, while her expression suggested a sort of sheepish embarrassment.

"I'm so sorry I didn't come up to greet you sooner," Rhonda said. "I've been crazy busy at work and . . . and I have more excuses ready but figured pie forgives all."

"Oh, thank you so much," Ruby said as she brought the pie over to the kitchen island. She went to grab some plates. "I hope you'll stay and have some with us."

Rhonda again got that sheepish look on her face. "Actually, I have to run out. My boyfriend is taking me out to dinner."

"You made us a pie on date night?" Ruby said. "That's incredibly nice of you."

"It was actually a frozen pie I bought a few weeks ago but forgot to bring up to you. I just defrosted it."

A moment of silence ensued. Then Ruby laughed delightedly, and Rhonda joined in. "Frozen pie is my favorite kind," Ruby said. "I'm sorry. I should introduce myself. I'm—"

Here, my breath caught. I was sure my wife was going to say, "Ruby Dawes," but instead she surprised me by saying, "Tanya Uretsky. And this is my husband, Elliot."

We all shook hands. Rhonda took notice of Ruby's yoga mat.

"Are you good at yoga?" she asked.

"Not bad," Ruby said. "I've been practicing it for a few years now. Why? Do you do yoga?"

"No, but I've been wanting to try it for a while now. I'm getting married—well, after I get engaged, but it's going to happen—and I heard yoga is great for getting in wedding dress shape."

"The best," Ruby said. "And congratulations on the engagement. That's wonderful."

"Well, he hasn't proposed yet, but I helped pick out the ring."

Ruby held up her finger, showing Rhonda the impossibly small diamond ring I bought her. "I picked this out, too," she said. "I have my romantic side, but I knew my husband has an even bigger 'I'd buy a ring we couldn't afford' side."

She was right, of course. Thank goodness I had Ruby to keep me in check.

Rhonda smiled. "It sounds like Matthew and Elliot would get along great."

Who's Elliot? I was thinking. Then I got it.

"I'm in school, studying acupuncture, and Elliot works from home. We're here a lot. Come up anytime and I'll show you some yoga poses that will help you get started."

"That would be great," Rhonda said. "I really wish I could stay. You guys seem really cool. Most of the people living here keep to themselves."

"We've noticed," Ruby said, chuckling.

I'm thinking, *It's just like the last place we lived.* Ruby was still attending school, but we had stopped inviting friends over to our place for obvious reasons. We were essentially alone on an island of our own creation.

"Well, look, I have to run, but it was really nice to meet you. I'm sorry again that it took so long to send the welcome wagon."

Ruby already had a spoonful of pie in her mouth. "Great to meet you, too," she said, her words garbled from the pie. She swallowed, pointing to the aluminum pie plate. "Honestly, this is the best frozen pie I've ever had," she said.

Rhonda laughed. "You guys *are* great. Dinner at my place next week. Deal?"

"Deal," Ruby said.

We took turns shaking hands good-bye, and then Rhonda was gone.

"See, it's not so bad here, after all," I said. "You've already made a friend."

"Honey, real friends know your real name."

Later that night, Ruby and I were lying in bed. Ginger, tucked firmly between us, purred with the intensity of a revving engine. Ruby was reading from one of her textbooks, a meaty tome titled *Al-*

ternative Medicine Best Practices, and I was watching the Bruins at low volume. I used a wireless video sender to transmit the signal from the cable box to the TV I had brought over from our old apartment—our old home, which we both missed so terribly. Even though at the moment we were both doing something perfectly normal, what we weren't doing was relaxing.

Ruby made a frustrated noise. "I think I've read the same page for the third time," she said.

"What's got you so riveted to that page?" I asked.

Ruby sighed and said, "I'm serious. I can't study, John. I can't concentrate on anything at all."

I turned over onto my side and eased the book from her hand. It dropped to the bed with a muted thump.

"What's going on?" I asked.

"What's going on?" Ruby laughed because it should have been obvious to me. "I think I have to drop out of school, that's what."

"But your professors promised they'd give you extra time on your assignments. Nobody wants you to drop out."

"They can give me all the time in the world. My heart isn't in this anymore. Besides, what good is alternative medicine," Ruby said, patting the textbook, "if I can't use it to make me better? I don't need herbs and needles. What I need is this stupid, superexpensive drug that makes me feel like absolute shit."

Ruby flipped over onto her side, hiding her face from me, but I could tell by the way her shoulders heaved up and down that the tears were flowing. I ran my fingers through her hair like a comb and then traced the contours of her slender neck with the palm of my hand. Ruby pressed her body up against mine, her way of saying she needed my touch.

The softness of her silk pajamas blanketed me in a familiar comfort. I rubbed her back, keenly aware of how her weight loss continued to reveal more and more of her bones. The longer I rubbed, the more she sank into me, until our bodies melded together. With each breath she took in, I did the same, and eventually her tears stopped altogether.

Ruby turned to face me. Her fragile, vulnerable expression put a walnut-sized lump in my throat. I wanted to fix this. Fix it now. What I'd done instead was add to her misery by compounding it with guilt. I knew why she couldn't concentrate. Her school subjects weren't the problem. The issue was what I had done.

"Tell me what you need," I said, stroking her hair. "Tell me and I'll do it."

"I just want to go home," Ruby said, her voice drenched in misery. "I miss our life, John. I miss it so much. This just isn't fair."

"It isn't forever."

"No, it just feels that way."

Ginger stretched and yawned to make her presence known.

"Hi ya, sweet pea," Ruby said, scratching Ginger's furry little head.

If Ruby had her druthers, she'd adopt again. Her heart was wide open that way, and her love for animals, especially those unwanted and abandoned, seemed boundless. And that love didn't apply solely to four-legged critters. Winnie Dawes could have decided to abandon ship, literally, to come stay with us awhile, and Ruby would have welcomed her without any lingering animosity.

Winnie had called a few times to, in her words, "check in," but I wasn't expecting to turn the futon into a guest bed anytime soon. Sadly, Winnie would have no idea we were living here under false pretenses. She'd never once visited us in our Somerville apartment.

"What would happen if we got caught?" Ruby asked.

"We'd be arrested, that's what."

"I've never done anything illegal in my life."

"You've gotten high."

"I didn't inhale."

"Liar."

"Okay, besides that."

"How about speeding?"

"I'd say what we're doing is a heck of a lot worse."

"What would you prefer? Give up?"

"No, I'd have preferred that we didn't buy the cheap health insurance from Atrium."

"Me, too," I said. "Believe me, if I could take it back, I would."

"It's bad karma what we're doing, and you know that's true."

"I don't know if I believe in karma. We didn't do anything wrong, and you got sick."

"That's not how karma works. It looks at what you do with the hand you're dealt. It doesn't deal out the cards. It's the circle of cause and effect. Karma is the consequence of our actions."

"Didn't know you knew so much about it."

A fresh look of concern crossed Ruby's face. "I can't help but feel that we're stockpiling a whole lot of bad karma by doing this."

She turned her back to me and shrugged off my touch.

"No, it's not your fault. It's mine. I screwed this up, and I need to make it right. Please. Just stick with me on this. We'll get through it together."

Ruby flipped over to face me. For a while we just stared at each other.

"We're going to have to make it up to Elliot Uretsky. Somehow, we're going to have to make it up to him."

"He's not being hurt by this," I said.

"No, UniSol Health is," Ruby replied, disgusted.

"Do you think UniSol is the good guy here? You want to talk karma? How many claims do they deny unjustly on a daily basis? I'm sure they've done their fair share of wrong."

"Two wrongs don't make a right," Ruby said.

"No. But this wrong is working out right, and we've got to keep going to the end. That's all that matters."

"That's not all," Ruby said. "Karma. That matters, too."

CHAPTER 10

We were sitting in Dr. Lee's office, which looked a lot like Dr. Adams's office, with the exception of a well-stocked saltwater fish tank, hoping the karma gods were on sabbatical or something. We were holding hands and waiting as patiently as could be.

"The waiting is the hardest part," I said into Ruby's ear.

She shot me a surprised look. "Really?"

"Yeah," I said. "I'm used to fixing buggy software. When something is broken, all I have to do is write a few lines of code and I can see right away if it's been fixed."

Ruby shook her head dismissively. "No, I mean, are you really going to give me a softball like that to hit?"

"What do you mean, softball?"

There were others in the waiting room, so Ruby sang in a whispered voice the lyrics from the tune made famous by Tom Petty and the Heartbreakers. I knew the song well enough to have performed it myself at karaoke, if I ever sang karaoke. Ruby held up her finger. One more point for her. Add one to the tally that could not be counted. Ruby kissed my cheek and smiled.

A door opened to our right.

"Mrs. Uretsky?"

Neither of us looked up.

"Tanya Uretsky?" the woman announced again.

Ruby jumped a little as the recognition sank in. I did, too, and we both stood a bit shakily. The woman speaking was the receptionist, and she motioned us to the window.

"Dr. Lee can see you now," she said.

For a place that dealt with cancer on a daily basis, the receptionist's manner was surprisingly upbeat. I figured she was cheery for
everybody, but decided to see her sunshiny demeanor as a sign that
Ruby's results would come back positive.

Dr. Lee, a stylish Asian woman who wore hipster black horn-
rimmed glasses, had the films of Ruby's latest imaging work.

"How are you feeling, Tanya?" Lee said, giving us both a friendly
handshake hello.

"I'm doing okay," Ruby said.

Ruby's strained expression told me that the identity theft was eating away at her, same as her cancer.

"Well, I have your CT and PET scans here," Lee said. "I was looking
for signs of active disease to compare it to the first sets of scans we
took." She illuminated her light board so we could see the images
clearly. Not that we could understand them; they looked like a
Rorschach inkblot test to me.

"And?" I asked, my voice dripping with anticipation.

"And"—Lee's voice rose in pitch, another positive sign in my
book—"the amount of activity has definitely decreased. I would say,
being cautiously optimistic here, that the nodes are definitely responding to the drug."

Ruby's face lit up in a way I hadn't seen since the day I proposed
to her, down on one knee, on the roof deck of a restaurant over-
looking the Charles River.

"That's . . . that's good news," Ruby said, her voice lifting with excitement.

"That's good news," Lee concurred, her serious expression breaking into a slight smile.

"So what now?" I asked.

"Now we keep doing what we're doing," Lee said. "Our plan of action is working, and we should stick with it. I'm still of a mind to
schedule you for the node dissection, because there could be microscopic cancer left in the nodes, but this is definitely a positive sign."

The plan of action was, of course, for Ruby to digest more of the
illegally obtained drug, Verbilifide. When we first sought Dr. Lee's
medical advice, I had no doubt that she'd come to the same diagnosis and same recommended course of treatment as Dr. Adams. It was
just a matter of going through the initial testing all over again. Through-

out it all, I remained in awe of Ruby's strength. A lesser person would have broken under the strain. Goodness knows I wouldn't have been surprised if Ruby's blood work revealed some sort of Amazonian lineage.

We left Dr. Lee's office with that clichéd extra kick in our step. Ruby, smiling in a way I hadn't seen in eons, was light on her feet and quick with a laugh. I felt extra alive and fully aware of our good fortune. *Grateful,* that was the best word to describe how we were both feeling at that moment. We were so incredibly grateful for everything, absolutely giddy with euphoria. For a brief flash we weren't weighed down by the guilt of what we'd done, the crime we'd committed to get to this point. Rather, we were elated. I kept thinking about what Dr. Lee had said.

Our plan of action is working. . . . Nodes are definitely responding to the drug.

My heart filled with hope and joy, and I thought back to the day I first developed feelings for Ruby. It wasn't love at first sight for me, more like smitten at ninth sight, because it was on the ninth day of our college history class together that—in a blink—I became spellbound by Ruby's dazzling smile. Everything about that moment is frozen in my memory: the way her strawberry blond hair draped like a fine silk cloth over her shoulder, the green sweater she wore that made her eyes sparkle, the freckles that skirted across her cheeks. I'm probably one of the few people in the world for whom the Peloponnesian War evokes lustful thoughts.

I was sitting behind Ruby, yes, listening to the lecture, yes, taking notes, when she turned around to ask me a question. I had noticed her the first day of class, of course, but I'd never had her smile at me before. I got lost in that smile, forgot all about the Peloponnesians and their bloody conflict. When she smiled at me, the only thing I wanted to learn more about was Ruby Dawes.

After class I asked her out on a date, pizza at Captain Nemo's in Kenmore Square, and she promptly agreed. Over cheese slices we talked about school, my passion for climbing, and her love of the outdoors. The subject of parents came up, and so we bonded over having both lost our fathers. It wasn't a heavy conversation, more like we'd been friends for a long time and there was comfort in rehashing our realities.

She knew a lot about music. I credit her with introducing me to some old school bands: the Pixies, the Red Hot Chili Peppers, Guided by Voices, and Jane's Addiction. She considered herself alternative on the inside, because the way she dressed, sporty casual, didn't fit the image of a brooding, darkly dressed, cutting-edge music aficionado.

We left Nemo's and went back to my apartment, which at the time I shared with two Italian exchange students, who were trying—sadly, without much success—to master my native tongue. We hung out in my bedroom for a while, talking about things people who are attracted to each other talk about, which amounted to just about everything except the one thing we both wanted to do, which was to kiss. When our lips finally touched, I had a pillow between us. I don't know how that pillow got there, but I decided to keep it there, as a barrier to prevent me from trying to push things too far too fast. It was Ruby who pulled that pillow away.

"It's okay, John," she said between our intensifying kisses. "I want you to touch me."

We didn't make love that night, or even that month. What we did was get to know each other better. She became my best friend, a soul mate. Our attachment was instantaneous and never wavered. I remember when I first told Ruby that I loved her. It was a spring afternoon, just like the one we stepped into from Dr. Anna Lee's air-conditioned offices.

"What should we do to celebrate the good news?" I asked Ruby as we strolled down Harvard Avenue.

"I vote for a pint of mint chocolate chip ice cream and a DVR marathon of *Ellen*," Ruby said.

It was a little slap of reality. Our combined elation didn't mean that Ruby's stamina had improved. Thanks to Verbilifide, Ruby's stamina had all the staying power of an ice cube in the desert.

"Hot fudge?" I asked.

"With rainbow sprinkles," Ruby said.

"Done deal," I said.

"What I really want is a kiss," Ruby said.

I obliged, with much tenderness.

"I love you, John."

"I love you, too."

We both breathed in the day as we walked the few blocks toward our new home. With each step, I let that good feeling linger, savoring it greedily. We arrived back at the apartment, carrying a single bag of groceries containing the ice cream, hot fudge, and of course, the sprinkles.

While I was putting the groceries away, the telephone rang. Instinctively, I reached for my cell but realized it wasn't my cell phone that was ringing.

My heart thrummed in my chest.

The phone in the apartment had never rung before, and for good reason. We used our cell phones to call the people we needed to call. We checked messages on our voice mail at the old apartment. The only reason this apartment phone worked at all was that I wanted to have utility bills in Uretsky's name. I obtained online access to Uretsky's health insurance account after I took over his identity. The helpful customer service representative who doled out Uretsky's account numbers reset the online portal password using a new Yahoo e-mail address that I had created.

From that portal I was able to change Uretsky's address to the P.O. box I'd rented from Post Boxes Unlimited, and the phone number to the new one I got for this apartment. I checked with the phone company to make sure my new number couldn't be traced back to this address. That meant the only one with access to this number was an official representative from UniSol Health.

Why would UniSol be calling us?

The phone rang again. The way the phone sounded—long rings, clattering bells (it was a corded Trimline phone)—made an especially ominous noise.

Maybe it's a wrong number, I said to myself.

It rang again.

"Aren't you going to answer it?" Ruby asked.

"It's probably a wrong number," I said.

Ruby grunted and pushed past me to answer the phone. She put the phone to her ear.

"Hello. . . . Hello? . . . Anybody there? Heeellloooo?" I watched her eyes dance about confusedly as she waited. She hung up.

"I guess it was a wrong number," I said.

She gave a quick shoulder shrug as if to say, "Oh well." A feeling of relief swept through me. Then the phone rang again.

This time I picked it up.

"Hello," I said, speaking quickly.

I don't know why, but the hairs on my neck started to rise.

"Hello?" I spoke the word like a question this time. "Is anybody there?"

A voice answered me, raspy and deep sounding.

A chill ripped through my body and my skin prickled when I heard a man say, "My name is Elliot Uretsky, and I believe you stole my identity."

CHAPTER 11

My body went rigid, freezing my jaw open and my eyes wide. Ruby, who was standing nearby, gripped my arm, fingernails digging hard into my skin, prying for information. She leaned over, putting her face close to mine, willing me to look at her. Out of the corner of my eye I could see Ruby's mouth saying the words, "Who is it? Who is it?" I held up my hand, a wave. *Leave me alone,* I was saying to her. *I've got to think! Holy crap!* I switched the phone to my other ear, keeping my back to Ruby. She moved in close, her body pressed up against mine, ear attuned to whatever snippets of conversation could be heard.

"I'm sorry, but I'm afraid you've got the wrong number," I said into the phone.

A long pause ensued that seemed to drag for eternity. My stomach clenched, releasing a wave of nausea through me.

"We both know that's not true," Uretsky said. His resonant baritone voice sounded throaty and coarse, while his vocal inflection, if graphed, would come out flat like the EKG of a dead man. Calm as a windless sea.

I took in a deep breath but found it impossible to slow my racing heart. Fear rode the back of my throat as I flashed on what was to come. Uretsky would phone the police, we'd be arrested, and Ruby would lose access to her medication. My subconscious acted on behalf of my frozen thoughts, doing what I'd trained it to do since I started taking climbing seriously—look for an escape route. Only, I couldn't see any way off this particular mountain. Through a twisted reversal of fortune, I'd become Brooks Hall, swinging pendulum-like from a rope, hovering helplessly above the infinite, while Uretsky assumed the role I had once played, wielding that knife, angling to slice the safety line in two.

Karma . . .

I pulled the phone away from my ear, readying myself to end the call, but something made me stop.

We could run, I was thinking. *We'll run! But how will Ruby get her medication?*

I felt Ruby's nails digging harder into my shoulder.

"Are you still there?"

Uretsky's voice made me shudder, the way a dark storm cloud could whenever it slipped over a ridgeline to make an unexpected appearance.

You can't hang up on him, I thought. *He called you for a reason. He could have just gone to the police directly. Why did he call?*

Ruby swiveled me by the shoulders, forcing me to face her.

Maybe . . . maybe he'll take pity on us. . . .

"Who is it?" Ruby demanded to know. "Who?"

I mouthed the name "Uretsky" and watched a look of terror stretch across Ruby's face. Her features contorted—eyes gone wide and wild, mouth falling open as though her jaw had come unhinged. Her hand went to her mouth; next, her color blanched.

"Please," I said into the phone. "Please, let me explain."

"Oh, I'm interested in your explanation," Uretsky said. "Why don't you tell me all about it?" His voice filled my head like an enveloping blackness, a suffocating smoke that made it impossible to speak. "I'm waiting," he said.

"My wife . . . my wife is very sick."

"Yes, I know," Uretsky said.

I recoiled as though I'd just been hit in the face.

He must have called UniSol and gotten access to the account again. That's how he knew about Ruby's cancer. That's how he found our phone number. Our only saving grace was that he couldn't know where we lived. Our home address was nothing but a post office box, and the phone number he called couldn't be used to trace us to here. But he still could go to the police, and if he did, it wouldn't take much to find out our real identities.

"Mr. Uretsky," I said.

"Elliot, please," he said, with a slight chuckle, chilling as a moon-less winter night. "We should at least be on a first-name basis. After all, you're me. But you know my name, and I don't know yours. Your real name, that is."

"Elliot," I said, swallowing hard. "What I did was very, very wrong, and very stupid. But I did it out of desperation. My wife has cancer, and we didn't have insurance for the drug she needed. There was no way we could afford her medication without better health insurance. I didn't mean to hurt you. I swear that's true." I started to speak quicker because I was struggling for breath and on the verge of hy-perventilating. "Please, you've got to understand. We were desper-ate. You're married. What if it were your wife?"

"The old walk a mile in your shoes, eh?"

I nodded emphatically, though of course, Uretsky couldn't see me.

"Yes. Yes," I said. "Think about if it were your wife who was sick."

"Hmmm . . . that's a good idea. Let me think about that."

The only sound to punctuate the lengthy quiet that followed was Uretsky's own heavy breathing. The sonorous breaths were like that of a sleeping man. Was he heavyset? I wondered. All I had to go on was his Facebook avatar, which was nothing but a picture of Mario from the video game *Super Mario Bros.*

I glanced over at Ruby, who appeared to have gone catatonic. She sat on a stool at the kitchen island, kneading the fingers of her hands; her eyes, unblinking, remained fixed on an empty spot on the hardwood floor.

Eventually Uretsky let out a long, protracted sigh—a signal to me that he had come to some sort of a decision.

"I'm done thinking," he said.

"Please . . . Elliot . . . don't report us to the police. We'll work something out."

"I have no interest in reporting your crime—to the authorities, or anyone else, for that matter," Uretsky said.

I breathed out a protracted sigh of my own.

"Thank God. Thank you, Elliot. Thank you for being so under-standing."

"Oh, I never said that I was understanding. I just said I'm not going to report you to the police."

I stammered before speaking. "What do you want? What can we do to make this right?"

My blood was burning now, like I had downed a pot of coffee with several Red Bull chasers.

"Do you like games?" Uretsky asked.

"What do you mean?"

"Games. Do you like games? How much clearer can I be?"

"I . . . I guess . . . but to be honest, I don't really see what you're getting at."

"Well, I like games," Uretsky said. "I like games a lot. Online games especially. They're so much fun."

Of course Uretsky was a game fanatic. I'd seen how many hours he logged playing *One World*. I felt the room darkening, an illusion, just a trick of the eye, I knew, but still, everything around me seemed to dim. I sensed what he was going to say next. Don't ask me how, but I just knew—gut instinct. I asked the logical next question, anyway.

"Tell me what you want," I said.

"Naturally, I want to play a game."

I took in an uneven breath as my eyes closed tightly.

I was right.

CHAPTER 12

My voice got stuck in my throat, but eventually, I was able to ask, "What kind of game do you want to play?"

I heard him take in a readying breath, one that seemed to suck the air right out of my lungs. "It's a game I've made up," Uretsky said. "You inspired it, in fact. It's called *Criminal*. Want to know how to play?"

"You know what? I think this conversation is over," I said.

"You hang up on me," Uretsky said quickly, his tone flush with hatred, "and I'll make sure that bitch wife of yours dies of cancer."

He essentially spit out the words *dies of cancer*. A knot built up in my chest. Ruby, who must have heard some or all of Uretsky's admonition, covered her mouth with her hands. She closed her eyes tightly, perhaps to will this nightmare into nothingness. When she opened them, those blue eyes I loved so dearly were ringed with red. Her lower lip quivered, and I could feel Ruby's anxiety start to build.

"Do you want to know how to play *Criminal?*" Uretsky asked again. The calm had returned to his voice. The old Elliot was back. "The answer, by the way, is yes. Yes, Elliot. I'd love to know how to play *Criminal*. Please, tell me all about it." Uretsky paused, long enough to let me know that he was awaiting my reply. "Go ahead. Now you say it."

He was goading me along—take a little drag, walk on the train tracks, make the jump, live on the wild side. "How . . ." I gulped before I could continue. "How do you play . . . *Criminal?*"

"Well, I'm glad you asked," Uretsky said, ebullient. "I think the best games are the ones where you improve yourself. Get better, you know? The more experienced you are, the better you do. So my game is all about making you a better criminal. That's where I got the name. Do you see?"

"Please . . . whatever you want."

"I want you to play my game," Uretsky said, the harsh edge to his voice returning. "Now then, at this particular moment in time, I'd say you're a pretty crappy criminal. Wouldn't you agree?"

"I don't . . . I don't know how to respond to that."

"The correct response is yes," Uretsky said. "I mean, I caught you. And it was damn easy, too. So, let's *both* agree that you're pretty bad at being a thief and get on with it, shall we?" Uretsky's breathy voice again raised the hairs on my neck. "So here's the game in a nutshell. You've got to prove to me that you're worthy of being labeled a real criminal."

"Okay, this has gone far enough," I said, a touch of anger in my voice.

"Oh, we haven't even begun to dance."

"If this is your way of scaring us—"

"Let me tell you how to play round one."

"It's not going to work."

"Do you know the Giorgio Armani store on Newbury Street?"

"Yes," I said, exasperated. "What does that have to do with anything? What do you want from us, Elliot?"

"I want you and your wife to go to that store, and I want each of you to shoplift a scarf valued at greater than a hundred dollars."

"What?"

"I want you to steal two scarves."

"Why?" I asked.

"Why?" he repeated, as though the answer should be obvious to me. "Because a criminal is a thief, no matter what the crime—a stealer of identities, a taker of lives, a remover of objects. To advance in my game, you must each steal one scarf with a value greater than one hundred dollars."

"I'll do no such thing," I said, sounding indignant. This had to be a prank, some trick intended to scare us. A tick of relief swept over me, as I believed with increasing conviction that this was true. Uretsky wanted to mess with us for what I'd done to him, and I fell for it, hook, line, and stinking sinker. It made sense. He was an avid gamer, maybe even a hacker type, someone who preferred that justice be served outside the usual lines.

I covered the phone with my hand and said to Ruby, "It's okay, baby. This is a prank. I'll take care of it." To Uretsky: "Tell me, Elliot, since you don't know who we are, how would you even know that we stole the scarves?"

"Good one," Uretsky said. "You're thinking. That's what a smart criminal must always do. I thought of that as well, so I went ahead and marked the price tag of two scarves on display, both of which have the requisite dollar value, with the initials E.U. and T.U. That's for Elliot Uretsky and my wife, Tanya, your doppelgängers. Those are the scarves you are to steal. Now, I've placed a hidden camera in the store, so I'll know when they've been stolen."

"Sounds logical," I said, humoring him.

"You have forty-eight hours from this very moment. Forty-eight hours starting right now."

"Okay. Sounds good. We're on it."

Could he pick up on my sarcasm?

I was shaking my head. I wasn't sure what else I could do to get him off the line.

"I haven't told you what happens if you lose," Uretsky said.

I was growing tired of him wasting my time. The tone I took was intended to communicate that. "Why don't you tell me?" I said.

"If either of you fails in your attempt to steal the scarves," Uretsky said, "if you get caught trying, or don't even bother giving it a go, I'm going to murder somebody close to you."

A shock of electric fear ripped through my body, but I soon recovered. *He's a hacker. He's a gamer. He's a prankster.* Still, I remembered the growl in his voice when he called my wife a bitch and told me he'd let her die of cancer. *Could he be for real?*

"Who?" I said, my voice betraying a slight waver.

"Somebody close to you," Uretsky repeated.

He had just tipped his hand. That's when I knew this guy wasn't for real; it was a scare tactic only.

"Nice work trying to freak us out, but you don't even know who we are."

"Forty-eight hours," Uretsky said.

"Or you're going to go to the police."

"I told you," Uretsky said. "I'm not going to report you to the police—no matter what. If you don't follow through, I'm going to kill somebody close to you. Game on."

"You're a sick person. You know that?"

"Game on," he said again.

I slammed the receiver down and waited, but the phone didn't ring again.

Ruby hoisted up her hands. The confusion on her face begged for any clarity. "What was that all about?" she asked.

"That was about nothing," I said, with an edge to my voice. "He's just pissed off and trying to freak us out. That's all. Everything's fine."

At the time, I believed this to be true.

CHAPTER 13

Seventy-two hours later, twenty-four hours past Uretsky's twisted deadline, I was starting to think about Plan C. Climbing had taught me to value contingency planning like a drink in the desert. Plan B involved my stealing another identity and starting our unfortunate, albeit necessary, scam all over again. My worry was that it might push Ruby over the edge, which was why Plan C required an altogether different approach for getting her medication. Unfortunately, I didn't have any idea what approach to use. Obviously, the Uretsky identity was something that had to be shed like a worn-out snakeskin.

On the good news front, Uretsky hadn't called back, and it went without saying that nobody close to us had been killed. Not that I warned anybody close to us to be extra vigilant. That wasn't a willy-nilly decision on my part. Uretsky, my logic went, couldn't know who to target without first reporting our crime to the police. Since no police had come, I assumed no report had been made. I was therefore left to conclude that my first assumption had been correct—Elliot Uretsky enjoyed dishing out his own special brand of punishment. The game he had invented was his twisted little way of saying: "Look, I'm not going to turn you in, because I do feel bad for you, but I'm going to scare the living daylights out of you so that you'll find a new identity to steal, chump."

Another thing I didn't do was to share with Ruby all the gory details of my conversation with Uretsky. Hadn't I already put her through enough? She didn't need to be privy to his threat. So I didn't warn anybody close to us—no family, no friends. And of course, nobody died.

What I did do was sulk around the apartment for most of those anxious days, thinking of other possible moves we could make—i.e., Plan C—while half expecting the police to show up at some point to cart me off in handcuffs. When they didn't come around, I figured we'd dodged a bullet fired by a deranged man.

Meanwhile, Ruby had less than a two-week supply of Verbilifide left, plus the specter of major surgery on the horizon, and all I needed to do—assuming I was through playing the identity theft game—was come up with a few hundred thousand dollars in that time frame.

"I'm glad he caught us," Ruby said.

"I'm not. How are we going to get your medication?"

"I'll take something different, something Atrium will cover. When the generic becomes available, I'll start taking that."

"You have to take the best drug for you, not just any drug."

"Then we're going to have to go into debt or get on *The Today Show.* Maybe we could start a Kickstarter campaign or use INeed-CashNow.com."

"Is that really a Web site?" I asked.

Ruby smiled. "Yeah, I looked it up."

"Assuming that we don't get a windfall payout from INeedCash-Now.com, how many credit cards do you think I can get? We'll never get out from under."

"We can do anything we set our mind to," Ruby said, kissing me on the lips en route to the bathroom with her make-up kit in hand. "You need to have faith."

"I'm not big on faith."

"Well, get big," Ruby said.

She was already packing to leave and downright giddy about abandoning my plan—Plan A—not that I could blame her.

"Did you call the Realtor?" Ruby asked, her voice echoing from the bathroom.

Ginger could be seen pacing the room as well, equally eager for a return trip home, it seemed.

"Yeah. I can break the lease and forfeit our security deposit. The couple renting our place is willing to relocate for a little 'sorry for the inconvenience' cash. But we've got to stay in this place until the end of the month, regardless. You know, we could stay a while longer—"

From the kitchen, through the bedroom, I could see Ruby poke her head out the bathroom door.

"That was a joke, right?"

"Joke," I said. "That was very much a joke."

"I've hated every second we've been here, John," Ruby said, returning to her packing.

"We're together, and you're alive," I said.

Ruby's head poked out from the bathroom door again. "Don't try to guilt me with the gratitude thing," Ruby said. "That's not fair. You know what I mean. This hasn't been my favorite experience."

My hands went into the air in a show of surrender.

Plan C (whatever you are), it is.

My cell phone rang. Thanks to Uretsky, the sound of any phone made me jumpy. I checked the caller ID and saw it was David Clegg calling. I let the call go to voice mail. A few seconds later, Clegg texted me.

John, I need to talk with you. Can we meet? Call me.

"Crap," I said to myself.

"What's up?"

Ruby came out of the bathroom, holding a cardboard box of things she had packed, and saw that my expression had darkened. "What's up?" she asked again, now pointing to my cell phone.

"It's Clegg," I said. "He wants to meet up with me."

A look of concern crossed Ruby's face. "Maybe he wants to meet you because he knows something," Ruby said. She spoke in a whispered voice, as if Clegg could somehow hear her.

"Knows what?" I whispered back. Why was I whispering?

"That we stole someone's identity." Ruby made a "Duh-uh" expression and lowered her gaze in disbelief of my ignorance. "He's a cop, John. Think about it."

My throat closed with the first sputter of nerves. I unlocked my phone and called back Clegg. He answered on the first ring.

"What time do you want to meet?" I asked.

CHAPTER 14

I saw David Clegg a few times each year, but never on the anniversary of Brooks Hall's death. Clegg would disappear on that day, and nobody knew where he went or what he did. He'd just up and vanish, and then return a day later, never telling anybody where he'd gone, his wife and kids included. I never asked Clegg how he marked the somber occasion, though he knew I spent it writing a letter to Hall's widow, Amanda.

On the first anniversary of the accident, I got a call from Amanda's attorney, requesting that I write to her. I was asked to provide a general update on my life. Apparently, Amanda wanted to know how I was feeling, coping, and adjusting in the aftermath of that tragic day. I suppose it was her way of staying connected to Brooks. It wasn't an easy letter to write by any means. Half of it was a rambling apology, while the other half was apologizing for apologizing.

The following year I sent Amanda another letter, unprompted this time, and the attorney didn't contact me to complain. I was more open about my feelings and better able to express myself, conveying the real bone-gnawing guilt that sabotaged my sleep and clung to me like an angry shadow. It became a tradition after that. I didn't expect Amanda to respond to my letters, and she never did. Still, I kept those letters coming, thinking that if she didn't want to hear from me, she'd let me know. Maybe I was helping her—that was my hope, anyway. I later found out, through other sources, that she had remarried and now has two kids, twins, one named Brooks. The Internet gives up a wealth of information if you know how to look. But not everything can be known via a clever Google search. I took precautions to make certain Amanda never found out that I was the guy who set up an online fund-raiser for a children's charity that both Brooks and Amanda supported. I didn't want her knowing I was involved, thinking the donations shouldn't be tainted with the memory of what I'd done.

Clegg and I usually meet up at Chaps Sports Bar in Kenmore Square. Even though Clegg lives in Hingham, he works in Boston, so it makes for a good meeting spot to grab a drink. This time, however, I insisted we meet at O'Brian's Sports Bar, which was a couple of blocks from our Brookline apartment. I didn't want to travel very far in case Ruby needed me for something. In truth, I wished Ruby had come along with me, but she insisted I go alone.

"He might not want to talk with me around," she had said.

I relented, but only after Ruby had made plans of her own, drinks—well, Diet Cokes—with her friend Elisa at the Deco Bar, a short distance away from O'Brian's on Beacon Street. Ruby needed to get out, it seemed to me, enjoy some fresh air, so I encouraged her.

At six o'clock in the afternoon O'Brian's would be sparsely occupied or packed to the edges, depending on the Red Sox schedule. The Sox were playing Tampa Bay in Tampa, so there were plenty of open seats at the long oak bar. Clegg used to dress in his police officer blues, which made him easy to spot and usually kept the stools next to him unoccupied, but that was before his promotion to detective. Clegg's new uniform was a tweed blazer and khaki slacks. Of course, he also carried a holstered firearm, pepper spray, and handcuffs, but those items weren't on display when I showed up.

Clegg raised a half full glass of Sam Adams, signaling the bartender to bring me the same while getting one on deck for himself to drink. He stood, and we exchanged bro hugs, basically light taps on each other's backs while we clinched in a weak embrace. It was both difficult and comforting for Clegg and me to hang together. In a way, we were cursed, because neither of us wanted to relive the past, while at the same time we didn't want to forget it, either.

Reading people was something better left to Ruby, but still, I appraised Clegg carefully, looking for behaviors that were directly antithetical to his usual mannerisms. I could tell *something* was wrong: clouds in the eyes, an atypically weighty demeanor, but I didn't get the sense that it had anything to do with me. I wished I could have told him about Uretsky, because that guy, for all his ghoulish antics, still lingered front and center in my mind.

Clegg might have been several years older than me, but his unwrinkled face and full head of dark hair would win him a prize at any carnival's "guess your age" booth. His nose was slightly crooked, set that way from years of youth hockey, which, when combined with his icy blue eyes brimming with street smarts, tinted his every expression with a hint of menace. Clegg could be smiling, and you'd still think, *This guy wants to kick my ass or arrest me.* Fit and trim because he continued to climb, Clegg was the closest thing the Boston PD had to a detective who looked like an actor playing a cop.

"You're late," Clegg said, not bothering to check his watch for the time. Cops like Clegg just knew.

"Sorry. Unexpected delay."

The unexpected delay was that I didn't want him to see me leaving an apartment that I shouldn't have been leaving. I looked him over again, searching for any reason I should be nervous, or more nervous than usual. Clegg had a way of setting people slightly on edge. Four of his past partners had asked to be transferred within a month of their assignment, and though Clegg has received numerous commendations from the BPD, he's also been a regular visitor to Internal Affairs. A self-described amalgam of "Dirty" Harry Callahan and the narcotics sergeant Martin Riggs from the *Lethal Weapon* franchise, Clegg relished life on the edge, which explained his passion for climbing and his penchant for pissing off his superiors.

I loved the guy like a brother.

"So what's been going on?" Clegg asked.

"Nothing much," I said.

"Nothing much," Clegg repeated, acknowledging the ridiculousness of my response while taking a swig of his beer as I did the same with mine. "How 'bout I get more specific? How's Ruby?"

"She's hanging in there," I said. "We won't know for a few more weeks if her medication is working or not, but we've got reason to stay positive."

"Well, at least *you've* got each other."

I nodded quickly, because it was true. Then paused because it was odd the way Clegg had phrased it. He emphasized *you've* as if to imply that he didn't have someone, which I knew not to be true, because he was married to Violet. I got a sinking feeling that another casualty of that day on the Labuche Kang was Clegg's marriage to his high school sweetheart.

"I swung by your place the other day," Clegg said, "but you weren't home."

Because I don't live there anymore, I wanted to say.

"Yeah? What day was that?"

"Tuesday."

"Tuesday?" I said, musing. "Tuesday . . . not sure where I was. Probably a doctor's appointment with Ruby. What were you doing in Somerville, anyway?"

"Looking for an apartment."

"Oh, no," I said, groaning. "What happened, man?"

"She wants a divorce," Clegg said.

Funny how Clegg's divorce bombshell felt like a relief compared to what I thought we might be here to discuss.

"Why?" My voice carried a harsh edge, like it was Violet's fault.

"She says I'm depressed. Hates that I still climb."

I did, too, but only because I was envious that he could still do it.

"Are you depressed?" I asked.

"My therapist seems to think so," Clegg said and chuckled.

"I'm really sorry. What are you going to do?"

"What can I do?" Clegg shrugged. "Look, I don't blame her. I haven't been a lot of fun to be around. To be honest with you, I can't believe we lasted as long as we did."

People carry guilt in different ways. Mine kept me from going up an escalator. From what I gathered, Clegg could tune his out with Johnnie Walker and a few chips of ice.

"What about your kids?" I asked.

Sammy and Tate were four when I spared their father's life. Now they were going on eight, prime years for parenting.

"It's going to be hardest on them."

"Is it really over? Can you salvage it?"

"Resentment is its own form of cancer, Johnny. And that's the cold, hard truth."

"So what happens now?"

"What happens is I move out. The kids broke down crying when I told 'em. That's when Violet begged me to look for an apartment or small house closer to Hingham. Thinking it means she'll agree to joint custody, but who knows. Look, I'm sorry to drag you away from Ruby to cry on your shoulder, but I needed someone to help me drown my sorrows."

"Fellow cops don't do the trick?" I asked.

"Divorce is as common as a cold in my precinct."

"What are you? A glutton for punishment? I'm a married man. Wouldn't you *rather* hang out with divorced guys?"

"Nah, they'd tell me that they're happier now," Clegg said. "That would just make me feel worse."

"Well, it's good to know you have feelings," I said.

"Cut me and I still bleed," Clegg said dramatically. "Of course, I'll also stomp on your face and then fill your mouth with pepper spray."

"Have I ever asked if you're a registered loose cannon?" I said to him, smiling.

"If that registry exits," Clegg said, "then my name is most certainly on it."

Clegg ordered us some hot wings as the bar began filling up with more of the after-work crowd. We had been talking for an hour or so when a woman with platinum blond hair, dressed in a business suit, sat down on the stool beside me. She hung her purse on the back of the stool and ordered a drink.

"How goes your game?" Clegg asked me.

"It's growing and going," I said.

"It was a real lifesaver," I wanted to say. Well, before Uretsky called, that is.

From the corner of my eye, I caught sight of a guy around my age, thin, hood over his head, sunglasses on indoors. He bumped clumsily up against the blond woman's stool. He wasn't that quick or that skilled in his fumbling attempt to snatch her purse. The purse got caught on the back of the stool, but he pulled on the strap hard enough to snap it.

"Hey!" the surprised woman shouted. The commotion turned heads, but shock and surprise kept every patron firmly rooted in place. The thief accelerated as he raced past my bar stool. Clegg, still holding his sticky chicken wing, nonchalantly reached behind with his free hand to grab hold of the fleeing man's sweatshirt. With startling quickness, Clegg yanked the man to the floor and at the same instant leapt up from his stool. The man fell with a hard thud, and I heard the air rush out of his lungs. Before he could wiggle away, Clegg was kneeling on his back, wrenching his arms behind him to snap his silver bracelets in place.

"Yo, clown town," Clegg said, his voice calm and his breathing even. "Looks like you picked the wrong bar to snatch from."

Applause filled the room as I handed the woman back her purse and Clegg hoisted the handcuffed man to his feet. I motioned to Clegg, because I'd obviously played no real part in his apprehension. Still, the victim thanked us both profusely.

"This job would be great if it weren't for all the criminals," Clegg said to me as he took out the handcuffed man's wallet to check his ID. Next, Clegg got out his cell phone, presumably to call for backup. "Here's your living proof that crime doesn't pay, Johnny," Clegg said, turning the thief to face me. The man looked remorseful only because he'd been captured.

Why did Clegg just say that to me? I wondered. *Here's your living proof that crime doesn't pay.* Could he know?

Clegg cupped his cell phone's receiver and then, turning to me, said, "Brookline dispatch. I'm on hold." The crowd kept still and hushed, watching the spectacle of a plainclothes police officer pressing a handcuffed man up against their neighborhood bar.

A minute or so ticked by with Clegg holding his phone tight to his ear. His expression revealed a growing frustration. He kept nodding and occasionally would say into the phone, "Yeah . . . all right . . . okay . . . What's going on?" He listened awhile, then something about Clegg's expression changed—he got a disgusted look, but not one that conveyed any agitation. "Really? No shit," he said. "Really? That's all sorts of messed up. . . . No, don't worry. . . . Yeah, I'm sure . . . I'll keep him occupied." Clegg ended the call, then said to the guy he nabbed, "Hey, buddy, looks like you're going to have to wait awhile in my car until we get some Brookline PD here to take you to the station for booking. Promise me you're not going to mess up my backseat?"

The guy said nothing; he just looked away.

"Want to walk with me, John?" Clegg asked.

"Sure," I said.

The bartender comped our tab, brushing us outside, as though worried we might attempt to fight his goodwill gesture. There were cheers and a rousing round of applause as we vacated the premises. Clegg held up his hand, acknowledging the patrons' appreciation with a slight wave, the way a baseball player might try to appease the crowd after a game-turning home run. We walked half a block with people on the street staring at the three of us, speculating as to the circumstance.

It didn't take long for Clegg to get the handcuffed perp settled into the backseat of his unmarked police car. "No messing up my ride," he instructed again.

The guy didn't reply.

"What's the delay getting the police here?" I asked.

"Some big blowup just down the road has almost every cop in Brookline tied up," Clegg said. "It won't be too much longer."

"What kind of blowup?" I asked.

"Oh, some dude came home to find his girlfriend murdered."

"Yikes," I said.

"Yikes is right," Clegg said. "You don't know the half of it."

"I'm assuming you do."

"I'm close with the dispatcher, so I got the skinny. Looks like the guy who did it cut off the girl's fingers."

"Shit."

"He put two fingers on her lips, one in each ear, then two covering her eyes."

"What the hell?"

"Get it?" Clegg asked.

"No," I said.

"See no evil. Hear no evil. Speak no evil."

"Holy shit," I said.

"Holy shit is right."

"Where did this happen?"

"Right down the road," Clegg said, nodding in the direction where I now lived.

"No. What address? I mean."

It couldn't be, I was thinking. *It couldn't be.*

"Why?" Clegg asked.

"I want to know which way to avoid when I'm heading home."

"No worries. I'll drive you."

"No, I've got to meet Ruby."

"Four-fifty-seven Harvard Avenue," Clegg said.

I felt the ground give way and had to steady myself using the door handle of Clegg's car. I found my balance, but the ground below me turned unsteady like the sea. Four-fifty-seven Harvard Avenue was the building where we had rented an apartment as Elliot and Tanya Uretsky. I knew at that moment exactly what Uretsky had meant when he said he was going to kill someone close to us. He didn't mean close by relationship. He meant close by proximity.

He knew who we were. He knew where we lived. My cell phone rang. I took it out and looked at the caller ID. The number came up as unknown. It rang again.

I answered it.

CHAPTER 15

"Hello?" I said into my phone. My strangled voice came out shaky, more like a whimper than a word. I moved away from Clegg, turning my back so he couldn't see me, couldn't overhear me, either.

"Hello, John," Uretsky said. His distinct rasp, the resonance of his baritone voice, that unsettling calm were as familiar to me as a Beatles song. "Yes, I know your real name, and no, you can't know how. I want you to listen very carefully."

"What have you done?" I said, speaking in a low voice. I took a few more steps away from Clegg. "What the hell have you done?" That came out harsh, a low, growling whisper. My heart was thrumming wildly.

"*Listen* means don't talk, dumb ass," Uretsky snapped. "Are you listening?"

"Yes," I said, breathing out the word in one long hiss.

"Your wife is wearing an olive-green sweater and blue jeans," Uretsky said, speaking quickly now. "She's with a girl named Elisa, and I know that they're at the Deco Bar on Beacon Street. I also know that Ruby has been drinking club soda and lime all night, because alcohol and Verbilifide don't mix very well. I know that Elisa is a pretty, dark-haired girl who won't stay pretty for long if you don't do exactly as I say. Do you understand?"

Clegg surprised me with a tap on my shoulder. I recoiled from his touch, as though his hands were an electric cattle prod. I must have looked like a wild man to him, my eyes flickering, mouth agape, and sweat beading up on my brow.

"Johnny, you all right?" Clegg asked. "You look white as my ass."

The phone was still pressed to my ear as Uretsky spoke. "Tell that cop friend of yours that it's Ruby. Tell him she's not feeling well."

He knew I was with Clegg?

My head darted about in all directions. I glanced into the glimmering windows of the apartments across the street, into storefronts, crowded restaurants, and bars, which existed aplenty in this section of town. He could see me! Good God in heaven, Uretsky was watching me! I kept looking around, noticing the multitudes of people milling about on this warm spring evening, many with cell phones mounted to their ear.

"Say it, John," Uretsky urged. "Tell him that Ruby isn't feeling very well and you need to go."

"Yo, bro? Are you all right?" Clegg asked.

"Ruby," I managed.

A flash of concern washed across Clegg's face, genuine, as though Ruby were family. "What's going on?" Clegg asked in a voice steeped with worry. "Is everything all right?"

"Tell him she's fine, but you have to leave," Uretsky instructed again.

I repeated those exact words, as though in a trance.

"I'll drive you," Clegg said.

"He's got a prisoner to deal with," Uretsky said into my ear.

How does he know that? Where is he?

"You've got your hands full," I said to Clegg, nodding my head in the direction of his police car. I couldn't see into the car's dark interior, but I assumed the man Clegg had apprehended was still seated inside, waiting for the Brookline police to cart him off to jail. I tapped Clegg's shoulder a few times. "I'm all right," the gesture was intended to say. "Just let me go." Hoping that allayed his concerns, I started to back away from Clegg slowly.

"Johnny!" Clegg shouted at me.

Turning my back to him now, I began a trot that soon broke into a run, yelling over my shoulder as I accelerated, "I'll call you!"

Clegg shouted, "Johnny," again, but I gave him no response. I kept the phone, with Uretsky still on the line, fixed to my ear but didn't speak until I had turned the corner, a block away from where I had left Clegg standing, his expression unmistakably and understandably confused.

"You still there, John?" I heard Uretsky say.

I slowed my pace, soon coming to a full stop. I couldn't yet catch my breath, so I had to double over, resting my hands on my knees to increase the airflow. "I'm here," I said, panting. "I'm here."

"Good boy," Uretsky said. "So listen, you've obviously lost round one."

"Why?" I said. My voice sounded constricted, as though Uretsky's hands magically extended through the phone to choke my windpipe. "Why did you do it? Why did you kill that woman?"

"Because she was there. Isn't that why you once climbed mountains? Because they were there."

Uretsky chuckled hauntingly, while I staggered into an alley directly behind a Chinese restaurant and proceeded to vomit up my dinner of chicken wings and beer. The sour stench from my stomach mixed foully with the smells from the kitchen.

"You're insane," I yelled before several gagging dry heaves put me on my knees. A cook from the restaurant, draped in white clothes blotched with food stains, flung open the back door to check on the commotion. I shielded my face with the back of my hand and slunk deeper into the alley, away from his prying eyes.

"My mental state is not your concern," Uretsky said. "Do you know what is?"

I couldn't answer—the nerves connecting my brain to my mouth seemed severed.

Uretsky answered for me. "Your concern should be that poor woman you let down."

"I didn't kill her," I stammered.

"Of course you did," Uretsky snapped. "You didn't even *try* to steal the scarves."

"I didn't think you were serious."

Uretsky scoffed, a loud "Ha!" "I told you very specifically the penalty for failure. It's your fault you didn't believe me, not mine. You lost round one after I gave you every conceivable chance to win.

I wish you could have seen what I did to her, John. It would have definitely inspired you to try a little harder. You were at home while I was doing it. In fact, I was right below you."

"Please . . . don't . . ."

Then I thought, *Right below me*. Could it have been our downstairs neighbor, Rhonda?

"She was begging me," Uretsky continued. "Big, thick tears rolling down her cheeks. I gagged her, of course. I didn't want her screams bringing anyone to her rescue. You've got to think these things through, John. It takes thought to be on the wrong side of the law, but you'll learn that soon enough. Anyway, I used these pruning shears I bought at Home Depot to cut her fingers. They snapped off just like I was breaking a stubborn branch. Snap. Snap. Snap. I figured she'd pass out by finger four, but it happened right after I cut off the second one."

"Oh God," I whimpered.

"God? Really? God?" Uretsky laughed a little. "You know, most criminals don't find God until they're in the slammer," he said. "And you've got a long way to go before that happens to you. Now, if you play my game, and this time you try to win, I can assure you, you'll never find yourself confined to those ugly four walls."

I couldn't speak.

"Are you listening, John?"

How to describe my shock? It welled up inside me, all consuming, entirely paralyzing. It was an inescapable blackness, a fast-acting cancer swelling from within, hollowing out my guts, turning my blood to molasses, slowing my heartbeat to a tick and my breathing to a trickle.

"Please . . . stop. . . . I don't want to hear this. . . ."

"Too late for that," Uretsky said. "Now, pay attention. Pay very close attention. I'm using a phone that cannot be traced. Don't even bother to try." I said nothing, so Uretsky continued. "Also, if the name Uretsky comes up in connection with the investigation into the gruesome murder of a youngish woman at four-fifty-seven Harvard Avenue, I'm going to kill again—and it will be someone you know, maybe a friend, a mother, or just a passing acquaintance. Contact with you is all I need to mark them for death. The point is—and this is a promise—someone will die, and die horribly, and their blood will be on your hands. Just so we're perfectly clear, that means you keep your pal David Clegg in the dark about everything. No mention of me. No mention of our game. Do you understand?"

I tried to answer but still could not find my voice.

"Do you understand?" Uretsky screamed the question with enough force to bloody my eardrums.

"Yes!" I shouted back, crying as I spoke. "Yes! I understand! Damn you, I understand!"

"Good," Uretsky said, placid again. "Another rule," he continued. "You can't move out of the apartment you rented in my name under any circumstance. You're to remain in the apartment above that poor murdered woman until you either win or lose my game. Is that understood?"

I nodded, dumbly—he couldn't see me—and numbly.

"Is that understood?" Uretsky asked again.

"Yes," I squeaked out.

I thought of Ruby, recalling the joy on her face as she was packing our bags to move. What would her look say when I told her that I'd stolen the identity of a raging psychopath, and that he was holding us hostage in an apartment I had rented under false pretenses? What would her reaction be when she learned we had no way out of this nightmare but to do as we were told?

"Good," Uretsky said. "Because it's time for you to play round two. The punishment for failure is that you'll be arrested for insurance fraud and Ruby will lose access to the medication she needs to keep alive. In addition to that, I'll still kill again, another woman, and it could be anybody who is even remotely connected to you. Sound like high enough stakes to you?"

"What do you want me to do?" I asked.

"Like I said before, a criminal, no matter what the crime, is always a thief of something. You stole the truth the moment you took my identity. Now you must play the part."

"How? I don't understand!" I was shouting. "How do I play the part?"

"Oh, you'll see. It's no fun if I spoil all the surprises."

I kept yelling at Uretsky, pleading with him to talk to me. I was on my knees in a wretched alleyway that stunk of rotted garbage, with shards of glass digging painfully into the fabric of my jeans, shaking. "How do I play the part? How do I do it?" Occasionally, a sob would escape my lips, but not enough to stop my continued questions, even though Uretsky's call had long gone dead.

CHAPTER 16

A young Brookline police officer, male, close-shaved head, round face, escorted Ruby and me up to our apartment. He informed us that the victim was a thirty-two-year-old dental hygienist named Rhonda Jennings. We knew her as someone about to get engaged to her boyfriend, interested in learning yoga, and who was once kind enough to bring us a frozen pie. Rolls of yellow crime-scene tape cordoned off the landing directly below where we lived. "Don't touch anything," we were instructed. "Keep your hands to your sides." If our police escort knew my real feelings, he might have said instead: "Don't get sick in the stairwell. Don't sweat so much. Don't pass out, even though you look like you're about to do just that."

Before we were allowed back in the building, Officer Teddy Walsh—his name, according to the badge he wore—had us answer some questions on the sidewalk.

"Did you know the woman who lived below you?"

"We met her once," I said.

"How long have you been living here?"

"A few months," I said.

"Have you seen anybody suspicious hanging around . . . loiterers, somebody who just looked out of place?"

"No."

Officer Walsh wrote down my answers in a little white notebook. Meanwhile, all around us strobe lights of every color in the rainbow lit up the night sky. More yellow crime-scene tape dangled from banisters and clung to door frames like macabre streamers. The answers I'd given Officer Walsh were all the truth. Could this be my next test?

Round two in Uretsky's twisted game? So far, I didn't need to lie to the police; I needed only to keep the truth well concealed. Was that playing the part? I wondered.

I'm going to kill again. . . . Contact with you is all I need to mark them for death.

At that moment, I wanted to tell him everything. Shout out my confessional like he was a faith healer, and I, a man with a broken spirit. I managed to temper my desire, though it boiled inside me.

A criminal thinks things through. . . .

Hadn't Uretsky said that, or something close to it? Wouldn't he be prepared for me to talk to the police—to confess everything? No matter what I did, even if I sacrificed my own freedom to admit to all I had done, Uretsky would still make another kill. And the blood of that kill *would* be on my hands. No question about it. I had to wait this out. Figure out how to "play the part." For the moment, at least, I was Elliot Uretsky's hostage, despite my freedom to go where I wanted and do whatever I pleased.

The police officer asked to see our identification, so we showed him our Mass IDs—the ones with the name Uretsky printed on the front. Our names needed to match the labels on the mailbox in the foyer and on the apartment lease. We were Elliot and Tanya Uretsky, at least until the real Uretsky tired of playing his game.

"Are you all right?" Officer Walsh asked Ruby.

Ruby had the dazed look of an accident victim. Her vacant eyes remained downcast, and her answer came out as soft as the flapping of butterfly wings. "Yes . . . I'm fine," she said. "Just scared and sad for that poor woman."

"I understand that this is traumatic," Walsh said. "We have counselors who can help if you need assistance."

"Thanks," Ruby said.

I wanted to say, "Nobody can help with what we need."

Instead, I said nothing.

Ruby sat on the futon, head in her hands. I sat beside her, but she recoiled from my touch.

"I don't want to be near you," she said. "I can't be near you right now."

"We need to stick together on this," I said.

"Why didn't you tell me? Why didn't you tell me exactly what that monster had threatened to do?"

"I didn't want to upset you."

"Upset me? Really? That was your reason? John, I think you've done a hell of a lot more than upset me!"

Ruby's face contorted into a sort of animal snarl. How many times had I seen Ruby truly irate? The answer: never. Of course she got mad at me, often deservedly so—sometimes, just because—but on those occasions she'd go quiet, like a stealth submarine running silent, running deep. This time, she stood and crossed the room, her arms folded tightly against her chest and her back turned.

"What should I have done?" I asked.

Ruby pivoted in a fluid motion to face me. "Told the truth, for starters!"

"And then what?" I didn't want to yell, but it was hard to keep my emotions in check. A woman was dead, and if you traced the blame, it originated with the identity that I stole. "What would we have done differently?"

"Maybe gone to the police," Ruby said. "Maybe then Rhonda would still be alive."

"And tell them what, Ruby? What? That we stole an identity and our victim is now terrorizing us?"

"What were you thinking, John?"

"I thought he was trying to just scare us. I didn't think he would do it. . . . I didn't think he could! He couldn't have known who we were. How the hell was he going to kill somebody close to us?"

"How did he find out who we are, John? How? You said there was no way to trace our actual address from the post office box," Ruby yelled from across the room.

"I don't know."

"Well, find out, dammit! You find out!"

Ruby crumpled to the floor like a folded napkin. She wasn't just crying tears—she was wailing like a woman in mourning. She lay on her side, crying like that, shaking, and struggling to speak. "I'm not strong enough to handle this, John," she was saying. "I'm not going to be able to make it. I can't do this. I can't—"

Her words were halted by another tsunami of tears. I got down on the floor beside Ruby. She wanted me close to her, I could tell, so I tucked her into my arms, spooning her the way I did when it was bedtime, just before sleep found us. I rocked Ruby in my arms in that spooning position, and I knew as the horror sank in that nothing about our relationship would ever be the same.

"I love you, baby. I love you," I said over and over again.

"We've got to tell the police," Ruby said.

"We can't," I said. "He'll kill again. He'll do it, and we can't stop him."

"You've got to make him stop. Please make him stop."

"I will," I said. "I promise. All I have to do is play the part. Whatever that means."

We were still on the floor when the phone rang. Ruby pulled away from me and got into a kneeling position quicker than a cat. The muscles of her jaw tightened; her fingers, knuckles white from the applied force, dug hard against her thighs. I whirled around, glaring at the phone like it was a predator set loose in the apartment.

It rang again.

"Are you going to answer it?"

It rang again.

"What if he hangs up?" she asked. "What if this is our only chance to do what he wants?"

It rang again.

"Answer it, John! Answer it!"

I picked up the phone.

"Hello?"

My voice had the croaky sound of having been roused from a deep slumber.

"Elliot Uretsky?" asked a man.

I didn't recognize the voice, but I knew it wasn't the real Elliot Uretsky calling to terrify us again.

"Who is this?" I asked.

The cold bite to my voice was intended to intimidate.

"My name is Henry Dobson," said the man. "Am I speaking with Elliot Uretsky?"

"You are," I said, lying.

Play the part. . . .

"Sorry to call so late."

I closed my eyes and fought to keep down what little was left in-

CHAPTER 17

Our apartment buzzer buzzed at nine thirty and zero seconds the following morning. The visitor was expected, but even so, Ruby and I flinched at the sound. We looked absolutely horrible—not a wink of sleep for either of us. We had watched the news and read the papers online but hadn't left the apartment—our prison.

Rhonda's parents, a pleasant-looking gray-haired couple from Michigan, made a tearful plea on the local evening news—rebroadcast for the morning news as well—for anybody to come forward with information to help apprehend their daughter's killer. The gruesome details of how the body was left—the demonic redistribution of her severed fingers—was somehow kept from the media.

"That's us, John," Ruby said. "We're the ones who need to come forward. We're the ones who need to help poor Rhonda's parents."

"And then we'll be the ones who will live with another dead woman on our conscience. We've got to play out this next round. Then we'll come forward."

"You think Uretsky is the one who alerted UniSol about us?" Ruby asked.

I nodded. "Play the part," I said. "We've got to convince the investigator that we are who we're pretending to be. It's got to be what he meant."

I said it calmly, but I wasn't feeling calm. I was racked with guilt—guilt that once I had intentionally killed a man, and then, years later, unintentionally killed a woman. I felt guilty for Ruby's sickness, for stealing an identity, for dragging my wife into this. I felt guilty for playing Uretsky's game and guilty for thinking of quitting. *Blood will* side my stomach. I glanced over at Ruby and saw that her hands were covering her mouth, ironically in a gesture not too dissimilar from that of the wise monkey warning against speaking evil. I thought of the woman who lived below us, whose severed fingers were meant to communicate the same.

"What do you want, Mr. Dobson? This isn't a particularly good time to talk."

"Then I'll make it brief," Dobson said. "I'm a fraud investigator with UniSol Health, and I'm afraid we might have a serious problem with your claim."

be on my hands. . . . I felt trapped and hopeless and sick myself, a sickness of my own damn making.

I buzzed Dobson in and waited. Minutes later I heard a soft knock. I opened the door, blocking Ginger's escape attempt with my leg. A man stood in the doorway. I took a close look at our judge, jury, and potential executioner. I guessed him to be in his mid- to late thirties, partly because he was balding, with clusters of sandy brown hair barely allowing for a comb-over. As for body type, he was thin up top, but thick in the middle, another sign of middle age. A bushy mustache accentuated his thin lips, and he wore glasses, round, wire-rimmed style, held in place behind ears that stuck out from his head. Dressed in a blue oxford shirt, red tie, and tan slacks, he reminded me of the accountants Ruby once worked with back when she was a graphic designer for a financial services firm. Just a regular guy.

He knows, I was thinking. *He knows everything. How will I be able to play the part?* I thought back to what Clegg said to me. *Here's your living proof that crime doesn't pay. Your proof is a balding guy with glasses, waiting with bated breath to bring down the hammer of justice upon your stupid, stupid head. Happy days, John Bodine. You've really made a mess out of things.*

Truth is, I'd be fine with a prison sentence for what I'd done. Maybe the national media attention would guarantee Ruby enough donations to fund her Verbilifide treatments. Maybe Uretsky knew all that, which was why he vowed to kill another woman if I failed to play the part. Win or lose at Uretsky's game, I was certain of one thing: if Uretsky didn't kill me, the guilt eventually would.

I unconsciously straightened my posture while extending my hand to Dobson. He set down his well-worn, black leather flap-over portfolio to shake hello. The man's smile seemed genuine and congenial, though his teeth were noticeably coffee-stained yellow.

"Elliot Uretsky?" he asked.

I nodded. My stomach churned at the sound of my stolen name. *Uretsky.*

He spoke from his throat, not his gut, so his voice came out muffled and a bit nasal. If asked, I'd place his upbringing somewhere in the Midwest.

Maybe near where Rhonda Jennings's family lives.

My stomach clenched and released spasmodically as I said, "That's me."

"Henry Dobson," the man said, strengthening his already firm grip on my hand.

He let go of my hand and removed from his rear pants pocket a brown leather wallet, well worn, too. He flipped the leather billfold open, showing me his UniSol Health investigator's identification, which he kept protected behind a clear plastic shield. He held the wallet close enough for me to read the name, Henry Dobson, and see that his face matched the picture on the ID.

"I didn't realize this was the building where that murder took place," Dobson said, still standing in the hallway.

"Last night," I said, somehow summoning up a convincingly calm composure.

"I got stopped by the police on my way in," Dobson said. "That's when I found out."

"Horrible, isn't it?" I said.

"You hear about murders on the news all the time," Dobson said. "But I never thought about the people who live in the buildings where a murder takes place. Until now, that is. And here I am, adding to your troubles."

I kept blocking the door to our apartment. I wasn't ready to let him inside just yet.

"Do you mind telling me what this is all about? My wife isn't feeling very well."

The real Elliot would be a bit indignant at the intrusion, I had decided. To play the part meant needing to find the right balance between anger and cooperation. In actuality, Ruby was in the bedroom, hiding out until she had to make an appearance, not that Dobson needed to know all that.

"Of course she's not," Dobson said. "And I do apologize for the intrusion. I just have to do some quick verification work. You see, somebody called our fraud line and reported you."

"Fraud line?" I asked.

"We have an anonymous tip line for folks to report medical fraud. You ask me, it's been a mixed blessing so far. We've uncovered some fraud, but we've also got our fair share of angry exes or envious coworkers wanting to stir up trouble. Regardless, we've got to investigate all reports."

So that was it—Uretsky had called the UniSol tip line to report our crime.

Play the part.

"How do you know?" I asked.

"Know what?" Dobson replied.

"If someone is committing fraud."

Dobson smiled, pushing his mustache up against his nose. "I'm really good at my job," he said.

If Dobson brushed the back of my neck, he would wonder if I suffered from hyperhidrosis, excessive sweating, and perhaps would ask why I never filed any medical claims for treatment. Dobson indicated with a nod toward the living room that he wished to come inside, and not wanting to be truculent, I opted to let him in.

Ruby emerged from the bedroom, her skin so white, it appeared almost translucent. Her hands were trembling, too. It was a subtle waver, but I could see it easily because I knew Ruby. Dobson did not, so if he happened to notice and think it out of the ordinary, he'd probably assume it was a condition of her cancer. Meanwhile, Ruby looked at me with these benumbed, wide eyes and a defeated expression that broke my heart. My guilt revved up well past the red line once again. I put on a false exterior—one of pure confidence—hoping Ruby would absorb some of my self-assurance. She stood, albeit shakily, and came to greet us in the small foyer.

"Hello," she said to Dobson, her voice weak.

"Hello," Dobson said, giving Ruby's outstretched hand a proper shake.

When they each let go, I saw Dobson nonchalantly rub his hand against his pant leg, perhaps to clear away the perspiration he'd picked up from Ruby's palm.

"Would you like something to drink?" Ruby asked, straining a smile. "Tea, perhaps?"

Dobson smiled warmly, but those yellowish teeth must have looked like bared fangs to my wife.

"No, thank you," Dobson said. "I really don't want to take up much of your time. I'll just be a few minutes. Routine questions, that's all. I'm sorry to be of any inconvenience at this difficult time. I promise to be out of your hair as quickly as possible."

I saw Dobson glance nervously at Ruby's gorgeous strawberry blond locks. Perhaps he thought Ruby had lost her hair to chemo, and his last statement could have been construed as a thoughtless remark. I preferred a sensitive investigator to a hard-nosed one.

"Before we sit down, do you mind if I have a look around?" Dobson removed a clipboard from within his portfolio and held it up for me to see. "Part of my investigation requires that I do a quick inventory of your living arrangements. We need to make sure you're actually residents here."

I felt like now was as good a time as any to show my indignation.

"I have to be honest, this is feeling like quite an intrusion. We're suffering a pretty significant ordeal already. I really don't appreciate UniSol treating us like criminals."

If you catch on to me, I was thinking, *another person, someone I know will die.*

Dobson made a face, as if to suggest this wasn't the first time he'd heard that complaint. "It's uncomfortable, and I completely understand your frustration," he said. "Unfortunately, some of the more brazen fraud attempts we've investigated have involved apartments rented under false names or P.O. boxes used for mail drops. Believe me, if there's a way to commit a crime, somebody is going to think how best to do it." Dobson laughed, perhaps to shake off the uncomfortable aura that had settled over the room. "I promise, I'll be quick," he added.

"Do you mind if I ask what exactly you are looking for?"

"Evidence that Elliot and Tanya Uretsky reside at this address," Dobson said. "Pictures. Mementos. Mail in your name, that sort of thing. It's pretty easy to tell with just a cursory inspection when someone is using an apartment for illicit purposes. Of course, you can refuse my search request. I'll have to report that back to UniSol, and they'll probably expand the claims investigation, which regrettably could impact your claim status until it's resolved."

My mouth fell open. "That sounds like blackmail," I said.

Ruby gripped my arm.

"Easy," she was saying to me. "Take it easy, John."

"Again, I completely understand," Dobson said. "I promise, it's just a quick check around. It's obvious to me that you are who you say you are."

I allowed my face to show pure outrage. Meanwhile, Ruby appeared ready to make a dash for that blue bucket tucked under the sink.

"By all means," I said, gesturing toward the bedroom where we'd slept for less than three months.

My acting chops were limited to a middle school production of the play *Harvey,* in which I gave an infamously dreadful interpretation of the Dr. Chumley character. I guess that past episode wasn't fully reflective of my inner thespian, because, somehow, I managed to maintain an air of pure indignation as Dobson walked into the bedroom, peeked into our bathroom, and then returned to the living room, seemingly satisfied. At least, he made several marks on his paper that were suggestive of his satisfaction.

"Just a few quick questions," Dobson said, "and then I'll be gone."

"I really don't appreciate being put through this," I muttered while I took my seat at our rented pinewood dining table. The ceiling mounted light above us was a cheap model that cast wide shadows, making it difficult for Dobson to read his paperwork. Ruby took a seat opposite to me, with Dobson plunked down in the middle of us both.

Play the part. . . . Play the part. . . . Play the part, I was saying to myself.

Every other second I thought about Rhonda. I could tell Ruby was thinking the same. I recalled Uretsky's chilling words. *I wish you could have seen what I did to her. . . . It would have definitely inspired you to try a little harder.*

"I just need to see some identification. Again, you can refuse. . . ."

I held up a hand to stop him.

"Here you go," I said, handing over our Massachusetts ID cards with the name Uretsky on the front.

If Dobson wondered why we didn't have driver's licenses, he didn't ask. He just jotted down some information on his sheet. Meanwhile, at his request, I produced several bills, cable TV and electric, all in Elliot Uretsky's name thanks to the paperwork I had previously filed. Dobson seemed satisfied with that as well. His writing speed accelerated proportionally with my desire to have him leave. Perhaps he sensed his welcome wearing out.

"What now?" I asked.

Dobson pushed his chair back and shoved his clipboard back into his leather case. "Nothing," he said. "I do feel terrible for having put you through all this rigmarole, and I greatly appreciate your time and cooperation. Damn system. We've got to check into every whistle-blower's accusation. Believe me, you're the last people I'd want to investigate. Personally, this is very hard for me."

"Why's that?" I asked, curious.

Dobson smiled, albeit somewhat sheepishly.

"Prostate cancer," he said, putting a hand on his belly. "Early diagnosis saved my life. So while I love my job and get a lot of satisfaction bringing the bad guys to justice, I don't derive much pleasure having to investigate a couple going through what I know to be a difficult ordeal. And my timing couldn't have been worse." His eyes went to the floor and might as well have burned a hole into Rhonda Jennings's apartment below. "I'm not just giving you lip service here. I know. This is a tough battle you're facing, and I hate being another obstacle in your way. But that's the job."

Ruby seemed to have lost her earlier nervousness. Despite all our troubles, she connected with Dobson on a level I couldn't, not without being a cancer survivor myself.

"I'm so sorry," Ruby said to him.

"No," Dobson replied. "I am."

"So we're all set, then?" I asked.

I wanted Dobson out of our apartment, shared painful experience notwithstanding.

"All set," Dobson said.

"What now?" I asked.

Play the part. . . .

"Now you get healthy and take care of each other," Dobson said.

I noticed he wasn't wearing a wedding ring, and there was a hint of sadness to his voice. Perhaps he was a bachelor who, despite our health struggles, felt lonely in our presence. I thought of Clegg. He hadn't called, hadn't tried to reach us to check up on Ruby. Maybe he went by our Somerville apartment again; maybe the professors from

Spain answered the door this time. They were still there. I had told them they didn't need to move out.

Before he left, Dobson checked his phone. "Another appointment," he said to me, holding up the device and shaking his head grimly. Ruby and I escorted Dobson to the front door, where he paused. He took out his wallet and handed me his business card with the UniSol Health logo embossed in gold on the front. "You shouldn't need to get in touch with me," he said. "But take this just in case."

"Thanks," Ruby said.

Ruby was talking to Dobson about cancer treatments when the phone rang. I felt my pulse drop. Dobson noticed something was wrong. "You all right?" he asked. "Your color just changed."

The phone rang again.

"Yeah," I said.

I left him and Ruby and went back into the apartment. I picked up the receiver, noticing that Ruby was watching me. Dobson, too, for that matter.

"Hello?" I said.

"Good for you, John." Uretsky spoke into my ear. "Looks like you've won round two, but we're not done yet. Not even close. We've got round three to play, and this time, John, you're going to rob a liquor store. Details to come."

I heard a click. The line disconnected. I hung up the phone.

"Who was that?" Ruby asked, her voice dripping with dread.

"Wrong number," I said.

CHAPTER 18

I told Ruby about Uretsky's call the moment I heard Dobson descending the stairs. She didn't break into tears, didn't seem all that shocked to me, either. If anything, she looked numb, just like me.

"He wants you to rob a liquor store?" Ruby asked.

I nodded.

"Which one?"

"Well, I don't know," I said. "He didn't say. He just hung up."

"How could he have known that we successfully played the part?" Ruby asked me.

I went from standing in the kitchen area to kneeling on the futon, watching Dobson through the apartment window as he crossed Harvard Avenue. Thankfully, I didn't have to look down to see him—probably would have sent me into a dizzy spell—but from my futon perch I could follow him as he weaved in and out of the mid-morning crowds. Puffy clouds drifted lazily across an azure sky; it was a perfect June day, the kind that let people know summer lurked just around the corner.

But something else lurked around the corner, too, something waiting just for me, an evil beyond any I could have imagined.

How could he have known?

Ruby's question haunted my thoughts.

"He must have broken in here and bugged our apartment," I said, leaving the futon to stand beside Ruby in the center of the living room. "That's the only explanation I can think of."

"You mean he's listening to us? Right now?" she said.

"I'm guessing," I said. "I don't know." I began to pace, trying to walk off a toxic cocktail of agitation, frustration, and fear building inside me.

"I can't stay here," Ruby said as a look of disgust came across her face while surveying the apartment. She saw ghosts lurking in every corner, or at least that was what her eyes suggested. *He's been in here. He's listening to us. He knows our every move.* "We've got to get out of here, now," she added.

"We can't leave," I said. I sounded emphatic and meant to. "Uretsky told me that we had to stay put. You know the consequences. He's proved he'll do what he says."

"This has gone far enough," Ruby said. "We're going to the police, and we're going now."

"No!" I shouted, my voice both sharp and angry.

Ruby jumped, and I felt terrible for startling her.

"We can't do that," I said more calmly, but still unable to mask my frustration and upset. "He'll kill again. Don't you get it? He'll kill again." I spoke those last three words through clenched teeth, slowly and forcefully.

He'll. Kill. Again.

"Well, maybe you can't or won't go to the police, but I can."

Ruby stormed off into the kitchen, while at the same instant my cell phone chirped out the first notes of the Beatles song "Help!"

That ringtone told me I just got a customer service complaint. Anytime a player of my *One World* game sends an e-mail to Customer-Support@OneWorldGame.com, I get a text message containing the sender's name and the subject line of their message sent to my phone. This way, since I don't always check my e-mail, I'm alerted to every new support issue as soon as it hits my in-box. "Help!" Get it? Usually, people e-mail customer support when there's something wrong with the game, something my automated monitoring services might not have picked up. My iPhone buzzes intermittently with these alerts, so typically, I just glance at the sender and answer later, usually in a marathon customer support session. I didn't imagine I would be doing customer support anytime soon, but habits are like a reflex, so I looked at the phone.

When I saw the sender, I just closed my eyes tightly and willed it to be different. The message came from Elliot Uretsky's game account. The subject line of his message: **Read me.**

CHAPTER 19

I had two computers in the apartment, a laptop and a desktop; the others had recently been sold to fund this catastrophe of mine. I went to my laptop computer, set up on a table in the bedroom; logged in to my game administrator account; and clicked on Uretsky's message. The message came up in my e-mail program all right, but the contents were sparse—a single link and, below that, a phone number.

Ruby stood behind me, looking over my shoulder. I could hear her shallow breathing and feel the force of her fingers pulling against the back of my chair.

"What are you going to do?" she asked.

"I'm going to call the number," I said. "The link—it's encrypted. There's no way I can tell what's going to happen if I click it."

"And the number?" She said that like it was the worst idea in the world. "Who do you think you'll be calling?"

"I'm guessing it's Uretsky," I said.

"Think about this, John," Ruby said. "Are you sure this is what you should do?"

I looked up at Ruby and wanted to cry. The past twenty-four hours had simply stripped her of all her strength. It was horrible to see. Even with the weight loss, the side effects of the drug—painful nodules popping up all over her body, the swollen joints, the stomach pains she battled daily—I could always see her inner strength. It was gone, like a switch had been flicked, and its glow extinguished. Hopelessness was all I saw in her eyes.

"I don't know what else to do," I said.

I picked up my phone and called the number in Uretsky's message.

Uretsky answered on the third ring. "Hello, John," he said. "Long time no talk."

That voice—the monotone rasp and deep-timbered baritone—triggered an olfactory illusion. I smelled something sour and fetid, the stench of rot and decay.

"Please," I said. "We can stop this. Stop this now."

"Click the link, John," Uretsky said. No inflection to his voice, no rage or upset, either, just a direct command.

"What is it? What is it for?"

"Just click the link."

My hand moved to the computer mouse. I felt in a trance, a creature without a will of its own, being manipulated by a master. The mouse cursor hovered over the link as though building up the strength to make the leap.

Click the link.

"What am I going to open?" I asked.

"A Web site," Uretsky said. "I made it. I'm using an anonymous proxy server, so don't think you can trace me via my IP address. You can't."

Uretsky was right, of course. Anonymous proxy servers are a special type of server that act as a go-between for a home network and the Internet. It's like sneaking out to the Internet, snatching some bits of information, and coming back home without anybody knowing you ever set foot outside your house. If Uretsky said it was untraceable, I was inclined to believe him.

"John—" Ruby said, gripping my shoulder now instead of the chair.

My shaking hand caused the cursor to dance over the hyperlink as a mirror of my erratic movements.

"Go ahead and click, John. I'm waiting."

I did it. I pushed my finger down and lifted it up. The click of the mouse sounded like an exit door slamming shut, then locking. *No way out now.*

A Web browser popped open. The background was black, and in the center of the Web page there appeared a rectangular area containing an embedded video application. The video feed was playing—a live stream, I speculated. I gasped at what I saw. Ruby did as well, taking in a wet, heavy breath and expelling the kind of moan she made during a nightmare.

The video showed a dark-haired woman, white and thin, bound with duct tape at the wrists and ankles, with a ball gag stuffed into her mouth and secured around her head with black leather straps. She was seated on a wooden chair beneath an exposed lightbulb that dangled from a cord in an otherwise empty concrete room. The woman's eyes were wide with desperation. I recognized her but still needed a second to make the connection. When I did, I felt consumed by sickness and sadness.

"Oh my God, John . . . that's . . . that's . . ."

"It's Dr. Adams," I said. "It's your doctor."

I could see Dr. Adams struggling to break free, but a rope tied around her waist and secured to the chair kept her immobilized. The chair must have been anchored to the floor, because it didn't move an inch, even though she was thrashing about like a fresh caught fish dropped onto a dock.

"What is this? What are you showing me?" Uretsky might have answered me, but all I could hear was blood pounding in my ears. "What—what—" I was stuttering, completely transfixed by Dr. Adams's struggle, feeling every one of her jerks and spasms as if I were attempting to break free.

"You've already met Dr. Lisa Adams, I presume," Uretsky said. "If you've forgotten, she's the one who helped save Ruby's life."

"People will be looking for her," I said.

"You'd think so," Uretsky said, sounding surprised. "But she lives alone. No evidence of a boyfriend, or any that I could find. I checked on her schedule, and she's off for a few days—like not on call off, not scheduled to go to the office off. So we've got time to play with her before anyone cares. She's either going to be dead or she'll be saved, by you."

"Me? What do you want me to do?"

"I told you," Uretsky said, the pitch rising in his voice, annoyed, as if I should have remembered. "You're going to rob a liquor store at gunpoint. I thought if you could see what you were playing for, maybe you'd take the challenge a little more seriously."

"You're insane!" I screamed into the phone. "Do you know that?

You are a monster! A sick freak!" I was spitting all over my iPhone, shaking with an incredible rush that boiled up inside me. A wave of hatred so deeply rooted and profound took over and for a moment I felt like a rabid animal on the loose. I didn't want to just kill Uretsky—I wanted to take out his eyes with a fork while I slowly crushed his windpipe and sliced his flesh with the heel of one of my crampon climbing shoes.

"Are you through?" Uretsky said when I finally stopped shouting.

Ruby's eyes were locked on the computer screen, watching poor Lisa pointlessly try to break free. If her cancer cells could talk, they would be saying, "We didn't know there was anything worse than us."

"Let her go," I said.

"I will," Uretsky said. "And that's a promise. But only if you win."

"The liquor store," I said.

"That's right, John. The liquor store."

"I can't do this."

"I think you owe Dr. Lisa Adams at least a college try. She's a real person, John. This woman's got *feelings*."

He said the word *feelings* like it was a joke to him.

"How come you won't show yourself? Are you a coward?"

Uretsky laughed. I amused him, or so his laugh implied. "Is this the reverse psychology part of our conversation? Do you think you can goad me into doing something by making me kowtow to my ego? Is that it, John?"

"Let her go. Don't make me do this," I said.

"You're in the middle of a game," Uretsky said. "You don't make up the rules. I decide. And I say if you walk away from this game, then Lisa here dies. Snip, snip, snip go the fingers, just like Rhonda. Got it?"

"Give me a minute," I said. "I've got to think. Got to think."

"Let me ask you something, John," Uretsky said. "How well do you know yourself?"

"What do you mean?" I asked.

"Your strengths, your weaknesses. How well do you know them?"

"I don't know," I said.

"Let me ask you something else," Uretsky continued.

"I'm going to hang up now," I said. "I can't speak to you."

"If you do, gone go Lisa's little fingers. So don't hang up."

I paused. "Okay," I said. "You win. What do you want to ask?"

The more I talked to him, the calmer I felt. Was that his intention? I wanted to know what he wanted from me, even though I was afraid to find out.

Uretsky said, "Do you think there is a chasm between good and evil? Do you think a good man can be pushed by circumstance into committing evil acts?"

"I think you're evil," I said.

"And are you good?" he asked. "Were you good and virtuous when you cut the rope that sent Brooks Hall plummeting to his death? Were you being a good boy when you stole my identity?"

"I had good intentions," I said. "I didn't see another way out. There wasn't another viable option. I'm sorry for what I've done, but what choice did I have?" Why was I justifying myself to him? Because he had struck a painful nerve, that was why. He was questioning things about me that I questioned about myself.

"You had other choices," Uretsky said. "But you were driven by fear. Weren't you? You were driven by the fear of death and the fear of losing your beloved Ruby to cancer, to be specific. You acted out of fear, not rational thought."

"You don't know me. You have no right to pass judgment."

He was right, of course.

"I suppose that's true," Uretsky said, almost with a sigh. "I don't know you. Not fully, that is. But I want to know you. I want to know you so much better. How far can you be pushed? That's the burning question here. I want to *see* with my own eyes how far you'll bend before you break. That's the game we're playing, John, and there's no way out. Think about poor Lisa, here. Is there really anything worse than having your fingers snipped off by a rusty pair of pruning shears, your life force drained from you, your windpipe crushed by the constricting power of two hands squeezing tighter and tighter? I think not. I think that's a gruesome death."

"I don't know," I said, my voice shaky. "I don't know." I started to cry, small tears pricking at the corners of my eyes. I was listening to the ranting of a madman and watching the agony of a woman whom I was powerless to help. Well, not powerless, because there was one thing I could do.

Rob a liquor store.

"Will you knowingly take another life, John? Will you let me kill this woman, or will you try and save her? That's what's on the table. That's the choice you have to make. Can you live with yourself if she dies? More guilt? Are you weak or are you strong? So much of our character is defined by adversity. How will you play this, John? Do you want me to kill her?"

"No," I said, with my face buried in my hand, my voice weak and trembling. "No, I don't."

"Are you afraid that I will kill her?"

"Yes."

"Are you afraid of Ruby dying of cancer?"

"Yes," I said. "Yes."

"I love your fear," Uretsky said, his voice a sharp whisper. "I wish I could eat it. It would fill me up. Tell me more. Are you afraid of Dobson figuring out that you were playing a part?"

"How did you know?" I asked. A second ago I had been held spellbound by Uretsky. That spell was broken. Now I wanted answers. "Dobson, I mean. How did you know?"

The phone felt sweaty pressed up against my ear. The air inside the apartment turned thick and soupy, as though I were on a mountaintop without enough oxygen to sustain me.

"Check under the lip of the kitchen counter," Uretsky said.

I stood, my legs shaky and uncertain as I stumbled over to the kitchen. Ruby stepped out of my way, the panic in my eyes transferring panic into hers.

I felt underneath the lip of the granite-colored laminate counter of the kitchen island. My fingers grazed against something stuck to the underside of the counter and held in place by a sticky adhesive. I pulled, it didn't give way easily, but eventually a small object—not much heavier than a quarter—came free. The object, obviously a listening device, was about the length of my ring finger and pinkie put together. A small battery attached to a green-colored circuit board abutted a black plastic rectangle stenciled with the lettering ZA-2. Two thin antennae extended several inches outward from the rectangular compartment.

"Did you find it?" Uretsky asked.

"I found it," I said. "Are there others?"

"No," Uretsky said. "That's the only one."

I showed Ruby the listening device and mouthed: "You were right." She took the device from me, palming it in her hand like it was a bug or the feces from some rodent. She put the device on the kitchen counter and smashed it with the bottom of a saucepan. The force of the strike echoed throughout the tiny apartment like a gunshot.

"Do you want me to stop?" Uretsky said as soon as the din died down.

"Yes, you son of a bitch," I said, snarling. "I want you to stop right now."

"Then you'll have to keep playing the game."

I went back to my desk, sat down, and watched Dr. Adams continue to struggle against her restraints. Her determination, the force of her attempts to break free, had the arc of a firework, bright and intense one moment, dimming until vanished the next.

"I'll call her office. I'll tell them she's been kidnapped."

"And I'll know it, and I'll kill her."

"If I refuse your demands?"

"Then I'll keep killing women. And those killings will go on and on, and you'll know that only you possess the power to stop me. Their blood will be on your hands. And I'll give proof to Dobson about your insurance fraud scam, too. You'll be arrested for that crime, and Ruby will be left all alone. Defenseless. Unprotected. Do you get what I'm saying? But you won't care about that, either, because you can handle the blood of the innocents. You're comfortable with inflicting death, suffering, and pain. Game over. Well played, John Bodine. Very well played."

"I hate you," I said.

"No, not yet you don't," Uretsky said. "But you will. I'm going to teach you the real meaning of hate."

"Tell me exactly what you want me to do," I said.

And so Uretsky told me.

CHAPTER 20

R uby and I went to a 7:00 p.m. movie. The film was irrelevant—an action comedy featuring well-paid, well-known actors traipsing about in exotic locales, having lots of chases, driving and crashing lots of cars, firing guns and wisecracks with equal frequency. We didn't get any snacks. Neither of us could eat. We sat in the back of the theater. I watched the happy couples in front of us laughing at all the jokes and nibbling away on their munchies. It was impossible for me to focus on the make-believe world of this film while I was being held prisoner by my reality.

My conversation with Uretsky brought back a quote from Franklin D. Roosevelt. I hadn't thought about that quote since I stopped climbing, but when I came across it in a book I was reading, I thought it appropriate for a guy who trudged himself to great heights and into potentially perilous situations. Roosevelt said during his Pan American Day address of April 15, 1939, "Men are not prisoners of fate, but only prisoners of their own minds." I used to think about those words while navigating a particularly tricky route—ascending a steep section of rock, negotiating a path around a crystal forest of seracs, which are nothing but giant ice pillars that are prone to collapse. To think I would die on the mountain was, for me, akin to summoning that very fate. Freeing my mind from negative thinking assured me—or so I believed—of a safe ascent and descent.

Here I was, secure footing, no ropes required, and yet I was a prisoner of my mind. Sure, I could go to the police, but I could not free myself from Uretsky's grasp. Whenever I tried, I saw Dr. Adams struggling with her restraints and then flashed on her dead body, fingers missing. I imagined the police, with Dobson in tow, coming to arrest me. I pictured Ruby, alone and vulnerable, being stalked by a predator with pruning shears while I sat helpless in a jail cell. Men might not be prisoners of fate, I thought, but I was certainly a prisoner of Elliot Uretsky.

By the number of explosions and gunshots that sounded in rapid succession, I guessed the film was nearing its denouement. Ruby must have sensed the same, because she nudged me and asked, "What time is it?"

I checked the time on the iPhone, covering the bright display with my hands.

"Eight forty," I said, whispering in her ear.

"I think we should have kept a lookout. We would have been able to identify him if we had."

I shook my head slightly. "We don't even know if he's here," I said. "All he said was that if we left the theater before the film ended, he would know it, and we'd lose the round. You know what that means."

"Dr. Adams," Ruby said. "We did this to her, John. All she did was try and help, and now she's going to die."

"No, she's not," I said. "I'm not going to let that happen."

Soon as the movie ended, Ruby and I got up from our seats and headed for the exit. We were the first people out the doors of our theater, but I saw a number of men—some with their kids—already entering the men's room directly to our right. We stepped aside to let the rest of the crowd filter out. Ruby and I waited against the wall until the people entering and leaving the restroom dwindled to a trickle and eventually stopped altogether. The next round of movies was starting up.

"Wait here," I said.

Ruby looked horrified. "What if he tries to take me?" she said.

"He won't," I said.

"How do you know?"

"I just do," I said. "God help me, but I'm starting to understand his game, his rules, the way he thinks."

"But, John—"

"You just scream, scream as loud as you can if anybody even

comes near you. But nobody will. Trust me on this, Rube. I'll be right back. I promise."

I pushed open the restroom door and entered the bathroom. There was nothing special about the space—urinals, stalls, sinks, and a wastebasket overflowing with crumpled-up brown paper. There wasn't a security camera to be seen, of course. That was all part of Uretsky's plan. He could be filmed coming into the movie theater, but we didn't know what he looked like, so he couldn't be identified. He could enter the restroom, carrying something, probably concealed underneath his coat, but there would be no evidence or recording of what he left behind.

I looked under the stalls for shoes but didn't see any poking out. I checked the door. Nobody was coming in. The bathroom was empty. Time to make my move. I dug my hands into the overflowing wastebasket, feeling sticky, wet paper towels, crumpled soda cups, and half-eaten bags of popcorn. If anybody came into the bathroom, I was prepared to say that I'd accidentally tossed my wallet into the trash. Nobody came in. I kept feeling around, digging my hands deeper and deeper into the oily mess, until my fingers brushed up against what felt like a plastic bag.

Bingo.

I hauled up the bag, spilling the discarded contents resting above it onto the floor. I was cleaning up the droppings and putting them back in the wastebasket when the bathroom door opened and somebody came inside and caught me, literally, holding the bag—a thirteen-gallon white kitchen garbage bag, to be precise.

"People have no respect for public places," I said to the man as he squeaked past me to get to his chosen urinal.

He didn't say anything in reply. I wouldn't have said anything to me, either.

I left the bathroom, returning to the carpeted hallway of the Cineplex. Ruby saw me with the bag.

"Anything strange happen?" I asked her. "See anybody hanging around, watching you?"

"No," Ruby said. She pointed to the bag. "Is that it?" she asked.

I hefted up the bag to show Ruby that it had weight, and said, "I haven't looked yet, but I assume so."

"Uretsky put it there?"

I nodded.

"John, what are we going to do?" Ruby's voice pierced my heart with the sound of pure desperation.

"We're going to get out of this," I said. "You've got to trust me."

We walked in silence back to the car, a bright red Ford Fusion that Ruby referred to as Ziggy, in honor of the David Bowie CD of the same name, which always seemed to be in the CD player whenever we went for a drive. We parked in the garage, away from other cars, but I still looked around to make sure we were far from prying eyes when I finally opened the bag.

I showed Ruby the first item, a black ski mask with red stitching around the eye and mouth holes. Ruby had to look away. Next, I pulled out a white T-shirt and green army jacket. Uretsky had pinned a note to the jacket. His penmanship was impeccable.

Sometimes games provide instructions to help you along the way, read Uretsky's note. *Here's my instruction for you. Wear these clothes when you commit the robbery, and change back into your clothes afterward. That's what a real criminal would do. I'll text you with your next steps.*

There was something else in the plastic bag. I reached inside and took the object out. I held it in my hand, surveying its weight, and though I knew steel felt cool, it still burned like a hot coal against my skin.

"Do you have to use it?" Ruby asked.

"That's his rule."

"How will he know if you don't?"

"It'll be on the news," I said. "At least, I imagine it will be."

"Not it, John, you. You'll be on the news."

"I don't know what kind it is," I said. "I don't know anything about these things."

"Is it loaded?" Ruby asked.

I raised the gun, careful to point the barrel out the car window in case of an accidental discharge. It took a bit of fumbling, but eventually I figured out how to drop the clip. Sure enough, it was fully loaded.

"What now?" Ruby asked.

I showed Ruby the note Uretsky pinned to the olive-green army jacket that had been stuffed inside the white plastic kitchen garbage bag. She was still reading—or probably rereading—the note when my iPhone buzzed. I looked at my phone's display: Uretsky, who had sent me a text message. He had my phone number, but I knew his would be untraceable. Either he was using a disposable phone or he'd sent it using one of the many text-messaging services that provide the sender with absolute anonymity.

Uretsky's text read: **It's now ten o'clock. Giovanni's Liquors on Kent Street in Somerville will close in exactly one hour. You have that amount of time to rob the proprietor at gunpoint of one hundred fifty dollars cash.**

Uretsky sent Giovanni's exact street address, but I already knew the store well and could get there without GPS guidance. The liquor store was just a few blocks from where we lived before I became Elliot Uretsky. I'm sure that was intentional. The next text from Uretsky made me fire up Ziggy's four-cylinder engine and burn rubber peeling out of the parking garage.

He had sent me a picture of blood-stained pruning shears.

CHAPTER 21

I tried to keep my speed down as we crisscrossed Boston's maddening one-way and dead-end streets. Now, it's a myth that the winding roads of Boston were originally carved out by aimlessly wandering cows. In truth, it was probably bad planning and topography that determined the haphazard layout.

Despite the dizzying and vexing street design, I somehow managed to avoid making any wrong turns. We didn't get pulled over by the cops, either. The ski mask and gun were resting on the floor between Ruby's feet, and I was sure they would have generated more than a question or two.

Ruby, meanwhile, had my cell phone out and was using Google Maps to plan our escape route.

"I could park on Kent Street," Ruby said, talking fast and in a loud voice. The anxiety came shooting out her throat like an angry swarm of bees.

"Go on," I said, punching the gas to pass a slow Honda.

"You come out of Giovanni's, and then you run left," Ruby said, staring at the display screen. "Kent Street will be the first street you come to. You jump into the car, and I'll turn left onto Somerville Ave. Then I should be able to take a right on Lowell Street."

"What about the plates?" I said. "Somebody might see our plates as we're driving away."

"What do you want me to do?" Ruby shouted at me. Her hands and arms were shaking. Strawberry-colored splotches—stress marks—marred her face and neck.

I heard an angry horn blast to my right, and I jumped a little, not realizing I had drifted into the wrong lane. I got Ziggy back on course and waved to the irritated driver, who delivered a proper Boston salute.

"It's okay. It's okay," I said to Ruby. My brain kicked into another gear, one honed from years of climbing, which had heightened my ability for impromptu thinking.

"Here's what's going to happen," I said. "You park on Kent Street. You get out of the car. You walk away. You'll leave the trunk open. Got it? You leave it open." I glanced over at Ruby, then back to the road. A fender bender would mean a death sentence for Dr. Adams. "Got it?" I asked again, this time more forcibly as I changed lanes.

"Got it," Ruby said, a stab of disgust to her voice.

"When I get to the car, I'll climb inside the trunk and close it myself. You wait twenty, thirty minutes, and then get back into the car and drive away. Don't open the trunk to let me out until we've got Ziggy parked in the alley behind the Harvard Street apartment. It's dark back there. Nobody will see me climbing out."

Ruby stayed quiet for a moment, showing me her profound displeasure. "Shit, John," she said. "You know something? You sound like a real criminal."

I parked Ziggy a few blocks away from Kent Street, and then I checked the time. Ten thirty at night already. The minutes were passing.

"I'll walk from here," I said. "You'll have plenty of time to get Ziggy over to Kent Street. You can hang out at the Arrow Lounge while you're waiting the twenty or so minutes I need to pull this off. It's close by."

Ruby and I had been to the Arrow Lounge before. We both knew this neighborhood well. Hell, I'd bought booze from Giovanni not that long ago. I reached over and picked up the gun from between Ruby's feet, dropped the clip—this time without fumbling—and emptied the bullets into the palm of my hand.

"What are you doing?" Ruby asked.

The look I gave suggested the intent of my actions should be obvious. "What do you mean, what am I doing? I'm not going in there with a loaded weapon. Did you think I was?"

"John!" she yelled, sounding more frightened than angry. "What if Giovanni is armed?"

I shrugged my hands.

"You'll have no protection," she went on.

"I'm not going to shoot Giovanni, no matter what," I said.

Ruby covered her mouth with her hands. "Maybe we should just forget this," she said in a muffled voice. "Let's go to the police right now. Let's do it."

I grabbed my phone and showed Ruby Uretsky's last text message—the one with a picture included. She sucked in a horrified breath, grimaced, and quickly looked away.

"That's Rhonda Jennings's blood on those pruning shears," I said. "Next, it will be Dr. Adams's. I can't face the guilt of causing another death. You can't either, Ruby. She helped save your life. We need to do the same."

"How would he even know you robbed the store?" Ruby asked.

I threw my hands in the air in a "Beats me" gesture. "Like I said, maybe he thinks it'll be on the news. I don't really know. I mean, how did he find out our real identities? How did he know I was talking to Clegg outside O'Brian's? How?"

Ruby's expression became contemplative. She turned her head and gazed out Ziggy's fogged-up window.

"What is it?" I asked her.

"When we got back to the apartment . . . after . . . after what happened to Rhonda, you told me that David arrested somebody right before Uretsky called."

"Yeah, that's right," I said, nodding.

I glanced at the time. Five minutes had ticked past; time kept moving like it was high on speed.

"The guy he arrested was inside Clegg's car when Uretsky called."

I nodded again. "So?" I asked, back to watching the time.

"Could you see inside the car, John?" Ruby asked.

I swallowed hard.

"No," I said.

"I'm just saying—"

I understood right away. "You think that the guy Clegg arrested was Uretsky?" I recalled the man's face: boyish features, sharp nose, thin frame, buzz-cut hair. Could he be Elliot Uretsky? "But he'd be in jail if that were so," I said.

"He could have posted bail."

I nodded. "But that doesn't explain how he knows so much about us," I said. "Or how he made a phone call with handcuffs on."

"Not if . . . not if Clegg . . ."

"What are you saying?"

"I'm saying, what if Clegg is in on it?"

"You think Uretsky is working with Clegg?"

My incredulousness was evident.

Ruby nodded, and vigorously. "What if David snapped? Survivor's guilt, or something like that, and he blames you for picking him over Brooks. You said he's getting divorced, right?"

I nodded.

"Maybe that pushed him over the edge," Ruby continued. "Some kind of stress-induced insanity. I don't know. I'm just thinking out loud here."

I brushed the idea off like it was something crawling up my neck.

"No," I said. "That's crazy."

I wouldn't admit it—not then, anyway—but Ruby had dug a foothold into my rock of denial, and I'd begun to imagine the impossible. I recalled what Clegg had said to me inside the bar. *Here's your living proof that crime doesn't pay.* Why did he say that?

I glanced again at the time. Ten forty.

"We'll talk about this later," I said. "After." I moved to open the door.

Ruby reached across her seat and grabbed my arm. "John, what if there are other people in the store?"

I gripped her hand. "I'm going for the cash, and then I'm gone."

"Yeah, well, what if somebody tries to stop you? You know, plays the hero."

"I'll wait until the store is empty."

"What if you can't?"

"I don't know, Ruby!" I didn't mean to shout at her, but my nerves were already frayed and on edge.

"Maybe you can hand him a note?"

"A note?"

"Explaining what's going on," Ruby said.

"And then take his hundred fifty dollars?"

"Tell him you just need to pretend to steal the money."

"He won't go for it. He'll think I'm crazy."

"How do you know?"

"Because I'd think I was crazy."

"I want to kill him," Ruby said.

"Me too," I answered.

I tried to move, but Ruby wouldn't let go of my arm.

"What if he sees you running toward Kent Street?" she asked.

"Who?"

"Giovanni. What if Giovanni sees you running toward Kent Street?"

This made me pause.

"Shit," I said.

"The police might start searching the cars."

"Make it an hour," I said.

"An hour?"

"Leave me in the trunk for an hour. They can't just pop the trunk without having probable cause. A parked car isn't probable cause."

Ruby looked pleased by something. "I don't know if you'll even have enough air for an hour. I'm not going to wait that long. There's a railroad track running perpendicular to Kent Street," she said, remembering. "I saw it on the Google map. Maybe they'll think you ran down the tracks."

"Maybe," I said.

She clutched my hands and looked intently into my eyes. "Don't do this, John," she said.

"I don't have a choice."

I took off my shirt and put on the clothes Uretsky had provided for me. Just the feel of the fabric made my skin itch, and the thought that Uretsky might have once worn these clothes made me want to burn them. I decided I'd do just that—each article of clothing I'd incinerate into ash. I got the shirt and jacket on. Next, I pulled the ski mask over my head, just to test it out.

"How do I look?" I asked Ruby.

I watched Ruby gulp down her concern.

"Scary, John," she said. "You look really, really scary."

CHAPTER 22

Ituckled the gun into the waistband of my jeans, stuffed the ski mask inside the pocket of Uretsky's green army jacket, and kissed Ruby good-bye. It was a long kiss, more desperate than passionate, the kind that spoke of final farewells. Forget the maxim "Live each day like it's your last." If I lived each day feeling like this, I'd go totally insane.

I hurried along the concrete sidewalk, a block away from Giovanni's, and kept my head low. Taking a glance down Kent Street, I saw ample parking for Ruby. Thankfully, there were already several parked cars in addition to the available spaces. A deserted street might have drawn unwanted police attention to a lone car. Parking here required a resident permit, which we happened to have. Was it happenstance that Uretsky picked a store for me to hit in our neighborhood or part of his planning? I had no way to know. I just kept walking.

I knew this neighborhood well—it was far removed from the livelier locales of Somerville—so it was no surprise to find the streets quiet at this time of night. A weeknight in a quiet neighborhood meant fewer cars on the road, too, and fewer witnesses to my upcoming crime. Was that part of Uretsky's planning as well? Did he want this to be a layup, because he wanted me to get away and keep playing his twisted game? Another maxim came to me, the tried and true: *Only time will tell*.

Yes, time would indeed tell all.

Low scudding clouds, dirty and gray as the sidewalk, glowed eerily above the city lights, providing a foreboding canopy under which I walked. I took another glance at my cell phone. Ten fifty-five. Five minutes until showtime. I had shut my ringer off because I didn't want anything to distract me while I was pointing an unloaded gun at an innocent man's chest.

Ruby had sent me a text message. I love you, she wrote. Be safe. Please be safe. XOXO I LOVE YOU I LOVEYOU I LOVEYOU

"I love you, too," I whispered to the air.

I texted her back. I'll be safe. I love you more than anything. Then I shut off my phone.

I quickened my pace crossing the sidewalk in front of a shopping plaza. The wide parking lot that abutted a Family Dollar Store, Papa John's Pizza, and a dog grooming business created an open area that left me feeling vulnerable and exposed as I passed. I crossed over a side street, relieved that a yellow-brick café called City Munchies provided some shelter. The lights above the café's orange-colored awnings were on, but those inside the store were not. *Quiet streets could mean a quiet liquor store.* I hoped Giovanni had serviced his last customer before I went barging in. Witnesses were bad enough, but hostages would be a heck of a lot worse.

I'm doing this for Dr. Adams, for Rhonda, for Ruby. . . .

Giovanni's occupied the lower level of a three-story, vinyl-sided building. I saw a few lights on in the apartments above the store, meaning people were at home—people who might see me dashing out Giovanni's front door, headed straight for Kent Street. I said a silent prayer, not just one evoking God's name, but a real honest-to-goodness prayer, something I'd never done before, even on my most perilous climbs. Nature had always been my religion, but at that moment I needed a dose of the more powerful to guide me.

I decided to do a walk by first, check things out, and get a lay of the land. A quick glance inside the liquor store would allow me to scope out the scene before I went barging in with gun drawn. The neon glow from an array of beer signs hanging in the store windows lit my face as I ambled past. I took a quick glance inside, so focused on my surveillance that I momentarily lost my footing. I regained my balance and finished crossing in front of the store, taking quicker steps than before.

On what had to have been the most conspicuous walk by in crime history, I managed to catch a quick glimpse inside and saw the guy working the cash register. I assumed he was Giovanni. If so, Giovanni was a portly fellow, with a dark oil slick of pomade-covered hair, wearing a short-sleeved button-down black shirt that showcased two beefy—and hairy—forearms. He looked bored leaning up against his counter, aggressively chewing on something—an entire pack of gum, or so it seemed to me. I didn't see anybody else inside.

I stood in the doorway of the adjacent hardware store. My chest heaved while I labored for breath. My throat closed up, heart rate jacked, blood thudding in my ears, hands slippery, and my skin clammy to the touch. I took in a bunch of short breaths the way a free diver readies himself to take a plunge.

"You can do this. . . . You can do this. . . . You can do this . . . ," I said aloud.

The front door shouldn't be locked, I thought, though I didn't check it on my flyby. I could imagine Giovanni's stunned expression were he to see a man in a ski mask, pulling haplessly on his locked front door. That would make the news for sure.

I took several furtive glances up and down the street while withdrawing the ski mask from my jacket pocket. I pulled the mask over my head, feeling the wool scratching against my face. I was hit by an instant uptick of adrenaline, the mask somehow emboldening me. I reached into the waistband of my jeans and gripped the gun with my sweat-slickened fingers. I looked left, then right. It was clear in both directions.

Springing from the shadows of the hardware store, I made a dash to the adjacent building, grabbed hold of the door handle to Giovanni's Liquors, and pulled the door open. I burst into the store with my arm outstretched and the unloaded gun trained on Giovanni. It didn't sound like me shouting: "Get your hands up. This is a robbery!"

But it was.

CHAPTER 23

By the time I came through the doorway, Giovanni had his hands high in the air. I could see the white folds of fat where his shirt had lifted up, black hairs peppering his ample midsection. Under the glow of overhead fluorescents, I ran across the linoleum toward the cash register while Giovanni was saying, in a thick Italian accent, "Don't shoot! Please don't shoot! Please!" His plaintive cries rung in my ears but didn't deter me.

I wanted to rip off my mask and tell him everything. Show him the picture of the bloody pruning shears Uretsky would use to sever Dr. Adams's fingers, but I knew he wouldn't believe me, so I didn't lower my weapon.

I thought there weren't other patrons in the store when I burst inside. Prejudging situations I couldn't foresee was what got me off so many mountaintops, but this time around, that sixth sense failed me, and in a big way. A bespectacled elderly woman with a hard-bitten face and crinkly hair—mostly gray—wearing a ratty navy overcoat, emerged from behind the aisle of peach schnapps, holding two plastic bottles of the worst kind of vodka. I didn't expect to see an old woman in the store at this late hour, but she had veins that looked like they had absorbed a lot of alcohol over the years.

The lady shrieked when she saw me and dropped both bottles onto the floor. They thudded and rolled but didn't break. I looked at her long enough to see her slip into an aisle, one black orthopedic shoe disappearing, followed by the other.

I returned my attention to Giovanni. How must I have looked to him—gun shaking in my outstretched hand, head covered by a dark mask with red stitching around the eyes and mouth? He looked frightened enough, but his mouth kept on working.

Chewing. Chewing. Chewing.

I approached Giovanni with prudent steps, as if I was crossing a ridgeline and not a floor. Without turning my head, I called out "Ma'am" to the old woman who had vanished down an aisle behind me. "Please come out where I can see you. I promise I'm not going to hurt you."

Giovanni was shaking. He looked pale and sweaty, but that didn't stop him from working whatever he had in his mouth.

"Ma'am," I shouted again. "Just come out where I can see you." I didn't like the quaver in my voice. It sounded nervous. I closed the short gap between the cash register and myself with shuffling side steps. Twice I glanced behind me, but seeing no sign of the old lady, I snapped my neck back to look again at Giovanni. I got close enough to poke Giovanni's chest with the gun barrel. Close up, I could see his big teeth gnashing away on something black and pink. *Gum mixed with tobacco?* That's what it looked like to me. My suspicion was confirmed when I spied a dribble of brownish spittle that slid between his lips and snaked down his chin. Giovanni risked lowering his hand to wipe away the dribbling mess. He lowered his hand calmly, without asking permission, which made me think he was pretending to act nervous. I should have paid more attention to that fleeting thought.

"I'm really, really sorry about this," I said. "I don't want to do this, but I need a hundred and fifty dollars in cash from your register, or a woman will die."

"What?" Giovanni said.

I could see him try to puzzle through my explanation for this crime. *Cash from your register*, he got, and got that pretty clearly, too. The *woman will die* part? Well, that must have been nonsensical.

"Please," I said, glancing behind me again for signs of the old woman. "If you give me a hundred and fifty dollars, you'll save a woman's life. I'll repay you. I promise."

"You a crazy man," Giovanni said, gesticulating with his raised hands. "Please don't hurt me, crazy man. Please. I give you what you need. Please. A hundred fifty dollars, right? I get it. Right now. I get it for you. Just don't shoot."

Giovanni patted the air with the palms of his hands, a gesture that implored me to remain calm. Then he bent at the knees and started to drop out of my view. He didn't ask my permission to move. That should have been my second clue that something wasn't quite right.

All of this happened in a matter of seconds, but that was all the time Giovanni needed. He popped back up like a jack-in-the-box, wielding a twenty-eight-inch metal bat.

I'd never seen a 250-plus-pound man vault a four-foot counter, but Giovanni went up and over like he was hurdling a laundry basket. Before I could back away, he swung the bat at me, level with my arm, while shouting a string of expletives in Italian. I could see the veins on his neck bulge like thick strands of climbing rope. His protruding muscles were rippled from years of hauling boxes of booze.

I dodged his swing just in time to avoid a direct strike. The head of the bat, however, connected with my gun hand, and I felt a flash of pain rocket up my arm. The gun fell with a clatter—no risk of discharge there.

Giovanni charged. Streams of brown spit sprayed from between his snarled lips. His eyes, clear and focused, narrowed on me. He raised the bat again and swung.

I ducked, allowing the bat to strike a triple-high stacked display of Two-Buck Chuck wine instead of my head. Half a dozen bottles set atop a sealed cardboard box shattered on impact, spewing a geyser of red wine that splashed my face and clothes in a splatter that looked a lot like blood.

Giovanni came at me again, the bat slung over his right shoulder, like a plus-size Babe Ruth with a vendetta. He backed me up against a magazine rack, so there was no place for me to go but down to the floor. I shielded my head with my hands, readying myself for the strike, but it didn't happen.

I looked up just in time to see Giovanni's feet slip out from underneath him—the wine had turned the linoleum into an ice rink. He crashed hard onto his back, shaking the floor on impact. The bat dropped from his hand and rolled noisily into the shattered wine display.

I rose from my crouch and went for the cash register. I was thinking I could grab the cash and make it out the door before Giovanni regained his footing. Ah, but "the best-laid schemes o' mice an' men go often awry," or so the Robert Burns poem goes (Ruby was an English lit major in college). I made it to the cash register all right, but when I got there, I saw that Giovanni wasn't trying to get up off the floor. Instead, he lay on his back with his legs kicking wildly and his hands clutching at his meaty throat, gulping for air. He made a slight coughing sound, but nothing more. One of Giovanni's thrashing feet kicked the gun down an aisle and out of my view.

I forgot all about the cash and thought only of Giovanni. Was he having a heart attack? I wondered if he might be having a seizure, but saw his skin turn a disturbing bluish gray and his fingernails darken. I went over to him and bent low. I approached cautiously.

"Can you talk?" I shouted. "Are you all right?"

Obviously, he wasn't. Giovanni responded with another wheezing cough, all the while keeping his hands wrapped firmly around his throat. *Choking,* I thought. *He's choking to death on that hunk of gum and tobacco he'd been chewing.*

I knew how to administer first aid, so I didn't feel panicky about what to do next. It would be impossible for me to get him into a standing position to administer the Heimlich maneuver. I needed to employ a different approach.

Still wearing my ski mask and green army jacket, I straddled Giovanni's thighs. I placed the heels of my hands, one on top of the other, against the middle of his fleshy abdomen and administered two thrusts, pressing inward and upward to help dislodge the object.

Before I could administer the third thrust of five, I felt a heavy thud against my head. I winced, but the blow was more startling than painful. I looked to see what struck me and saw the old woman, purse in hand, hoisting the makeshift weapon above her head, ready to make another strike.

"You get off him!" she yelled, though the force of her voice had clearly diminished with age. "You stop hurting him right now."

I felt like John trying to save a life, but the woman's petrified expression reminded me that I still had my frightening black ski mask on.

"Ma'am," I said. "This man is choking to death. I'm trying to help him."

At least I had the wherewithal to address her as "Ma'am." Meanwhile, she had the wherewithal to strike me again with her purse, repeatedly. Ignoring the blows, I administered three more thrusts. Whirling around, I straddled Giovanni again, this time facing his head. He bucked beneath me like a wild stallion, but my thighs dug into his side hard enough to hold me fast. I pulled apart Giovanni's jaw and reached my hand into his mouth, grasping hold of his thick, slimy-to-the-touch tongue, and pulled it away from the back of his throat. The blows from the old lady's purse struck my shoulder again.

"Please, ma'am!" I shouted. "Let me save his life!"

"You should be ashamed," she said, delivering three quick, successive blows with her purse.

Whap. Whap. Whap.

I managed to work my finger deep inside Giovanni's cheek and, using a sweeping, hooking motion, slid it across the interior of his mouth to the other cheek. The tip of my finger sunk into a pliable substance blocking his windpipe. Caution here was critical, else I risked pushing the tobacco wad deeper down his throat. Feeling like I had a good hold, I removed my finger from Giovanni's mouth, carrying with it a saliva-soaked blob of tobacco leaf and gum.

Giovanni inhaled a breath that was loud with relief. He lay on the floor, panting, the proper color already returning to his skin and nails.

I climbed off Giovanni, and the old lady backed away several paces, positioning herself between the front door and me.

"Please give me a chance to get away," I said to her. "I'm doing this to save a woman's life. I'm not a bad person. Please."

I tried to imagine that my ski mask made me look like some sort of superhero, but suspected that I looked more like the devil.

"Turn your life around, young man," the old lady said.

I thought I knew what she meant by that, but I wasn't sure. I said a prayer, my second in a night, that I was right. The old lady vanished out the door as I made a dash for the cash register. I fumbled about with the buttons until I found the one that opened the drawer. I took a hundred fifty dollars—five twenties, five tens.

Giovanni worked himself from his back onto his stomach, where he lay heaving in a puddle of wine. The red liquid pooled around his body like blood spilled from a grave wound.

I went to him and knelt close to his face.

"I'm so sorry," I said. "I'll make it up to you. I promise. Are you okay?"

Giovanni muttered something in Italian.

I don't speak Italian, but I'm pretty sure he didn't say, "Thank you."

I retrieved the gun, which wasn't too far away, and raced to the front door, half expecting to see the old lady standing in the middle of the street, screaming for help. I looked both ways, but the street was deserted. No cars. No pedestrians. Nobody. The old lady was gone.

Turn your life around, she had said. I wondered if that meant she'd give me a chance to get away. I guess saving Giovanni's life inspired her to believe that I could be redeemed.

I listened for the sirens but didn't hear any. I pulled off my ski mask, used it to wipe down the front door handle, and took off running. I got to Kent Street, no problem. I looked behind me, but Giovanni must have still been on the floor, wine-soaked and all, trying to regain his breath. Nobody came barging out the door in pursuit.

I turned the corner and saw Ziggy parked where I expected. I pulled on the trunk, and it popped right open. I climbed inside, shaking off the last remnants of the adrenaline rush, feeling like my heart could burst from exertion. Reaching above me, I grabbed hold of a hook and pulled the trunk closed.

Enveloped in darkness, I didn't know how many minutes had passed before I heard the sound of police sirens, but they came, all right, seemingly from all directions. It wasn't too long after that that I heard the squawking sound of a police radio. It was coming from directly outside the car where I was hiding.

CHAPTER 24

Life in fast-forward—that was what the next few moments felt like, anyway. Press the button on the remote, the one with the two sideways triangles, and watch everything zoom along, herky-jerky, quick and nonsensical until it's over. Only this scenario zipped right along with me locked inside the trunk of a car, cocooned in absolute darkness. Radios crackled. Sirens wailed. Footsteps fell. I heard Ruby's voice. It made me ache for this nightmare to be over, to return to our apartment on the other side of town, lie half naked on our futon, scratch Ginger's belly, watch *Design on a Dime,* and quiz Ruby until I begged her go to bed.

I sensed Ruby was standing alongside Ziggy's trunk—with me stuffed inside it—because I could hear her engaging with the police. She asked questions: "What's going on? Is everybody all right? Was anybody hurt?" She couldn't have known if I was inside the trunk or not, but I heard her say, "Thank goodness." She rapped her knuckles on Ziggy's backside, but I didn't rap back.

"I hope you find him," I heard her say.

A door opened. Ziggy's weight shifted. An engine fired up. The car lurched forward. The wheels turned. The car lurched some more. It jostled me about. We inched along. Eventually, I felt we'd traveled far enough from the police that I rapped my knuckles against the trunk, just to let Ruby know I was safe inside.

The car stopped. I swallowed down a lump of dread. Had I signaled her too soon? Did someone hear me?

Ziggy moved again, quicker this time, the wheels picking up speed.

And we were gone.

Not much happened after I climbed out of the trunk. Ruby and I hugged, we kissed, and we both got a little teary-eyed. Okay, a lot teary-eyed. We went up to the apartment, walking past the yellow caution tape that designated Rhonda Jennings's home a crime scene. Back inside our apartment, I flopped down on the futon, wearing only my jeans. Ginger took up roost in my lap. Ruby stuffed the ski mask, green army jacket, and the white T-shirt I wore into a black plastic garbage bag.

"We'll have to get rid of these," she said. She tied the bag after filling it with rubbish from the kitchen and the bathroom wastebaskets. "What are you going to do with the gun?"

"We'll drive out to Concord and toss it into the river," I said. Ruby and I knew a secluded spot in the Great Meadows sanctuary, where we both liked to hike. It would be perfect place for getting rid of the gun unseen.

Ruby returned to the living room and sat beside me on the futon. She rested her head on my shoulder, which in turn caused Ginger to rev up her purring. As a threesome, we were family, and the family was together once again. Everyone was safe.

"I was so freaking scared, John. I don't ever want to feel that scared again."

"Yeah, me neither. But I don't think that's going to happen," I said.

Ruby gave me a fractured look, one that recognized our predicament: her cancer, Rhonda Jennings's death, Dr. Adams's kidnapping, Giovanni, Uretsky, and his game. Until further notice, fear would be our norm, not the exception.

"What do you think will happen now?" Ruby asked.

"I think we're going to hear from Uretsky," I said.

"Could he have been watching the liquor store?"

"Maybe," I said. "I don't know."

Could he have been the old woman in disguise? I kept that a private thought, though it seemed to me that Uretsky was the sort who would have enjoyed playing that kind of game.

"Do you want to talk about what I said earlier?"

I shook her off like a pitcher changing the sign.

"I've been thinking about it more," Ruby continued. "David might be involved."

"He's not."

"How do you know?"

I shrugged. "It just doesn't make sense," I said.

My body still felt all charged up from the robbery and getaway, so I took in a few deep breaths and expelled them slowly. Then I ran my hands back and forth through my short hair, feeling the sweat that still dampened my scalp.

My sudden movement irritated Ginger. She meowed softly and dropped to the floor, silent. Ruby got up, scratched Ginger's head, and went over to the laptop on the kitchen island.

"How will you give Giovanni his money back?" she asked.

"I'm just going to hand it to him," I said. "I'll say that some neighbor people heard about the robbery and collected some funds to help out."

"You don't think he'll recognize your voice?"

I hadn't thought about it. "Good point. Maybe you should give him the money," I said.

Ruby had her face in the laptop when she agreed. Then she said, "Boston.com has breaking news about the robbery."

"It'll be on the morning news for sure," I said.

Ruby gasped. "John, they have video posted."

"Video?" I said, getting up off the futon to see for myself.

The video, grainy and recorded from a fixed position—probably a camera mounted above the front door—showed me barging into the liquor store and training a gun on Giovanni. Ruby and I watched the baseball bat attack, the slip and fall, Giovanni choking on tobacco and gum, and my attempts to dislodge the object while the old woman struck me with her handbag. The headline read: BREAKING NEWS: SOMERVILLE GUNMAN SAVES LIQUOR STORE OWNER FROM CHOKING, THEN STEALS HIS MONEY.

Ruby watched the video several times. "How did they get this up there so fast?"

"The police must have given them permission."

"Would they do that?"

"I don't know, Ruby," I said. "You watch all the same TV shows that I do. The cops can do what they want. I'm not worried. I never showed my face, and I didn't leave any fingerprints behind."

My phone buzzed in my pants pocket. I took it out, holding it at arm's length, as though it were a bomb. I knew who was calling.

"Uretsky?" Ruby asked.

I glanced down at the display and nodded. "Unless you know somebody else who can call us from 888-888-8888," I said.

I pressed the answer button on my phone, silencing the vibrations of the ring.

"Hello?" I said.

"Well done, John. Congratulations. Very well done."

Uretsky.

I felt a stir of sickness just hearing his voice.

"This is over," I said. "I did what you wanted. It's over. Let Dr. Adams go."

"In part," Uretsky said. "I e-mailed you a link. Open it."

Ruby stepped away from the computer to give me access. I opened my *One World* administrator Web page and sure enough saw an e-mail from Elliot Uretsky, with a time stamp of eight minutes ago. I clicked the link and was directed to a Web page that displayed a presumably live video feed of Dr. Adams still seated on a wooden chair. She seemed to be unconscious, but I could see her chest rise and fall with breath.

A figure emerged from the shadows and stood behind Dr. Adams. This same figure came around to the front of Dr. Adams's chair/prison and bent down to get face level with the camera. Ruby grabbed my arm when the face of a man wearing the same ski mask I wore during the robbery filled the screen.

"Hello, John," Uretsky said. He spoke in the same deep, monotone voice I had grown to despise. "Nice to chat with you in person. How do I look? Do you like my disguise? They were on sale, a two-for-one deal."

Ruby had said that I looked scary, but this time I witnessed for myself the horror of my appearance.

"We're like twinsies," Uretsky said. He stuck his tongue out of the mouth hole of the ski mask and flicked it in and out rapidly, the way a lizard feels the air.

"We're nothing alike," I said.

"Don't be so quick to judge," Uretsky said. "Now, let's get down to business. You've done well. I kept up with your endeavors on my police band radio."

Ruby looked at me, and I could tell what she was thinking: David Clegg.

"What about Dr. Adams?" I said.

"I knocked her out," Uretsky said. "Slipped a little narcotic into her water. After our chat, I'm going to give her a lift to a secluded spot I like. They'll be no trace of me, and she'll have no clue as to why she was taken."

"So that's it," I said. "You'll leave us alone now."

Uretsky laughed.

"No, John," he said. "Far from it. You still haven't won my game. You still have to prove that you've got what it takes to be a real criminal. But I am curious about one thing."

"I don't have to answer your questions," I said.

"Did you think Giovanni was going to attack you?"

"I said I don't have to answer you."

Uretsky wagged a finger in front of the camera. "Uh-uh," he said. "I make up the rules, and I can change the rules. Life isn't fair that way. So you'll answer my question, or you'll watch this woman die. Got it?"

The room warmed to the heat of a sauna. "I got it," I said, swallowing hard.

"Good. Glad we've cleared the air. So tell me, did you think Giovanni would attack you?"

"I had no idea, but I didn't rob him with a loaded gun."

"You got rid of the bullets?" Uretsky said, his surprised voice rising in pitch. "Very trusting of you, John. I wouldn't have done that, but it's interesting that when you entered into a life-threatening situation, you chose to leave yourself vulnerable."

"Is that what this was really about?" I asked. "Are you monitoring how I'll behave under certain conditions?"

"No, John. We're playing a game," Uretsky said. "It's really quite fascinating to watch. You see, I knew Giovanni would attack you. In fact, I picked that store because he's been robbed in the past and he always fights back. What would it have taken for you to keep the bullets in the gun? Would you have gone in armed had you known he was a rattlesnake and not to be messed with?"

"I never would."

"Ah! Never say never."

I expected he'd say that. I decided to change the subject. "I'm going to track you down," I said.

"Remember my warning about involving the police. I'll know if they're looking for me."

"Don't worry. I'll find you on my own," I said. "And when I do, I'll have no trouble keeping bullets in the gun."

Maybe I wouldn't toss it in the river, after all.

"Oh, I think you'll be surprised at what you find," he said.

"What do you want from us? What do you want?" I tried to keep from shouting but had a hard time controlling my anger.

"Easy, tiger," Uretsky said. "You'll know soon enough. But take some advice from me. Rest up. You're going to need your strength."

"What the hell are you planning?"

"Surprises. In two days you'll know. Two days, my friend."

"I'm not your friend."

"No. You're my parasite, living off my name. But if you insist on a hint of what's coming your way, I'll tell you this. The snake and lotus flower are gripped in Qetesh's hands."

"What?"

The screen went black.

Ruby and I stared at the black rectangle a few moments. I was half expecting Uretsky to reemerge and yell, "Boo!" If he had, I would have jumped, that's for sure. Thankfully for us, the rectangle stayed black.

"You saved her, John," Ruby said, rubbing her hand between my shoulder blades while she kissed my head. "You saved Dr. Adams's life."

"We think," I said.

"No," Ruby said. "I know it. He's not going to kill her."

"Two days," I said. "What do you think is going to happen in two days?"

"I don't know," Ruby said. "I wish I did. What did he mean by the snake and lotus flower thing?"

"Who did he say? Kesha?"

"Isn't she a pop star?"

"It was something else," I said. "It sounded like it began with a *Q*. Qatash or something."

Ruby launched a Web browser on the laptop and did a search for "Qatash," "Lotus Flower," and "Snake." Only four results returned. If I had to guess, we were misspelling the most important word. Ruby did another search, this time for the words "Somerville," "armed robbery," and "choking." The results page returned a bunch of links with five videos listed as a top hit. The videos were of my robbery.

"How did these get up here?" Ruby asked.

"There's a button on the Boston.com video to share it to YouTube," I said.

"John, look at this," Ruby said, indicating the screen. "The view counter says twenty-five thousand."

I groaned. "Twenty-five thousand views in less than an hour. Shit."

"What?" she asked.

"Not only did I just commit a crime, but the video's gone viral."

"What are we going to do?"

"About the video?"

"No, not about the stupid video," Ruby snapped at me. "Uretsky. Two days. The snake and the lotus flower. Quidditch, or whatever the hell he was saying."

"I'm going to find him," I said. "I'm calling David Clegg, and I'm going to find him."

"But what if Clegg is working with Uretsky?" Ruby said.

I kissed Ruby on the forehead, letting the feel of her skin warm my lips before letting go. "Then I'll be that much closer to getting him," I whispered.

CHAPTER 25

I waited in Ziggy while Ruby went inside Giovanni's liquor store, carrying an envelope we had stuffed with three hundred dollars in cash. His money, plus what we could afford as a hardship gift. Ruby would say that she took up a collection from concerned local citizens. It was the morning after the robbery, but I measured time in the number of days before Uretsky would try to make me commit another crime. That would be a little less than two, assuming he started the clock after I robbed the store.

The news was on the radio. I listened to yet another report on the strange kidnapping of Dr. Lisa Adams. Naturally, Ruby and I had been listening all morning. Adams didn't know where she'd been taken, who took her, or what her kidnapper wanted. All she knew was that one moment she was tied to a chair, and the next she was back in her bedroom. There was no evidence of sexual assault. No physical assault, either, aside from several rope burns. Dr. Adams was free to get a lifetime of therapy for no other reason than she knew us. At least she was alive.

We both had strength, but it was like a faucet—off and on. One moment we'd be fine; the next one of us would break down. We'd think about Rhonda. We'd think about what happened to Dr. Adams. We'd feel guilty and trapped, but we also knew we had to carry on. We didn't see an alternative.

I watched through the front window as Ruby talked to Giovanni. He talked back to her, his hands contributing equally to their conversation. I saw him shooing her away, not angrily. He kept bowing his body, waving with his hands, gestures that implied "Thank you, but no thank you." Ruby tried twice more to give him the envelope, but each time Giovanni shook his head.

Now, Ruby has one of the best puppy dog looks going. I swear that look is like a siren's song when she wants it to be. So I'm pretty sure she flashed Giovanni one of her finest, because he touched his hand to his heart and then put both hands on her shoulders. He smiled—a resigned-looking grin—made several successive head nods, and motioned for the envelope. Ruby gave it to him, waved good-bye, and headed for the front door.

However, something made her stop. I assumed Giovanni called for her attention, because he held up a finger and was making a "Wait here" gesture. He vanished from my view but reappeared moments later, holding a bottle of wine. With the roles reversed, it was now Ruby who tried to refuse the offer. Giovanni insisted and Ruby relented.

She left his store and walked to the corner as we had planned. I started up Ziggy, made a U-turn, and picked Ruby up where Giovanni couldn't see us. She climbed in and handed me the bottle of wine.

"He says it goes great with fish," Ruby said.

"What else did he say?" I asked.

"If he could find the guy who robbed him, he'd give him a hug for saving his life."

"That's nice," I said.

"Then he said he'd get his bat out and finish what he started."

I laughed, but only a little.

We drove in silence awhile. Then I said, "It's making me sick."

"What is?"

"Rhonda Jennings."

Ruby got quiet. "Me too," she said. "But what could you have done? How could we have known?"

"I just wish, is all . . ."

"Wish what?"

"That there was something I could put inside an envelope and make that right, too."

We stopped by Dr. Lee's office on the way home. Ruby needed more Verbilifide, and we decided to keep using the Uretsky name to get it. In for a penny, in for a pound, or so the saying goes. We had enough stress, and to add to it by coming up with another way of getting Ruby her meds just didn't make any sense. We also figured Uretsky already knew about Dr. Lee, same as he did Dr. Adams. What could we tell her? "Be careful"? "Look out for strangers wearing masks"? Right now we just needed to get the drugs and get out of there. Soon we were back inside the cramped examination room, which had become as familiar to us as our bedroom—at either apartment.

Dr. Lee, looking professional in her white lab coat, surveyed Ruby underneath the harsh glare of the overhead fluorescent lighting and didn't take long to make her assessment.

"Are you feeling all right?" she asked. Her worried tone concerned me.

"I'm okay," Ruby said.

"You don't look very well," Lee said.

"It's just a bug," Ruby said. "I haven't been sleeping well."

Lee made a "hmmm" sound as her practiced eyes continued to study Ruby's face. She looked over at me. "John doesn't look so great, either," she said.

Ruby nodded toward me. "Yeah," she said. "It seems like we've both caught the same thing."

Back at the apartment, Ruby held fast to her suspicions about David Clegg, and I couldn't make her think otherwise.

"Who else could have known that you were talking to Clegg?" Ruby asked. "It had to be the guy David arrested—the guy in the back of his police car. Think about it, John."

"I have thought about it," I said. "And we've got to find Uretsky without alerting the police. Clegg is the only person who can do that for us."

"By doing that, you could be alerting Uretsky. That's what I'm saying."

"I know."

"Then don't do it."

"What should we do?" I asked, tossing my hands in the air. "Just sit and wait for him to call us with the next crime to commit? Do we sit, or do we fight?"

"You don't know the consequences," Ruby said. "You'll be violating the rules of his game."

"It's a risk," was all I said.

"Well, I don't like our odds," she said.

I called Clegg, anyway, while Ruby went to the bedroom to rest. I wasn't worried about Uretsky overhearing my conversation. Ruby had smashed what I believed to be the only listening device planted in the apartment. If there were leaks, some way for Uretsky to learn of my inquiry, I would be found out regardless if I contacted Clegg by phone or in person. What I wanted was an answer to my question, and I wanted it now.

Clegg sounded glad to hear from me. We chatted about his divorce, the apartment in Hingham he had found, and Ruby's health prognosis. He didn't bring up climbing, but I could hear in his voice that he had a trip planned. It's like a jealous intuition that I have. I used to get that same squeak of excitement before departing on a major expedition myself.

I got to the point. "I need a favor," I said.

"Yeah? What's that?"

"I've got a problem with one of my game players."

"What sort of problem?"

"He's just harassing some other players. Nothing too horrible."

"Kick him off," Clegg said.

"He's threatening to hack me," I said.

I had thought for all of six seconds about what lie I'd tell, and this one seemed to work just fine.

"So what can I do?" Clegg asked.

"Tell me if he's ever been arrested for hacking."

"I could look him up if you give a name and address."

I gave Clegg the name Elliot Uretsky, spelled it for him, too, along with the address I gave UniSol to help steal the same man's identity. Clegg keyed in the information, and I waited.

I sat at the kitchen counter, refreshing YouTube on the laptop, watching my video stats skyrocket. In the time it took for Clegg to come back on the line, another fifty thousand people had witnessed me—ski mask and all—save a man from choking to death while a little old lady beat me silly with her purse. Hell, I'd have watched it, too.

"I got nothing," Clegg said.

"Nothing," I repeated.

"No priors. No arrests. No speeding tickets. This guy is clean. So if he's a hacker, he's never been busted for committing any computer crime. At least not in Massachusetts."

"Is that the only place you can check?"

"I didn't look for outstanding warrants," Clegg said. "That's in LEAPS—our Law Enforcement Automated Processing System."

"Can you look?"

"Sure thing, buddy. Hang on."

Clegg put me on hold. Instead of Muzak, the Boston PD played PS announcements about drinking and driving and the importance of wearing a seat belt. Ginger wove in and out between my legs like a slinky slalom skier while I waited.

"Lucky cat," I said, scratching her head. "You don't have anything to worry about. All you have to do is be a cat."

Ginger meowed as if she understood and agreed wholeheartedly. Within a span of five minutes, I had become jealous of both Clegg (for climbing) and a cat (for its peaceful existence). I checked the video and groaned. Forty thousand more views. Damn, this thing was going to make the national news.

Clegg came back on the line. "Well, I got something," he said.

My pulse jumped, and my leg involuntarily kicked out and sent Ginger scampering away.

"Tell me."

Clegg said, "Nothing about his hacking chops, but if your game buddy is plotting an attack, then he's going to do it from the shadows. It looks like the report was filed a couple months ago by a neighbor."

"What report?" I asked.

I felt a sick drop in my stomach. That was around the same time I'd become Elliot Uretsky.

"You'll be surprised," Uretsky had said to me.

You'll be surprised.

Clegg said, "A neighbor of his filed a 'be on the lookout' message about three months ago with the Medford police."

"What does that mean?" I asked.

"It means somebody wants to know where the Uretskys are, and nobody has seen them."

CHAPTER 26

The next day Ruby and I drove to Medford to scope out the house where Elliot and Tanya Uretsky resided. I keyed the address taken from Uretsky's game account—38 Skyview Lane—into my phone's GPS. Twenty minutes later we were parked on a wide, pleasant street across from a single-story, vinyl-sided ranch home with a detached single-car garage. Thick beige curtains blocked out every window.

My thumb is brown when it comes to gardening, but even I could have spruced up this place. The trees in front of the house were sparse and scraggly. There were bushes all around, but those looked as shaggy and unkempt as the front lawn that begged for a trim. The home itself appeared dark and uninviting. I surveyed the landscape, looking for lawn furniture or toys or any sign of habitation, but saw nothing of the sort. The garden, brown and untended, seemed especially out of place in a neighborhood full of neatly landscaped properties with colorful flower beds.

Ruby and I climbed out of the car. She was wearing a wide-brimmed sun hat and smelled of SPF 50 sunblock. Her jeans and long-sleeved shirt were for added protection. She seemed shaky on her feet, so I wrapped an arm around her waist to give her some added support. We had grown to hate the drugs keeping her alive almost as much as we hated the cancer that was killing her.

"Are you feeling up to this?" I asked.

Ruby nodded, though I could see she felt about as healthy and ready as Uretsky's lawn.

I checked the mailbox, a big black metal oval mounted on a faded wooden post. It was full, but not overly so. There were bills (nothing from UniSol Health), along with the current issues of O *Magazine* (addressed to Tanya Uretsky) and *The New Yorker* (also addressed to Tanya Uretsky). I put the mail back in the box, ignoring the temptation to check out this week's cartoon contest.

"Where is the rest of their mail?" I said to Ruby. "If we're to believe Clegg, these people haven't been seen in months. Shouldn't there be a mountain of it?"

"That's still a big if in my mind," Ruby said, meaning whether to believe Clegg. My look conveyed my disagreement. "Anyway," Ruby continued, "maybe the post office is keeping it."

"Then why is today's mail here and nothing else?"

"I dunno," Ruby said. "Uretsky is probably hiding out. He doesn't want his neighbors to see him."

"Hiding out with his wife?"

Ruby shrugged.

"Something is wrong," I said. "Something is very, very wrong with all this."

"What?" Ruby asked.

"I just don't get the feeling that a psychopath lives here."

"Why? Because it's not all spooky?"

I shrugged. Ruby was right—the place didn't feel scary as much as lonely.

"Can we ever really know what our friends and neighbors are up to?" Ruby said.

"Follow me," I said.

There weren't any lights on inside the home, but I tried to get a peek through some of the windows. Unfortunately, the closed curtains made it impossible to see, and it was too dark inside the house to get a good look through the front door sidelight windows. I couldn't see into the garage—no windows there—so Ruby and I worked our way around back.

The backyard was a small, unfenced square of land, not more than a quarter of an acre, but as poorly maintained as the front. I saw a grill and some all-season furniture on the stone patio, but those were dusty from disuse. A dark shadow seemed to have been cast over this place, impervious to the sweet scent of spring air and an afternoon sky that was bright blue and cloudless. Birdsong filled our ears, though no birds seemed to be nesting in the few trees that dotted Uretsky's property. It was as though the land here had gone sour, and the animals seemed to know it.

We walked back to the front of the house and climbed inside Ziggy.

"Somebody is coming to get the mail," I said to Ruby. "And I don't think it'll be Elliot Uretsky."

"You want to wait in the car?" Ruby asked.

I nodded.

"Would it be in poor taste if I read that O *Magazine* while we waited?"

I shrugged, got out of the car, opened the mailbox, and got her the magazine. She flipped through the pages while we waited some more. We didn't talk much. Ruby took out her phone and checked the stats on my video.

"You've been viewed over two million times now," Ruby said.

I took out my phone and checked as well.

"You mean two million fifty-eight thousand," I said.

"Fifty-eight thousand people just watched that video?" Ruby asked, unbelieving.

"I think I'm big in Japan," I said.

Ruby groaned.

The robbery, just as I had feared, made national news. It was on the CNN home page and was covered by just about every other news outlet around the country. Defense attorneys made endless online pleas for me to come forward so they could represent me. I had reached celebrity status. I had also unwittingly set off a massive ethical debate. Did my single act of goodness offset my unconscionable act of evil? Opinions seemed to vary but were not in short supply.

The comments were great. Everything from I should be given the key to the city to I should be given an enema by a lifer named Bubba at Concord prison. I was feeling the love, that's for sure. Web sites about the robbery sprang up overnight like runaway weeds, many paying homage to the masked bandit who stopped his robbery in progress to administer CPR. If *Entertainment Tonight* was to be believed—yes, my robbery was now considered entertainment—Giovanni's business had never been better. There's no such thing as bad PR. I hated what I had done, but to look on the positive side, choking was responsible for about twenty-five hundred deaths per year. Perhaps someone, someday, would save a life using what he saw in that video.

"I can't believe you're a viral video." Ruby put her hands to her head. "I'm going to keep searching for snakes and lotus flowers."

"Let me know what you find," I said.

One day, I was thinking. *We'll know in one more day.*

An hour later I saw a woman approach in Ziggy's rearview mirror. She was just north of middle age and walking a chocolate Lab. She stopped at the Uretskys' mailbox. I got out of the car, hoping that I wouldn't startle her. She whirled around and put her hand to her chest. Her dog didn't bark.

"Oh, you startled me," she said.

The best-laid schemes o' mice an' men . . .

I smiled, but judging by her expression, I might as well have had the ski mask on.

"Hi there," I said. "Sorry about that. I was wondering if you could help me out."

Ruby got out of the car, and I saw all the worry in the older lady's face slip away. Nothing says "nonthreatening" like a sun hat.

"Hello," the woman said to Ruby, warmly now. "How can I help you?"

Ruby stepped forward and introduced herself.

"I'm Ruth Shane. I'm a neighbor. And this here is Bucky," Ruth said, patting her dog's shiny coat.

Bucky approached Ruby, sniffed around her, and started to bark.

"Bucky!" Ruth snapped. "Calm down."

Bucky circled, winding his leash around Ruby's legs, sniffing and barking. Ruth yanked him back to her side. Bucky whimpered some, then pulled away to stand beside Ruby once again. He sniffed, barked, and looked up at my wife with eyes that looked brokenhearted.

"Bucky, what's gotten into you?" Ruth said. "I'm sorry."

"Maybe he smells our cat," I suggested.

"Bucky doesn't care about such things. At least, he hasn't before. But if it was your cat, I wonder why he didn't bark at you?" Ruth seemed to say this to herself.

Bucky settled down, so we all shook hands. I introduced myself as John, since Ruby was Ruby, finally.

"I'm looking for Elliot Uretsky," I said.

The woman looked pained. "Oh goodness, are you family?"

I lied. "Cousin," I said.

"I didn't know Elliot had any family in the States," Ruth said. "Are you from Ukraine, too?"

"No, we're distantly related," I said. "We haven't actually met. I went on a family tree kick a while back, so I've been trying to locate as many of my relatives as I can."

Ruby looked at me like I had two heads.

"That's so wonderful," Ruth said. "Young people these days don't put enough value on family, if you ask me."

"I've been trying to reach him, but I haven't been having any luck," I said.

"I'm not surprised," Ruth said.

"Is that why you're collecting his mail?" I said, tapping the mailbox. "Is he out of town?"

"I am collecting their mail," Ruth said, her pleasant voice now tinged with worry. "But it's not because they're out of town. At least, I don't think they are. You see, I reported them missing to the police several months ago. I've been collecting their mail ever since. The police offered to put a stop to it—the mail, I mean—but I don't mind, really. It's taking up only a couple of boxes in the garage. It'll be easier for them to go through it all when they come back." She paused and reflexively put a hand on Bucky for comfort. "If they come back," she said, finishing the thought.

I thought about handing her the *O Magazine* we had in the car, but that felt a little too creepy. We'd keep the magazine. Hell, I was already a criminal. "How long has it been since you've seen them?" I asked.

"Three months, thereabouts," Ruth said.

Three months is well before I became Elliot Uretsky, I thought.

"I never saw Elliot all that much," Ruth continued. "Mostly, I'd see Tanya working in her garden." She pointed to the brown patch of land that lay barren like a stain on the earth. "I kept telling Tanya to plant more perennials, but she preferred what she preferred."

"Why do you think they're missing?"

"Well, because nobody has seen them, of course."

"What about their friends?" Ruby asked.

"Oh, they are private people."

"Coworkers?" Ruby asked.

"They both work from home," Ruth said. "He's a computer consultant, I think."

"And Tanya?" Ruby said.

"She makes jewelry and sells her work online." Ruth showed us her earrings—dangling silver triangles with an embedded green gemstone. "She gave me these before they vanished. Beautiful, aren't they?"

"Beautiful," Ruby said.

"Anyway, when March came around and I hadn't seen Tanya outside once, I just got the feeling that something was wrong."

"What did the police say?" Ruby asked.

"Well, that's the crazy thing," Ruth said. "Did you know that it's not that simple to report an adult as missing? They could just be gone."

"Is their car still here?"

"No. It's gone. The police checked the garage."

"Did the police go inside the house?"

"They did but didn't see anything suspicious. They think they just up and left."

"You must think that, too, because you're collecting their mail."

"I'm collecting their mail, but I don't agree with the police," Ruth said.

"What do you think happened to them?" I asked.

Ruth turned around and pointed toward a yellow clapboard house fronted by green shutters set slightly askew and a lawn that stuck out because it rivaled the Uretskys' for its lack of landscaping.

"I told the police to look at Carl Swain," Ruth said.

Bucky seemed to slink away at the mere mention.

"What's wrong with Carl?" Ruby asked.

"I've seen him lurking around the Uretskys' house. Peeking into their windows."

"That is creepy," Ruby said.

"Carl would drive by slowly if Tanya were out gardening. I've seen it happen several times. I told this all to the police, of course, but they never got back to me."

"So you think Carl Swain has something to do with the Uretskys' disappearance?" I asked.

Ruth nodded. "And so does Bucky."

"Your dog?" I said.

Bucky perked up, and his tongue dropped out of his mouth. Ruth said, "I believe animals have a sixth sense."

"I've read somewhere that dogs can detect cancer and other diseases," Ruby said, looking at me.

I looked back. It could explain Bucky's powerful reaction to Ruby and not to me.

Ruth nodded. "That's true," she said. "Some dogs have fifty times the scent receptors as humans."

"So does Bucky bark at this Carl fellow?"

"He won't let me walk him on that side of the street," Ruth said, the pitch of her voice dropping to signify the ominous connection.

"Has Bucky met Carl?"

"On a number of occasions," Ruth said. "And if you thought he barked at Ruby, you should have seen his reaction to Carl."

I admit that Ruth got me curious. I didn't really believe in doggie detectives, but I was desperate to find Elliot Uretsky, and willing to believe that Bucky's barking at Carl Swain was some kind of lead.

"Maybe Carl has cancer," Ruby suggested.

Ruth's eyes narrowed. She made several furtive glances at Swain's house, as though afraid of being overhead.

"I believe I have a sixth sense, too," Ruth said. "And if Carl Swain has cancer, then it's a cancer of the soul."

CHAPTER 27

We returned to Uretsky's neighborhood the very next day, arriving exactly one hour later than the time we saw Ruth out walking Bucky, the psycho-sniffing dog. We didn't want her to think we were stalkers—which, of course, we were. We sat in Ziggy, just like a couple of private dicks on a stakeout. We were parked directly across from the little yellow house with the crooked green shutters. Unlike the Uretskys' house, the garage here was attached, and a structure was built on top of it, too, an addition of some sort.

"What are you going to do if you see him?" Ruby asked.

Ruby rested her hand on my leg. I loved the feel of her touch, though it made me miss our more playful and more naked touching sessions. One look and I could tell that Ruby was missing them, too.

"I don't know," I said.

"You don't know! That's your plan?"

"I just want to see him."

"And then what?"

"Then I think I'll know if he's involved in some way."

"Now you, Ruth, and Bucky all have the sixth sense?"

"Wasn't that about seeing dead people?"

Ruby punched me in the arm. "This isn't funny, John. Ruth thinks Carl had something to do with Uretsky's disappearance. He could be dangerous."

"Tell me this, then. If the Uretskys have disappeared, how is it we're being terrorized by Elliot Uretsky?"

"So why are we even here?"

"Because what else do we have to go on? Maybe Swain saw something during his Peeping Tom sessions. Something that could help lead us to Uretsky."

Ruby couldn't argue that point, or she could but didn't feel like arguing, so we went back to waiting.

I broke a minute of silence by asking, "Do you want to play twenty questions?"

Ruby shot me an annoyed look. "No, I don't want to play twenty questions," she said. "I want to go home, and by *home,* I mean to the apartment you rented to a couple of Spanish-speaking professors."

"I just want to wait a little longer," I said, kissing Ruby on the cheek. "I love you."

"You better," Ruby said before giving me a quick kiss on the lips.

We returned to silence. Twenty or thirty minutes later my cell phone rang. It was Clegg calling—or returning my call, to be more precise.

"Hey, David," I said. "Thanks for getting back to me."

Ruby looked at me, shaking her head in dismay. "I have a sixth sense, too, you know," she said.

"Sorry I wasn't around yesterday," Clegg said. "What's up?"

I could tell that his "Sorry I wasn't around yesterday" was code for "I was preparing for a climbing expedition." Sensitive guy he was, he knew better than to tell me.

"Remember that LEAPS thing, or whatever you used to look up information on Uretsky?" I said.

"Sure," he said.

"Can you look up somebody else for me?" I asked.

"A buddy of Uretsky's?" Clegg asked, not missing a beat.

"Something like that," I said.

"Sure thing. Give me the name and address."

I gave him Carl Swain's name and Carl's address.

"I'll check the Triple I, too," Clegg said.

"What's that?" I asked.

"Interstate Identification Index. It's basically Google for criminal history."

"Sounds good," I said.

"It'll take a bit, so I'll call you back," Clegg said.

"Good again."

"Kiss your lovely bride for me," he said.

"With pleasure," I said. I got out of the car.

"Stretching?" Ruby asked.

"I'm going to take a look around."

"I'm coming with you," Ruby said, reaching for the door handle.

"No. Stay in the car. I'll be less conspicuous alone."

"No, you'll be just as conspicuous," Ruby said. "But maybe it's better if I stay and keep a lookout. Make sure your cell is on. I'll text you if I see anything to be worried about."

I nodded, leaned forward, and kissed Ruby, as Clegg suggested, and away I went.

Twice, I walked past the front of the house feeling, just as Ruby had predicted, completely and ridiculously conspicuous. It looked like one of those homes without any lights on during Halloween— the kind you'd scurry right past because on the night when bogeymen were most real, this was the exact sort of place they'd like to congregate. The windows were dark and dirty; sprigs of weeds came shooting up through cracks in the front step bricks. The lawn, more brown than green, looked mostly dead, and while some lovely pots filled with dirt were set out front, the plants within them were nothing but thin sticks with black leaves. In another bit of creepy construction, there were no windows on the extension built on top of the single-car garage that was connected to the side of the house.

It looked like nobody was home, but I knocked on the front door, anyway, just to check. No answer. I tried the doorbell. It didn't work. So I cut across the forgotten lawn and stood close enough to Ziggy to get Ruby's attention. "I'm going to check out back," I said in a half whisper.

Ruby rolled down her window. "What?" she asked loudly.

Now it was my turn to shoot her an annoyed look. "I'm going to check out back," I said, speaking in my normal voice. I gave up trying to not appear conspicuous. It was obvious that we were both lacking in the detecting department.

"Be careful and keep your phone on," she said.

The back of the house, like the Uretskys', proved to be as ugly as the front. A dilapidated trampoline with one leg missing took up a good portion of the postage-stamp lawn. Rusty toolboxes were strewn about with no tools inside—none that I could see, anyway. The trees were cut down to stumps, and the stone birdbath next to one of them, cracked and ugly, held brown, dirty rainwater. The lawn was a dead patch of dirt where nothing, not even weeds, would grow. The basement door had a window covered by a curtain, and the other windows out back were too high for me to see inside without a stepladder.

I did a three-sixty and got the same feeling Ruth Shane had expressed the day before. The place felt poisoned.

I'd decided it was time for me to head back to Ziggy when my phone buzzed. I looked and saw a text message from Ruby. Some of the words were misspelled, but the content of her message told me that she had sent her text in great haste.

Woman wiith gunn run!

CHAPTER 28

Left or right—which way should I go? Wrong way, and chances were I'd run into an armed woman. Instead of bolting, I hesitated, overthinking and not reacting. For a few seconds my feet stayed rooted to the ground, with half my brain screaming to run and the other half debating which way.

Five seconds at most. That's what it took to decide. Five quick ticks of the clock, but as it turned out, it was three ticks too many. When I broke left—which happened to be the right way to go—I almost made it to the side of the house when I heard a scratchy, hoarse-sounding female voice shout from behind me.

"You stop or I shoot!"

I stopped, all right. The world around me turned gray, as if all its color had gone swirling down a fast-draining tub. My eyes closed tightly, while my hands went unprompted above my head.

I heard footsteps approaching, slow moving. Either she was being cautious or she couldn't move quickly. I kept my hands up and turned around . . . nice . . . and . . . slow. I can't say which I saw first, the woman or the double-barreled shotgun pointed at my chest. We'll call it a tie.

The woman, rollers in her hair, wore a faded white nightgown in mid-afternoon and had no shoes on her feet. Her cheeks were sunken, as though the bones beneath had dissolved over time. As for her face, she radiated toughness, a look enhanced by her leathery skin, which had crinkled the way a potato dries in the sun. Her lips creased back into a snarl, while her eyes, milky and blue, could not conceal the hatred that probably accompanied her every waking second.

"Who are you?" she said.

I could tell by the rasp that she inhaled at least three packs a day. She stood about twenty feet from me, but that gun shortened the distance between us considerably. This was probably how poor Giovanni felt, scared and cornered, though he had an aluminum bat stashed at his disposal, whereas I was unarmed.

The woman took a threatening step forward. "Who are you?" she asked again. "And what do you want?"

I kept my hands in the air and didn't take a single step. I went rigid like the Tin Man, but I had a heart, and that organ was pounding away mightily.

"I'm looking for Carl Swain," I said. My dry throat put a little crack in my voice.

"What for?" she asked. The word *for* came out sounding like "fo-ah." She took another step forward, keeping the gun pointed at my chest. Her toes curled in the dirt to show me that she was digging in. Hopefully, that meant she wouldn't be coming any closer. Then again, she could blow me away just fine from this distance.

"I'd like to ask him about Elliot and Tanya Uretsky," I said.

"Carl's not here, and you shouldn't be here, either," she said. "So get off my property, or I'm going to shoot, and then I'll call the cops."

She raised the gun, taking aim with her eye. The skin of her arms where it had loosened from the underlying muscles flapped like two white, sun-spotted wings. Her toes curled deeper into the dirt. I was taking a cautious backward step when I caught movement behind her. It took me a couple blinks of the eye to realize that it was Ruby.

"Stop!" I heard Ruby shout. "You stop it right now!"

The woman whirled around and trained the gun at Ruby's head. My breath caught in my throat, and I lunged forward, ready to tackle the woman to the ground and wrestle the gun away, but Ruby held up a hand that told me to stay put. So I stayed put.

Wearing her sun hat and glasses, Ruby looked about as threatening as Annie Hall, but she did not back down. Rather, she took a couple steps forward, her finger wagging at the weathered woman like a scolding schoolmarm's. Ruby, who was a card-carrying member of the ASPCA, who checked food labels for genetically modified organisms, who loved to do yoga before she got sick, who contemplated veganism, and who read Mahatma Gandhi's biography twice, did not appear ready or even able to preach the power of nonviolence. Instead, she strode right up to the woman and stopped maybe a foot away.

"You put that gun away right now!" Ruby said. My wife ripped off her sunglasses so the seriousness of her expression could not be misunderstood. "Right now!" Ruby said.

The woman hesitated, the standoff in full effect. Ruby didn't back down, but the woman eventually did. She set the butt of the gun on the ground, the barrel aiming skyward, with one of her knotty hands still positioned near the trigger mechanism, ready to make a quick move if necessary.

"How dare you point a gun at my husband?" Ruby said. "How dare you? You could have killed him!"

"What's he doing sneaking around my property?" the woman said.

"We weren't sneaking," Ruby said. "We knocked on your door."

"And I rang the bell," I added.

The woman twisted her neck around to glare at me through those milky, dying eyes. Guess she didn't need to know that part.

"You get off my property, and don't ever come here," she said. "We have enough trouble just living as it is. Why don't you leave us alone? My boy hasn't done nothing to no one. You just leave and leave him be."

Now, I may not be a professional detective, but even I could deduce that this angry old woman was Carl's mother. I walked past Mama Meanie, taking quick and purposeful steps. Carl's mom eyed me with contempt, holding on to the shotgun in a way that reminded me of the *American Gothic* painting. I only wished that she brandished a pitchfork.

Ruby took hold of my hand, and we slinked away backward, instinct telling us that vigilance was still necessary.

The woman followed us to the front of the house. Once again we were back inside Ziggy; once again we were driving away from this neighborhood. I kept looking in the rearview mirror, half expecting to see Carl's mom standing in the middle of the road, leveling her shotgun and readying it to take a lucky shot. But I saw nothing more than a sunny street and rows of pleasant-looking houses—pleasant except for two of them, Carl Swain's and Elliot Uretsky's.

CHAPTER 29

Leaving never felt so good. Ruby and I were in recovery mode, still breathing hard, still trying to regain our equilibrium. I was driving through neighborhoods I didn't know very well, using my GPS to guide us back to the apartment on Harvard Avenue—a place I couldn't really call our home—when my phone rang.

Ruby saw it was Clegg calling, which did nothing to improve her battered spirits.

"Maybe you need to screen your users better, John," Clegg said before I even got out the word *hello*.

"Explain," I said.

"The Triple I query I ran on this guy Swain came back jackpot. Not only is he a neighbor of this Uretsky guy, but he's a level three sex offender. We've got one count of assault with intent to commit rape, indecent assault and battery on a person aged fourteen or older, and two counts of rape."

"Crap," I said. Ruby looked at me. I mouthed the word *rapist* and watched her pale skin turn even paler. "Shouldn't he be in jail?" I asked.

"He served seven years, then got out," Clegg said. "Average time behind bars is eleven for rapists, in case you wanted to know."

I didn't want to know. Seemed like infinity would be a more fitting sentence for a scumbag like Swain, but what do I know about the law.

"Got any physical stats on him?" I asked.

"White male, forty-six, six feet, two-ten. Hair brown. Eyes brown."

"Can you send me a picture?"

"Sure. Or you can look him up yourself on the SORB Web site."

"SORB?" I asked.

"Sex Offender Registry Board."

"One more question," I said, signaling to make a left turn. "The address I gave you, is that Mom's place or his?"

Clegg looked it up. "By *Mom* I'm assuming you mean Lucille Swain, and yes, she's the registered owner of the property on that address," he said. "So, is this guy giving you grief? I've got plenty of contacts in the Medford PD who would love to pay this piece-o-crap a visit."

"No. Not really. I'll just deactivate his account. Thanks for the help."

"Okay, hombre," Clegg said. "Call anytime."

I ended the call, wondering if the next time I tried to reach Clegg, he would be someplace far away, feet high above the earth, smelling the purity of the sky and feeling his soul come alive. I wished I could join him.

"What do you make of that?" Ruby asked after I put my phone away. I shouldn't have been talking and driving, anyway. At least it wasn't another crime.

"Well, let's assess the situation," I said. "The Uretskys seem to have vanished."

"True," Ruby said.

"But Elliot is a murdering psychopath who is still antagonizing us."

"True, as well."

"We know he's going to try and make me commit another felony, and we have no clue what his snake and lotus flower thing means."

"Kesha," Ruby said.

"It's not Kesha," I said, "but yes, Kesha. Meanwhile, the Uretskys' neighbor, Ruth Shane, is convinced that Carl Swain has something to do with their disappearance, or at least Tanya Uretsky's disappearance, and it turns out she has some real reasons to think the way she does. Swain is a registered sex offender with a gun-toting mama."

"So what do we do?"

"We wait for Uretsky to contact me. Today should be the day. And we take it from there."

* * *

We didn't have to wait long. We were back in the apartment on Harvard Avenue, or "John's Place," as Ruby had taken to calling it. Ruby was feeding Ginger, and I was washing the potatoes we would have with dinner. Neither of us had grown accustomed to the fact that while embroiled in this nightmare, Ruby and I were required to observe the rules of life. We had to eat. We had to sleep. We were still alive, and though trapped beneath the shadow of pain and guilt cast by the deaths of Rhonda Jennings and Brooks Hall, we were obliged to live.

I kept my phone by the sink. When it chirped, I drew in a ragged breath, glanced at the text message, and yelled out, "Uretsky!"

Ruby came running over to read it. I assumed his text was untraceable; a guy who knew how to configure routers to hide out on the Internet knew how to send untraceable texts, too.

Uretsky's text message read: **Have you figured out my clue?**

I texted him back—what the hell, why not? I was honest, too. I saw no reason to lie. It wouldn't help us any. I wrote: **We couldn't spell your clue.**

He wrote back: **LOL! I didn't think of that.** Honestly, this deranged psycho used LOL! Like we were pals having a conversation over a Facebook status. **The snake and lotus flower are gripped in Qetesh's hands.**

I showed the phone to Ruby and said, "Google Qetesh. Q-E-T-E-S-H."

Ruby went over to my laptop and typed in the correct spelling. She read for me verbatim what Wikipedia had to say about it. "Qetesh is a Sumerian goddess adopted into Egyptian mythology from the Canaanite religion, popular during the New Kingdom. She was a fertility goddess of sacred ecstasy and sexual pleasure."

"What the heck?" I said, mulling that over. "Google the snake and lotus flower and Qetesh."

Ruby did just that. "There's a stone carving of Qetesh that shows her standing on the back of a lion. She's holding snakes in one hand and a lotus flower in the other. According to what I'm reading here, these are symbols of creation. John, what is he planning?"

I heard the slight tremor in Ruby's voice. Her alert eyes were wary.

What do you want from us? I texted to Uretsky.

The bastard typed a three-word reply: **Check your in-box.**

CHAPTER 30

I'd been through this before, so I expected everything that happened next, or I should say that I wasn't surprised. I followed the instructions and looked at the admin e-mail account for my *One World* game. Right at the top of the queue was an e-mail from Elliot Uretsky. The time stamp on the e-mail read one minute in the past, and the message contained only a link, which I clicked without hesitation.

An on-screen prompt appeared, asking me if I wanted to allow a two-way video chat. No, of course I didn't want to, but I did it, anyway. I had to. I also knew that the Web page that loaded ran through the same anonymous proxy server Uretsky had used before, to broadcast poor Dr. Adams's misery.

The black rectangular shape centered on the Web page gave way to a depressingly familiar image, one that filled me with horror and rage all over again. I gazed upon the concrete windowless room, nondescript in every way except for a single lightbulb that dangled above a sturdy oak desk chair. I couldn't feel the dampness of the room, but I could hear the echoes of dripping water from a corroded copper pipe—but only when the woman beneath that pipe wasn't making muted cries for help.

I couldn't see the gag silencing those cries, because a bag made from a velvety silk cloth, one that shone like a panther's fur in the dim room, had been placed over her head. Her hands, white skin tanned to a shade of brown, were bound to the arms of the chair, and I assumed her feet were secured as well. I also assumed the chair was bolted to the floor; otherwise, her thrashing would have toppled it over.

Uretsky's face filled the screen—not his face, really, but the mask of Mario from the *Super Mario Bros.* video game. Uretsky had used the same character as his Facebook avatar. The red hat, bulbous nose, and trademark mustache of Mario were all there, but Uretsky had cut out eyeholes where the mask's eyes should have been, and he cut a hole for his mouth as well.

"John, how nice to see you again," Uretsky said. That voice, soulless as the dead, chilled my skin. "You're looking unwell, if you don't mind my saying so."

"What . . . ," I said, trying to catch my breath, finding it hard to speak. "What are you doing?"

Ruby got her face in front of the laptop's camera and shouted, "Stop it! Stop it now! You let her go!"

Uretsky screamed loudly in response, with a high-pitched shriek, not unlike the noise of a boiling teakettle, a yell so piercing that we were both silenced.

"I can't think when you two are shouting at me," Uretsky said.

"Well, we can't talk to you with that mask on. Take it off, you coward."

"Can't do that, John," Uretsky replied. "You might take a picture."

"You're not a felon. I checked."

I regretted the words the moment they slipped out of my mouth.

"You checked up on me?" Uretsky said, his voice rising with surprise.

"On the Internet." I spoke quickly, crafting a suitable lie without much fumbling. "I used a Web search to look you up. Not the police. I didn't violate the rules."

Uretsky stepped back from the camera, pondering. He nodded, slowly and several times, and I thought I could see the faint outline of a smile inside that grotesque mask. "Oh, very well. You didn't cheat. So, what did you find?" he asked.

"Nothing," I said. "But I do know about Carl Swain."

I fixed my gaze upon Uretsky's eyes when I said Swain's name, searching every pixel of the grainy video feed for a slight glimmer of recognition, a hint that I'd struck a nerve. Did he know Swain? Was there some connection? Behind the ovals he had cut out for eyeholes, I saw nothing but the black infinity of death. If Uretsky wondered about my non sequitur, he didn't say.

"I've made sure to keep my face off the Internet. You don't know what I look like, and that's part of the fun. I want to keep this mask on, and I want you two to keep playing my game. Is that understood?"

What other choice did I have but to nod?

"Now then," Uretsky continued. "Have you figured out what you're to do next?"

"Qetesh," I said.

"Yes, Qetesh, a luscious Sumerian goddess. Her name means 'holy woman,' " Uretsky said. "A goddess of sacred ecstasy and sexual pleasures. So, do you get it yet?"

"No," I said.

"Well, it's going to be a dandy good time," Uretsky said. "But I decided that you'll need a bit more incentive than Dr. Adams's life to pull this one off."

Uretsky stepped away from the camera, giving us a clear view of the woman strapped to the chair, still struggling mightily, albeit futilely, to break free. Uretsky, mask on, materialized behind the woman, as though conjured from the ether. In a sweeping motion, he ripped off the hood covering the head of his prisoner. Ruby gripped the back of my chair in response.

"Mom?" Ruby's shaky, uncertain voice caught in her throat. Eventually, after recognition set in, once the brain had time to process the inconceivable, Ruby shouted, "Mom!"

It took me a moment longer to register what I was seeing, but there she was, Winifred Dawes, Ruby's mom, tied to that chair and somehow Uretsky's prisoner.

Ruby began to scream. Her anguished cries, so visceral, so instinctual, went far beyond any sound I had ever heard from my wife. "Mom!" Ruby shouted again and again before the sobs took over.

Ruby, hyperventilating, couldn't speak for a minute or so. She lost her footing, and I gave her my chair, while I leaned in close to get level with the camera. Ruby's eyes stayed fixed on her mother. I didn't know if Winnie could see her daughter, but the pain etched on her face whenever Ruby spoke told me that, at a minimum, she could hear her voice.

"Please . . . please, Elliot," Ruby managed to say. "You could just let her go . . . let her go, now. Okay? You could do that."

Winnie, with her short and spiky hair, bleached blond in some spots, left brown in others, and her skin pruned by the persistent Caribbean sun, should have seemed a familiar sight, but here, in this dark prison, she was barely recognizable. Her bright blue eyes were as wide as two quarters, but I couldn't get a good look at her face. She kept shaking her head, as though her hair were on fire. The ball gag in her mouth, I suspected, had once been in poor Dr. Adams's mouth, too.

"I'd make the introductions, but I know you're already well acquainted," Uretsky said from behind Winnie. "And you're going to have to push the limits to save this sweet lady's life . . . or not."

"Let her go," I said. We still had a chance to save Winnie's life if we did whatever Uretsky had in mind. Perhaps that was why my voice came out sounding oddly calm. "She's done nothing to you. Come get me instead, dammit!"

Winnie nodded a vigorous yes. Son-in-law or not, she'd switch places with me in a heartbeat. I couldn't blame her. That was just the survival instinct kicking in.

"Doesn't work like that," Uretsky said. "You've got more crimes to commit, John . . ." Here Uretsky paused . . . waiting . . . waiting . . . and then he said two words that truly chilled my bones. "And Ruby."

I hated that he'd even spoken my wife's name. The privilege wasn't his. Besides, this wasn't about her; it was about me, and what I'd done to him, or so I thought.

But in that very next instant, I knew. Qetesh. Sacred ecstasy. Sexual pleasure. Uretsky wanted Ruby to commit the next crime, not me. And I knew what the crime was, too.

"Please," I said. "Don't do this. There's got to be another way."

"No," Uretsky said. "The show must go on." The mask made Uretsky's low voice sound hollow and breathy, more terrifying. "Now, Ruby, aren't you at all curious how I managed to get your mom to be my guest here?"

Each ragged breath Ruby took sounded like a record skipping. She managed only to say, "Please let her go. Mommy, I love you. Don't worry. We're going to save you. I'll do anything."

Uretsky put the bag over Winnie's head again. He came around in front of her chair to face the camera.

"I called your mom and pretended to be one of John's climbing buddies, told her we were the closest of friends," Uretsky said. "I also broke the good news that you'd gone into complete remission, that the meds had worked wonders, and I was putting together a big surprise party in your honor. You and John knew nothing about this, of course, but I was arranging the flights and accommodations for all the out-of-town relatives. Guess who picked her up curbside at the terminal?"

Behind Uretsky, I could see Winnie thrashing about like her chair was electrified.

"This isn't an acquaintance's life hanging in the balance. It's Mom. Good relationship or not, she's still your mother, Ruby. How far are you willing to go to save her? What will you do? Can you be transformed? Those are my questions. Questions that demand answers."

"What do you want me to do?" I said.

"Not you," Uretsky said, confirming my darkest fear. "Ruby is going to have to participate this time."

"What do you want?" I asked again.

"Qetesh represents divine sexual pleasure. Ruby is going to provide someone with the real deal."

"She has cancer, you sick bastard," I said.

"The crime she is to commit is one of the oldest known professions."

Ruby got her face level with the camera. She didn't flinch from Uretsky's eyes—eyes swimming with madness. "Tell me," she said.

"You will go to a bar of my choosing, and there you will proposition a stranger for sex in exchange for cash. You will whore yourself to this strange man and bring him to a hotel room that I've set up for this rendezvous. I've taped an envelope to the front right tire of your car." Ruby and I glanced at each other, thinking the same thing: He was here? "Inside that envelope you'll find the address to the hotel I've rented under the name John Bodine, and the key card to your room. You will also find the name and address of the nearby bar where you will select your client. You will let him have his way with you, whatever his desire, and then, once it's over, you'll take his money. You have twenty-four hours to complete this task. Simple as that."

"And if I don't?" Ruby asked, her voice a whimper.

Uretsky held up the pruning shears for us both to see. "Then I'll strip your mother of her fingers, one by one, before I strip her of her life."

CHAPTER 31

With five hours to go before Uretsky's deadline, I found myself at a bar, my guts twisted and my pretended calm threatening to come undone. I'd promised myself I wouldn't drink—I needed to keep a clear head—but after overhearing Ruby's conversation with a man neither of us knew, I'd either order a whiskey or throttle the bastard.

It hurt me desperately, the worst kind of ache, the remorseful kind, every time I looked at Ruby. I could think only of what she was going through and of all the pain I had caused her, distress piled on top of distress. Sure, I had stolen Uretsky's identity with the very best of intentions, but that excuse rang particularly hollow when it was Ruby who had to complete this repulsive task, not me.

Even so, I could not crumble under the oppressive weight of regret. Climbing had taught me to do the exact opposite, and those instincts are difficult to suppress. Up on the mountain, when a rope system fails or a seemingly steady rock is found to be dangerously unstable, I didn't anguish over my predicament. Instead I acted, immediately and decisively, to ameliorate the threat. My life depended on it. The time for self-reflection came after the climbing was done. So until Ruby was safe and Winnie free, until Uretsky was no longer our black cloud, I was going to keep climbing and fighting to stay alive, and Ruby, who had never climbed a day in her life, would have to do the same.

We didn't sleep a wink after hearing Uretsky's demands. We were too busy putting together a contingency plan.

"What if I can't go through with it?" Ruby asked, a thin band of tears lining the bottoms of her eyes.

I told her it was all right. I'd already come up with a way she wouldn't have to.

We contemplated abandoning Plan A (Ruby sleeps with stranger) for my Plan B, but Ruby decided—for her mother's sake—that she would have to bow to Uretsky's will. The decision had to be hers and hers alone. Hadn't my intervention already dropped enough misery on our family?

But every dangerous climb required a contingency plan, so I spent the hours before our deadline arrived putting the pieces in place for Plan B.

Just in case.

Oh, how I hoped we would use it.

We spent some time searching for an outfit Ruby could wear, only to discover the cancer had sucked so much life from her body that nothing she owned fit anymore. She sat on the floor of the closet, clothes tossed all about in a pile, crying, sobbing, really.

"You take care of this," she said, but only when the tears allowed her to speak. "It's so repulsive I can't even think about it. Get me something I can wear. Just get this fucking over with!"

I went to the Gap down the street and bought her a steel-gray satin sheath dress for about eighty bucks. In fact, I bought two, and for good reason. We would need two dresses for Plan B to work. Ruby put the dress on, looked at herself in the mirror, and said, "I'm going to burn it after this is done."

"We'll make a pile," I said, in reference to the clothes from the robbery that we had yet to dispose of.

She gave me a forlorn look. We left the house and went to the bar.

Though her body was full of sickness, and her heart filled with dread, Ruby still managed to turn every head in the Red Bell Lounge, Uretsky's chosen watering hole for this crime. I walked close by, keeping a protective and vigilant watch over my wife, even though we had agreed to act like strangers. Ruby shot me a look that forced me to back away.

"Don't blow this," her eyes were saying.

Every surface of the lounge, including the front of the bar, was draped in rich red velvet, the color of blood. The lounge was crowded with an eclectic clientele, which made it easy to discreetly work the room.

Ruby saw a lonely-looking guy sitting at the bar. She broke away from me and approached him with a surprising confidence. She got maybe five feet from him, stopped, and turned to look at me. Her mascara painted several black lines down her cheeks because her tears wouldn't stop flowing.

While Ruby raced off to the bathroom to reapply her makeup, I searched the bar for anyone who might be paying extra close attention to us. Perhaps that person would be Uretsky, watching. Maybe that was why he insisted we find our "john" at the Red Bell, or maybe it was for our convenience, because this place was so close to the hotel. Then again, I had already figured out how Uretsky would verify that Ruby had gone through with it. I had figured out his plan and crafted a plan of my own.

Plan B.

Ruby came back from the bathroom, looking poised and ready to try again. Twice more she attempted to solicit a man for sex, but with each attempt she broke down. Ruby's body simply wouldn't allow her to betray her heart. Consensual or not, what Uretsky demanded of her made it rape by proxy. It was a knife wound to both our souls.

Instead of attracting prospects, Ruby's tears became the ultimate repellant, an uncontrollable act of self-preservation. After the second prospect dashed out of the bar, she said, "We've got to go through with your plan."

I said a silent prayer of thanks.

CHAPTER 32

An hour later we were ready to try again. Our new mark was in his late thirties, but I put his body age a good ten years older than that. In this dimly lit watering hole everything about him looked dark, from his short hair, groomed in a Clooney way, to the rings around his sunken eyes, to the stubble dotting his "I'm the man" face. He looked like a guy who enjoyed taking whatever he wanted. Perfect.

Take my bait, you jackass.

He wore a pin-striped blue suit, the kind that graced many a corner office.

Our plan required a modestly impaired individual, but this guy exceeded our needs by at least three cocktails. I picked him after he swallowed down a Dewar's and soda like he was doing a Jell-O shot. We waited long enough to make sure he'd come alone, and it was obvious to us both that he was a regular. I checked his finger for a wedding band. I didn't want to be responsible for any marital disharmony. After all, he was going to pay for sex tonight, just not with my wife.

Ruby, who had been sitting at the far end of the bar, got up and sat on the stool next to our guy. Her eyes, though haunted, were at least dry. It appeared as though Plan B gave Ruby the strength to take things to the next level. The guy might have been talking to the bartender, but almost immediately his eyes were communicating only with Ruby. He would drink, glance over at her, sip, glance again, wet his lips, and again he'd glance. He reminded me of an animal on the hunt. He wasn't just undressing Ruby with his eyes; he was consuming her.

I moved as well, putting myself close enough to eavesdrop on their conversation. I didn't know what was going to happen, but I sure as hell was going to know what was said. In hindsight, I probably shouldn't have listened at all.

"Is your name Princess?" the man asked.

That was when I ordered the whiskey.

Ruby hesitated. Plan B required she use a specific name, and I worried that maybe she had forgotten. "Actually, it's Jenna," Ruby eventually said. I heard her swallow away the flutter in her voice, but I was pretty sure Mr. Dewar's and soda didn't pick up on her evident nervousness. He was too focused on other things, like imagining my wife naked.

"Can I buy you a drink, Jenna?" the guy asked.

Ruby swiveled to face him, uncrossing and crossing her legs. "I'll have a Chardonnay," she said.

He ordered the wine with a cat-who-ate-the-canary grin.

"What's your name?" Ruby asked.

"Andrew," he said, slurring. "Anndrjrew," it sounded like. "Jenna's a pretty name," Andrew said. "You're a pretty girl."

"Thank you," Ruby said. She avoided Andrew's probing gaze, as though looking at him was like trying to stare directly into the sun. Andrew didn't seem to care.

Ruby's Chardonnay arrived, and she pretended to take a sip. Their conversation continued, with Andrew doing all the talking and Ruby doing a lot of listening and head nodding and forced smiling. It wasn't hard to overhear what was said. Drunken Drew liked to talk loudly.

Here's what I learned: he was single and a stockbroker and an asshole. He bragged about his money and connections—the Beamer he drove, the vacation property he owned, the restaurants where he didn't need a reservation, the clubs that would let him cut the line. This went on for some time, and with each passing minute, Andrew positioned himself closer and closer to Ruby.

I watched his hand maneuver with the subtlety of a predator on the prowl, inching through the tall grass, getting closer to Ruby's leg, until it came to rest on her thigh. The actress Ruby disappeared in a blink, and the real Ruby took her place. Her body stiffened at his touch—recoiled, really—but Andrew kept his hand on her thigh. Either he didn't take notice of her discomfort or he didn't care. What he did seem to care about was talking, which he did whether Ruby appeared interested or not.

I finished my whiskey in two healthy swallows, got up from my stool, and walked behind them. I was pretending to stretch my legs, but really I wanted Ruby to see my face. The pain in her eyes filled me with profound sorrow, but I tried not to let it show. I mouthed the words, "You can do it." That seemed to give her a little jolt of confidence.

Ruby leaned in close. I cringed because her lips nearly brushed Drunken Drew's ear. I couldn't hear what she whispered, but she talked for a good long while and I saw Drunken Drew nodding vigorously as she spoke. Though her exact words were not audible, I knew what she was telling him.

"I have a massage business," she was saying. "I'd love to give you a massage. Would you like that? I know I would. I have a hotel room just around the corner, too. We could go there now, if you'd like."

Andrew's next move didn't surprise me any. He asked for the check, and impatiently. My heart sank. I closed my eyes tightly when they got up together and headed for the door.

Keep climbing. . . . Just keep on climbing. . . .

Andrew stumbled once on his way out of the bar. He was laughing, a sloppy drunk—the most detestable kind. Keeping close behind them, I emerged into the warm night air feeling more than a modicum of gratitude that our plan appeared to be working. Thanks to Uretsky's arrangements, I wouldn't have to endure the sight of Andrew groping my wife for long. The hotel room at the Holiday Inn was a five-minute walk from the bar.

Walking behind what others would assume to be a happy—but inebriated—couple, I had no choice but to watch everything Andrew did to Ruby. Drew, staggering and unsteady on his feet, put his arm around Ruby's slender waist and then pulled her in close to his body. I saw him slide his hand down to her butt first, giving it a hard squeeze and next a rub. It took every bit of self-restraint not to rush him. I wanted to throw him to the ground. Honestly, I wanted to kick him in the head. It was like a burst of road rage, only we were three pedestrians.

Rather than charge, I took a calming breath. My machismo wasn't going to help us.

Ruby slapped Drunk Drew's hand away, and they stopped walking. An exchange took place, with Andrew saying something and not looking happy about it, and Ruby saying something and looking equally displeased. Then Andrew grabbed Ruby's cheeks and kissed her hard on the mouth—a slobbery, disgustingly wet kiss. He forced their faces together, trying to push his tongue inside her mouth, as Ruby tried unsuccessfully to pull away.

I had to stand there and watch, unable to help.

Ruby pushed Andrew, more forcefully this time, while somehow managing a smile. I heard her say, "Wait till we get to the hotel room." Again, Drunk Drew nodded. He started walking faster, too. I kept my distance, following them.

Inside the lobby, Ruby took the elevator to the third floor. I opted for the stairs. I could see the hotel room Uretsky had rented for Ruby to use—room 324—from the stairwell exit. I waited in the stairwell until Ruby had her key card inserted and the door to room 324 opened.

I was on the move before the door clicked shut. This was the first moment Ruby had been out of my sight, and anxiety squeezed my throat. I took out a key card of my own.

It opened room 325.

CHAPTER 33

A woman watching television, splayed out on the king-size bed of room 325, propped herself up on her elbows and smiled warmly as I entered the room. She lay on top of the covers with the steel-gray satin sheath dress I'd bought at the Gap bunched up around her waist.

"Oh, good. You're here," she said, her accent unmistakably Boston. "I've been dying for a friggin' smoke."

"No time," I said. I had stipulated no smoking until after her job was done, but I guess she'd forgotten.

She shrugged away my denial. "So what now?" she asked.

"Hang on," I said.

I took out my phone, tried to slow my breathing, and texted Ruby next door. I worried Andrew might get aggressive before Ruby had a chance to get him to take a shower. If she didn't text me back right away, the plan was for me to go barging in, fists at the ready. The act might cost Winnie her life, but there was no way I was going to sit in the room next door while a drunk from the neighborhood bar raped my wife.

Me to Ruby: **What's going on?**

Ruby: **He won't take a shower.**

I breathed a heavy sigh that the situation—at least for now—was under control.

Me: **Tell him he gets nothing if he doesn't.**

Ruby: **I did.**

Me: **Make him do it. You can do it. Text me back.**

The woman on the bed asked me, "So? Are we ready?"

"Almost, Jenna," I said. "Almost."

Although I'd seen Jenna once before—just hours ago, when I let her into the hotel room—her resemblance to Ruby still struck me. Her legs and arms were long, waist narrow, hair the same length and color of my wife's. Of course there were differences. Jenna's face was a bit more angular and ragged, having lost some of its natural beauty from a combination of smoking, drinking, and a hard-living lifestyle.

Her ad in the Boston *Phoenix* read: *Gorgeous girl next door Jenna redhead, all natural, including bush. Sensuous, kind, & patient. Photos online. Ask about my specials!* I checked out the photos and confirmed that I had picked the right girl for the job.

Escorts don't advertise fees for sex. That would be illegal, but I counted on convincing her that I wasn't a cop. As it turned out, that "convincing" required my agreement to pay her four times her usual fee to "socialize." The unplanned expense would drain our bank account to dangerously low levels, but I could offset that some by selling more equipment. Because of her grand payday, Jenna didn't mind being sequestered for a couple hours in a hotel while Ruby and I searched out a suitable mark.

Jenna and I discussed my special needs when we spoke by phone. I told her that my wife and I were into kinky sex and role-playing games. I explained that it was our anniversary, and my wife wanted to play out a fantasy whereby she pretended to be an escort. She was going to seduce a man and bring him back to a hotel room, but she didn't want to have sex with him. We wanted a real "pro" to do that for us, but we wanted to watch. I told her we had placed a hidden camera in the armoire at the foot of the bed. This was all true—a camera was hidden there—only Uretsky had set it up, not me. I'd found the camera when I went into room 324 to search for such recording devices, knowing Uretsky would need some way to verify Ruby had done the deed. It was early afternoon so the camera's red record light wasn't on. I figured Uretsky wasn't expecting Ruby until sometime after dark. He had no need to waste battery life filming an empty room. I searched the entire hotel room but found only the one camera.

I came up with Plan B—a flash of inspiration—after I saw the hotel rooms had interior doors that opened up to the adjacent rooms. The doors were locked, of course, but could be unlocked if both parties wanted. I guess Jenna could have done our bait-and-switch routine by going through the hallway entrance while Andrew took his shower, but that presented an additional risk. The camera might pick up a slight change of light from the hallway that could arouse Uretsky's suspicions. I would have risked it, but it was a moot point when I learned that room 325 was unoccupied. It didn't stay unoccupied for long. I rented it for the night.

I met up with Jenna at the Holiday Inn shortly after my shopping stint at the Gap, and we did a walk-through of my plan. I unlocked the interior doors and showed her the camera stashed inside the armoire. I told her she could walk in front of the armoire, because the camera wouldn't show her face, but on the bed, when she was having sex with a man I didn't know who would be named Andrew, she had to keep her back to that piece of furniture at all times. If we saw her face in the recording, I explained, it would ruin the fantasy for us.

Did I feel horrible lying to Jenna?

Well, yes, I did. But I rationalized it, too.

Jenna was a sex worker, and we were paying her handsomely. Naturally, I was concerned about bringing anybody near Uretsky's web, but not overly so, not to the point where I wouldn't go through with it. "Keep your back to the camera, and everything will be just fine," I kept telling Jenna.

I reminded myself that Jenna wasn't our first choice. She was Plan B. Ruby had tried to seduce a man on her own—more than tried. She did everything in her power to save her mother, but her body simply wouldn't allow it. Now Jenna had Winnie's life in her hands, and she'd save it, too, as long as she kept her back to the camera.

My phone buzzed. I looked down to see a text from Ruby.

He's in the shower.

I texted back: **Okay. We're ready. Make sure the lights are off.**

I suspected Uretsky's camera was optimized for low-light recording, but a dark room would provide more cover than a well-lit one.

"Okay," I said to Jenna. "It's time."

Jenna got up from the bed and adjusted her dress. She looked at me with eyes a little teary.

"Are you okay?" I asked her. For a moment, I was completely distraught. What if she got cold feet?

She touched my face and smiled. "Of course I'm okay," she said. "I'm looking forward to this."

"What's wrong, then?" I asked.

"It's just that you're so sweet to do all this for your wife," she said. "My asshole boyfriend won't even buy me a flower."

CHAPTER 34

The plan worked, but it wasn't the least bit pleasant seeing it to fruition. After the switch was made, Ruby and I sat next to each other on the edge of the king-size bed in room 325, waiting. We stayed in that room until it was over. The walls were thin enough so we could hear everything. We listened to Jenna seductively moan and coo in ecstasy. Her cries of pleasure turned louder as the passion progressed.

As soon as I heard her, I worried Uretsky would find it odd that Ruby took so much pleasure from the act. I couldn't very well have instructed Jenna to behave as an unwilling partner. Such direction would have seemed contradictory to the fantasy Jenna believed she was creating for our benefit. If pressed, I would tell Uretsky that Ruby didn't want to give him the satisfaction of seeing her suffer. That could not have been further from the truth. Each time Jenna cried out in pleasure, Ruby cringed in pain. We sat in silence while Drunk Drew had sex with a woman he thought was my wife, but was too intoxicated to notice the switch.

When I tried to hold Ruby's hand, she pulled away.

"I don't want to be touched," she said.

"I'm sorry," I said. "I'm so sorry for everything."

Ruby looked at me and fought back tears. "I want you to know that I'm never going to stop loving you, John." She spoke in a whispered voice, as though Jenna and Drunk Drew might overhear us talking.

I didn't say anything. A good husband knows when it's time to just listen. Meanwhile, Jenna's moans of ecstasy, faked or not, grew louder and more intense.

"I didn't appreciate the motto 'Live for today' before I had cancer," Ruby continued. "Every day I've lived with this disease, I've felt tainted by its presence. It's as though somebody took a gigantic eraser to the best parts of my life and wiped them away with a quick sweep of the hand. It didn't matter how great my yesterdays were, because I'd have to live through this today, knowing that my body was working hard to kill me."

"I understand," I said.

"No, I don't think you do," Ruby said. "Because the situation we're in right now feels a thousand times worse."

I kept my eyes fixed on Ruby, but words failed me. I looked away, only to have Ruby grab my chin and force me to reconnect.

"You begged me to go along with your identity theft plan. I didn't want to do this, but you made me. You begged me. That's what I want you to really understand."

Jenna cried out again, and I could tell it was the finale. Ruby and I didn't speak until ten minutes later, when Jenna entered room 325 through the unlocked interior door, counting her money from Drunk Drew. Including what I owed her, Jenna's jubilant expression implied that she had had one of the best workdays in her life.

She looked Ruby and me over and smiled. "You guys are my freakin' favorite couple ever," she said. The word came out sounding like "ev-ah."

"Is Andrew gone?" I asked Jenna.

"Yeah, he's out of there. I'd hang around and chat, but I'm dying for a smoke."

I paid Jenna while Ruby snuck back into room 324. If Uretsky was watching us, we wanted him to see Ruby leave that hotel room, not her body double.

"Thanks for everything," I said.

"No. Thank you," Jenna said.

I thought that would be the last time I'd ever hear Jenna's voice.

I was wrong.

We got back to the Harvard Avenue apartment shortly after one o'clock in the morning. I tried to get in touch with Uretsky to tell him we'd completed his task and he should let Winnie go, but I didn't have a phone number for him. I sent an e-mail through the *One*

World game instead. No response. I text messaged him by replying to one of his earlier texts. He'd used a bunch of different numbers to contact me, so I sent a bunch of different texts.

Again, no response.

Ruby sank to the floor, her head buried in her hands. Ginger sauntered over and rubbed her furry little body against Ruby.

"I can't take this anymore," Ruby said. "It's too much. . . . It's too much for me."

I knelt beside her.

What could I say to make it better? What could I do?

Nothing.

"It's going to be all right," I said, stroking her hair. "I promise. Everything is going to be all right."

That would be the second thing that night about which I was wrong.

The apartment phone rang and woke us at seven o'clock the next morning. We had passed out—not fallen asleep—on the hardwood floor. Ruby, who lay huddled in a fetal position, rolled over onto her back and jumped to her feet before the second chime sounded. She rose too quickly, so I gripped her shoulders to steady her. My fingers felt her bones. The fragility of her body reminded me of a robin's egg in the springtime.

"I don't feel well," Ruby said.

She didn't look well, either.

Her sallow skin and sunken eyes suggested that she had greatly downplayed her current condition. Cancer? Uretsky? Which poison was killing her fastest? It didn't much matter. My wife, my beautiful wife, the love of my every single waking moment, was dying before my eyes.

"Just sit down," I said. "I'll get the phone."

I led Ruby over to the kitchen stool and helped get her settled. My stomach tightened as I reached for the phone that kept ringing. I suspected it was Uretsky calling, but Henry Dobson, the UniSol investigator, had this number as well. Maybe he was calling with a paperwork issue, or perhaps it was a wrong number. Those were just thoughts of the wishful thinking variety. I knew the truth. I looked over at Ruby as I picked up the phone. Her hands covered her mouth. Her nervousness and apprehension seemed to equal my own.

"Hello, John," Uretsky said. "We need to talk." He spoke in a voice that reminded me of an upset parent's disappointment with an unruly offspring.

"We did what you wanted," I said.

"I sent you an e-mail, but you didn't respond," Uretsky said. "I figured you might have fallen asleep, so I called to wake you. Ruby must be tired. Emotional strain extracts a heavy physical toll on the body, you know."

"Let Winnie go," I said. "Do it now. We did what you wanted. The game is over."

"I'm afraid I can't do that," Uretsky said.

"We did what you asked. You know it, too," I said, my voice rising in pitch, pushed up by a stab of anger.

"How do you know I know it?" Uretsky asked.

I saw no reason to lie. "I found the video camera," I said.

"You checked the room?"

"That wasn't against your rules."

The ensuing pause made me shudder.

"You're right, John. That wasn't in violation."

It wasn't much of a gamble telling Uretsky about the camera. I knew he operated with certain rules in place, and somehow, God help me, I was able to determine what constituted an infringement of his twisted thinking. I'd come to some other understandings about Uretsky as well. This wasn't about revenge for my stealing his identity, and it sure as hell wasn't about teaching me to become a real criminal. That was just an excuse for him to play his evil game.

Uretsky was a master manipulator who, for whatever reason, wanted to use and control me. He got off on terrorizing us. This was all just a game to him—a living, breathing game without any pixels or reboots or cheat codes. Our terror wasn't manufactured by lines of code, but rather by our deeds, and he loved every single authentic minute of it. Uretsky had forced us into the ultimate test of good versus evil for the simple curiosity of seeing how far he could bend us before we broke. His game play aside, Uretsky had proven one thing for certain: we all possessed a capacity to commit acts we wouldn't dream of.

"I sent you an e-mail," Uretsky said. "I'd like you to watch something with me."

With the phone pressed between my ear and shoulder, I motioned for Ruby to hand me my laptop.

"Is my mom all right?" Ruby asked me. "Is she?"

"Oh, yes, Mother is doing just fine," Uretsky said into my ear. "But we've got another problem."

"He said she's fine," I whispered to Ruby, covering the receiver with my hand. "But something is wrong."

"I want to see her!" Ruby demanded. "I want to see her right now."

"That's an impossibility," Uretsky said. "Tell her that, John."

I told her. Ruby responded by shutting her eyes tightly.

I powered up my laptop, opened my e-mail, and saw a message from Uretsky time-stamped fifteen minutes earlier. The message contained a link. The link opened a Web page that contained an embedded video file, like a YouTube page.

"I'd like to watch this video with you, if you don't mind," Uretsky said.

"Of course I mind," I said. "Do I have a choice?"

"For Winnie's sake, I'm going to answer that in the negative. The link you clicked has given me control over your computer, so I'll go ahead and press play."

My chest tightened the moment the first frames flickered on the screen. The video, taken from inside hotel room 324, showed Ruby cajoling Drunk Drew into taking a shower.

"What is this, Uretsky?" I said. My voice came out singed with ire. "You want me to watch my wife having sex with another man?"

"I want you to watch," was all Uretsky said.

A chill ripped up my spine.

Could he know?

The video quality looked surprisingly good—not grainy or jerky. I watched Drew stumble and trip while unbuttoning his pants on his way to the shower. The video captured Ruby closing the bathroom door and turning off the room lights, just as we had planned. Although the camera lacked motion capability, it was in fact low-light sensitive, such that I could make out the floral pattern on the bed covering before Andrew emerged from the bathroom, dressed only in a towel.

"Why are you making me watch this?" I asked, making sure I sounded shaky and wounded.

A figure stepped into the camera's view. She wore a sheath dress from the Gap and did a perfect job keeping her back to the camera. I studied the footage closely. In the limited lighting Ruby and Jenna were virtually indistinguishable. I watched Jenna take a drink of water from a bottle set atop the night table, and then the video stopped playing.

"I hit pause, in case you were wondering," Uretsky said.

"Why?" I asked.

"Just remember that moment," Uretsky said. "Let's continue."

The video playback resumed. I watched Andrew and Jenna kissing, my pulse pounding with what proved to be unwarranted anxiety that Jenna had shown her face to the camera. Andrew's hands fumbled greedily all over Jenna's body. Inevitably, those same hands slid up and underneath Jenna's dress. He probed Jenna's flesh in all the places that would have driven me to rage had he been touching my wife instead of a professional. Jenna didn't speak as she maneuvered Andrew over to the bed. Andrew let his towel drop from his waist, flashing the camera with a full frontal assault of his fleshy midsection and tumescent penis. He got himself prone on the bed. Jenna took another sip of water, hiked her dress up waist high, and straddled Andrew's back.

Uretsky paused the playback once again.

"Did you see that?" he asked. "Are you with me, John?"

"I see that my wife is about to give a strange man a massage," I said.

Uretsky sighed, as if disappointed. "Let's keep watching."

The video resumed. The bathroom door opened a bit on its own, exposing a wider sliver of light that better lit the room. The light provided a clearer view of the action as well. I didn't time it with a stopwatch, but if pressed, I'd guess the massage lasted around five seconds at most. Andrew flipped over onto his back. Jenna reached across the bed and took another drink of water while Andrew fumbled to put on a condom. Jenna lowered herself down onto Andrew with her dress and heels still on. I heard a soft moan escape from her throat. She arched her back when his thrusting began.

The video stopped playing.

"Did you see it?" Uretsky asked.

"See what?"

"She took three drinks from that water bottle. Three times she reached for the bottle and drank. Three."

"So? My wife was thirsty."

"Your wife is right handed," Uretsky said. "Maybe if she drank with her left hand once, I would have believed it. But three times? No, that's not what right-handed people do. They drink with their right hands."

An intense wave of apprehension swept through me, as though I'd been caught in a sudden and raging blizzard, trapped on the side of a mountain. My breathing tightened. My hammering heart thundered in my ears. Ruby reached out to steady me, but her eyes were affright as well.

"I figured out what you'd done, and I followed that whore you hired to her home. Too bad for her she lives alone."

"What have you done?" I said. My dark voice came out just above a whisper.

"I'll show you," Uretsky said. "Watch your laptop."

Uretsky, who still had control over my computer, loaded up a new Web page in the browser window. The page was blank except for the words "Now I know everything."

"Ready?" Uretsky said. "Keep watching. It's a slide show of sorts."

An image faded into view beneath those words. It showed Jenna lying on her back on a beige-colored carpet, her face frozen in a silent scream. Ruby screamed, too. A feeling of nausea overcame me as the room began to spin. The image of Jenna faded—one picture blending into another—and up came an image of Uretsky's bloody pruning shears.

"No. No. No," I said, hiding my face in my hands.

I looked up just in time to see the picture of the pruning shears dissolve slowly away. In its place came another string of words, which I managed to read even though my whole body was shaking with the intensity of a seizure. The words I read were "See No Evil, Hear No Evil, Speak No Evil."

I positioned myself to block Ruby's view of the laptop's display screen. In my heart I knew what was coming next. A picture materialized on screen in the same manner as the others, fading into view beneath a grim headline.

That's when I screamed.

CHAPTER 35

I closed the laptop and dropped to my knees. The bar stool fell sideways at the same time Ruby lost her balance reaching for me. She toppled out of her seat and landed right on top of me, cushioning her fall with my body. I clambered back to my feet, straining to reach the laptop—pawing for it—but Ruby had the better position and got there first.

"Don't look at it!" I shouted at her. "You don't want to see!"

"Mom!" Ruby cried out, fumbling to flip open the top cover.

I guess Ruby thought it was a picture of her mother that had made me scream and fall to the floor. I wasn't trying to be protective of Ruby when I told her not to look. I was speaking the truth. A lifetime ago—at least that was how it seemed—I had created a mental picture of what Rhonda Jennings looked like when the police found her body, but that image paled entirely when compared to seeing the real flesh and blood thing.

The blood.

It was everywhere, but it didn't cover the purple bruise marks on Jenna's throat where Uretsky had choked the life out of her. Jenna's face, moonlight white, was marked with bloody crimson streaks that appeared painted on, and with crude brushstrokes. Her cloudy eyes, open and lifeless, were partially covered by one of her severed fingers. The finger's ragged flesh, lumpy and torn at the knuckle, appeared to have been ripped off her hand, not sheared. Two of Jenna's fingers jutted out from her ears like heinous, bloody antennae. Another two, those a pulpy mess as well, had been set upon her pale blue lips in a purposeful manner.

See no evil.

Hear no evil.

Speak no evil.

Ruby stared blankly at the screen. A baleful scream, low at first but rising in pitch, escaped from her tremulous mouth. She threw the computer against the wall with enough force to break it open on impact. Chunks of flying metal and glass spread out like shrapnel, with a few pieces nicking me in the face and neck. Ruby grabbed hold of the apartment phone, which I had let drop in front of the kitchen island.

"Damn you!" Ruby screamed into the phone. "You monster! Let my mother go! Let her go!"

I couldn't hear Uretsky's reply, but Ruby let the phone fall from her grasp as though it had become too hot to hold. I watched it swing back and forth in front of the kitchen island, moving slowly like the pendulum of a grandfather clock. Ruby dropped to the floor, huddled into a protective ball. I picked up the phone, put it to my ear, and heard Uretsky's singsong voice to the tune of "Camptown Races" saying, "Put John on, or your mother dies. Put John on, or your mother dies. Put John on, or your mother dies."

"I'm here!" I shouted. "It's me! It's John."

Uretsky stopped his singing.

"Johnny!" he exclaimed, sounding excited to hear from me, as though we were old friends newly reunited. "You hanging in there, Johnny?"

"Please . . . ," I said, tears again stinging my eyes. "You didn't have to do that. She didn't do anything to you."

"*You* did this to her, not me. You tried to pull a fast one on me, didn't you? Rules are rules, and you broke 'em. Now, there's a price to pay when you don't follow the rules."

"Just let Winnie go," I said. "What can I do?"

"Not that easy. You've got to play a penalty round."

"I'll do anything."

"I think you're going to come to regret that statement," Uretsky said.

"Tell . . . me . . . how," I said, my shaky voice barely audible.

"You sure you want to keep playing? You can say, 'Game over.'

That's always an option. Of course, I'll kill Winnie if you don't play along, and I'll probably come after Ruby next."

"Tell me what to do to free Winnie," I said in a low voice.

"Okay. You made the choice, so it's game on! Thatta boy, Johnny! Now, listen to me, and listen close, because I'm not going to repeat myself." Uretsky's voice had dipped in volume, a return to the serious business of the game. "There's a warehouse in South Boston, on the corner of West Third and B Street. It's in a part of town that doesn't see a lot of foot traffic. Across from that warehouse is a single-story brick building with a Dumpster in the back parking lot. You're going to go Dumpster diving. Inside that Dumpster, you'll find three five-gallon canisters of gasoline buried beneath the rubbish. You're going to take those gas cans over to the warehouse and enter through the green door, which I've left unlocked for your convenience."

I could feel my insides shriveling up into nothing. "Then what?" I asked.

"Then I want you to use the accelerant to soak a pile of wood pallets on the first floor. I suggest you save some gas to make a trail to the door. You don't want to be close to those pallets when they go up in flames."

"You want me to start a fire inside the warehouse?" I said.

"That's exactly what you're going to do. Strike a match and start a fire. I have a scanner, so I'll know when the fire department gets the call. I have other ways of knowing you've followed my instructions to the letter."

Cameras. He's got cameras in there. No way to fake it. No way out. Do what he says.

"Escape without getting caught," Uretsky continued, "and I'll let Winnie go. If you fail in any way, Winnie will look a lot like Jenna, maybe even worse. That's the deal, and it's nonnegotiable."

"Let her go first and I'll do it," I said.

"Nonnegotiable," Uretsky repeated. "You have one hour from this very moment to become an arsonist. Best of luck."

CHAPTER 36

Ziggy no longer had the familiar feel of just being our car. It had transformed into something sinister when it became our getaway vehicle for the Giovanni robbery. It sickened me to put Ziggy into ignoble use once again, but it was "game on" and I had to play. For Winnie's sake, I had to play.

I plugged the address Uretsky had provided into my GPS, and soon we were on our way to the site of a future arson incident in South Boston. I had divided the allotted time into three critical sequences: thirty minutes to reach our target (morning commuter traffic would still be a problem); ten minutes to get the gas canisters; twenty minutes to spread out the fuel and strike a match. I might have had a plan in place, but my thoughts were with Jenna and Winnie.

Ruby's pale complexion and her body's persistent trembling suggested that she was thinking the same.

"What are we doing?" Ruby said, her voice cracking from the strain. "What the hell are we doing?"

"We're going to save your mother."

Ruby held her head in her hands, her body convulsing. Her face flushed as she began to sob so hard, she could barely breathe. "What he did to that poor woman. How could he do that? How?"

"We can't think about that right now," I said. "We've got to think about your mom."

"Every time I close my eyes, all I see is what he did to Jenna. That image—it's never going to go away. Never."

Somehow I managed to navigate my way through the barrage of

traffic without getting into an accident. But Ruby was right. The image of Jenna would last us a lifetime. My eyes saw the road, but my heart saw only blackness, death, and Jenna's bloody fingers. What I'd once thought to be our incorruptible morals turned out to have all the flexibility of a pipe cleaner—with disastrous or near disastrous consequences.

For Rhonda Jennings, who would never marry.

For Giovanni Renzulli, who almost choked to death before two million YouTube viewers.

For a redheaded prostitute named Jenna, whose mutilated body had yet to be found.

We had saved Dr. Adams's life. How far would we be willing to go to save Winnie's—or our own, for that matter? At what point would we be asked to do something we'd simply refuse to do? How far could we be bent before we broke?

I lost sight of myself, my morals, the moment I became Elliot Uretsky. What other crimes was I capable of committing? I wondered. I really didn't know. That might have terrified me most of all. Uretsky didn't know, either, but he was determined to find out.

"It's my fault," Ruby said, her sobs slowly abating. "I should have just gone through with it. I'm the reason that girl is dead."

"Don't do that to yourself," I said.

Ruby flashed me an angry look. "Why? Because you don't blame yourself for what happened to Brooks Hall?"

"That's different," I said.

"No, it's not. It's no different at all. You cut the rope. I couldn't sleep with a stranger. We both made choices that cost innocent people their lives."

"But I knew what was going to happen to Brooks. You didn't know Jenna would be murdered."

"It was a risk involving her with Uretsky in the first place. I knew that much," Ruby said.

I didn't say anything. How could I? She was right.

I parked a few blocks from the warehouse. I worried about surveillance cameras capturing video of two arsonists climbing into a red Ford Fusion to make their escape. We each wore Red Sox baseball hats, the ones I'd bought last year, during our annual anniversary have time to go hunting for Uretsky's hidden cameras. Either I did it the way he wanted it done, or I didn't. But how could I start a fire that would be the least risky for the responding firefighters?

I caught sight of something that gave me an idea.

"No, we're not going to let your mom die," I said, pointing.

"How is a fire alarm box going to help us?" Ruby asked.

"Because we're going pull the alarm before we start the fire," I said.

I checked the time on my watch and set its stopwatch feature to zero. We had fifteen minutes to get that fire started.

date at Fenway Park. Ruby's hat served a dual purpose, conceali
her identity from the cameras while shielding her sensitive skin fr
the sun. I gave Ruby a pair of sunglasses to wear. Meanwhile
donned a handkerchief to hide my face. I wanted to do this alor
but Ruby wouldn't allow it.

We walked to the intersection of West Third and B Street. Su
enough, I saw the Dumpster behind the single-story redbrick buil
ing with a flat roof and a white garage door. The parking lot housir
the Dumpster was empty. In fact, the only things in abundance in th
desolate part of town were broken bottles and crumpled aluminu
cans. I looked to my right and saw the warehouse we'd been i
structed to torch, directly across the street from the Dumpster.

The three-story brick warehouse looked dark and empty, wit
many of the windows boarded up, covered in newsprint, or broken.
thought about how the flat tar roof would burn when the fir
reached that floor. I imagined the smoke would be thick, black, an
toxic, transforming a dumpy cityscape into the lead story on the si
o'clock news. Would it be a three-alarm fire? Four?

And then I thought about a firefighter climbing up his steel lad
der, hose slung across his shoulder, vanishing into a smoke-filled
window and never coming out.

In my single-minded mission to save Winnie, it simply hadn't oc
curred to me that a firefighter—or plural—could die while battling a
blaze that I started. I pondered the conundrum while my stomach
roiled. *Walk away and Winnie dies. Set the fire and maybe somebody else—or plural—dies or gets burned to the point where death
would be preferable.*

What do we do?

Ruby saw my hesitation.

"What are you thinking about?"

I told her, and by her blank look, I saw that she understood the
gravity of our situation.

"Do we let my mom die?" Her voice held no trace of sarcasm—
same as me, she honestly considered just walking away.

How far would we bend?

I paced in a tight circle, cursing aloud to nobody but the pigeons
enjoying a mid-morning snack of trash. I needed to start a fire. I had
to burn a pile of wood pallets using three canisters of gasoline. I didn't

CHAPTER 37

The green, rust-speckled Dumpster smelled of ammonia, rotting food, and gasoline. I saw the chain used to secure the flip-top lid on the blacktop beside it, coiled like a metal snake poised to strike. I could see where the chain had been cut, presumably with bolt cutters and undoubtedly by Uretsky's hand. I pried open the lid and let it drop with a clang. Hesitating, I did a quick double take and agreed with Uretsky's assertion that this desolate part of town saw very little foot traffic. Still, I pulled my hat down lower and the handkerchief covering my face up a bit higher. I climbed onto the lip of the Dumpster with ease. For a second or two, I crouched there, with my legs spread wide and my sweat-slickened hands down between my knees, gripping at the lip for balance.

"Apparently, he likes to hide things in the trash," I said, remembering that he'd hidden a gun in a bathroom waste receptacle at the movie theater.

Beneath a cloudless sky and pale yellow sun, I jumped in and sank waist deep into the spongy refuse. The smells were more intense down here. Gag worthy, in fact. It was a potpourri of scents taken from the worst places imaginable: think the Port Authority bathroom, a field of rotting vegetables, a trash-filled car left baking in the sun.

I felt about blindly, reaching my hands lower and lower into the seemingly bottomless mass of foul-smelling trash. I dug and dug until the tips of my fingers brushed against a plastic handle. Gripping that handle, I yanked the object toward me. Almost immediately, my throat closed as my gag reflex kicked into overdrive. Evidently, I had brought to the surface, along with the first canister of gasoline, a fetid rag that stunk of excrement. Maybe it was something else, but it sure didn't smell that way to me. It was a reminder that Uretsky was always playing games, using any opportunity he could to torment me.

It didn't take long to find the other two containers of gas Uretsky had stashed down there. I set them in a neat little row on the blacktop beside the Dumpster.

I checked the time and swallowed hard. I didn't know whether Uretsky first choked his victims and then cut off their fingers, or if it went the other way around, but if we didn't pull the fire alarm in ten minutes, Winnie would have a few seconds of terror to find out.

While I was busy fishing containers of gas out of the trash, Ruby looked up some information on her smartphone. "There are two firehouses nearby," Ruby said. "There's one on K and Fourth Street and another on D and Third."

"Perfect. So the fire department will get here in two minutes, tops," I said.

"Tell me what you're thinking."

"You pull the alarm, and I'll stand by the warehouse door with a match. We wait forty seconds, and then I light the gas. The pallets will burn for no more than a minute before the fire department gets here, and we're already gone. Uretsky sees the pallets are on fire via his hidden camera—no false alarm, either, as it'll be on the police scanners—and we'll have met his demands without creating a towering inferno."

Ruby thought a beat, searching for any holes in my plan.

"It'll work," she said. "But is he going to honor the rules of his game?"

I nodded. "He will," I said, certainty in my voice. "It's the only thing honorable about him."

I was preparing to dash across the street, gripping the three red plastic gas canisters, when I heard an approaching car. I grabbed Ruby and pulled her down behind the Dumpster with me. We watched as the car—some sort of sedan—turned right onto B Street. Only when the sound of its wheels and engine had gone did we dare breathe again. We popped up from behind the Dumpster like wary prairie dogs.

Once again I hefted the gas canisters. Dropping into a crouched position—as if that would render me invisible in broad daylight—I broke for the warehouse across the street. I didn't dare think about someone spotting me from a darkened window of the nearby buildings.

I checked my watch.

Ten minutes to go.

I went to the door that Uretsky said would be open, tried the knob, and found it was locked. I cursed under my breath. Again, Uretsky had proved he never tired of toying with us. Rather than search for an unlocked entrance, I decided to break the glass of a first-floor window to get inside. I assumed I could open the locked door from the inside; if not, I'd have to find another way out.

I looked around for a solid object to use, found half a brick, and pitched it baseball-like through a first-story window. Shards of broken glass fell to the ground, sounding like wind chimes plinking in a soft breeze. I motioned for Ruby to cross the street, and she came over in a crouched posture, same as I had done.

"Help me up," I said to her.

My breathing wasn't labored. I was surprised, too, at the calmness of my voice. I wasn't relaxed, but I wasn't hurried, either. The adrenaline rush made me so focused on my goal, I forgot to be completely terrified. Perhaps that's how real criminals feel before they commit their crimes—more amped than afraid.

Ruby locked her fingers together, and it seemed the adrenaline had got to her as well. Even in her weakened condition, she had no trouble giving me the needed lift. I set my forearms on the windowsill, relieving Ruby of my body weight, and clumsily used my elbow to push the remaining glass inside to clear away the jagged edges. I had just enough room to swing my body around until my legs dangled on the inside and my torso extended outward.

"Pass me a canister," I called. I had my body perfectly balanced on the sill, making it easy to reach down and grab hold of the gas. I tossed the first canister into the warehouse, then the second, and soon enough I had all three of them down there. The rising vapor stung my eyes and burned the back of my throat, but that didn't stop me from sliding off the sill as if I was being sucked down the gullet of some gas-breathing monster.

Ruby called, "John, are you all right?"

"I'm fine!" I shouted back.

The warehouse was dark inside except for places where the paper coverings on the windows had peeled back to allow slivers of light inside. Dust motes swam in and out of those light shafts, agitated by my presence. I took out the portable flashlight tucked in my back pocket and shone the beam around. The warehouse was nothing more than a big open space with concrete support columns staged evenly throughout.

Almost immediately, I saw the pile of broken wooden pallets Uretsky had instructed me to burn. I shone my flashlight around some more, wondering if I could spot one of Uretsky's hidden cameras. I saw huge piles of debris scattered about, but I didn't inspect them closely—there simply wasn't enough time or reason. Nor did I worry that they would catch fire. Judging by the distance from the pallets, I felt confident the fire department would get here before the closest—and largest—pile could burn.

"Hello!" I yelled out. "Anybody here?" My heart was pounding in my chest, and my shaky voice mirrored my nerves.

Are you watching me right now?

I shone the light on my watch and shivered.

Six minutes to go.

CHAPTER 38

Iused two of the gas containers to give the wood a good soaking and carried the third over to a rectangular border of light some thirty-odd feet to my right. I figured that light border was the same door I had tried to open from the street—the one Uretsky had promised was unlocked. Trying the knob, I found the door opened easily from the inside. A little bit of light spilled into the room, and that was when I noticed a stairwell to the other floors directly in front of me. Even though the pallets would burn for just a minute, I figured I should check the second and third floors for any people, as I had on the first.

I noticed the time before heading up.

Five minutes.

I climbed the rickety steps quickly, nervous that the flimsy boards would splinter from my weight. I got out on the second floor and shone my flashlight into the darkness. The upper level was a twin to the one below it. I jumped at the sight of a fat, hairy brown rat as it scurried in and out of my flashlight beam. I had a feeling it would escape the flames just fine. The wood floor creaked and groaned under my weight, and I wondered just how quickly it would burn if it caught fire. Very quickly, I decided.

But it won't catch fire, because the fire department will get here in less than two minutes.

"Hello!" I shouted. "Anybody here? I'm not the police. Please answer me!"

I trained my flashlight on a few scattered piles of debris, just like below, but no movement. Again, only my echo answered back. I called out once more, and I waited—waited—but no answer. I looked at my watch.

Four minutes.

I raced up to the next level, the top level, and to save time, only popped my head out of the stairwell and repeated my call.

"Hello? Anybody here?"

My voice spilled into the darkness. I listened a few seconds for rustling noises, any movement at all, but heard nothing. As I descended the stairs, the powerful odor of gasoline reminded me I wasn't a concerned citizen on the lookout for people in danger, but rather the person about to set a fire that would put them in harm's way. Taking Uretsky's suggestion, I made a trail of gasoline from the wood pallets to the door as quick as I could. When I exited the warehouse, I had to blink until my eyes adjusted to the light. My breathing was labored from all the gas vapors still swimming in my lungs.

I saw Ruby across the street, standing in position.

I held up my right hand—*Get ready*.

I checked my watch.

Two minutes until the deadline.

I lowered my hand as though starting a drag race. Ruby pulled the fire alarm, and I expected to hear a piercing shrill, but there was no sound at all. I reset my stopwatch and started it again. Five seconds later—ten at the most—I heard the sound of sirens in the distance. Ruby looked at me with a fresh concern. I couldn't believe how fast the fire department had responded.

I struck a match and let it drop. I stood in the doorway with my mouth agape and watched as the burning trail of gasoline wound its way across the floor on a collision course with the gas-soaked pile of wood pallets. In an instant the darkness of the warehouse erupted into a bright and blinding fireball. There was a powerful *whoosh* sound as all the air in the room seemed to get sucked toward the flame.

A ball of fire shot upward, licking at the varnish on the wood ceiling above. Flames crackled and spit angrily in all directions. Soon I couldn't see the wood pallets anymore. Smoke began to billow up from the fire and unfurled across the ceiling like a noxious black tide.

Meanwhile, the sirens from a fleet of fire engines sounded louder—

help was on its way. Ruby and I needed to make our getaway, and fast. We couldn't be seen anywhere near the fire I had just set. I raced across the street and grabbed hold of Ruby's arm.

"Start walking," I said, pulling down my handkerchief, taking it from a disguise to part of my wardrobe. "Just act normal. Just be natural."

Of course, I was breathing heavy and hard on our leisurely stroll—nothing at all natural about that.

I could see the fire engines coming, racing toward us.

Take that, Uretsky!

Ruby and I walked nonchalantly down West Third, thinking the fire trucks would zoom right past, but before they reached our location, the trucks took a sharp right turn onto C Street as if headed for City Point, a Southie neighborhood near Castle Island. I looked behind me and saw black smoke seeping out of the warehouse's broken first-floor window.

"John, what's going on?" Ruby asked. The sirens began to fade off into the distance. "Why aren't they going to the fire?"

My phone rang.

I answered the call.

"We've done what you've wanted," I said. I didn't have to ask who was on the other end of the line. I just knew. "Where's Winnie? Let her go."

"Aren't you wondering why the fire trucks aren't coming to save the day?" Uretsky asked.

My legs went weak.

Uretsky spoke again. "Did you know that when an alarm is struck, the fire department automatically dispatches three engine companies and two ladder trucks to the scene?"

"What's going on?" I asked. "Where is Winnie?"

Uretsky ignored my questions. "Did you know that South Boston has two engine companies and two ladder trucks total? Total! A third engine would come from Columbia Road, maybe even Edward Everett Square."

"Stop playing games!" I shouted, shaking. "Where is Winnie?"

Uretsky went on speaking. "But if two fires break out at the same time, the fire department won't divert the trucks from one fire scene to another. The second call could be anything—a false alarm, even.

Can't risk sending engines from a real fire to a fake one. So if all the engines in South Boston are tied up answering a call when another fire in Southie breaks out, the dispatchers will send engine companies and ladder trucks from another firehouse farther away. Just so you know, the closest ones to you are on Harrison Avenue in the South End and maybe Atlantic Avenue in the financial district."

"Why are you telling me all this?" I asked.

"Because it's going to take at least another ten minutes for the engines from those locations to reach the fire you just started. Now, I bet you didn't think I'd set another fire in City Point right before your deadline hit."

My stomach clenched. I had to hold on to a parked car for balance.

"Too bad for Winnie," Uretsky said.

"What . . . what have you done?"

Uretsky made a little "tsk" sound with his mouth, as though he needed to recall some details that had gotten away from him. "Let's see. . . . Oh, that's right. . . . I gave Winnie a big narcotic cocktail and left her unconscious on the first floor of the warehouse that you just set on fire. I tucked her behind the big pile of trash nearest to the pallets, but I'm pretty sure the fire department won't reach her in time. Well, at least she'll die in her sleep—unless, of course, you go back to save her. Once again, I'm wishing you good luck, John. This time, you're really going to need it."

I looked behind me. Black smoke poured from the warehouse window. I watched as the smoke rose like the fingers of the devil's outstretched hand, reaching up to scratch and scar a beautiful and cloudless sky.

CHAPTER 39

All I said to Ruby was, "Your mom."

I broke into a run for the warehouse. At first Ruby kept pace with me, but she soon pulled ahead. She reached the warehouse door first and made a move to go inside. I grabbed her from behind and yanked her back.

"You can't go in there!" I shouted.

Foul-smelling smoke continued to pour out the broken window and seeped from underneath the shuttered door, too.

"She's my mother!" Ruby yelled back at me, her face twisted in agony.

"You'll never be able to pull her out," I said. "You don't have the strength. Think about it! The drugs. The cancer. You'll never get her out, and you'll probably die trying. I'll go."

Ruby screamed, "No!" as I pulled the door open. A plume of smoke sent both of us staggering back several feet. Ruby yelled, "No!" again, but that was after I had vanished inside the burning building.

My first thought was that the movies made it look easy—cover your nose and mouth with your arm, get low to the ground, and go barging into a raging fire. What they don't show is the survival instinct kicking in. They ignore the invisible wall that pops up and halts your advance the moment that first poisoned gulp of air slides down your throat. Your eyes close up and water, your lungs cough in rebellion, while the heat lashes at your skin and produces nearly intolerable pain. I felt every bit of that and more, and I'd taken only three steps inside. The fire had been raging for a grand total of two minutes. The fire department would be here in seven minutes at most, maybe sooner. But "sooner" might mean "too late."

From behind me I heard Ruby screaming, "John! Mom!" She continued to call my name as I plunged deeper into thick plumes of smoke that turned the warehouse into the darkest night imaginable. The pestilent fumes burned my lungs. I fell to the floor, forced there if I wanted to breathe. Down low, I could see an inch or two in front of my face, but no more. Waves of heat washed over my body. Imagine holding a hand to a flame, unable to pull it back, not even after the skin begins to sear.

Bit by bit the pain ratcheted up.

One thought kept me going: *Save Winnie. Save Ruby's mom.*

I crawled forward, moving an inch at a time, trying to orientate myself within this dark and alien world. How far in were those burning pallets? How far from that was the first pile of debris?

The only thing saving me was the size of the warehouse. Smoke was spreading out across the ceiling, with thousands of square feet still to cover. If Uretsky had put Winnie on the upper floors, it probably would have been easier to reach her. He knew that. The fire had yet to burn a hole into the ceiling. The accumulating smoke had no place to go but down on top of me, like a thick black curtain signaling the end.

Breathe.

Crawl.

Breathe.

I tried to scream, "Winnie!" but the smoke suffocated my voice. Even if I could have shouted, the snap and crackle of the fire would have drowned me out.

At this point I wasn't thinking about being brave, or trying to make amends for what I'd done; I was thinking, *I want to get the fuck out of here*. That desire beat like a war drum in my head, getting louder and louder as I crawled farther from the exit. For a second, I thought this was just a nightmare from which I'd soon awaken. And when I did, I'd be in bed, in our Somerville apartment, with Ruby right there beside me, and it would be B.C., before the cancer, and our life would be beautiful again.

At that moment, a tendril of fire reached down from the ceiling and whipped the ground inches from my face, as if to say, "This is a nightmare, all right, but you're not dreaming."

I couldn't think clearly under the constant roar of fire. My lungs were burning for air. Did I have enough oxygen to make it back out? Still, I moved forward, slithering on my belly as quickly as I could.

I covered my mouth with my arm, as if that would protect me from the smoke. My lungs seemed to laugh at the attempt. A hacking cough exploded from inside me, hard enough to shake my bones. Once I started, I couldn't stop. Above me, I heard the floor moan and hiss as the flames below it converted trapped moisture into steam. I reached a place where the fire burned hotter, and I knew that I was directly across from the wood pallets used to start the blaze.

If I hadn't just been in the room, I might not have been able to orient myself in total darkness. But I remembered that if I headed in a northwest direction, the pile of debris closest to the pallets was about twenty feet from my current location. I moved ahead, my fingers doing the work of my eyes, and ended up crawling maybe another fifty feet before I found the trash pile. Cardboard boxes, concrete bricks, an overturned sofa, trash barrels, and scraps of sheet metal that had formed a makeshift wall kept me from seeing Winnie while I was dousing the pallets with gas. But I found her. Unconscious. Inert.

I didn't have time to see if she was alive. The smoke was descending more rapidly. I figured I had fifteen seconds at most to drag Winnie out of the building before we could both kiss the land of the living good-bye. My chest screamed for relief, poisoned by a thirst for pure air. Every breath exited my body as a cough.

Still, I had enough strength to grab hold of Winnie by her wrists. I was on my knees, with my head bent low, crawling backward toward the door, pulling hard. Winnie came along with me, I assumed on her back, but I couldn't see her through the smoke. I couldn't see the light of the door, either, but at least I could hear sirens, so I figured I was getting closer.

I'm not going to make it.

Every fiber of my body screamed out for oxygen. How bad my lungs hurt. How hot my skin felt. A deeper darkness overcame me.

This is what forever feels like.

Before I knew what was happening, before I blacked out, I sensed myself being pulled. A human chain had formed—someone (a fire-fighter?) on one end, Winnie on the other, and me in the middle. I don't know how long it took to drag us outside, but in that kind of situation, a second passes like eternity.

The next thing I knew, I was on the ground with an oxygen mask on my face.

Rebirth.

I looked to my right and saw a group of EMTs working on Winnie. I could tell she was unconscious. But was she breathing? Was she alive?

Ruby stood with the EMTs working on her mother for about half a minute. Then she came rushing over to me. I motioned to the EMT to give us privacy—it was too hard to say the words. He understood and backed away, but only a little.

"She's alive," Ruby said, brushing away her tears. "She's alive be-cause of you."

Fire trucks were everywhere: hoses and water and people with oxygen masks, wearing thick fire-retardant coats, rushing into the burning building, doing what firefighters do best. I pulled away my oxygen mask. I needed to feel Ruby's touch. Her fingers came away black with soot. She was holding on to me, trembling, calling my name over and over. She kissed my forehead and stroked my black-ened arms.

"We don't know her," I said, coughing out the words.

"What?"

"Winnie," I said, still coughing. "We don't know her. We can't ex-plain that."

"I know," Ruby said.

God, how I loved her.

"What did you tell them?" I asked. "The firefighters, I mean."

"We were passing by and saw the fire. I pulled the alarm. You heard a woman call out for help. You went in to save her."

This time I said it. "Ruby, I love you so much." Then I said—or more accurately, managed to wheeze—"We've got to get out of here. I don't want to make the news again."

Ruby nodded. "They want to take you to a hospital," she said.

"I'm fine," I said. "I don't have to go." Then I coughed. A lot. I couldn't see my reflection in a mirror, but if my arms were any indication, my face was almost entirely black. I coughed again and spit out something black and nasty on the ground. "Find out where they're taking Winnie," I said, "and then let's get out of here."

I saw a police officer, youngish, fittish, and wearing a look of concern as he approached. He knelt beside me and asked, "How are you doing?"

"Fine," I said, just as I started to hack and cough. Again, I spit out something terrible.

"You need to go to the hospital," he said, not a question but a statement of fact.

I waved him off. "No, really. I'm fine," I said. "I'm actually allergic to hospitals. They give me hives."

That inspired a little smile.

"Look, I need your statement for the police report," he said. "Do you think you can manage that?"

Maybe he caught my apprehensive look, but he probably thought I was about to cough again. In truth what really got my heart rate going was a vision of a thousand reporters all clambering for an exclusive interview with the hero who saved a mysterious woman from a burning inferno. If somebody recognized me on the six o'clock news, the police would be one step closer to linking us to Winnie.

"I don't want the reporters hounding me," I said.

"Your personal information will be redacted from the police report. They can't know you if you don't want to be known," he said.

I grimaced as I took a breath and probably flashed the cop my blackened teeth in the process.

"Okay," I said.

"Good," he said. He took out a pad and pen from his utility belt. "Let's start with your name."

I didn't hesitate. "Elliot Uretsky," I said.

CHAPTER 40

The news people faced an incredibly busy day of reporting, and it was all because of me. They had three major stories to cover, but the two fires in Southie, and the mystery woman who was rescued by the mystery man, were not the lead items. Not even close.

But let's start with those fires in Southie, both of which were labeled as arson by Boston's FIU, Fire Investigation Unit. As it turned out, Officer Christopher Walsh—the guy who took down my police report at the scene—was right about the press. I'm sure they would have loved to interview me, and if I hadn't been the one who started the blaze in the first place, I would have granted that request. I would have said things like, "I'm not a hero. . . . I was just in the right place at the right time. . . . I just wanted to help. Yada. Yada. Yada." But in truth, I wasn't a hero, was I? I was an arsonist. Fortunately, my name (okay, the Elliot Uretsky name) was not made available to the press via the police report, because I hadn't been arrested for any crime—at least, not yet.

Having the media all over the first fire in Southie helped me stay an enigma. By the time Ruby and I were leaving the scene of the second fire, the news trucks were just rolling in. We slipped away in the gathering crowd before anybody could point the newsies in our direction.

The reports about Winnie were pretty vague. They knew that she was a woman, but they didn't have a picture to show the public or any identification to go on. I had no idea what Uretsky did with her purse and wallet. Maybe it burned in the fire. They could have filmed her inert body splayed out on a stretcher as it got loaded into the back of an ambulance, but I guess that's considered poor form—even for the local news. According to the Channel Seven reporter, this Jane Doe had been taken to Mass General Hospital, where her condition was reported as critical.

We knew a little bit more than the reporter did, but that was because we had gone to see her.

After the fire, Ruby and I returned to the apartment. We both showered, and I turned the bathroom black with soot. I still couldn't get a decent breath, but with every cough and everything I expunged from my aching lungs, I was clearing a pathway for some actual respiration. Once we'd cleaned up, we drove Ziggy to Mass General, parked in the garage, and ten minutes later identified ourselves to the staff working the ICU as the people who pulled the Jane Doe out of the Southie fire. We asked if we could see her for just a moment, if that would be all right with them.

"It's important for closure," I said.

If any of the staffers found it odd that Ruby got emotional in this woman's presence, they didn't say. Tears in the ICU are a common occurrence, but I bet the staff didn't often witness one stranger sobbing over the medical plight of another. Of course, they didn't know this was a daughter holding her mother's hand.

Winnie was on a ventilator, her arms an octopus of IV drips. All sorts of other machines were attached to her, all humming and beeping away, but I didn't know their purpose and didn't think it wise to ask. It might seem odd to take such an interest in Jane Doe's medical condition. Thanks to HIPAA, we didn't glean all that much about her prognosis, either. She was suffering from severe smoke inhalation; that much we were told, though it was unclear when—or even if—she would regain consciousness.

I overheard two nurses talking about the toxicology report they were expecting from the lab at any moment. I'm sure when the police read through that report, they'd have some questions for Elliot Uretsky—aka me. How did I manage to hear this woman calling out for help if she had enough drugs swimming in her system to knock out an elephant? Those questions might come up, and if they did, either I'd BS my way through them or I'd make a call to Clegg and ask for a lifeline. Right now I needed to be a rock for Ruby, who sat silent by her mother's bedside, swallowing down tears as sour to her as the smoke lingering in my lungs.

But of all the stories to make the evening news, Winnie and the two fires in Southie were merely footnotes. We got back to our place a little before five o'clock in the afternoon and parked Ziggy in the reserved spot out back. We entered the apartment building through the back door, which meant we didn't see any of the action going on out front. I immediately turned on the TV, curious what the reports would have to say about the fire.

That's when we heard the lead story—the really big news item of the day. It hadn't been confirmed yet by the police, but there was growing speculation about a possible serial killer on the loose in Boston. According to the somber-sounding newscaster, the body of a mutilated woman had been found inside her Winthrop apartment. Authorities were not releasing the woman's name pending notification of her family, but they did have some disturbing information about the crime to share with the viewing public.

The woman's fingers had been severed and placed ritualistically on her body. And some bright reporter with a nose for the news managed to link the gruesome details of the murder victim to a similar act performed on Rhonda Jennings. Somebody read the police reports and matched the modus operandi of the two crimes. Somebody didn't need a lot more information to connect those terrible dots. Now the race was on between the people trying to control the flow of information and those who wanted to expose the truth. We sat riveted to the news, watching the reporters trying to make sense of it all.

The news people had all their bases covered. One television crew was out in Winthrop, at Jenna's apartment, one was at the Boston police headquarters, and another was stationed right outside the apartment on Harvard Avenue where Rhonda Jennings once lived. Ruby went over to the window and confirmed at least four news trucks from different television stations parked right outside. Thank goodness we'd come in through the back door, or we would have been accosted like our other neighbors, who were just trying to come home for the night. On the TV, the Channel Seven news anchor was asking the same questions anybody would ask.

Was this the work of a single killer?

How many other killings had there been?

What did the placement of the fingers mean?

Was it part of a demonic ritual?

In addition to rampant speculation, the media had given this killer a name. In a mere couple of hours from the discovery of the bodies to the linking of the two murders, the SHS Killer had been born: see, hear, and speak no evil. SHS. Maybe twenty years ago it would have taken a day or two for the name of the SHS Killer to become part of the cultural lexicon. But with the advent of instant communication networked to just about everybody, fear could travel at supersonic speed and a name could catch quicker than a fire in Southie. One minute, people were watching the end of *Ellen* and the next they were tweeting and updating their Facebook profiles with warnings to stay vigilant, walk in groups, and avoid going out at night unless absolutely necessary.

We watched the five o'clock news blend into the six and were witness to the police battling a swelling tide of panic. They urged caution while warning against jumping to conclusions.

"At this point, we cannot confirm or deny reports of a serial killer," the police commissioner said on camera. "We do have two murders with strikingly similar characteristics, and we're asking anybody with information to come forward to help us solve these terrible crimes."

The words tumbled about in my head. *Anybody with information*—well, that would be me. I had all the information, but yet I felt powerless to do anything about it. I could give up Uretsky's name, along with my role in the fire, Jenna's death, the robbery of Giovanni's Liquors, Rhonda Jennings's murder, and our medical fraud in the process, but would that stop the killings? Uretsky and his wife, Tanya, were both MIA. What realistic hope did the police have of tracking them down?

Ruby must have been thinking along the same lines. "We've got to tell them what we know," she said.

"The police, you mean?"

"Yes, John, the police. We've got to tell them about Elliot Uretsky."

I nodded, because I agreed with her. We needed help. We needed the police. And yet the consequences of a confession were immense.

"I just need to think about it," I said.

"What's there to think about?" Ruby asked, her voice a burst of hostility. "Make the call, or I will."

"We need to make arrangements. For you . . . for us," I said, stammering to get out the words. "I'm going to jail for what I've done. You don't have to."

Ruby's eyes turned downcast as she ruminated on what I had said. "We could run," she suggested. "We'll vanish. We'll figure it out."

"Or we wait until we hear from Uretsky," I said. "Keep playing his game."

"Who knows what he'll ask us to do next?"

"Let's not rush," I said. "We can't go far from your medication right now. We need time to figure out what's best. Okay?"

Ruby nodded and looked out the window. "There's more news trucks out there," she said. "A lot more."

We watched those trucks for a while, kneeling on the futon with our arms wrapped around each other. I shivered even though my body still felt like it was on fire. For some reason, I didn't mind looking down this time. Normally, I get the shakes glancing out a second-story window. I guess a deeper and far more profound horror had sequestered my acrophobia in some sort of mental lockbox. Hell of a way to find me a cure.

Twenty minutes later, our apartment phone rang. I knew who'd be waiting for me on the other end of the line.

Despite every voice inside my head screaming not to do it, I answered the phone.

CHAPTER 41

"Quite the scene we're causing," Uretsky said as soon as I picked up the phone.

"What you did to Winnie . . . to us . . . Please, this needs to stop." I needed the kitchen island countertop to keep myself upright. "You win. You win everything," I said, pleading with him. "Please just let us go."

It was odd to hear myself beg, but beg I did. Desperation seeped from my pores as rivers of sweat. Hopelessness stifled my breathing. I had so much rage welling up inside me, so much hatred, that I was amazed I could put together a coherent thought. All I could do was to plead for some sort of mercy and pray that he might tire of toying with us.

"You've watched the news reports, I trust," Uretsky said. "Crazy stuff, John. Crazy."

"You need to stop this," I said. "This needs to stop."

"You don't control me," Uretsky said. "I control me. You can just react to what I do."

"You're going to keep killing," I said. I meant it as a question, but it came out as a statement of fact.

"I am," Uretsky said. "Unless you stop me."

"How do I stop you?"

I hated how weak I sounded. My voice came out pleading, shaken, and defeated.

Uretsky just laughed. "By winning, of course," he said.

"You want me to commit another crime?" I asked. The anger in my voice encouraged me. "What do you want me to do now? Mugging? Carjacking? Drug smuggling? I guess there's a lot to choose from."

"You sound excited, John," Uretsky said, chuckling. "Are you actually looking forward to what's next?"

"How many more?" I asked.

"Crimes, you mean? Not for you to know. It's a game, remember?"

I looked over at Ruby, still kneeling on the futon. If her ashen complexion were any indication, the end of this game was very near at hand. We couldn't take much more.

"I'm thinking about turning myself in to the police," I said. "That means you won't have me to play with anymore. You'll be all on your own, and they'll come looking for you. They'll come after you with everything they've got."

"It won't help," Uretsky said. "I'm as hidden as hidden can be. They can't trace any of my communications to you. These calls, the texts, they're all done through a bunch of anonymous proxy servers and so many Internet hops it's like the Easter Bunny traveled around the world. I'm untraceable. I can't be found. But I can be stopped. Are you ready to stop me?"

I let my apprehension pass through me like a shiver.

"I'm ready," I said.

Did I mean it? I didn't know. But it was what came out of me, because now I wanted to stop him. I wanted to beat him. To be honest, at the most primal level, inside a place I cringed to acknowledge, I wanted to win.

"Have you ever heard of the Machiavellian Scale?" Uretsky asked.

"I've heard of Machiavelli," I said.

"Well, the Machiavellian Scale is an assessment of the lengths one would travel to gain an advantage in interpersonal encounters."

"And your point is?"

"My point is that a prince should imitate the fox in cunning as well as the lion in strength. A wise prince should never keep his word when it would go against his interest, because he can expect others to do the same. Those aren't my words, by the way. That's from Machiavelli's *The Prince*. It's poetry."

"Like I said, your point?"

Ruby was watching me intently, so she probably saw my jaw tightening.

"My point is that I've always had the advantage in our burgeoning little relationship, and you the disadvantage, and I think it's high time I tipped the scales a bit more in your favor."

"Why?" I said.

"Because I want you to succeed," Uretsky said. "I want this to be a fair fight. I mean, I think you've done your dandiest to thwart me, but it seems I'm always one step ahead. No arguing there. So are you ready to take the advantage? Are you ready for that big, bold step toward ending the game?"

"And if I'm not?"

My phone buzzed. I glanced and saw that I had received a picture text message. The sender's name was just a series of numbers, but I knew where it came from. I went quiet, thinking about what to do next.

"Look at it," Uretsky said in a hushed tone, that breathy whisper of his.

I did as requested and saw a picture of a playground and an attractive black woman pushing her young son on a swing.

"There's no geolocation information embedded in this image," Uretsky said. "Nothing to help the police identify my whereabouts. You don't even know what city I'm in, or what state for that matter. But I'm going to tell you about the woman in this picture, because it's very important. Her name is Tinesha, and she's a single mother of three, and if you don't do exactly as I say, she's going to be reported missing. You can go to the police. Go right now, but I'll know if you do, and I promise you, she'll go missing. I picked her because you know her, John. Is she familiar to you?"

I studied the picture intently but couldn't place the face. "No," I said.

"I'm not surprised. We interact with so many people on a daily basis, we can't possibly keep track of them all. But I assure you, the connection to you is there. Now, you can quit playing my game. But I'll know if you do, and she'll go missing. The only way for her not to go missing is for you to succeed. Is that understood?"

"I thought you were tipping the scales in my advantage," I said.

"I am," Uretsky replied. "I just want you to know there are consequences for failure."

"What do you want me to do?"

"I want you to figure out what my next clue means. No crime this time, just your smarts. That should make it easier for you to play along. Do you have a pen and paper ready, John? Get those items now."

I found a scratch piece of paper and a pen nearby. My throat had gone dry as I looked at the picture of Tinesha at the park, knowing that I held her life in my hands, and not just her life, but all lives tethered to her.

"I'm ready," I said.

"Good. Write this down exactly as I say it. I won't repeat myself. Forty-two, twenty-six, twelve, seventy-one, six, fifty-seven. Do you have it? If so, repeat those numbers back to me now."

I was still scratching down numbers, but I was able to repeat the sequence without error. "What does this mean?" I asked.

"That's for me to know and for you to figure out," Uretsky said. "Now remember, for Tinesha's sake, every minute and every second counts. Text me when you have the answer. Once again, John, best of luck to you. Game on."

CHAPTER 42

Ruby studied the sheet of paper with the numbers scrawled on it.

42, 26, 12, 71, 06, 57

"It's code," Ruby said. "How the heck are we supposed to crack some code? John, we've got to take this to the police. They have experts in cryptography. They can figure this sort of thing out."

The look I gave Ruby conveyed my disagreement. "He'd told me he'd know if we did that," I reminded her. "He'll kill the woman in the picture. We know that he will. He picked her because she's somehow connected to us. We can't let her down."

"We've got to get out from this, John!" Ruby said, pulling her hair to show her exasperation. Ruby slumped down on the futon, and Ginger took the opportunity to move in for a little snuggle. Despondent as she was, Ruby couldn't resist giving Ginger what she needed. The cat purred delightedly while Ruby studied the numbers some more. "How will he know if we take this to the police?" Ruby said. "We tell them it has to be contained. We tell them everything."

"I don't know how he'll find out, but say that he does. Maybe there's a leak," I said.

"By a leak, you mean Clegg?" Ruby said.

I shot my wife an angry look. "Are you back on that?" I said. "Do you still believe that Clegg is helping Uretsky?"

"Think about it, John," Ruby said. "Who was the guy Clegg arrested the night Rhonda was killed? We don't know anything about him. Maybe he's helping Clegg out. Maybe Clegg got a computer guy to set everything up. He's had time to plan this. I don't know how

Clegg is doing it, but I have a gut instinct about him. You've always trusted my gut. Why aren't you trusting me now?"

I thought back to Ruby's vision board, her penchant for asking the universe for answers. It was true she seemed to always be in the know.

"So if it's Clegg," I said, "then is he helping Uretsky or pretending to be him?"

"I don't know," Ruby said. "We don't even know what Elliot Uretsky actually looks like." Ruby correctly judged my expression as one of dismay. "What's wrong?"

"I should have asked Ruth Shane what Elliot looked like when we were at Uretsky's house," I said, angry with myself. "She'd know. Maybe she even has a picture of him. If we had that, we could have matched it to the mug shot of the guy Clegg busted and we could be done with this debate."

"Fine. You should have done that," Ruby said. "But there was a lot going on, and we've got to do something right here and right now. I say we go to the police."

I looked down at my phone and once again fixed my gaze on the smiling faces of Tinesha and her son. It was sickening to think that Uretsky was there—hiding in the shadows, watching them from a distance. He took this picture, and he sent it to me for a reason. What did he want us to do?

Uretsky's words came back at me like an arrow shot from a bow.

Are you ready for that big, bold step toward ending the game?

Ginger leapt off the futon and onto the floor when I sat down beside Ruby.

"There's no crime this time," I said to her. "We just have to solve the clue. We already have Jenna and Rhonda on our conscience. Dr. Adams and your man, too. Do we really want to add a fifth victim to the list? Because that's what's going to happen here."

I showed Ruby the picture on my phone. Unfair of me, but I couldn't let Jenna and Rhonda's fate become Tinesha's as well.

Ruby stared at the display screen for a long while. She didn't pick up on the connection to me, either.

How did I know this woman?

"We have nothing to lose by trying," I said, "And Tinesha has everything to gain. We've got to try, Rube. We've got to try."

In one hand, Ruby held the paper with numbers on it, and in the other, my iPhone with Tinesha's picture. She appeared to be weighing the two choices, as though her hands had become scales.

"Do you want to be responsible for what happens to her?" I said. "Because I don't."

Ruby's gaze fell to the numbers. "Have you Googled them?" she asked.

"No, but I'll give it a try."

Since Ruby had thrown my laptop against the wall, I used my iPhone to Google the number sequence. I showed her the results, which were pages full of climatological data—sequences of numbers that happened to have all our numbers in it, but not in the order that Uretsky had given them to me.

"So this is pretty much useless," Ruby said. "What now? How long do we have to figure this thing out?" Her question made me pause. Ruby didn't have patience to wait for an answer. "John, I said how long?"

"I don't know," I said. "He didn't tell me."

"He's always given us a deadline," Ruby said.

"Well, this time he didn't."

Ruby looked at me, unblinking. "That's strange," she said.

We spent the next couple of hours trying various cryptographic approaches, many of which I got off the Internet. We tried substituting letters for numbers, but that just yielded a string of gibberish.

"There's no key," Ruby said. "He can't expect us to solve this without a key."

We were working at the dining table, with every inch of available surface covered by our spread of papers, all failed attempts at cracking the code. I found a Web site that listed two dozen different ciphers: Caesarian Shift, Double Transposition, Playfair, and the list went on.

"We don't have time to learn all of these," I said, "let alone apply them."

"Time," Ruby said, her voice trailing off.

"What?"

"He didn't give us a time limit," Ruby said.

"You're back to that," I said.

"He hasn't done that before," she said. "We had a time limit for the other crimes, shoplifting, armed robbery, prostitution, arson. Only this time we don't have any limit at all."

"Play the part," I said. "He didn't give us a time limit for that."

"That's because we weren't the drivers for that. Dobson was coming to us. We didn't go to him. But here he wants us to take action to get an advantage, not wait for it to happen. Just following his own logic, there should be a time limit."

"I still don't see how that helps us," I said.

"You need to tell me exactly what he said to you."

"He just gave me these numbers. He told me not to go to the cops—that he'd find out if I did. He told me he wanted to tip the scales in our advantage. He said we didn't know what city he was in, or what state. If we didn't play along, Tinesha would go missing." I was talking fast, probably too fast, but I wanted to remember every possible detail, so my mind was free-form thinking and recalling.

"Not helpful," Ruby said. "What else?"

I couldn't think of anything else that struck me. "He just ended the call by saying that every minute and every second counts," I said. "That was all."

Ruby's eyes went wide. "John, don't you get it?"

"What?"

"Open your eyes and your mind. He didn't give us a time limit, but he said the seconds and minutes count? Does that make sense to you?"

"I don't see how that helps us with these numbers," I said.

Again, Ruby looked at the sheet of paper. Her head was bent low, eyes studying. "Do you remember that climb you did in Colorado when I called your cell and asked where you were?"

I nodded. It was a long time ago, over eight years, but I never forget my climbs. "I think I said we were going to try for a three-peak day. We'd just climbed Mount Democrat and Mount Lincoln, and Mount Bross was up next."

"That's not what you told me," Ruby said. "When I asked where you were, you initially gave me your location in latitude and longitude and I laughed, because you were so focused on your climb, you forgot who you were talking to."

My eyes went wide, and a tingle swept through my body. "You think these numbers are location coordinates?"

"Minutes and seconds," Ruby said. "Longitude and latitude can be expressed as degrees, minutes, and seconds or as decimal degrees. You taught me that. I don't think this is a code with a key for us to crack."

"What do you think it is?" I asked.

"I think it's a place that Uretsky wants us to go."

CHAPTER 43

We stood at the edge of a forest and gazed numbly into a thicket of trees. What secret was hidden here? What did Uretsky want us to find, or worse—to do? The Middlesex Fells Reservation covers over twenty-five hundred acres and is a welcome retreat for city folk seeking a day of hiking, mountain biking, horseback riding, or rock climbing. The hilly tracts of rocky land should have been a picturesque sight, but we had a different sort of picture troubling our thoughts—that of a woman at a playground, pushing her son on a swing.

I listened to the enveloping stillness and heard the forest come alive—the chirping of chickadees and other birds, the rustling of leaves in a light wind. A squirrel scampered up the side of a tall tree, its clawed feet clicking as it climbed out of my sight. The late afternoon, usually pleasing against my face, felt like nothing at all. The dampness of the bark and the moss would have normally brightened my spirits. This was a place of true scenic beauty, great for picnics and exploring. Horrible things weren't supposed to happen here.

Maybe Ruby was right. Maybe Uretsky wanted us to commit another crime right here, right now. Maybe it involved Tinesha, but I doubted it. The only thing I believed continued to weigh heavy on my conscience. Tinesha, however we knew her, would become Uretsky's next victim, unless we intervened.

At first Ruby had balked about coming here.

"It's probably a trap," she had said.

I had texted Uretsky after we figured out his clue, and he promptly texted back.

Go there and see for yourself.

He didn't credit me with a job well done. No virtual pats on the back, Johnny old boy. Just a tersely worded "Go there and see for yourself." I reminded Ruby that we had saved Dr. Adams's life by robbing Giovanni's Liquors but had helped to end Rhonda Jennings's by our own inaction.

Ruby fell silent. Obviously, she agreed. Still, she couldn't ignore her gut instinct about what to do next. "We should tell the police," she said. "They should come with us."

"He doesn't want to hurt us, and he wants us to go alone," I said.

Ruby's arms folded, a look of indignation crossing her face. "You can't know that for sure."

I thought. "We're too much fun for him," I said. "I just know that he wants to keep playing with us, not hurt us. But if we take a chance and bring the police along, I don't think Tinesha is going to live to see morning."

Instead of responding, Ruby reached for her sun hat and put her jacket on.

"Let's go," she said.

It was close to five o'clock in the afternoon by the time we pulled into a parking area just off South Border Road. We locked the car and walked across the street. That's when we stood at the edge of a forest and gazed numbly into the trees. I held in my hand a pocket GPS from Garmin, procured back in my climbing days. Once I had a good satellite signal, I brought up the Mark Waypoint screen and scrolled up to select CURRENT COORDINATES. This produced an entry field that allowed me to key in the exact coordinates cryptically relayed to us through Uretsky:

N42 26 12   W71 06 57.

I showed Ruby the route we had to take. There was no path to follow.

"Do we just start trekking through the woods?" she asked.

"It is called an eTrek," I said, flashing her the GPS.

"I didn't bring bug repellent."

"Don't worry. I'll check you over for ticks," I said.

Ruby gave me a look—that look—and started off ahead of me.

Something made her stop. She turned to face me. "What's out

here? What the hell are we going to find?" She knew I couldn't an-swer the question, but she did look a little less bothered.

Initially, bushwhacking through the forest was easy enough, but the underbrush quickly grew thicker, and the mass of vegetation under-foot tripped one of us up every few steps. I used a stick to clear away some branches, but our trek was like a boxing match; we'd duck one tree, only to get thwacked in the face, neck, and arms by another. Every hundred yards or so, I checked my GPS for course corrections.

The route took us through one steep trough that required us to inch our way down. I could hear Ruby's labored breathing behind me. The hike would have been moderately challenging without her cancer. At some point she stopped and, resting against a tree, took a long drink of water from the camel pack. The scrub provided excel-lent shelter for chipmunks and other woodland critters seeking a hideout. I wondered what else the land could be hiding. Had Uretsky put something here that he wanted us to find? If so, what could it be? How would it give us an advantage?

Ruby slumped to the forest floor, breathing hard. "I need to rest a bit," she said.

I looked up. We still had plenty of sunlight.

After a few minutes we continued, walking west, swatting flies and branches in equal measure until we came to a sudden stop at a steep cliff face. My breath caught when I looked down at the jagged rocks jutting out from the clay-colored surface. As my eyes focused on the depth, the ground below began to swirl, the brown of dead leaves re-volving until all color slipped into black. I felt the horizon pitch and roll, as if it had come unfurled from the earth.

I staggered backward and felt Ruby's hands grip my shoulder to steady me. Seeing the height of the cliff, without any warning, with no time to prepare, hit me hard—instantaneously, I became light-headed, dizzy, and nauseated. I took ten steps in retreat before I found my bearings once again.

"We'll take . . . the long . . . way down," I said to Ruby between breaths.

The unsettling sensations lingered but eventually quieted down.

Ruby looked very troubled. "Is it getting worse, John?"

"You mean my acrophobia?"

A branch I had cleared catapulted backward and nearly knocked

Ruby off of her feet. "Hey!" she said, surprised. "I'm your wife, re- member!"

"You're my everything," I said, apologizing with a kiss on her cheek. "And to answer your question, yes, I think it's getting worse, but hasn't Uretsky made every facet of our lives worse?"

We marched on, with Ruby keeping close behind me. On my GPS display, the little triangle that represented "us" continued to close in on the x that represented our destination. A hundred yards to go . . .

What would we find?

Fifty yards . . .

I looked back and saw Ruby valiantly battle through a thicket of branches. Was her heart beating as fast as mine? Was her pulse racing, too? She knew we were getting closer.

Twenty yards . . .

I pushed my way between two pine trees—the forest version of a car wash. That's when I had this thought about paths, the ones we take and the ones we don't. I'd tried my best to live free from regret, but at that moment, I regretted becoming Elliot Uretsky so pro- foundly that I knew I'd never forgive myself. No matter what the out- come, I had an incurable disease called regret. Life, I thought, was full of paths, like the one Ruby and I were forging through this forest. There are paths made for us, and paths that we make. Sometimes we stumble upon a route we think about taking but, for some reason, don't. Or worse, we walk one way and look back wistfully at the way we had left behind.

Ten yards . . .

I looked back at Ruby—pale, her pert nose blackened by dirt. A herd of flies roamed about her head like a haphazard halo. I won- dered what path I took that led me to her. What made her apply to the same school as me? Why did we take the same class? Was it a se- ries of choices, or was it all somehow predestined?

Ruby came toward me, her body trembling with exhaustion. Be- hind me was one final coppice to clear before we'd reach our desti- nation.

"I love you," I said, holding her tight. "No matter what we find. I love you."

I pushed my way through the trees, with Ruby following.

We emerged into a small clearing with trees all around us. In the center of the clearing I saw loose-packed dirt, as though it had been dug up recently. No plants were growing in that patch of dirt, but set upon the barren oval was a large X composed entirely of stones. X marks the spot.

Ruby shrieked when she looked to her left. I cried out, too, after I looked. Leaning up against a nearby tree, I saw two shovels. Long wood handles, hard steel spades. I went over to the shovels, and I saw that each had a tag on it with a note written in neat printed lettering.

One tag read *Ruby's.*

The other tag read *John's.*

CHAPTER 44

When the shovel blade hit the dirt, it made an eerie scraping sound. Still, it slid easily enough into the loose-packed soil and went right up to the handle. I pulled out my first scoopful of richly dark earth and tossed it to my left, partially covering the pile of stones that had been used to mark the spot with an *X*. Ruby drove her shovel into the ground as well, but with a little less force. She applied pressure to the footrest to bury the blade and afterward pulled out a shovel full of dirt to add to the growing pile. It took ten scoopfuls of dirt to put sweat on my brow. Four more and I needed to wipe the sweat away with the back of my hand.

"John, I hate that we're doing this," Ruby said, extracting another shovelful of soil. "What's buried down here?"

"I don't know," I said. "But I'm going to keep digging."

And so we dug. Our blades sinking into the earth the way a knife might vanish inside flesh. We moved shovelful after shovelful of dirt. After a while we'd dug a wide, round hole in the ground at least a foot deep. Thick earthworms moved about in our growing mound of excavated soil, waving for our attention. Our hands swatted away a persistent horde of black flies. The sun, still visible overhead, cast a weak light that barely scraped its way through the canopy of trees.

Ruby slouched to the ground, her breathing uneven and tired. She wiped clear some sweat, leaving behind a belt of dirt that traveled across one flushed cheek to the other. She sat while I dug. Scrape. Lift. Toss. Scrape. Lift. Toss. Two feet down now, still nothing but dirt.

"Maybe he's just toying with us," Ruby suggested. "You said he likes to do that. Maybe there's nothing down here."

My shovel sunk up to the handle with another thrusting plunge of the blade.

"There are no roots, no rocks," I said, breathing heavily from exertion. "This ground has been dug up before. The soil is still loose, not at all compacted. He wants us to keep digging until we can't dig anymore, or we find whatever he's buried down here."

"He didn't tell us we had to dig," Ruby reminded me. "His text just said to go there and see for ourselves. Not dig. We don't have to dig."

"I want to see," I said. "I *have* to see."

"Why?"

I had to think about this. Why was I digging? What was I after?

"Because I have to finish what he started," I said.

"This isn't one of your climbs, John," Ruby said.

My shovel went back into the earth. I tossed the dirt aside as the mound to my right grew to the size of a mini-mountain. Two feet down soon became three. Before I knew it, I was waist deep inside a four-foot hole. Ruby couldn't help out anymore, but only because there wasn't enough room in the hole for both of us to dig. I worked alone, pulling the shovel back to ready for the strike, driving the blade into the ground, time and time again. Each thrust I expected more of the same—easy entry, easy exit, more dirt to move. But that didn't happen this last time. No, this last time my shovel blade hit something hard. It made a clanging sound, as though I'd struck a rock.

I pushed the shovel in once again, looking for the edge of the hidden object, and eventually found it. I slid the blade underneath the blockage and lifted the shovel, using the handle for leverage to dislodge the item. Up came the side of a green plastic garbage bag with something inside. Something I hit. Something that made a clanging sound.

A horror-stricken look came over Ruby as I pulled the bag out of the hole. It was light to lift, easy to move. Brown rivulets of dirt slid down the sides of the bag after I tossed it out of the hole. I climbed out myself and brushed away dirt that had caked up on my blistered hands. For a quiet moment, Ruby and I stared wide-eyed at the plastic bag. Almost immediately, I noticed a change in the air—a scent, a smell, that I didn't like one bit.

"What are you going to do?" Ruby asked.

"I'm going to open it," I said.

"John—"

I wasn't listening. I was too busy untying the bag.

The instant the top came apart just a little bit, I recoiled at the stench. My nostrils burned with the putrid smell of death and decay. Ruby gagged several times before turning her head away in disgust. I gagged, too, retching as I clumsily turned the bag upside down, spilling the contents onto the ground by my feet. I buried my nose in my arm to help block out the smell. At first I couldn't register what had fallen out with a thump—no, make that two thumps. Slowly, as the initial shock gave way, my brain began to connect the dots and I understood what I was looking at.

Two severed heads had fallen out of the bag.

Ruby's screams pierced the quiet woods loud enough to send resting birds scattering in flight. I didn't scream, but I think I was moaning as though wounded. The heads didn't look real. Rather, they looked to be made of wax, or maybe even beaten-up mannequin heads. But the flies that began to swarm around them said they were real. The stench that forced me to cover my nose and mouth did the same.

One of the heads—the one that rolled a few feet to my right—had long brown hair that was matted down and stringy. I could see molted blue skin on the nape of the neck. The neck itself appeared to have been severed from the body with near-surgical precision. That head had come to a stop facedown, so I couldn't see the eyes or mouth, but I could see that duct tape had been used to secure two objects to where the ears should have been. Without closer inspection, I couldn't make out what they were.

My eyes shifted to the other head, which hadn't rolled as far. This head belonged to a man. The skin was tight to the skull, but a lot of tissue remained. Like the other head, the hair was matted down, but the color was dark. The skin around the man's ample nose had browned and peeled at the tip, revealing a pinkish layer underneath. But that was just the start of the horror. The man's lips were mostly gone, so his teeth looked to be protruding from his mouth in a twisted, wicked grin.

I could see on this head what I couldn't see on the other, which was how I lost the voice to scream. My mouth formed the shape of a scream, but the only sound to come out was a whisper of air. I studied the head absently, vacantly, as though all my senses had been overloaded by a profoundly sickening horror. Affixed to the head, with several judicious applications of duct tape, were severed fingers: two planted on the eyes, two dangling down from the ears like decaying earrings, and two adhered to those protruding teeth.

See no evil.

Hear no evil.

Speak no evil.

CHAPTER 45

I didn't know how many hours had passed. Ten? Maybe fifteen? We weren't in the forest anymore, that's for certain. We were at Boston police headquarters, or at least I thought we both were there. Ruby and I weren't together for the first time since becoming vessels for Uretsky and his game. The cops had separated us. They never questioned you in the same room. But our stories would match up perfectly because we had agreed before making the call to 911 that we were going to tell them the truth, the whole truth, and nothing but the horrible truth.

We didn't stick around the woods very long after the heads came tumbling out of the garbage bag. We didn't dig anymore, either. Ruby started to run, frantically, back the way we had come. I followed her, calling her name, while branches lashed at my face and roots tripped up my steps.

When I caught up to her, she was hysterical, tears streaming down her face. But then again, so was I. What we had just seen would have made anybody hysterical. I wasn't sure we were going to make it back to the car hiking in such a distraught state, but eventually we did. I made the call to 911, and before too long the sounds of chickadees and scampering squirrels were drowned out by a fury of sirens.

The cops brought in police dogs and GPS equipment. There were fire trucks and ambulances and some sedans driven by guys who looked like they were from the FBI. Thankfully, I didn't have to show anybody how to get back to those heads. I gave them the coordinates, instead.

We didn't stick around to see the crime-scene folks work the area. Instead, we were ushered away, driven to Boston by a cop who promised me that Clegg would be there once we arrived.

Clegg was there, all right, but he didn't get a chance to speak with us—not for long, anyway. We had to be interviewed first. Nothing he could do about that. Clegg did ask me if I wanted a lawyer present. I didn't. I just wanted to tell my story.

And so I did, to two detectives, a burly, doughy-looking fellow named Gant and a bald one with a thin mustache, Kaminski. They were nice enough, probably because I was just answering their questions. I had on a grimy blue T-shirt and jeans layered with dirt. They wore suits and hard-edged attitudes.

I told them about Ruby's cancer and stealing Uretsky's identity so we could afford her medication. I told them about Uretsky's phone call and how I believed he was just trying to scare us. "That's why I didn't try to shoplift those scarves," I said, "and why Roberta Jennings was subsequently murdered."

I recounted my life of crime—lying to Henry Dobson, the investigator from UniSol; robbing Giovanni's liquor store with an unloaded gun; orchestrating Ruby's stint as a prostitute and finding the substitute, who ended up paying the ultimate price for her trick; and finally starting the fire in Southie. I gave them what information I had about the people Uretsky had used to control me—people connected to me in some way: Dr. Lisa Adams, Ruby's oncologist; Winnie, her mom; and Tinesha, another mother who I somehow knew and who lived somewhere unknown to me. I told them what I could about the concrete room with a dripping pipe where Uretsky held his victims hostage.

Gant left the interview room for a while and returned, not looking particularly happy or sad. "We don't know of anybody named Tinesha who's been murdered, kidnapped, or reported missing," he said.

"Whose heads did I dig up?" I asked.

"We don't know that, either," Kaminski said.

Gant was shaking his head.

"What?" I asked him.

"Just so I'm clear, you're the guy wearing a ski mask in the surveillance video, doing CPR?" he asked me.

"That's me," I said, no pride in my voice.

Kaminski showed me his phone. "That video has got eight million hits."

It had shot up since the last time I looked, I thought.

"You beat out the baby who got scared by his mother blowing her nose," Gant said.

"No? Really?" I said. I probably sounded surprised, but I didn't know how else to act.

Kaminski went back to his smartphone. "Nah," he said, correcting himself. "That video has over twenty-three million views."

I don't know how much I helped them with their investigation into the SHS killings. I told them they could take all my computers, access my phone, and search my apartments—yeah, both of them—for anything helpful. I did ask that they give the Spanish professors living in my Somerville apartment a heads-up first. We talked a lot about my drive by in Uretsky's neighborhood, how he and his wife had been reported missing, and that the neighbor, a class three sex offender named Carl Swain, came from some very bad stock and enjoyed leering at Elliot's wife.

"I want to see Ruby," I said.

"Yeah, soon," Gant said. "She's doing all right. I promise."

I believed them, though that didn't stop me from worrying.

"So are you going to arrest me?" I asked.

"We don't know what's going to happen to you," Kaminski said. "To be honest, these are some pretty unusual circumstances. We do appreciate your cooperation, though. No matter what goes down, that's going to count for something."

It was well past midnight when Clegg entered the interview room and relieved Gant and Kaminski of their duties. He looked haggard in a rumpled suit, red tie askew, with bags under his eyes big enough to be checked by TSA. He took a seat across the table from me and glanced at the mirror, which I knew was two-way glass.

"John," he said. "Holy whopper."

"How much trouble are we in?" I asked him.

"I don't know right now," he said. "There have been some new developments."

My eyes went wide. "Like what?" I asked.

"We'll get to that," he said.

"When can I see Ruby?"

"Soon," Clegg said. "I just checked in on her. She's doing fine. You should have called me."

"I couldn't," I said. "You weren't there. He told me he'd find out."

"I can keep a secret. You should have called me. You should have told me what was going on. I've got your back, John. More than you'll ever know."

"Got it," I said. "I should have." I said it, but I didn't mean it. He was a climber. He knew better than most that some chances simply weren't worth taking. Or maybe Ruby's gut instinct influenced me more than I realized. "So what happens now?" I asked.

"Now I cancel my trip." Clegg winced a little. He had crossed an unspoken line we didn't cross—he was talking about the mountains.

"Where were you headed?" I asked.

"Just out west for a couple of weeks," Clegg said. He was nonchalant, making it sound like no big deal. We both knew that wasn't the case.

"Did you get anything off of my computers? Any clue where Uretsky might be hiding out?"

"That's the thing, John," Clegg said. He looked down at his hands, then back up at me with his bloodshot eyes. "We've got some new developments."

"Now you can talk about them?"

"In a minute," Clegg said. "This guy, whoever is killing these women, he's using you for whatever reason, and we're going to need your help catching him. Now, I've spoken with our chief, and he's agreed we're not going to arrest you for armed robbery, identity theft, or arson, as long as you're willing to help us catch this bastard. I told him you'd do anything. I'm not wrong, am I?"

"No, you're not," I said.

Clegg nodded grimly. "Okay, so brace yourself, because things are about to get a whole lot crazier. Our crime-scene folks finished excavating the dig site. They found something else buried down there," he said.

I swallowed hard, my body tensing with anticipation.

"They found two wallets with IDs inside them."

"Who? Who did Uretsky bury down there?" I asked.

"That's the thing, John," Clegg said. "The IDs belong to Elliot and Tanya Uretsky."

The room seemed to flip upside down.

"But that's . . . that's . . . impossible," I stammered.

"We had the lab rush a DNA match of the male head you dug up to a sample we took from the Uretskys' house," Clegg said. "It's not as comprehensive as DNA sequencing, but the genetic markers that make each of us unique came back positive for Elliot Uretsky. We're assuming right now the other head belongs to Tanya, but the lab hasn't confirmed that yet. They did come back with a preliminary on time of death, though. You see, bodies decompose at different rates depending on location. A rule of thumb is that one week on land equals two weeks in the water, and that equals four weeks in the ground. The heads you dug up have the same level of decay as if they were discarded on land four weeks ago. That means they've been in the ground for at least four months. It would match up to around the time the Uretskys were reported missing."

I was trying to catch my breath, still trying to process it all.

"John," Clegg said, registering my lack of understanding. "Elliot Uretsky is dead. He's not the one doing this to you."

"Do you realize what you're saying?" I said, my voice rising with alarm. "Do you know what that means?"

"You tell me," Clegg said.

"It means I stole an identity that somebody had already stolen," I said. "It also means that I have no idea who killed those women or who's been tormenting us."

"That's not all," Clegg said, his voice ringing distant in my ears. "It also means we don't know why he wanted you to make this discovery, or even worse, what he has planned for you next."

CHAPTER 46

An hour later Ruby joined me in the interview room. Assuming her appearance mirrored my own, I looked absolutely horrible. I'm guessing we were both just a few notches above roadkill on the beauty scale—dirty, worn out, and utterly exhausted.

More people had joined us, so we went over our stories again, but by this point I'd lost track of how many times. Clegg was in the room, as were Gant and Kaminski. The chief of police, a burly guy named Eric Higgins, joined the party as well. They brought in a sketch artist even though I told them it was a waste of time. They could draw a guy wearing a ski mask and a Super Mario disguise all they liked, but it wasn't going to help anybody catch a killer. I signed a stack of consent forms allowing the police to take possession of my computers, my phone, and such. I doubted much would come from it, and when I told a tech about the anonymous proxy servers used to avoid detection, the look he gave me suggested he thought the same.

I'd grown so accustomed to referring to our tormentor as Elliot Uretsky that it was a difficult adjustment for me to call him anything else. A couple of times during the interviews I referred to him as Uretsky, and that caused all sorts of confusion.

"The dead Uretsky or the guy you thought was Uretsky?" Kaminski would ask.

The press referred to him as the SHS Killer, but he wasn't just a media label to me. We'd forged an entirely different sort of bond. I started to think of him not as Uretsky, but as "the Fiend." My sobriquet befitted the man: a devil, a demon, a person of great wickedness. Uretsky might have been dead, but the Fiend was still very much alive.

The police were asking all sorts of questions, while I struggled to provide them with any useful answers. There simply wasn't much information to share.

At some point an FBI profiler joined our gathering, introducing herself as Special Agent Andrea Brenner. Agent Brenner was thirtyish, athletically built, with shoulder-length chestnut hair, arched eyebrows, a pronounced nose, and wide brown eyes that could not conceal her enthusiasm for this case. Honest-to-goodness psychopaths weren't an everyday occurrence, even for the FBI.

"How do you think this person found out you stole an identity he'd already stolen?" Brenner asked me.

"The Fiend, you mean?"

"If that's what you want to call him."

"I don't know," I said. "I'm guessing he contacted UniSol for some reason. Maybe he was trying to use Uretsky's insurance, same as we did. Maybe he was just trying to close up loose ends and found out someone was using the insurance. That would have raised a red flag because he had already killed Tanya and Elliot."

"What do you think he wanted from you?" she asked.

"I told you already. He said he wanted to teach me how to become a real criminal."

"Do you still think that's true?"

"No," I said.

"What do you think he really wants from you?"

I took a moment to answer. "I think he wants to see how far he can push me," I said. "He's curious to know what sorts of things he can make me do. He once asked me if a good man could be pushed by circumstance into committing evil acts. It's like an experiment to him. He wants to inflict the maximum amount of torture on me as possible. He gets off on it."

"In a sexual way?" Brenner asked.

Ruby looked exasperated. "You're the expert," she said. "We're just his victims."

Gant pressed his palms against the table and leaned his body between Brenner and me. "I know it's a challenge for you to find out what makes this guy tick, Agent Brenner," he said. "But we need to figure out who this guy is first."

"We have the same goal," Brenner said.

"I already gave you two names of people he could be," I said.

Kaminski nodded. "Yeah, the purse snatcher from the Brookline bar and"—he glanced down at his notes—"this Carl Swain fellow from Medford."

Ruby flashed me a look—one that said she still hadn't ruled out Clegg as a possible suspect. I guessed her theory held even more validity, in that the Fiend could be anybody. He could be a priest, a gas station attendant, a teacher, a purse snatcher, a level three sex offender, even a cop. He could even be a friend. Still, I couldn't bring myself to believe that Clegg was involved.

"Any luck tracking down either of those men?" Chief Higgins asked Clegg.

"We've got detectives on it," Clegg said, checking his watch. "It's three in the morning right now. We'll go see them in a couple hours. The purse snatcher is Edwin Valdez. He lives in Everett with his girl-friend. We've got Swain's address in Medford."

"A couple of hours?" I said, sounding incredulous. "What are you talking about, a couple of hours? Go get these guys right now. Go search their homes! Tear their places apart, and start with Swain, be-cause that's our guy. The more I think about it, the more sure I am. His neighbor told us he was watching Tanya Uretsky every chance he got. He lives on the same street as the Uretskys. He has a criminal record, for crying out loud."

Clegg kept his composure, though my outburst had rumpled his suit just a bit more. "We can't go get a search warrant based on your suspicions, John," he said. "We can go talk to him. We can ask for his cooperation. But we have no probable cause for a search warrant. No evidence. Nothing we can give to a judge. I'm sorry, but that's not how it works."

"You've got to be kidding me!" I shouted.

"Take it easy, John," Ruby said, gripping my arm.

"No, I'm not going to take it easy!" I knocked over my chair as I stood up. "One of these two guys, Swain or Valdez, took my mother-in-law and tried to get me to burn her alive. He used the fingers of four people, four now dead people, to parody some proverb. He kidnapped women. He threatened their lives. He murdered. There is a monster out there who wants to keep hurting people, including my wife and me. So I'm not going to just take it easy. You guys need to do your jobs and go get this fucker. Now!"

Higgins went red in the face. "May I remind you, son, that we can still arrest you for the felonies you've confessed to committing? Do you know how thin and tenuous a thread you're currently dangling from? You do as we say, or our cooperation ends right here and right now, and off to jail you go. *That's* how we do our job."

"John, it's late," Clegg said. "You've been through a lot. Trust us, we're going to investigate."

"It's interesting," Agent Brenner said, "that with John all the victims have been women, but he killed a man. He killed Elliot Uretsky. Why? What significance does that have?"

Blank stares all around.

Chief Higgins rose from his chair, his knees creaking as he stood, his face reverting back to the less threatening shade of pink. "Get someone to drive these two back to their home—wherever they live. But I want you both back here at this station at nine o'clock tomorrow morning to work with Special Agent Brenner. It's not a request. It's an order."

"Yes, of course," Ruby said. "We'll be here."

"I want two patrols put outside their apartment," Higgins said.

"Right on that," Gant said.

"We're going to put a task force on this," Brenner said, addressing Ruby and me. "So they'll be quite a few more agents involved starting tomorrow."

"That's fine," Ruby said. "Whatever you need from us."

Chief Higgins turned to Clegg. "I want you to release the identities of the two victims to the media. Thanks to some freaking leak in our department, the press already knows that the body parts recovered from the Fells are linked to the other two murders. The SHS Killer is getting a lot of attention, and rightly so. We might as well get as much information as we can from the public. Who knows what it might bring?"

Clegg nodded. "Yes, sir," he said. "We'll get right on it."

We stayed another fifteen minutes or so while more plans were being hatched to get the public messaging and communication strategies in order. Meanwhile, I was making plans of my own. I was thinking about how I was going to get the police the probable cause they needed to execute a search warrant on Carl Swain's house.

CHAPTER 47

Maybe we slept three hours that night. It wasn't restorative sleep by any means, but nature had plans for us we simply couldn't refuse. I don't know what I dreamt about in those few restless hours, but Ruby woke me several times to stop my screaming. We hadn't heard from the Fiend since the discovery of the Uretskys' bodies—or heads, to be precise—and that was more than a little unsettling, like knowing we were swimming near a ravenous shark but having no idea where in the murky water it lurked.

We weren't trying to hide from the Fiend. No, we wanted him to call us. In fact, the police gave us back our phones, hoping that he would call. Clegg told me that they installed some application that would help to triangulate the signal and track him down. Basically, to keep that shark metaphor going, they were chumming the waters for the Fiend, and using me as bait. They tapped our home phones as well, both in Brookline and in Somerville.

Speaking of Somerville, the Spanish professors who were renting our place had decided to move out, not surprisingly. Poor skittish Spaniards didn't even bother to ask for their security deposit back.

Our names hadn't been released to the press, so we were able to return unmolested to Harvard Street. For the moment, at least, we were unknown equations in an escalating manhunt that had every Boston resident glued to the news reports. Patrol cars were stationed outside our apartment, and the police were keeping a close watch over us, hoping the Fiend was doing the same. Funny, though, even with all that extra attention we were getting, neither Ruby nor I felt very safe.

To say the SHS Killer—I'm using the media's name for him here, not mine—was a major news story didn't do the coverage any justice. Every few minutes—my perception—television broadcasts were interrupted with late breaking developments or safety tips for the millions of citizens on edge. Most every report included the smiling faces of the SHS Killer's four known victims: Rhonda, Jenna, Elliot, and Tanya.

I don't know where they got the pictures of Elliot and Tanya. Perhaps they were photographs released by the police, maybe taken from the couple's home. Their images filled me with incredible sadness. He was a normal-looking guy—curly dark hair, nice smile, friendly eyes, a bit on the geeky side. She was shy-looking, and the way she dressed, floral blouse underneath a sweater vest, reminded me of a class picture from the 1970s. I knew I wasn't responsible for their deaths—not like Rhonda or Jenna—but we were still connected and in a very profound way. Though I never knew the Uretskys personally, we had grown close. Seeing their pictures humanized the tragedy, as if two friends of mine had been killed.

We got a ride back to the police station early the next morning, bleary-eyed and logy, but ready to get to work with the FBI's newly formed task force. The meeting got off to a late start because the unit chiefs from the Behavioral Analysis Unit-2 (Crimes against Adults) and the Violent Criminal Apprehension Program were flying in from different states. A supervisory senior resident agent from the Boston office was on hand, as well as other agents too numerous to remember and name.

After several hours we were able to work up a preliminary profile of our killer. What this accomplished in the grand scheme of things I couldn't say, but we were there to cooperate and answer as many questions as possible. We decided the SHS Killer (the Fiend) wasn't a dysfunctional loner. He was highly intelligent, and had not just tech smarts. He'd shown himself to be supremely organized, disciplined, too. This guy understood human nature—for instance, he knew how to lure Winnie to Boston and was well aware how hard it would be for Ruby to prostitute herself to a stranger. Ruby nearly broke down when Winnie's name came up in conversation. Her mother was still in a coma and might very well become the Fiend's fifth known victim, which would make me an unwitting accomplice to her murder.

The profiling work continued. The Fiend could be hiding in plain sight, married, perhaps even a father. He liked games, and liked computer gaming especially. He could blend into his surroundings. He didn't stick out. Winnie trusted him for a reason. We knew he was a white male because I saw the color of his skin, although not his face. He wasn't motivated by sex. Instead, he satisfied his urges by seeing how far he could push people, and then took delight in their killing, using their body parts to make a statement. He enjoyed inflicting unconscionable suffering and pain and didn't end his victim's agony quickly. He certainly wasn't ending ours. He preferred his victims to languish in their misery, though we didn't know why he'd killed only one male—that we knew of.

This question continued to bother Agent Brenner.

We agreed he took enormous pleasure in watching his victims suffer. Brenner postulated that he used Boston as his anchor point, and that most if not all of his killings happened in this state. That gave everyone an added sense of urgency to make a positive ID of Tinesha, because she might still be in danger.

"He has impulse control," Ruby said at one point.

"Why is that?" Brenner asked.

"He hasn't called us back since we dug up the Uretskys. If he couldn't control his urges, he would have tried to get in touch with us."

Brenner seemed impressed. "Maybe he knew we tapped your phones."

"No," Ruby said. "He's smart enough to get around that. There's a reason he hasn't been in touch. Like he's planning something."

No one disagreed with Ruby, and by the looks of it, nobody liked what she had to say.

We came to some other conclusions in the roughly three-hour session. For interpersonal traits we listed glibness, superficial charm, and a grandiose sense of self. But all this profiling meant nothing to me. It's hard to care about narrowing in on a killer's motivation when he's got you in his sights.

"Could he be a sex offender?" I asked, thinking of Carl Swain.

I'd seen Swain's mug shot, so I knew what the guy looked like. Square head, hard-pinched face, short hair, and beady, close-set eyes. He looked meaner than his mother, which surprised me.

"There's nothing in the profile to say he couldn't," Brenner said, "but we don't think the attacks are sexually motivated."

"Maybe he has a different motive for adults than he does for children," I suggested.

I took a glance around the crowded second-floor conference room and saw some head nods and an equal number of shoulders shrug.

"Could be," Brenner said. "We'll add that to our profile."

The FBI agents broke into a discussion about "agency" things. They brought up the need for a preplanned task force model—no idea what that meant—and a robust information management system to track tips and leads. Agent Brenner thanked us for our time and escorted us out of the conference room.

We returned home—back to Harvard Street—like Atlas supporting the heavens on our sagging shoulders. Clegg was coming over any minute to give us a progress report, and after that we were going back to the hospital to visit Winnie. I wanted to know if they had interviewed Carl Swain yet, and what, if anything, had they gotten from their chat with Edwin Valdez, the purse snatcher? Did Ruth Shane offer up anything helpful? But mostly I was interested in Swain—the guy with a cancer of the soul.

"I'm glad the profile we worked up doesn't rule Swain out as a suspect," I said to Ruby.

"Nothing we discussed today rules Clegg out, either," Ruby said.

I shook my head in vehement disagreement. "So he's killing strangers because he blames me for all the problems in his life?"

"No, John," Ruby said. "He wants to inflict the maximum possible punishment on you."

"Do you really and truly believe that, honestly?"

"If I had to rank our suspects, I'd put Swain at the top of the list, too. But it's just that I've been having this gut feeling—"

"Ruby, the universe doesn't always give us the answer we seek."

"It's worked for me every time," Ruby said.

I was about to say that I thought she was way off base when our apartment buzzer rang. I pressed the intercom, expecting to hear Clegg's voice.

"Hey, John. It's Officer Walker," said the policeman parked outside and assigned to keep watch over the apartment. "I've got a guy here named Henry Dobson. Says he knows you. Says he's an inspector from UniSol Health and he wants to come up."

CHAPTER 48

Ruby and I looked at each other. She just shrugged.
"Yeah, send him up," I said into the intercom.

We knew this moment was on the spectrum of inevitability. The Uretsky name was being broadcast every few minutes, across every media outlet, or so it seemed. You'd have to be a pretty bad inspector not to make the connection. We might have fooled Dobson once, but we had no intention of trying to make it twice in a row.

A few moments later I heard a knock on the door. We hadn't seen Dobson in quite some time, but he looked like the same frumpy, disheveled guy we'd met a while back. We did the handshake thing, and soon as we were all seated at the table, Dobson got to the point of his visit.

"I could have done this all with certified letters," Dobson said, "but I like you both and I thought you deserved to hear from me personally. It's about your insurance claim with UniSol."

I saw no reason to beat around the proverbial bush. "I guess you've figured out that we were lying to you," I said.

"Imagine my shock when I heard the names Elliot and Tanya Uretsky on the news," Dobson said. "Goodness, I thought you two were dead."

Ruby grimaced. "We're very much alive," she said. "And deeply sorry for what we've done."

Dobson sighed and looked away. "Well, I figured you were okay after I saw the Uretskys' pictures on TV and realized they weren't you. Of course, it got me thinking. I still didn't want to believe it, so I looked up all the Elliot and Tanya Uretskys in the United States, hoping there would be a number of them. Guess how many there were?"

"I'm going to go with less than ten," I said.

"Try two, and they lived in Medford, to boot. So that's when I knew . . . I knew I was going to have to issue an amended report to UniSol," Dobson said. His wan expression appeared steeped in disappointment. "You understand that I have a job to do. Once I make my report, they're not going to allow you to get any more medication. Your claim is going to be frozen and rigorously investigated."

"We understand," Ruby said. "In fact, we're already cooperating with the police."

"The police?" Dobson said. "So you've confessed to identity theft?"

"Once we heard the Uretskys were found murdered," I said, "we told them what we'd done."

I felt Ruby grip my leg underneath the table, so I patted her hand, my way of saying I wouldn't share the whole truth. Still, I thought dishing out a part of the story wasn't the same thing as a flat-out lie.

"We're not suspects in the Uretskys' murder, if that's what you're thinking," I said. "Nobody else knows we stole their identity. If the press finds out, they'll never leave us alone."

"I'm not going to tell them, if that's your concern," Dobson said. "But I am going to have to report your fraud, and for that I'm truly sorry."

I told Dobson about our struggles with Atrium Insurance and was surprised to see him looking so upset. Ruby reached across the table and cupped his hand with hers. I didn't like seeing how tightly the skin clung to the bones of her hands and how loose it hung on her arms. Her face looked thinner to me as well. *Damn you, cancer.*

"We did this to ourselves," Ruby said. "It's not your fault, and we appreciate you coming all the way out here to tell us in person."

Dobson appeared shaken. "To be honest, I've never had a case that made me want to quit my job," he said. "Until now. I wish I didn't have to do this. I really, really do."

Dobson stood up and shook my hand. Ruby came around the other side of the table and gave him a heartfelt hug. "Thank you. Thank you for helping us. I'm so sorry for lying to you," Ruby said in the embrace.

Dobson returned a sad little smile of his own. "I'm sorry, too," Dobson said. "I hope they catch him, whoever killed the Uretskys."

My phone buzzed while Ruby and I were escorting Dobson to the door. I checked the caller ID and saw Clegg's number come up.

"Maybe this is the answer," I said to Dobson as he headed out the door. Ruby watched Dobson descend the stairs, waving as he departed, while I answered Clegg's call.

"What's up?" I said, anxious for some good news.

"I can't come over," Clegg said. "We've got an all-hands-on-deck powwow back at the station. Higgins is none too pleased with our progress so far."

"What about Swain?" I said. "Did you guys speak with him?"

"We did, John. We asked if he would talk to us, and he agreed."

"And?"

"And nothing," Clegg said. "He doesn't have any information. He said he wished he could help us and that he liked the Uretskys because they left him alone. About what you'd expect him to say."

"What about the search warrant? Can't you get one?"

"There's no probable cause here. I told you that already. We did find Tinesha, however."

That gave me an uptick. "Who is she?"

"She works for Post Boxes Unlimited."

I groaned.

"What?"

"I used them to get my P.O. box. I guess that's how I knew her. All he needs is some connection to me to turn someone into a target."

"Maybe that's how SHS found out your real identities."

"Possible." I sighed into the phone. "What about Edwin Valdez?"

"He's MIA," Clegg said. "We're going to continue to look for him and talk to him only because you think it's important, but nobody else does. I don't either, John. The guy was handcuffed, or don't you remember? Tell me, how could he have called you?"

"Hands-free dialing. Voice-activated calling. There are ways," I said.

Maybe you didn't secure the handcuffs, I thought. Maybe you two were working together. . . . Maybe . . .

I waved my hand and banished that suspicion to where I thought it belonged—nowhere.

"Okay," I said. "Tell me, what's your take on Swain?"

"He gives me the shivers," Clegg said, "but then again, all level three sex offenders seem to have that effect on me."

"So how do we nail this guy? I don't know anything about evidence gathering and warrants, and you do. Tell me, you think that guy is clean?"

"Even if I do, you're not going to drop this, are you, John?" Clegg said.

"A murderer is running freely in this city, he's got Ruby and me in his sights, we're living every single moment in absolute terror, and if the cancer doesn't get to my wife first, then the stress we're under will. So, no, I'm not going to drop this, not for one freaking second am I going to drop this."

The line went silent for a while—long enough so that I thought maybe *his* call got dropped.

"Do you really want to go all the way with this, John?"

"I do," I said. "I really do."

"Okay. Then this is what we're doing. At ten o'clock tonight, head out the back door. My meeting with Higgins should be over by then. Nobody is watching your back entrance, so nobody will know you're gone."

"Why all the subterfuge?" I asked.

"Because I don't want anybody to know we're together, in case things go south. Pick me up in front of Chaps. Dress in black."

"Sounds ominous. Where are we going? What are we doing?" I asked.

"Me and you are going to break into Carl Swain's house and see what we can see."

CHAPTER 49

I went over to Ruby, who was sitting on the futon with Ginger on her lap. My pulse fluttered. I didn't know how she'd react to Clegg's offer. I looked out the window at the gathering darkness, wondering if the adrenaline rush would last up until ten o'clock, or if I'd pass out from nerves beforehand. I thought about it—all the crimes I'd already committed—and realized it wasn't my nerves that had me jacked to the nines, but rather a feeling of unbridled excitement. I was honestly looking forward to breaking into Swain's house.

What the heck was I becoming?

"I'm going out with Clegg in a couple of hours," I said.

Ruby gave me a curious look. "Where are you going?"

"We're going to take a little drive over to Carl Swain's house."

"No!" Ruby said.

"You don't even know what we're going to do."

"Nothing good, I can tell."

"Ruby, we've got to get the police some real evidence, and Swain is the guy. Clegg is willing to help us, so I hope you'll get over thinking of him as somehow involved. Forget the purse snatcher, too. It's got to be Swain. He's a sicko who was watching Tanya Uretsky like a hawk. Now, I'm going back to that house, and I'm leaving there with evidence that's going to give the police probable cause to execute a proper search warrant and make an arrest."

Ruby snarled in disgust. "Don't get all self-righteous on me, John," she said. "You're not in charge of capturing this killer. That's what the police are for. Have *Clegg* break in and get what they need if that's what it takes."

"Clegg won't go if I won't go," I said. "He needs a lookout."

"So, what? You're going to go all Rambo on me now?"

"I'm not just doing this for us," I said. "I'm doing it for Rhonda, for Jenna, your mom, and everyone else this Fiend has terrorized, including us."

"Then I'm going with you." Ruby got up, to Ginger's great displeasure.

"No," I said—and a firm no at that. "I'll be fine. I couldn't live with myself if anything happened to you. Please—"

"What about me? You're going to leave your cancer-stricken wife a widow?"

"Look, I'm not going to take any unnecessary chances. I swear. I'm going to be with Clegg the entire time."

"Oh, like that's supposed to make me feel better," Ruby said, her eyes downcast and her voice sharp with disappointment.

"You've got to trust him," I said. "And we've got to do something to get out from under this Fiend. There's no other way. I'm going, Ruby, and I need your support here."

Ruby folded her arms and shot me a disapproving scowl that eventually softened into something less hostile. She sighed and fell into my arms, and we swayed a bit with our bodies entwined. "I trust you, John. I *really* do. If you think this is the only way out from under him, then it's what we have to do, but," she said, holding up a finger, "but you're checking in every fifteen minutes. Text. Call. Whatever. Every fifteen minutes, no exceptions."

"No exceptions," I said, kissing her forehead, pulling her closer, and holding on tighter. "Just stay in the apartment while I'm gone. The police are out front, so you'll be safe."

I kissed Ruby on the lips and we sat awhile on the futon, draped in each other's arms. Eventually Ruby fell asleep with her head on my shoulder. When she awoke, I already had on my darkest clothes. Ruby stood up sleepily and greeted me at the front door, holding Ginger in her arms.

"Any last requests?" I asked her, zipping my black Windbreaker.

"Yeah, baby. Come back," Ruby said.

I smiled, a bit shamefaced, and held up a finger—one point for me, the gesture conveyed—and sang, "Any kind of fool could see, there was something in everything about you."

Ruby's worried expression didn't budge. Not surprisingly, she didn't smile back.

Clegg was waiting for me outside Chaps when I pulled up to the curb. Like me, he was dressed head to toe in black.

The first question he asked right after he climbed into Ziggy was, "How's Winnie?" That wasn't the sort of thing a killer would want to know. It made me feel even more foolish for having had a fleeting suspicion that my friend and former climbing companion could somehow be embroiled in all this.

"She's stable, but still unresponsive," I said. "Ruby and I are going to the hospital tomorrow to see her."

"If she dies," Clegg said, his eyes fixed forward, "the DA is going to charge you with second-degree murder."

I swallowed hard. "Thanks for being such a cheery conversationalist," I said.

"Just reporting the facts," Clegg said. "I don't think you fully understand the trouble you're in, John. Why do you think I'm going to break into this guy's house?"

"Um . . . because I saved your life once," I said.

Clegg chuckled. "Yeah, I suppose that has something to do with it. Let's go."

I drove away.

It wasn't a good feeling being back in this Medford neighborhood again, but for some reason—ill-advised, probably—I believed that we were in the right place and about to do the right thing.

We drove past the Uretskys' house, which had crime-scene tape splayed across the front door but no police detail keeping watch. Clegg had me park Ziggy a bit down the road from Swain's house, but with good enough sight lines to conduct some sort of surveillance. I texted Ruby, told her we'd arrived and that all was well. She texted back that she was fine, too, but worried to death and wanted me to know how much she loved me, simple as that.

Clegg and I spent a few minutes sitting in his car, watching Swain's dark house, looking for lights to come on or other signs that some-body might be at home.

"They could have gone out," I said. "Mom and son enjoying an ice cream."

"At ten thirty at night? I don't think so on the ice cream, but they could be out," Clegg said, agreeing.

"I was kidding about the ice cream," I said.

Clegg gave me a stern look. "We're about the break into some-body's house," he said. "Now is not the right time for levity."

Outside the car the hum of nighttime insects provided the sooth-ing soundtrack to suburbia. Clegg glanced at his watch and used binoculars to make a closer inspection. The house was deceptive in its construction. It was built on a sloping hill, so even though from the outside it appeared to be a two-story structure, there was actually a basement accessible from that patio area out back. We couldn't see if the basement lights were on without checking behind the house. My eyes were again drawn to that odd, windowless structure slapped on top of the garage. It could have been a room—an extension of the attic, perhaps. Maybe someone was hanging out upstairs right now, but there was no way we could tell without going inside.

"So what's the plan?" I asked.

"The plan is for you stay put and for me to go check around back."

"I'm going with you," I said.

"Hey, we're not Starsky and Hutch," Clegg said, removing a gun from his ankle holster. He did that thing cops do in the movies, when they make sure their weapon is ready for action—pulling back on something, hearing a click, looking for ammo, whatever. I didn't know shit about guns. He put on dark gloves and gave me a pair to wear as well. That got my adrenaline flowing again.

"I need you to watch the house and honk the horn if you see any lights come on. If the house is clear, I'll come back and get you. I want you to be there with me and see this for yourself."

"Why's that?"

"Because if the search comes up empty, I'm going to need you to drop Carl Swain from your memory banks and spend the rest of your energy looking out for Ruby while we do our job and catch this nut bag. Sound like a plan?"

"Anything you say, Hutch," I said.

"Screw you," Clegg said, getting out of the car. "And if *anything*, I'm Starsky."

I watched Clegg slide like a shadow across the street, then saw him work his way along the side of the house until eventually he vanished from my view around back. During my watch, the Swain home, lovely as it ever was, remained dark and uninviting. Using the binoculars Clegg brought, I tried to see if the curtains were moving, a flutter or a part, but these weren't the night-vision variety, so I had a hard time seeing anything. I don't know how much time had passed while I kept watch over the house, a while, anyway, when somebody knocked hard on the driver's side window and I jumped in my seat—okay, maybe I screamed a little, too.

I swiveled my head and saw Clegg standing there.

"The back door is open, and nobody is at home," he said. "Let's go have ourselves a little look-see."

I followed Clegg around back, seeing the same stuff I had seen before: the rusted, lopsided trampoline—who ever jumped on it?—the toolboxes, and of course, that ugly birdbath. The back door was shut, but Clegg turned the knob and pulled it right open.

"How'd you get it unlocked?" I asked.

Clegg flashed me a compact kit that contained a gleaming set of silver tools, the likes of which I'd never seen before. "Brought a lock-pick kit with me," he said, sporting a pleased-with-himself smile. "You should know the closest thing to a criminal, John, is a cop."

I flashed again on Ruby and her usually spot-on instincts.

Clegg removed two small flashlights from his back pocket and handed one to me. I followed Clegg inside, shining my light around to get a good look at the wood-paneled basement into which we had entered. It smelled musty, and I could almost feel the mold growing underneath the nappy carpeting. If ever there was a place to hang a velvet painting of a leopard in a tree or a sad clown holding a balloon, well, this was it. A patchwork couch with toy blocks for legs stood in front of a thirty-two-inch television that had a milk crate for a TV stand. A tall bookshelf on one wall, covered by a dark varnish and scratched like a well-loved Beach Boys record, was stocked with paperback novels that added to the moldy smell. An upright piano stood against another wall—a flea market purchase at best—which surely would have been out of tune had I dared tickle the ivories. There wasn't much in the way of evidence down here. Smelly piles of clothes, empty food containers, and stacks of yellowing newspapers, but nothing that said, "Hey. I'm the Fiend."

I heard a sound, a click of some sort, and quickly shone my light in that direction.

"Easy, John," Clegg said, gripping my arm. "I checked the house from top to bottom. Nobody is home. Houses make noises, so don't get freaked every time you hear one."

"Where could they be?" I asked, whispering.

"Who knows?" Clegg said, not whispering. "Maybe our little police visit spooked 'em. Maybe Mommy and sonny boy split town for a while, until the Uretsky heat dies down. Anyway, we've got the run of the joint for now, so let's have a good look around."

Four rooms comprised the entire lower level—the basement family room, into which we had entered, usable only by a family that didn't mind mold and filth in equal measure; a nasty bathroom that had a fetid stench all its own; a paneled bedroom with two twin beds set atop a different nappy carpet; and a utility room with linoleum flooring and plasterboard walls. Clegg and I searched the family room and bedroom thoroughly but came up empty. Nasty clothes, unclean rooms, and mold might get unsanitary marks from *Good Housekeeping,* but it wasn't going to inspire a judge to sign a search warrant order.

Clegg went upstairs, while I explored the utility room some more. My flashlight beam gleamed off the yellowing linoleum floor as I scanned the baseboard perimeter, looking for whatever, something useful, all the while surprised that my heart rate kept to a steady and even rhythm. Here I was, breaking into somebody's house, calm as if the owners had given me the key. The Fiend's game had trained me for this moment—transformed me into a pro's pro of the criminal variety.

I found a box of electronics, old cell phones, wires, speaker cables, and such, and was rummaging through that when Clegg called, "John! Come here! Come quick!"

I found Clegg in a carpeted hallway, standing beside an unfolded stairwell, which I presumed led up to an attic space. He had a grin on his face that made me think of the clichéd cat having eaten a certain yellow bird.

"You've got to see what's up here to believe what's up here, amigo," he said.

CHAPTER 50

My first thought: *How many computers does this guy own?* My second thought: *What the hell is all this crap?* I stood upright on a carpeted floor in the middle of a stuffy, airless attic.

Clegg found a switch that turned on a bank of overhead lights. A long particleboard desk ran parallel to the sloping ceiling. The desk was jam-packed with computers, four monitors, two laptops, and a couple printers, nice ones, too. Underneath the desk I found a jumble of wires, hubs, and Internet routers—a typical computer nerd setup with all the accoutrements associated with digital know-how.

But it was the other wall that had me all sorts of freaked out. Neatly arranged on pegs and shelving units was—and I knew this only from bad cable movies—a wide variety of BDSM equipment, an acronym made up of the interchangeable words *bondage, discipline, dominance, submission, sadism,* and *masochism.*

Clegg took out his flashlight and shone it on one particular item hanging close to my head. "Does that look like the kind of gag SHS used?"

I looked at the big black ball secured to a leather strap containing silver locking buckles and thought of Dr. Lisa Adams. I remembered her so clearly—tied to a heavy oak chair, a naked bulb dangling above her head, a ball gag that could have very well been this one stuffed into her mouth.

"Yeah," I said, my voice carrying softly on the stream of unpleasant memories. "It could be this one."

I didn't know what a lot of this stuff was, but Clegg seemed to have a good idea.

"I used to work SVU," he said. "We learned these things. Over here, you've got your basic bondage mittens," he said, shining a light on pouch-like coverings that could be secured around the wrists.

"I'm impressed that anybody could make a mitten creepy," I said.

"And here we've got a nice assortment of rings, not for your fingers, and here we've got your classic humbler."

"What's a humbler?" I asked.

Clegg paused, holding his flashlight steady on the apparatus with a cuff and a clasp mounted to a concave bar. The device could easily fit around the back of a person's legs. "Let's just say it's nasty, and leave it at that," Clegg said.

Some of the items I could figure out on my own—something to spread the legs apart, a straitjacket, ropes, shackles, black leather masks, hoods, restraints of one variety or another. What I didn't see were any masks of Super Mario with cutout eyeholes or even a black ski mask with red stitching around the mouth and eyes.

Clegg walked by me, headed to the other side of the attic, where a shuttered door offered the promise of a needed discovery—something that would make this cache of the ultra-creepy a slam dunk from a warrant perspective. Maybe the incriminating masks would be stashed in there. Perhaps we'd find videotapes of Dr. Adams's and Winnie's kidnapping and torture sessions. Maybe we'd even find the bloody pruning shears used to sever the fingers of the Fiend's four known victims. I wondered, too, about those computers. What did they have on them? Deranged pornography probably, the stuff that made use of all that equipment hanging on the walls, perhaps something else, something even more sinister.

Clegg whistled me over, and I soon found myself inside a large, windowless room about the size of the single-car garage that I figured was directly below us. The ceiling was sloped here as well, but there was still plenty of room for a wooden bed that had all sorts of loops and hooks and chains and things for strapping and holding and restraining people. The bed wasn't made, but a pillow and a crumpled pile of blankets convinced me that somebody actually slept up here.

"I'm guessing Mom doesn't change the sheets," Clegg said.

"Clearly, Swain hasn't vanquished all of his sexual proclivities," I said.

"I'd say you're right," Clegg answered.

"So what now?"

"Now you look at those computers and see what you can find," Clegg said.

I was about to tell him that was a great idea when a sound made my breath catch. It was a rumbling noise directly below our feet, a steady churn, and I heard the distinct rattle of a chain being moved by a motor.

"Aw, shit," Clegg said. "Looks like somebody's come home."

My heart was beating fast. Clegg didn't seem the least bit bothered.

"What are we going to do?" I asked. "There's no way we're getting out of this house without being seen."

In response, Clegg took out his smartphone and snapped a bunch of pictures. He took pictures of the bed, pictures of the computers, pictures of the BDSM collection.

He put his arm around me in a comforting gesture. "John," he said, speaking calmly, "we're going to have to leave here now. No time to search those computers, I'm afraid. But we've got something here." He showed me his smartphone. "I'll say that somebody anonymously sent me these pictures I just took."

"Can you do that?" I asked.

Clegg cracked a half smile. "Why not?" he said with a shrug. "I'm the police."

"You think that'll be enough?" I asked. All the while I was imagining that the person who'd driven into the garage was entering the house.

"It's the best we've got," Clegg said.

"How are we going to explain being here to the person or persons downstairs?" I asked.

Clegg went over to the wall and took down two black BDSM hoods from their respective nail pegs. He used a penknife, which he took from his back pocket, to rip open two sets of eyeholes.

"Put this on," he said.

"What?"

"We don't have much time," Clegg said. "Put on the hood, and do everything that I tell you to do."

I slipped the hood over my head. Without a lot of ventilation, my quick breaths made the hood stiflingly hot. I looked over at Clegg, who had a hood on as well, gun drawn, and a bunch of ropes in his hand.

"Okay, John," he said, his voice sounding muffled. "Time for us to leave."

That's when I heard a voice call up the stairs, a voice I recognized as belonging to Carl Swain's mother, Lucille.

My heart felt like it was moving to a calypso beat. Clegg motioned with his gun for me to take a few steps back. He stood on one side of the stairwell, while I took a position on the opposite side of the stairs. If anybody came up the stairs, we wouldn't be seen until they actually entered the attic space and turned around. I heard a creak as some weight was applied to the bottom step, followed by another creak, and still another. With the black hood on, Clegg looked like an executioner in waiting, and I assumed I looked the same.

"Carl? Are you up here, sweetie?" a scratchy voice called, and a head poked up through the folding stairwell opening.

Clegg waited until Swain's mother had ventured all the way up the stairs before making his move. He stuck the gun into the small of her back and said, "Get facedown on the floor now. Right now! Do it!"

Swain's mother turned her head to the right and then to the left, seeing both our shapeless, covered heads. She shrieked as Clegg pushed her to the floor. "I said, get facedown on the floor. Is anybody with you?" Clegg asked.

Lucille didn't answer.

"Is anybody with you?" he asked again.

"Yes, my son is here," she said. Her voice carried a noticeable tremor.

Clegg wrenched her arm up toward her shoulder until she cried out in pain.

"Tell the truth," he said. "Are you alone?"

"Yes! Yes! Please! I'm alone! Please don't hurt me."

"Where is your son?" Clegg asked.

"I don't know," Swain's mom said.

Clegg did the arm wrench thing again, and she shrieked again.

"Please . . . I don't know where Carl went. . . . He took off after the police questioned him about the Uretskys. That's the truth. Please don't hurt me."

Using one of the ropes, it took Clegg all of thirty seconds to secure Lucille's wrists behind her back. He used another rope to tie her ankles. Then he got the ball gag from off the wall. He knelt down so that Swain's mother could see his hooded face.

"You'll have to wear this," Clegg said.

Her protest lasted only a few seconds before Clegg forced the ball into her mouth. He tightly secured the strap around her head.

"Can you breathe all right?" Clegg asked.

Swain's mom nodded, her eyes widening.

"I'll make a call in a bit so you won't stay tied up for too long. Sorry about this." Clegg turned to me and said, "Down the stairs posthaste."

We got down the stairs, ripped off our hoods, and tossed them back up into the attic. Clegg kept his gun drawn, checking every corner. He couldn't trust the word of a woman he had just bound and gagged. Seeing no obstacles in our way, we dashed out the back door, ran around the side of the house, and before I could say, "Holy freakin' cannoli"—which is exactly what I ended up saying—I had the keys in Ziggy's ignition and the engine fired up. I drove down the street past the Uretskys' house with the headlights off and didn't turn them on until Swain's house was out of sight.

I was about say a lot of things to Clegg—"Are you nuts?" "Are we nuts?" "What did we just do?"—when I felt a buzz in my pocket and realized I hadn't sent Ruby a text in ages. My hands were shaking as I went to retrieve my phone. I thought it was strange, because she hadn't sent me a message, either.

I pulled the car to the side of the road a safe distance from Swain's house.

Where are you? I thought you were downstairs at the back door? she had written.

My blood turned icy. *No,* I thought. Why would she even think that? I never told her I was headed back. I never asked her to meet me downstairs at the back door. I had my keys. A horrible sick feeling crawled through my stomach.

I texted Ruby, my shaking hands making it hard for me to type: **Where are you?**

Clegg watched the whole thing unfold. "What's wrong?" he asked. "What's going on?"

No response from Ruby. I texted her again, ignoring Clegg, feeling my throat close up. **Where are you!** I wrote. **Answer me!**

I told Clegg to hang on. He hung. A few minutes later, the wait pure agony, my phone finally vibrated.

"What's going on, John?" Clegg shouted.

"Oh please . . . oh please," I kept saying, terrified to look at the phone's display.

"John!" Clegg yelled. "Talk to me!"

I glanced down at my phone, and a sob broke from my mouth, low and shaky, like a rumbling earthquake. The words written on the display blurred as my vision went blank, but I saw them long enough to make sense of it all.

The opening line of the message read: **You're not the only one who knows how to spoof a phone number.** The second line read: **You and I need to have a little talk.**

The third line was a link to a Web site.

CHAPTER 51

"It's Ruby. He's got Ruby!"

I tossed Clegg my phone so he could read the message for himself. My ears were buzzing. Soon everything went dark. Each breath felt like it would be my last. I blanketed my face with my hands, feeling sick with dread.

"I don't get it," Clegg said. "How did he do this?"

I don't remember speaking, but I had the vague sense of having explained all about phone spoofing—how hackers used the technique to make a call or send a text from one number and make it look like it came from another. I think I told him I used the technique myself to steal the Uretskys' identities. The buzzing in my ears made it hard to think.

"Turn the car around," Clegg said. I lifted my head and looked to him for clarification, but his cool eyes were as revealing as a fog.

"Where are we going?" I asked. "What are we going to do?"

"We're going back to Swain's house," he said.

"Why?" My voice sounded unrecognizable, so steeped in desperation. "Shouldn't I just call up that URL on my iPhone? I've got to see Ruby!"

"John, there are plenty of computers back at Swain's house," Clegg said, sounding like an experienced climber conversing with a skittish novice. "Let's use one of those."

"I still don't get it. Why go back there?" I asked. My body trembled with worry, while Clegg, as a counterpoint, didn't so much as twitch an eyebrow.

"If you're right, and Mr. SHS is Carl Swain, then I think what we're going to need is a hostage to exchange."

This time I parked Ziggy right in front of Swain's house. Clegg and I climbed out at the same time and slammed our doors shut synchronously, too. Distress had replaced prudence. Again we went around back, and again Clegg used his lock-pick kit to open the door. This time, Clegg followed my frantic dash upstairs. I made my way hurriedly to the attic's foldout stairwell, but before I could take a single step up, Clegg grabbed my arm from behind and pulled me back down.

"You don't want her to see your face," he said. "Let me go up first."

I nodded, unable to speak. What I could do, and easily, was imagine the absolute worst. My mind's eye saw Ruby tied to the same horrible oak chair as Dr. Adams and Winnie once were. An all-consuming despair overcame me as I thought about her struggling to break free from those restraints. I pictured the Fiend flashing those bloody pruning shears, threatening to do what he liked to do.

Clegg disappeared up those rickety stairs, the slanted ladder bending with his weight. Moments later I heard him shout, "Get facedown! Facedown, now!" He sounded just like a cop making an arrest. Then I heard some shuffling, followed by a bit of grunting, footsteps overhead, and then a door slamming shut. "Okay, come up!" Clegg yelled down.

When I got upstairs, I saw Clegg standing by the door to the small room that contained the bondage bed. The muffled sobs of Swain's mother filtered out into the larger room.

"She's in there," Clegg said, pointing to the shuttered door behind him. "I'll watch her. You do your thing."

"You had to lock her up?" I asked.

"You want to wear a hood?"

I turned on Swain's computer, grateful he didn't password-protect his machine. All his computers came with built-in cameras, which would be necessary to communicate with the Fiend—and to see Ruby.

Working quickly, I typed the URL from my iPhone into a Web browser. A password prompt came up, asking only for a first and last name. I typed "John Bodine" and got an access denied message. Then I typed "Elliot Uretsky." A live video stream came up, showing me that well-worn oak chair, the dangling naked bulb on a brown extension cord, the corded pipes dripping filthy rust-colored water. My whole body became weightless and heavy in the same instant.

However, instead of seeing Ruby seated on that chair as I had expected, there was a note penned with a black marker in neat all-caps handwriting on a piece of white rectangular cardboard. The note read: *Be back soon. Hang tight!* The scene, unchanging, could have been a photograph.

"What's going on?" Clegg asked.

"She's not there," I said. "Come look."

Clegg grabbed a bondage chair, yet another piece of disturbing furniture with straps and hooks and ways of holding people down, and jammed it underneath the doorknob of the room where we were holding Swain's mom captive.

"Is she still tied up?" I asked.

"Yeah, but I've learned over the years that people can be crafty. Better to play it safe."

He found the bondage hood with the eye slits cut out on the floor and slipped it over his head.

"What are you doing now?" I asked.

"Taking precautions," he said. "SHS knows your face, but he doesn't know mine."

Clegg read the note on the video feed while I paced in a tight circle and tried to keep from throwing up.

"What do we do?" I asked. I found it impossible to maintain eye contact with Clegg while he wore that hood.

"We wait," Clegg said, his voice muffled by the fabric covering his mouth. "Just like the note tells us to do."

CHAPTER 52

I slumped to the floor, legs useless, arms hanging limply by my sides. Clegg came over and knelt down beside me.

"Take off that hood," I said. "I can't look at you with that thing on."

Clegg shook his head. "Precautions," he said again. "I don't know when our guy is going to show up on the video feed."

"You're crazy. But you know that already, don't you?"

"If you want to save Ruby, I'm thinking we're going to both have to be a little bit on the crazy side," Clegg said.

I felt separated from my body, afloat and shapeless. "I can't live with myself if anything happens to her."

I wished I hadn't voiced that possibility, worried it might somehow make it all come true. Clegg didn't answer me. I could see his eyes through those slits in the black fabric of his hood but failed to pick up even a trace of worry.

"How can you be so calm?" I asked him. "I feel sick inside. I can't stop shaking."

"Same way you were calm when you decided which rope you were going to cut," he said. "When somebody's life is on the line, you act first, panic later."

I looked up at the computer, blinking, as if that would make Ruby appear. Between blinks the video feed went completely black. I rushed over to the computer, started moving the mouse around, manically pressing keys on the keyboard, doing everything I could think to do to make the black screen refresh and show me the room again. As much as I loathed reconnecting with that horrible setting, I didn't want a second to go by where I wouldn't be able to see Ruby.

A minute passed. Then two. Then five. The computer screen flickered as I fiddled with the keyboard and mouse, and when it refreshed, she was there: Ruby tied to that oak chair, her arms and wrists secured by thick ropes, a ball gag shoved into her mouth, her strawberry hair matted down by sweat. A jagged tear in Ruby's pink pajamas left one of her bony shoulders completely exposed. I could see red marks on her face and neck, along with other welts and bruises, too.

"Ruby! Baby!" I felt gutted by an invisible knife that sliced me from belly to chest. "Let her go. . . . Let her go . . . please," I begged. "Whoever you are. Come take me. I'll do anything."

A masked figure rose from below the camera's lens, slowly and purposefully, as if wanting to delay the reveal in dramatic fashion. I believed it was Carl Swain who appeared from below the camera's scope, but until I saw his face, he'd remain the Fiend. It took a moment to make sense of the grotesque disguise he wore, but soon enough I had it figured out. The blue police cap adorning the zombie policeman mask was ripped and faded, as if long buried in the ground. The gray crinkled face of the mask featured a twisted mouth and two rows of pointed teeth set askew into decaying black gums, all below white pupils encased in yellow eyes. The rubbery skin, pinched in places and made to look flayed in others, did a good job portraying rot and decay.

"Hey, John," the Fiend said, his voice muffled within that mask. "Long time no see. Miss me?"

"Let her go!" I screamed.

The Fiend cocked his masked head to one side in a calm manner. "Where are you?" he asked, lowering the level of his gaze to get a better look at the scenery behind me. "I see lots of interesting things tacked on the wall."

"You know where I am, Swain," I said.

Do I have it right . . . ? Are you Swain? The Fiend?

"Oh, you've figured me out, have you?" he said. "Actually, I do know where you are. I have a GPS tracker fixed to the bottom of your car. How'd you think I knew I could go and get me some Ruby?"

"Why don't you take off your mask and show your face, you coward?"

"No can do," he said. "See, I like our game, our little mystery. Do you know who I am? Can you be certain?"

A thick clump of Ruby's hair fell in front of her eyes. She rolled her head from side to side to shake away the irritation, but the hair, heavy with sweat, wouldn't budge. Her chest heaved and fell with each uneven breath.

Without thinking, I reached out and put a gloved hand on the computer monitor, touching the pixels of her hair, and imagined I could do for her what her own hands could not.

From behind me I heard a door open and turned my head to see Clegg dragging Swain's mother out of the BDSM bedroom. She was blindfolded. No problem finding one of those around here. The ball gag stayed in her mouth, and with her arms and legs still tied, the only way to move her was to drag her. Clegg, his face still obscured underneath the fetish hood, pushed Swain's mother in front of the computer's built-in camera.

"So if you know where we are," Clegg said, "then you know who this is. You let Ruby go, and nothing will happen to her." Clegg held Swain's limp and listless mother up to the camera like she was a puppet in a puppet show.

A dreadful feeling overcame me. "What are you doing?" I said through clenched teeth. "Ruby's life is at stake! Don't mess with him!"

"Trust me," Clegg said, his voice sharpened to a harsh whisper.

"I heard that," the Fiend said. "So now this is really fun. We've got two men in masks, two women with ball gags stuffed in their mouths, and you, John, the odd man out. I love it! Who's your pal under the hood? Look, I won't blow his cover, but is that your friend repaying a debt? A little police work outside the lines of the law? Oh boy, you guys inspire me."

"Please, my friend means what he says," I told him. "He'll hurt your mother, and I won't be able to stop him."

Swain's mother squirmed and squealed, trying to break free from Clegg, but her efforts were weak and futile.

"You know something? That's so unbelievably convenient," the Fiend said, sounding exuberant. "You can commit your next crime, right here and right now."

I stammered before I could speak. My body tingled. "What do you want me to do? Tell me."

"The SHS Killer—that's what they're calling me," the Fiend said in his distinctive rasp. "I'm becoming something of a cult figure around town, a real media super whore, and I want you to broaden that legacy."

"What?" I was unsure of what I heard, unable to make sense of it all.

Clegg must have squeezed or pinched Swain's mother. She cried out in pain. "We'll make an exchange," Clegg said, his voice a growl beneath that hood. "Mom for Ruby."

"No exchanges," the Fiend said. "It's time for John to step up to the plate in his criminal career and swing for the fences. Look at his progression. I admire you, John. Honestly, I do. You've put in a lot of hard work into all of this, but now it's time to take things to a completely new level. It's time for you to become a murderer like me. I want you to kill another person just the way I would do it. Choke the life out of someone. Then cut off the fingers and leave 'em . . . well, you know where.

"So if you want to kill Mommy Dearest, go right ahead and do it. But make sure you tell your police buddies where to find the body. Because if there isn't a new victim of the SHS Killer reported on the news within thirty-six hours, I'm going to give them one, and it will be your lovely wife, John. I'll cut off her fingers, one by one, and smile as she bleeds until I get bored with her misery. Then I'll choke her until she sees nothing, hears nothing, and speaks nothing ever again."

Before I could say another word, the live chat went dark, and my Ruby was gone.

CHAPTER 53

Clegg took off his hood, I guess because Lucille still had her blindfold on. She couldn't see the barrel of his gun pressed up against the back of her skull, but I'm sure she could feel the biting cold of its steel. Her body trembled, while these awful whimpering noises leapt from her throat.

"Did you recognize your son's voice? Shake your head yes or no!" Clegg kept her pinned to the floor by straddling her thin frame, holding the gun steady, finger cocked on the trigger.

Swain's mother rolled her head violently from side to side.

"He's disguising his voice," I said.

"What? Like Batman in those movies?"

"Yeah, just like Batman."

I couldn't believe that in my most desperate hour the Dark Knight had somehow become part of this conversation.

"Crap," Clegg said.

"What do we do?" I asked.

Clegg undid the ropes securing Swain's mom's wrists and made a careful examination of the skin. He undid her leg restraints as well. "Good thing these ropes don't leave a mark," he said.

My jaw fell open when Clegg removed a pair of handcuffs from the equivalent of his utility belt and secured those around her wrists. Afterward, Clegg removed her blindfold.

"What are you doing? I thought we couldn't let her see our faces."

Almost immediately, those sickly, yellowing eyes fell to me and widened with recognition. "You have the right to remain silent," Clegg said, removing the ball gag from her crinkled mouth.

Soon as the gag came free, she howled, "You!"

Clegg continued with her Miranda rights.

"You're cops?" she said.

"I'm a cop," Clegg said. "He's my friend. And she," Clegg said, looking at me while pointing at Lucille, "pulled a gun on us."

"I don't follow."

"We came here looking for Carl," Clegg explained. "Mom apparently didn't like us coming around, so she pulled a gun on us. There's a gun here, right?" he asked Lucille. She didn't answer, but Clegg didn't seem to care. "That's okay," he said. "I'll find it."

"That's a lie!" Lucille barked. Her mouth looked as snarled as the Fiend's zombie policeman mask. "You're both liars."

"No, I'm a police officer with the BPD," Clegg said. "And you're the mother of a level three sex offender who probably knew all about your boy's weird little BDSM hangout. So nobody is going to believe your story. Not even your lawyer. Say, how much kiddie porn does Carl boy have on these computers? Any idea? Well, we'll find out soon enough."

"So we just take her into custody?" I asked.

"That's what we do," Clegg said. "And then you and I need to go and have a little powwow about how we're going to get your wife back."

I sat alone at a Formica table in a waiting room at police headquarters in downtown Boston, vaguely aware of a CNN news report blaring from a wall-mounted TV. Even though the Medford police had taken Lucille into custody, Clegg still had to process paperwork for the booking, which left me alone with my dark thoughts.

Despair washed over me in great waves. Ruby. My Ruby. Where was Ruby? Carl Swain, meanwhile, had become the prime suspect in the SHS killings, finally. Bringing in Mama Swain added fresh urgency to an already frenetic investigation. Ruby became media fodder, her picture broadcast across every news outlet. Search warrants and APBs were being issued. Carl Swain was considered armed and dangerous and not to be approached.

I fought to hold myself together. I thought about survivalists, the people whose stories inspired my own adventuring—Shackleton; the sailors from the sailing ship *Essex;* Joe Simpson and Simon Yates, whose nearly fatal climb of Siula Grande was turned into the movie *Touching the Void;* the Uruguayan rugby team who survived ten weeks in the Argentine Andes. Their stories, their trials and tribulations gave me a shot of strength, a glimmer of hope that I would see and hold Ruby once again. Not knowing what else to do, I got down on my knees in that lonely waiting room and looked past the drop ceiling and fluorescent lights. I envisioned my affirmation. It was how Ruby had taught me to make things happen. Ask of the universe, and the universe shall provide.

I will find you, Ruby.

I will bring you home.

I will set right what I have made wrong.

Clegg entered the waiting room some time later and found me asleep on the same Formica table.

"John, let's talk," he said, shaking me alert.

I looked up at him, my eyes raw and red for sure. Clegg offered me an oil slick in a Styrofoam cup, which I declined. He took a long sip, evidently accustomed to the drink, and fixed me with a hard stare.

"We've got to face the reality here," Clegg said.

"How long have I been out?" I asked, my voice scratchy and hoarse.

"A few hours," he said. "You need it. For Ruby. You need to rest when you can rest."

"What are we going to do? How do we find her?"

"Our computer forensic guys might not be able to trace the location of the chat."

"But they're looking at Swain's computer?"

"Yeah, they're looking," Clegg said. "All the computers, the Uretskys', too."

Something Clegg had said triggered a thought—a clouded, still developing thought, but a thought nonetheless.

"Games," I said.

"What?"

"I found Elliot through my game, but how did he find Elliot?"

"What do you mean?" Clegg asked.

Shaking my head, I tried to dislodge the sleepiness that seemed to block my thinking.

"Elliot is the only male murder victim of the Fiend that we know of. We've been trying to figure out why, and I think I've come up with something."

"Go on."

"We need to find out if the Fiend and Elliot knew each other through my game. I mean, how did he come to know Elliot? Does he play my game, *One World,* or were they playing a different game? I know it's a game that brought us three together, but I don't know if it's the same game. We should look. We need to find the game linking Elliot to the Fiend. Can you tell the forensics guys to look at the games Elliot was playing, Swain too? There's a link there. I know it."

Clegg nodded. "Of course, John. Look, every cop is working on this. Everybody wants to find Ruby alive, but, John, I wouldn't expect a miracle here. This guy knows how to stay in the shadows, right?"

"He does," I said.

"Like I said, we've got to face the reality of this situation."

"By reality, you mean that we might not be able to find her in thirty-six hours?" I said.

Clegg looked at his watch. "More like thirty," he said.

"So what do we do?"

"Maybe . . . maybe we do what has to be done," Clegg said, his eyes murky.

"I don't understand."

A shroud of secrecy seemed to cover us both. "I know people," Clegg continued, his voice dropping in volume. "People who are not good people. These people that I'm speaking of have somehow managed to slip through the knot of justice. A search warrant issue. Some freakin' technicality. Some reason they managed to escape what should have been a slam-dunk conviction. Escape their punishment."

"I still don't get it," I said.

"Maybe we do what has to be done," Clegg said, repeating what he had said, but speaking each word slowly and emphatically.

I shook my head as though I'd been slapped.

"Are you saying what I think you're saying? Are you nuts?"

"No, I'm a cop. Look, it may be our only hope," he said, delivering this edict with all the feeling of a guy ordering an omelet.

"How could you even suggest such a thing?" I asked.

"I wouldn't be alive if it weren't for you," Clegg said. "My life may not be perfect, but I'm damn glad to be living it. No way I'm going to watch yours go down the toilet without doing everything I can to save it. End of story. Listen, I've read over the FBI's latest profile on the SHS. He plays by rules. He doesn't break them. He'll free Ruby if you comply because he wants to keep playing this game of his.

"Now, there's a reason I told you not to tell anybody what he asked you to do. Nobody knows that he wants you to commit murder. We can't off Swain's mom, now. She's too closely watched. But if another person dies, one of these justice jumpers, well, the cops are going to think the SHS Killer has struck again, and Ruby goes free."

A sour taste rode the back of my tongue.

"I can't think straight," I said. "I . . . I can't take all of this in."

"Sometimes we do what has to be done," Clegg said. "Did Swain's mom pull a gun on us? No. But we said that she did, because we had to. She's no good. She's protecting her son. Fiend or no Fiend, they're going to find kiddie porn on his computer. The forensics guys already told me it's there. She's a dirt bag, and she's getting justice, just in a different way. Sometimes that's how things need to work."

"I don't know. I need time to think about this," I said.

"We have some time," Clegg said. "But not much."

CHAPTER 54

On the day Ruby was kidnapped, Winnie came out of her coma. I felt like my prayers had gotten mixed up somehow. I'd been back in the apartment—yes, John's place—all of two hours when the hospital called with the news. My eyes, heart, and soul felt heavy with the absence around me. The silence filled my ears like screams. I desperately wanted to get out of here, but Ginger needed food, and I needed a bit more sleep. Soon enough, I wouldn't get another chance.

As it turned out, sleep eluded me. I lay on the futon, plagued by inescapable thoughts. I wondered how Ruby slept. Did she stay upright in that chair? Did he feed her? Were her hands ever untied so she could feed herself? Was he giving her water? Could she take her medication? Oh, I doubted that. Did he let her use the bathroom? But the questions I wanted answered above all were, *where* was my wife, and *how* would I find her?

The answers, though grim and difficult to fathom, brought me back to Clegg.

At first, his offer seemed insane. Actually, Clegg seemed insane. I knew the guy had a few bolts loose, but maybe his whole wiring was screwed up. But the more I thought about it, the less crazy the idea became. Who were these people who had, as he put it, slipped through the knot of justice? I wondered. Murderers, rapists, drug czars, I supposed. Were they more deserving of life than Ruby? Could I do the unthinkable? Husbands and wives hire so-called professionals to kill each other all the time—just watch *48 Hours Mystery* or *Dateline*—and they do it for anything but noble causes. He wants her money. She wants her lover and no complications. Assuming you don't get caught, divorce is a lot more expensive than murder. Their reasons are plentiful, and the excuses probably made sense to the perpetrators at the time of the crime. Did Clegg's offer somehow stand on different moral ground? I didn't know. I couldn't answer, so I did the only thing I could think to do.

I went to see Winnie.

Winnie's hospital room smelled of strong cleaning chemicals, which only heightened the scent of sickness. Propped up in her bed, Winnie had the dazed and confused look of a car accident victim shocked by her circumstance. The equipment attached to her, IV drips and heart monitors and such, paled in comparison to the apparatuses employed during her stay in the ICU. Winnie assessed me wide-eyed, as though I could be a mirage. But recognition dawned, and tears fell from her eyes in streams.

"John," she cried, her lips trembling. "What happened? What happened to me?"

Winnie hid her age with dyed hair and a perpetual tan, but her skin looked almost bleached. I saw bruise marks on her neck, thin wrists, and arms. The marks that looked like handprints or rope burns turned my thoughts to Ruby and the marks that would be left on her by the Fiend. I stood beside Winnie's bed and took hold of her shaky hand.

"What happened to me?" Winnie sobbed.

With my throat going tight and dry, I wiped clear her tears and used a damp cloth to help cool her forehead.

"Hi, Winnie," I said. "How are you feeling?"

"I don't understand any of this . . . don't know what happened. . . . Ruby . . . where is Ruby?"

"She's okay," I lied. "She'll come to see you soon."

"Who did this to me, John?" Winnie said. "Why would somebody want to hurt me?"

"I don't know," I said, finding the lies came easily, knowing the truth would be like shoving smoke down her already singed lungs.

"How long have I been here?" she asked. I could feel my resolve weakening, tears pushing against my eyes until they forced their way out. And when they started to flow, they wouldn't stop, and for the first time since this ordeal began, I thought, *Dead is better*. If anything happened to Ruby, if I couldn't free her from the Fiend, how could dead not be better?

"John, what's wrong?" Winnie asked, right before she coughed—the racking, hacking kind of cough that made people wince in sympathy.

"It's nothing," I said. "I'm just glad you're all right."

"What's happening?" Winnie asked.

"What do you remember?"

"Nothing. They said I was in a fire. I remember flying into Boston. I remember a phone call from someone, your friend, I think. What's his name?" Winnie squinted, trying to force the memory. "I can't remember," she said, her disappointment evident. "Ruby's cancer had gone into remission. I remember feeling so happy for her. That's it. . . . That's what I remember. Except . . . except . . ." Winnie cringed. "When can I see Ruby?" she asked.

I was gripping the side of the bed, trying to keep from crying more. That was when I noticed all the vases of flowers surrounding the empty bed in Winnie's two-person hospital room.

"Soon," I said, finding my composure by focusing on those flowers. "Where is your roommate?"

Change the subject. Get yourself together.

"Dead," Winnie said. "She died last night, not long after they moved me in here. She was young, twentysomething, and went into a cardiac arrest. It was quite unexpected and horribly sad. All these doctors and nurses were in here trying to save her. They moved me into the hallway. I didn't want to see it, anyway." Winnie was talking quickly, more like her old self, free-form speech without too many filters. "Her family has been in and out of here grieving all day. The mother is amazing, though. She's donating all of her daughter's organs—eyes, liver, everything. Poor thing had Parkinson's disease. I heard a nurse say they think that's what caused her heart attack. Who knows? So young, so sad. I guess her mother is going to donate her brain to a medical school, so maybe they'll find out.

"God, I want a drink. John, can you get me something to drink? Not water, I mean. Something with a bit of a kick. Maybe a glass of wine. Something to relax me. I'm *dying* for a drink."

Winnie's voice drifted to the back of my mind. I could hear her talking but wouldn't have been able to repeat a single word she said. I could feel the cogs of my brain beginning to turn, slowly at first, but quickening as the momentum began to build. I needed to leave the hospital right away. I needed to find Clegg. I looked up at the clock on the wall and shuddered.

I had twenty-four hours to produce a victim of the SHS Killer or Ruby would die.

And now I knew how I could do it.

CHAPTER 55

The War Room, the centralized meeting place for coordinated information exchanges about the SHS Killer, was located in the basement of the Boston police headquarters at One Schroeder Plaza. Gathered around a long conference table, and eyeing Clegg with a mix of curiosity and suspicion, were all the people essential to locating this predator. Chief Higgins sat across from me, red-faced and paunchy, and to his right were detectives Gant and Kaminski. Special Agent Brenner was also seated at the table, along with a few others from the FBI, the state police, and other agencies with acronyms that were meaningless to me.

I should have expected the hostile reception. Only Clegg knew about my plan, and it was his idea to call this gathering together without first providing details or specifics. Less chance of getting it shot down during one big powwow than if we piecemealed the approvals, he assured me. So nobody here knew what we were going to propose. This was *my* plan, and it explained why and how Clegg got me a seat at the table. He didn't want anything getting lost in translation, and neither did I.

Looking around, I could tell by the fidgeting fingers, long stares, tapping toes that most viewed this impromptu meeting as a giant distraction and profound waste of their time. Of course, they were wrong. The Fiend might have been a step ahead of me before, but this time things would be different.

Following the arrival of some last-minute invitees, Clegg began to speak as soon as the conference room door closed. These people understood the Fiend had kidnapped my wife. They knew that every tick of the clock brought Ruby that much closer to death, but they were not aware that the Fiend wanted me to commit murder in exchange for Ruby's life. As of that moment, we had less than twenty hours to make everything happen.

Papered on the wall behind Clegg were various maps, photographs, timelines, and charts—all the stuff of an investigation that I knew was going nowhere.

"We've heard from the SHS Killer," Clegg began, using the moniker most familiar to this group.

Brenner stood, palms flat on the table, face brightening. "When? How?"

Before this meeting, I had worked things out with Clegg and advanced the lie using some rudimentary computer scripting. Technically, we had obstructed justice by not revealing the Fiend's initial demands from the get-go. Since Clegg worried that we might need to produce an actual victim in exchange for Ruby's life, we couldn't have told them what we needed and produced that very thing without having suspicion cast right on me.

"I think it's best that John tell you what happened," Clegg said.

"Why? He isn't a cop," somebody shouted from the back of the room.

"No, numb nuts," Clegg barked. "He's the guy who came up with a plan to save his wife's life. So show him some respect, or show yourself out the door. Sound good?"

Nobody debated, so I stood up and went to the front of the room while Clegg passed around copies of the e-mail that I wrote myself.

"The person who kidnapped my wife contacted me through my game *One World*," I began. "He used Elliot Uretsky's game account to send me a message."

I had modified the transaction logs for my game server so that the IP address could not be traced. I figured the BPD forensic guys, or the FBI, for that matter, would try and track down the Fiend's location by IP, so I faked them. They were going to hit a dead end, no matter how hard they dug. My plan was all that counted, and I believed this little bit of subterfuge was necessary to set things in motion.

I waited for the folks gathered to get their copy of the simple note. It had sickened me to write it, but I had memorized it nonetheless. I began the letter "Dear John," thinking the Fiend would view the formality of his greeting as a pleasing bit of irony. Brenner and the other experts at the FBI would be dissecting every word, trying to match it to the profile that I helped to create.

I read the letter aloud, just to emphasize the urgency.

"Dear John, it's time for you to take your criminal career to bold new heights. I want another victim of the SHS Killer, and you're going to provide the goods. Man or woman, doesn't matter to me. What I want is a dead body by your hands, with two fingers set upon their dead lips, one in each ear, and two on each eye. See no evil. Hear no evil. Speak no evil. You have twenty-four hours to make this happen, otherwise Ruby is going to be my next victim. Signed, SHS."

"When did you get this?" Higgins asked, rolling the letter up like a wand, shaking it at me.

"Two hours ago," I said. "We're already late."

"John's prepared to turn over his computer to the FBI's forensic guys," Clegg said. "But he has another idea that I think we need to listen to."

Again all eyes fell to me.

"I want to give him a victim," I said.

"Sounds great," Gant said. "Only one small problem. We're the police. We catch killers. We don't employ them."

"My victim is already dead," I said. "I want to use a body donated to a medical school or some research facility. We'll need to make a bunch of calls to relatives of the deceased until we find someone willing to help us. I'm betting that somebody who wanted to use his body to help save lives or train doctors would want to help save my wife's life. Let's just hope the living relatives see it the same way."

Agent Brenner stood again. "How is this going to help us catch him?"

"It's probably not," I said. "Honestly, I don't know how we're going to catch him. Right now, I just want to get Ruby back. That's what matters most to me."

Clegg interjected, "For that, we're going to need Chief Higgins's help."

"Me?" Higgins said, sounding a bit surprised.

"We'll need to arrange a media press conference," Clegg said, "announcing the discovery of a possible new victim of the SHS Killer. You'll say that you can't provide any more details at this time."

"Why are we going to do that?" Higgins asked.

"To get his attention," Clegg said. "Obviously, we can't show a dead and mutilated body on the six o'clock news, but this monster is going to be on the lookout for some sort of news report. He wants another SHS victim. It's all part of his game. We keep a small circle that knows about this in case of any leaks. Everyone involved will think it's a real murder."

"So you think this guy is going to try to contact you after it makes the news," Kaminski said.

I nodded. "He'll demand his proof. That's when I'll send him a video recording of the victim. I'll tell him that Detective Clegg took it for me."

"Will he buy that?" Brenner asked the room.

Clegg said, "We've got to think this guy has already dug into John's past. He'll know that we're friends, so it won't come as a surprise to him that I helped out. Bent a few rules."

You were going to bend a lot more than a few rules, I thought as a hush settled over the room.

"What then?" Higgins asked.

"Then I'm hoping he lets my wife go," I said. My voice cracked. Clegg poured me a glass of water from one of the dew-coated metal pitchers set out around the table. I struggled to get enough air into my lungs. The room felt oven-hot. "Please," I said, pleading. "Don't say no to this. We don't have enough time. He'll kill her. He's going to do it. Please."

Before anyone could answer, the conference room door burst open. In stepped two breathless guys, neither looking like a pinnacle of fitness, or the beneficiaries of sunlight, for that matter. *Computer jocks,* I thought.

"Hey," the stouter of the two said. "Sorry for the interruption, but we just found something on Elliot Uretsky's computer that you've got to see."

"What is it?" Higgins asked.

"We think we know why the SHS Killer is using body parts to communicate the proverb 'See no evil, hear no evil, speak no evil.' "

"Why?" Higgins asked.

"Chief," the guy continued, "you've got to see this to believe it."

CHAPTER 56

I didn't need a badge or credentials to qualify me for inclusion in the big discovery. I was a major stakeholder in this affair—the guy who had played an integral part in the Fiend's twisted game, the only one related by marriage to his potential next victim, close friend of a lead detective, and not to mention the man with a plan. Those were qualifications enough, I suppose. Which must have been why nobody questioned my presence as I followed Clegg up a dingy staircase, through a warren of cubicles, and then along a maze of corridors that called for a bread-crumb trail. A parade of people followed, with Special Agent Brenner close on my heels.

Brenner gripped my arm gently as she pulled up alongside. She spoke softly, the tense quiet of the processional necessitating a hushed voice. "Just so you know, I think your plan is a good one," she said. "He's going to kill her if you don't give him a victim."

"Every second counts," I said, matching her whisper. "I hope what we're about to see isn't a waste of time." Assuming my frayed nerves didn't send me into cardiac arrest, I'd soon find out.

We came to a stop at a shuttered metal door secured by a keypad entry mechanism. On the frosted glass windowpane I read the stenciled words BOSTON POLICE COMPUTER FORENSICS LAB. With the locking mechanism engaged, the door popped open with a swoosh. Our group, a dozen or so strong, shuffled inside in an orderly fashion.

The open floor plan of the carpeted room featured four rows of workstations, none of which had been cordoned off into cubes, with storage space above and file cabinets underneath. Computers and monitors occupied virtually every inch of available work space. Their persistent hum and artificial glow gave me the feeling of being trapped inside some sort of living organism. Two fifty-inch monitors took up most of the front wall, while whiteboards scribbled with obtuse algorithms and equally cryptic notes occupied the two adjacent walls.

People settled themselves into plush seats, swiveling their chairs to direct their attention toward the oversize screens, as if about to watch a movie. Clegg knew I couldn't sit, so he stood with me. His composure contrasted sharply with my churned-up anxiety.

"You're doing great, John," Clegg said, quietly enough so only I could hear.

The buzz of electronics thrummed in my ears and seemed to grow louder, while the powerful air conditioners keeping the room meat-locker cool set bumps upon my skin. "Do you think they're going to do it?" I asked. "Will they help me pull this off?"

"They better," Clegg said, "or I just might end up paying back the debt I owe you."

I flashed Clegg a troubled look. "What are you saying?" I asked him.

He put a finger to his lips and signaled quiet. "Detective Brewer is about to speak."

Detective Aidan Brewer carried all the telltale signs of someone who had spent the past twentysomething hours working at his desk, gazing into a computer monitor's hypnotic glow. Dark puffy circles surrounded his raccoon eyes, marring a plump and boyish face. His brown hair appeared windswept, suggesting that he'd been in a storm of a different sort. He wore his black polo shirt tucked inside a pair of food-stained chinos, and his ample belly looked extra stuffed with fast food.

Brewer pressed a remote control device, and the monitors behind him flickered to show a screen shot of a computer transaction log. Written in green font on a black background, the transaction log provided a detailed accounting of all the Web sites and applications a particular computer had accessed—in this case presumably Uretsky's—including date and time stamps and the amount of computer processing power and megabytes used to complete various tasks.

"We've been dissecting Elliot Uretsky's computer and looking at the various Web sites he visited," Brewer said. He pronounced the word *computer* "compu-tah," a Boston native no doubt. "We were especially interested in games and found evidence that he was a big-time online game fanatic. He's a fan of the game *One World*, owned and operated by one of our suspects, John Bodine."

Clegg cleared his throat loudly. "John is in the room with us, Aidan," he said. "He's not a suspect anymore. In fact, he's the one who suggested you look closely at the games Uretsky was playing."

Heads turned and eyes fell on me, even though most were already aware of my presence.

"Okay, news to me," Brewer said. "Computer guys are always the last to know these things."

I could see Higgins fidgeting in his chair. We were both impatient. I wanted to shout, "Get to the damn point!" but knew that would be counterproductive. Instead, I opened my mind, allowing some positive energy to flow in.

I will find you, Ruby. . . . I will find you . . . and I will find you alive. . . .

"So Uretsky was a big gamer," Brewer went on to say. "He played a bunch of games. Some we've heard of, like *FarmVille* and *Kingdom Age*. Some we hadn't. Like the flash-based game *Streetwise*, in which you play a pimp with a vendetta to kill all your hos. A lot of these online games can be sickeningly violent, full of profanity and sex, and easy to access. Parents give their kids gaming consoles for Christmas, not realizing they can be used to play games that are a heck of a lot more violent than most of the titles rated mature."

"So what other game was Uretsky playing?" Detective Kaminski asked.

"Has anybody ever heard of a game called *See Evil*?"

No hands went up, including my own.

"We've contacted Sick World, the game's manufacturer. We're going to try to get a database dump of all the registered players, as well as anybody who has chatted or messaged Uretsky's game account."

"What's this game all about?" Clegg asked.

The projection behind Brewer flickered and flashed. The screen refreshed with an animated street scene, a cartoon drawing of some nondescript city corner. A hokey-looking cartoon character appeared on-screen, oversize head on a smallish body, animated to enter from screen left. The character, dressed in a nice dress shirt and jeans, had been drawn to have a high forehead, wavy brown hair neatly parted to the side, close-set eyes, and a handsome nose—a handsome face, in fact. He stood on the street corner, looking bored. A woman, animated as well, her breasts overexaggerated, waist impossibly narrow, hips seductively swaying—well, as seductive as a cartoon can be—materialized from the right side of the screen. Cartoon balloons appeared above the man's head.

"Hello," the balloon read. "My name is Ted Bundy. What's your name?"

Detective Brewer must have hit something on his remote to pause the game.

"*See Evil* allows the game player to pick from a preset list of notorious serial killers. You can be Charles Manson, Ted Bundy, Dennis Rader—that's the BTK killer—Dahmer, Gacy, and the list goes on."

"What's the point of the game?" someone asked.

"Basically, it's about torture and torment," Brewer said. "I'll show you."

The game came to life again, as the blond bombshell with a heaving bosom said via her cartoon bubble, "My name is Sugar. Do you want to hang out?"

"Sure," the Bundy avatar said, his eyes bulging and going watery with lust. "We can go back to my place."

"Not so fast," Sugar said, holding up an animated finger. "Can you tell me what year you were arrested?"

A box appeared on the screen containing several options.

a)   1972
b)   1974
c)   1976
d)   1977

Brewer selected answer C, 1976, and Sugar cooed delightedly, her animated body doing the equivalent of a shimmy.

"So this is like serial killer *Jeopardy*?" Chief Higgins asked.

"Yes, in a way," Brewer said. He pointed to a status bar on the screen, above which were written the words *Trust Index*. The index was currently at 10 percent trust. Brewer continued, "Players have to answer trivia questions about the serial killer they've chosen to play. Right now the game offers about twenty to choose from. The trust status bar goes up the more questions a player gets right."

"Can't they just go to Google for the answers?" Gant asked.

"I don't think the sickos who made this game care if you use first source material," Kaminski said.

"What happens when the status bar reaches a hundred percent?" Clegg asked.

"That's where things get really interesting," Brewer said. "I could tell you, but it's better if I show you."

CHAPTER 57

It took about a minute for Brewer to go through a dozen questions that virtual Sugar asked virtual Ted. As soon as that bar filled in completely, the city scene faded to black and a new scene took its place. I felt my stomach drop.

Sugar, animated to be wide-eyed and terrified, was tied to a sturdy oak chair, trapped in a grimy animated cellar. On the bottom of the screen were graphics depicting implements of torture: pliers, blowtorches, knives, thumbscrews, nails, to list a few. There were also selectable items of the living variety, like snakes and bugs. A new status bar replaced the trust one I'd seen on the previous screen.

This bar was titled *Fear Index*.

"The game play here is pretty simple," Brewer said. "You have to find the right mix of torture implements, applied in the proper sequence and for the correct duration, to raise the Fear Index."

Brewer clicked on the blowtorch graphic. Animation made the blowtorch appear lit. Using the remote as a mouse, Brewer maneuvered the blowtorch close to Sugar, her animated eyes popping out of their sockets while sweat sprouted from her forehead like a sprinkler. Her terrified noises sounded very realistic. The closer the blowtorch icon got to Sugar, the wider her eyes grew, the more she struggled to break free, the louder her moans, and the more cartoon sweat she secreted. When Brewer touched the blowtorch to Sugar's leg, her character shrieked in pain—again very realistic sounding—and her face contorted to display her agony. The color of her skin in that one spot went from peach to black, while the Fear Index increased by 5 percent.

"It's easy to play the game, but hard to find the right sequence," Brewer said. "In other words, it's easier to kill your victim than it is to keep her alive and increasingly afraid. You've got to keep track of a lot of variables to find the right combination that will make the fear factor complete. I'm sure there are hard-core gamers who have written code to help them solve the puzzle."

"This is all very fascinating and rather disturbing, Detective Brewer," Higgins said, "but how is this going to help us catch the SHS Killer?"

"I think that Uretsky was playing this game and became friends with another player. I think this other player might have gotten bored with all the cartoon violence. They arranged a little face-to-face meeting, but Uretsky didn't realize what was in store for him. It's fitting with what he's done to John," Brewer said, motioning with the remote control in hand. "This guy is all about playing games and creating an environment of fear."

Agent Brenner stood, her agitation apparent.

"While I appreciate your behavioral analysis, Detective, pardon me for saying so, but you're a computer jock. You're not qualified to make that sort of judgment."

"You're right," Brewer said, shrugging off her rebuke. "Maybe I am way off base here. But I haven't shown you what happens when you torture your victim to death before the fear factor is complete."

Brewer took the animated blowtorch to Sugar's animated body, covering every pixel of skin until she looked like wood turned charcoal from a fire. Sugar screamed in horrible pain throughout her virtual ordeal, while I just cringed, unable to distinguish between the simulated violence on-screen and what I feared the Fiend could be doing to my wife at that very moment. A new status bar appeared, this one showing the victim's health. It had started off at 100 percent but went down precipitously the longer Brewer applied the blowtorch.

A warning flashed on screen: *Ted, You're Killing Your Victim Too Fast.* When Sugar's body went limp, it was obvious that she'd been rendered to appear dead. The fear factor was only at 50 percent complete. All-caps words materialized above her head: *YOU KILLED YOUR VICTIM.*

That gruesome scene faded to black, and when a new image appeared, everybody in the room, myself included, released a collective gasp. The words *Sorry, Ted Bundy! You See No Evil*, the letters dripping blood, materialized above a cartoon drawing of a decapitated head. The lid of each shuttered eye was partially concealed by a severed finger dripping blood as well. Severed fingers protruded from the ears, and two more covered the lips. Below the bloody stump of a neck were the game's credits, written in the same drippy blood font.

"I may be just a lowly computer jock, and not a tried-and-true FBI agent," Brewer said, "but I think the SHS Killer got tired of playing this game virtually and decided it would be a heck of a lot more fun to do it in real life."

Higgins rose to his feet with startling quickness.

"Gant!" he said, barking out the name. "I want you working with Brewer on getting that user database from this game manufacturer. Pronto! Brewer, find out if Swain was playing this game as well. He might have been using an alias, so look hard. Kaminski, we've got to get the word out through the media about this game, too. I want anybody who has played it to get in touch with the Boston police. You know the drill. Work the media, get the press releases out there, and hit up the social networks, too. We might get something from that. We want to find people SHS has been trying to lure into a face-to-face meeting.

"Clegg!" Higgins continued, turning his attention to my friend. "I want you to pull together a team and work the phones, calling every medical school within a two-hundred-mile radius. We'll helicopter in a body if that's what it takes."

"So we're going through with John's plan?" Clegg asked.

"I'm not going to let this woman die."

Agent Brenner stood, hands glued to the back of the chair in front of her. "Chief Higgins," she said, her face flushed. "May I remind you this investigation is still under the direction of the FBI."

Higgins glared at Brenner. "Then I suggest you get your team involved, because this is what we're doing. I shouldn't have to remind you that Carl Swain is still an official person of interest, and at this moment we have no idea of his whereabouts. If you want to run this show, how about helping us find and apprehend him? We've got a clock set on a woman's life, and we don't have time to argue jurisdiction!"

"What about me?" I asked. The sound of my voice had a calming effect on the evident tension between the police and FBI.

"You, Bodine, you need to go home and wait," Higgins said.

"Wait for what?"

"Wait for this guy to contact you. I've got a very strong feeling that he's not done playing games."

I nodded because I agreed. Then I checked the time.

Twenty-one hours to go.

CHAPTER 58

Ipaced around the apartment—nowhere else to go, nothing else to do. Two agents from the FBI, both male and both with short hair, one who went by Robert and the other who went by Bob, sat at my kitchen table, playing cards. They'd been here for hours. One of them, Bob, the taller of the two, apparently was a technician of some sort, who would come in handy should the Fiend made contact. Takeout wrappers from D'Angelo's and McDonald's—theirs, not mine—filled my wastebasket to the brim. I couldn't eat.

Once again I was back to the waiting game, which reminded me of the day—two lifetimes ago, it seemed—when Ruby and I sat nervously in Dr. Anna Lee's medical office, waiting for our names to be called. Not our names, I remembered, but the Uretskys' names—Elliot and Tanya, our stolen identities.

I had my phone plugged in and charged. I moved my desktop computer out of the bedroom and into the living room. The FBI wanted me to keep my remaining computer, hoping the Fiend would initiate another video chat. I prayed that he would, not so that Bob, the computer savvy FBI agent, could try to track him down—I knew he couldn't—but so I could see Ruby again.

Ginger moved cautiously about the apartment. She wanted food. She wanted her head scratched. She wanted her belly rubbed. She had become extra needy, her way of expressing knowledge that something was wrong. I sat with her on the futon, consoling her, tapping my foot nervously.

And I waited . . . and waited. . . .

"Do you mind if I make some coffee?" Agent Robert asked.

"No," I said.

Clegg called. "Just want to tell you we're still working but got nothing to report," he said. "How are you holding up?"

"I want to puke," I said.

"Do it," he said. "You'll feel better. I'll be in touch."

He hung up before I could answer him.

I turned on the TV, flipped through the channels, and saw every news station reporting the latest breakthrough in the SHS Killer case. They didn't use the graphic from the *See Evil* game, just the logo from Sick World, the game's producer. People who played the game were asked to call a special tip line splashed across the screen but weren't given any specifics as to why. I wondered how many people would fess up to being avid gamers of the equivalent of torture porn. Then again, people plunked down a lot of money for films that were just as dark and twisted.

I did a bit of research simply for the want of some distraction. Ruby, that was all I could think about. Where was my wife? What was happening to her? I wanted her back with me like I wanted air. To me, there was no difference.

In my research explorations, I discovered that Sick World made a bunch of these games, but *See Evil* was by far their most popular. The head of Sick World was a twenty-nine-year-old California native named Peter Rosenheim. He had a Facebook page, set to private; a LinkedIn account, with fifty connections and no picture; and a Twitter feed with about a hundred tweets, all announcements for his games. A Google search didn't turn up much on Rosenheim, but I figured he was an underground sort of guy, adept at communicating with his user base while keeping in the virtual shadows. We were both small-time game developers, but Rosenheim cultivated very a different sort of following from mine. Still, Elliot Uretsky played my game and his, so there was overlap. The Fiend could be a registered player of my game. In fact, he could be online playing it right now, using my servers and code for his enjoyment while holding my wife hostage.

Who would play these games? Why would they play them? I dug up an article in WebMD about the attraction of torture porn. I wanted to understand the Fiend better—figure out for myself why playing *See Evil* no longer satisfied his sick fantasies.

The article discussed something called the "horror paradox." By our very nature, we're programmed to want to experience only pleasant emotions. As it turns out, when tension and fear get built up and released—the climax when good triumphs over evil—the brain produces lots of those pleasure sensations, hence the paradox. But games like *See Evil*? Well, I just didn't see anything pleasant or pleasing about it. Evil wins no matter what.

Maybe the Fiend played the game to cope with his own fears about violence but discovered within himself a hidden bloodlust. Or maybe he believed that he'd actually act out his fantasies, and hoped the game would serve as a release valve for his darkest impulses. Perhaps the game itself ignited a long-simmering sadistic streak—a deep desire for power and control. Whatever the cause, this psychopath had my wife, and I had just over eleven hours to get her back.

A vibration pulled me back to the moment. *My phone!* It had buzzed. I jumped up, grabbing it with fumbling hands. I took a look at the display screen. The two-word message sent my heart racing again.

Let's chat.

CHAPTER 59

A gent Bob was doing something with my phone, but I didn't care.
I rushed to my workstation in the living room, knocking over a
chair in the process. The mouse moved herky-jerky, imitating—in
fact almost exaggerating—my shaky hand. Checking the admin e-mail
queue for my *One World* game, I was not at all surprised to see an e-mail
from Elliot Uretsky. He wasn't speaking to me from beyond the
grave. It was the Fiend, pretending to be someone he was not, just as
I once had.

I clicked the link in Uretsky's e-mail, knowing it would open one
of those live video chat sessions. A Web browser did come up, with a
view window showing only a black rectangle—a precursor, I supposed, to a two-way video conference. I wasn't asked to provide a
password, as I'd been the last time. I guessed the Fiend knew he was
communicating with a trusted computer—the computer at the Harvard Street apartment.

Bob had his computer connected to mine, analyzing the data
packets from my computer connection in real time. He was looking
for the Fiend. The data he collected was being relayed back to a network operations center manned by scores of FBI agents. He sighed
and groaned and threw a pen across the room; whatever he was
doing, it wasn't going to work.

Agent Bob grunted in disgust. "This guy is using a pool of anonymous proxy servers to keep hidden. Some of our tracking tools are
being blocked by a firewall, too. He's good. Damn, he's good."

Agent Robert was on the phone, I guess speaking with the FBI's computer forensics operation center, while I watched the computer screen like it was a stove-top pot working toward a boil.

"We've got some early feedback on the text message he sent," Agent Robert said to Agent Bob. "They think he's using a burner phone."

"Burner phone?" I said.

Agent Bob said, "Burner phones are prepaid cell phones, replaced frequently, sometimes weekly. That's why we call them burners. Can we get a trace?"

Agent Robert dispelled the hope with a shake of his head. "We think it's a no," he said. "There's a theory he's sending text messages via a Google Voice account that he established using Tor or some other proxy server. We can't trace that."

In a flash, the black rectangle became an all-too-familiar basement setting. And there she was, Ruby, still tied to a chair, looking impossibly weak and frail. Her head lolled limply to one side; her eyes were open only a sliver. Her lips looked desert dry, cracked like scorched earth. Her skin was slack and sallow. Without the rise and fall of her chest from each tired breath, I'd have believed the worst.

"Ruby!" I shouted, dismayed that my voice failed to rouse her.

A figure entered the frame, and I prickled at the sight. Once again, the Fiend wore the mask of Mario, those cutout eyeholes a portal into a bone-chilling evil. I could see his mouth move, but couldn't hear a word being said. Frantic, I hit the volume button on the keyboard, but the sound level was already maxed out. I kept hitting the volume button, anyway.

"I can't hear you!" I shouted, pantomiming the message by pointing to my ear. "I can't hear you!"

The Fiend eyed me with curiosity, head tilted slightly to show his confusion, his masked face moving closer to the camera. Then he pointed to his ear and shook his head. He couldn't hear me, either!

"Volume! Volume!" I screamed.

We had a video connection, but something wasn't right with the audio transmission.

"What's going on?" I said to Agent Bob, pleading. "Why can't he hear me?"

"There's a problem translating digitally compressed data packets into audio sounds. I can't tell you any more than that without a lot more analysis."

I set my hands on the monitor, caressing the sickly image of Ruby. Agent Robert placed a reassuring hand on my shoulder, his touch comforting. The Fiend held up a finger to the camera—"One moment please," the gesture conveyed. I watched as he stepped out of the frame and came back moments later, holding a marker and pad of paper. I saw him write something on the paper.

Behind him, Ruby sat slumped in the chair, her wrists bound to the armrests and her ankles secured as well. I was sure it wasn't unintentional that the rope used to bind my wife could also be used to scale a mountain.

I kept my hand on the monitor, my finger tracing the contours of Ruby's weary face. I wanted to embrace her, relieve her suffering, but my touch could not be felt any more than my words could be heard. A vast digital ocean that could not be crossed or navigated separated us.

The Fiend showed me his pad of paper.

Technical difficulties, he wrote in a neat hand.

Another sheet of paper.

Wanted you to see Ruby was all right.

Another sheet of paper.

But she won't be without that body.

Another sheet of paper.

You've got eleven hours to go.

The video conference went to black, cut off with cruel abruptness.

For a while, I don't know how long, I sat benumbed, staring wide-eyed at the black rectangle lodged in the center of a Web page, praying it would flicker back to life again, but knowing in my heart that it would not. I heard the agents Bob talking animatedly, reviewing data packets sniffed from the session, dissecting every nuance of my nightmare in real time. All I could do was to sit and stare, feeling ashamed of my powerlessness, again asking the universe to guide me out of my darkest hour.

That was when I knew I'd come full circle. Not that long ago I'd feared the love of my life was going to die. I had tasted the bitterness, the profound sorrow, witnessed the crumbling of the future we'd planned. I imagined my life after the inevitable and thought about all the holidays and birthdays that would come and go without my beloved. I had cried and hated myself because I wasn't the one who was dying. I thought I'd found a way to save her, but I was right back where we started, only worse. This was my private hell, so I kept my thoughts to myself, speaking them only in my head, over and over again—a mantra of sorts.

My name is John Bodine. I'm twenty-nine years old. I'm married to the love of my life. And no matter what it takes, or how far I have to go, I'm not going to let her die.

I closed my eyes and opened my heart, asking of the universe with every fiber of my being, believing without a doubt that faith and clarity of vision would answer my wishes. I constructed a vision board in my mind. It looked just like the one Ruby had instructed me to build back when my depression lingered and my game needed a serious publicity boost. I envisioned a corkboard covered in purple fabric. On it, I imagined pictures of Ruby and me together. I filled our future with kids, laughter, and love. I said my affirmation over and over again, seeking strength from above.

No matter what it takes, or how far I have to go, I'm not going to let her die.

At some point, my phone rang, not once but three times. I didn't notice. I was too busy visioning. It was Agent Bob who tapped my shoulder to get my attention. I looked at the number and saw that Clegg was calling. I pressed to talk.

"We have a body," he said.

CHAPTER 60

Clegg and I followed Doctor William Cartwright, a skeletal man with stooped shoulders and a horseshoe of wispy brown hair, down a long corridor located somewhere in the basement of Harvard's medical school. Cartwright seemed a bit too titillated by the large police presence accompanying us for my liking—Clegg's, too, I could tell.

"The medical students aren't always prepared for gross anatomy," Cartwright said in a breathy voice. "Some of them find it horrific to see a dead person. Imagine that, doctors afraid of the dead."

"Imagine that," Clegg said. I could tell Clegg was annoyed, but Cartwright seemed oblivious.

"We'll have to scramble to get a replacement cadaver, as we don't keep a surplus of bodies," Cartwright continued. "Fortunately, we're still able to comply with Mrs. Grayson's request."

"Well, we're awfully sorry for the inconvenience we've caused, Doctor, but I thought you might be glad to help save a woman's life," Clegg said.

Cartwright cleared his throat, fanning out his long, thin fingers and then closing them into a tightly balled fist, one finger at a time. "Well, I'm speaking without a filter," he said. "I'm glad to be of help, though less pleased to be back here at midnight, Officer."

"Detective," Clegg said.

"Is the plan for us to receive the body after you . . . do what has to be done?"

"That's the plan," Clegg said. "The medical examiners will contact you when the body needs to come back."

Cartwright said, "From what I understand of this plot, the body will need to be cremated as it will no longer be of use to our students."

"Speaking of students, you know you can't talk about this to anybody," Clegg said. "It would be considered obstruction of justice."

"Of course," Cartwright said, somewhat indignantly. "I was well informed of my obligation on this sensitive matter. Gentlemen, if you'll excuse me."

Cartwright nodded his good-bye and shuffled on ahead, moving quickly to catch up with the medical examiners wheeling the stretcher that would carry out Ruby's only hope for survival.

"He's trying to help us, David," I said, wanting to settle him, though not at all surprised by Clegg's harshness. When agitated, Clegg could be downright ornery, and we were all highly agitated. I, for one, was definitely ready to snap. But I dug deep, finding the strength to keep moving ahead, one foot in front of the other.

Chief Higgins wasn't faring much better, at least according to Clegg. Apparently, even with the task force working nonstop and bulletins cast out to every law enforcement organization from here to Fresno, nobody had been able to locate Carl Swain or Edwin Valdez, aka the purse snatcher.

Clegg and I passed through a set of double doors that opened into a large room kept meat-locker cold. Racks of bagged bodies entombed in white plastic shells, four long rows worth, rested atop metal trays. Rollers beneath the trays made body retrieval easier. The overpowering smell of preservative, formaldehyde perhaps, hit me like a sucker punch, causing my eyes to water, my breath to quicken.

"Now, that's a scent only a mortician could love," Clegg said as we caught up with Cartwright at the end of a row of dead people.

"This is yours," Cartwright said, rolling out the tray on which the cadaver rested. "We're going to arrange for cremation, but you have instructed the widow that she'll need to pick up the remains, have you not? We can't ship human ashes, you know."

"Yup, that's all set. Thanks, Doc," Clegg said. "We'll take it from here."

"Yes, I'm sure you will."

Cartwright slunk out of view, and Clegg looked pleased.

"Why are you giving him such a hard time?" I asked. "He's trying to help us."

"That guy," Clegg said, "didn't want to give up this body. I had to go to the dean to get Cartwright to comply with Mrs. Grayson's wishes. The dean, it turns out, was a lot more understanding."

An ME unzipped the bag and nonchalantly pried open the sides like it was just another day at the office for him. It was time for me to do my job.

Someone had to make the call that the body would fool the Fiend. To my surprise, Higgins had asked Clegg to include me in this gruesome show-and-tell. The plan was mine to begin with, and it was my wife in jeopardy, so maybe that was why Higgins wanted my input. Maybe he worried a preserved body would look too different from a freshly killed one. Maybe he just knew that Clegg would bring me along regardless.

It looked like a wet and heavy cloth had been overlaid on an old and withered frame, but the counters were all there, the basic scaffolding of features that defined a face. He had caterpillar eyebrows, wisps of gray hair, and wrinkles that spoke of a long and fulfilling life. His arms were two twigs, chest sunken, a body ravaged not by disease, but by the aging process alone.

"Who is he?" I asked. "I need to know about him."

"He's an eighty-two-year-old retired pharmacist who wanted to donate his body to his alma mater. He was a pilot, a war vet, and from what I read in his file, an all-around nice fellow."

"Was it hard to get the permission?"

"Not hard," Clegg said. "We found the right person. There was a lot of paperwork to fax back and forth. Mrs. Grayson's son helped her do it. It took a while, but we got it done."

"Why'd she agree to do this?" I asked.

"The Graysons had a daughter," Clegg said.

"Had?"

"Had, as in the daughter's dead."

"Oh, that's terrible," I said in a respectful tone, as though expressing my condolences. "How did she die?"

"She was murdered," Clegg said. "About twenty years ago. When we told the wife we needed to use her husband's body, but we couldn't say how or why—police business was all we could tell her—Mrs.

Grayson wasn't too keen on helping. Then we told her about Ruby, or more specifically that a young woman's life might be saved, and she agreed to help, whatever it took. We had a lot of people making a lot of calls, John. For a while there, I didn't think it was going to happen."

I nodded, feeling a reverent appreciation for the Graysons' sacrifice.

"What now?" I asked.

"Now you tell me if you think our killer is going to believe that you took out an old guy."

"I think he'll believe that the most," I said. "I took a life at the end of a life. Yeah, this will work."

"He looks a bit like a marinated olive to me," Clegg said. "We're going to need to get some blood to add a bit of realism here."

"Will he be on the news?"

"Not his face, just a news report," Clegg said.

"We'll need proof."

"The profilers at the FBI think he's going to contact you after the news breaks. We'll get you a video clip you can send him. That should work."

I nodded.

"Okay," Clegg said. "Then we're a go. I'll prep it."

Without warning, Clegg hoisted up one of the man's frail arms and splayed open the fingers of his bony hand. He reached into his back pocket with his free hand and removed a pair of spring-loaded pruning shears.

"I hope this works," Clegg said, snipping off one of the man's fingers as nonchalantly as an ME opening up a body bag.

CHAPTER 61

It all went down. The best-laid plans of mice and men. The MEs, accompanied by a substantial police escort, brought Mr. Oliver
Grayson's body to a cordoned-off section of woodlands near the
Boston Police VFW Post in Dorchester. I guess I could have killed
somebody there in the predawn dark. A press release went out to the
news media shortly thereafter, around 4:30 that morning, six hours
before the deadline. "The police have found a body in Dorchester,"
the alert read, "another apparent victim of the SHS Killer." News
media descended on the scene the way vultures are drawn to car-
rion.

Yellow crime-scene tape held the press at bay, though reporters
did everything possible to gather information. They pushed and
shoved and shouted out questions. "Who is the victim?" "Male or female? Age?" "Any connection to the other victims?" "How did he die?"
"Can we see the body?" Police detectives assigned by Higgins to
manage the media gave vague answers to the firestorm of questions.

I stood in the background, watching as the events unfolded.
Everyone, it seemed, acted with authentic urgency. It looked like
controlled chaos. I wasn't in the briefing room when Higgins and the
FBI did all the planning, but if Academy Awards were given out for
the most realistic faked murder scene, I'm sure this would have won.

The discovery of a body in Dorchester, and its possible link to the
serial killer terrorizing Boston, dominated the morning news and
topped headlines on both local and national media outlets. Everyone, Special Agent Brenner included, believed the Fiend would con-

tact me via my cell. He'd done it before. He'd do it again. So I was kept under close supervision. The FBI set up a tech center that could triangulate a cell signal if he did make contact.

An hour passed. And then another. Four hours to go, and still no word.

The tightness in my throat matched that of my stomach. Not a second went by when I wasn't thinking of Ruby. I wanted to hold her, to feel her touch, feel her body pressed up against mine. I couldn't shake the feeling of being cursed. King Midas in reverse. Everything I touched turned to poison.

I said my mantra over and over again. *And no matter what it takes, or how far I have to go, I'm not going to let her die.*

"It's like fishing," Detective Gant said to me, depositing a steaming Styrofoam cup of coffee in front of me. "Bait the hook, cast a line, and wait for a bite."

I ignored Gant's tasteless analogy by watching the video of Oliver Grayson's dead body. We took the recording using my iPhone's camera just after sunrise. Morning dew collected around the head in a crown of beaded water. The sky ignited with streams of pinks and yellows, all the markers of a beautiful day. We wanted the video on my phone in case I had to send it to the Fiend. The illusion had to be complete and perfect. I killed Oliver Grayson. I took a video of the body as the sun poked out over the horizon.

Afterward, the MEs bagged up Grayson—again—and Clegg left to escort them to a funeral home where the body would be cremated. Wailing sirens added authenticity to the departure. I stayed behind, camped out in a conference room at the VFW headquarters, along with a host of other law enforcement types, playing the waiting game.

I watched the video several times. Grayson looked to me like the other victims of the SHS Killer. Poor Oliver had two fingers set on the eyes, two on his waxy lips, and fingers protruding from each bulbous ear. The added blood was ketchup, but on video I couldn't tell the difference. I didn't see a cadaver. I saw a dead body, a murder victim. What I saw was my obligation fulfilled.

Three hours to go. Still no word.

A song popped into my head. *The waiting is the hardest part.*

Tom Petty. Hadn't I sung that to Ruby in Dr. Anna Lee's office? Hadn't that won me a point in our never-ending game? How prophetic a tune, how true it was.

And then it happened. My phone rang. My first thought was that Gant was right: it was like fishing. I did feel that jolt of adrenaline when a slack line suddenly goes taut. Everybody in the room—Higgins, Gant, Kaminski, Brenner, Agents Bob, Brewer—all tensed as well. I could see it on their faces. They felt the pull on the line, too.

"Shut up! Everybody shut up!" somebody screamed. "Everybody shut the hell up!"

Silence descended like a curtain. Voices went from a murmur to complete quiet in a few breaths. My phone rang again, sounding out the haunting chime of marimbas. I heard Brenner whisper, "Make sure our equipment is a go." Burner phone or not, I knew that by triangulating the nearest cell phone transmission masts, coupled with cooperation from my cell provider and a lot of sophisticated equipment, they could pinpoint at least a general location of the Fiend.

I answered the call. "This is John."

"Of course it is," the Fiend said, his rasp on full display. "How are you, John? How are you feeling? Congratulations. Looks like you're in the big leagues now."

My teeth clenched.

"Where is Ruby?" I said.

"Easy, tiger," said the Fiend. "I still need my proof. I was disappointed the news didn't showcase my copycat's handiwork."

Brenner came over to me, gesturing excitedly for me to keep him talking.

"I have your proof," I said. "I took video of the body."

"Good boy. Tell me something. Are you trying to trace this call?"

"Of course not," I said, hoping the jump of my pulse hadn't betrayed the lie. "I just want you to release Ruby."

"Don't bother trying to trace this. You can't find me, John."

"I'm not."

"You're a bad liar," he said. "I thought we worked on that before."

"Dobson," I said, remembering my first criminal task.

"Poor fellow," said the Fiend.

Obviously, he was referring to Dobson.

"What does that mean?" I said, overcome with a sinking feeling.

"Oh, you'll see."

"What have you done?"

"Later. What I'd like right now is to see your effort," he said. "E-mail a copy of the video to GoodbyeJohnsRubyTuesday@hotmail.com. Don't try to trace that, either. Just send the file."

"Hang on," I said.

I put the phone on mute.

"He wants me to e-mail him the video of Oliver," I said to Higgins.

"Do it," Higgins said.

Brenner said, "We can't get a trace on this guy. His IP is bouncing all over the place. Are you experiencing any latency on the call?"

"No," I said. "It's coming through clear."

"I don't know how he's doing it," Brenner said, "but the call is definitely going through a proxy server that's making it impossible to trace."

"I don't think you're going to have better luck with the e-mail address," I said.

Brenner's haunted expression seemed to agree.

I e-mailed the video directly from my phone and heard someone talking. Maybe they thought the conversation was over. I turned off the mute button after Brenner had once again silenced the room.

"I sent the video," I said.

"Good." Then a pause. Then I heard, "Ohhhh . . . oh, John, lovely work. Was it hard?"

"Was what hard?"

"Taking a man's life," the Fiend said. "Did he struggle?"

"Of course," I said.

"Were his legs kicking? Did he thrash about? He looks so old and frail. Could he put up much of a fight?"

"No," I said. "He didn't fight much at all."

"So, you took out a weakling. Culled the herd, did you?"

"He lived a long time. It was the best of the worst. Now, you promised you'd set Ruby free."

"Did he froth at the mouth? Did he spit on you as he died?"

I didn't know how to respond. Did that happen to people who were choked to death? Could they even spit? Was he testing me? I decided he frothed but couldn't spit. That's what I told him, anyway.

"Jenna frothed at the mouth, too. Did it make you excited? Are you going to give Ruby a bit of that excitement when you're re-united?"

"Please," I said. "Please just let her go."

"Okay . . . okay. Come and get her, John. She's at one-fifty-seven Beacon Street in Boston, Apartment Seven-E."

"You're just going to let me come and get her?" I said, disbelieving.

"Yes. That was our deal. One murdered person in exchange for one sick wife."

"I'm coming now."

"Good. And bring friends if you'd like. I don't care if an entire armada of police shows up. But I do have one rule. One very specific rule. Nobody, and I mean nobody, is to attempt entry without first getting my permission. If anybody so much as rings the buzzer, she dies. Is that understood?"

"Yes," I said. "Understood."

"And, John?"

"Yes?"

"You're almost a real criminal."

"What do you mean, almost? I've done everything you've asked."

"Yes, you've done everything I've asked," the Fiend said, "but I haven't asked everything you'll do."

CHAPTER 62

The apartment, situated in an upscale neighborhood of Boston not far from Kenmore Square, was a nicely maintained five-story brownstone fronted by a convex awning with a green cover. Morning sunshine turned the day warm, triggering the scent of blossoms that sweetened the air. Police barricades sectioned off four surrounding city blocks. Helicopters buzzed the skies with the uneven trajectory of flying insects. Police ordered a mandatory evacuation of all residents living in the two adjacent apartment buildings and those directly across the street. Ambulances and fire trucks were called in to assist with the evacuation effort. Most everyone else, it seemed, went to the rooftops to get a bird's eye view of all the commotion happening at street level.

Clegg drove us to the site and got me acclimated to the massive and awe-inspiring law enforcement response.

"We've got SWAT on the rooftops and snipers in pretty much every place with a clear line of sight for a kill shot," he said. "We're using infrared thermography to see what's happening inside the apartment, but I don't think we've picked up anything yet. He could have Ruby in a back room, out of range for our equipment."

"What now?" I said.

"Now we wait until he calls."

"I hate the waiting game."

"Me too," Clegg said.

Somebody I didn't know came over and whispered something I couldn't hear into Clegg's ear.

"I'll be right back," Clegg said, leaving me to join Higgins and

Brenner, who were camped out nearby. They exchanged words, with Clegg nodding a lot, and the next thing I knew, Clegg was vanishing within a cloud of SWAT.

News media had been barred from flying in the restricted airspace, but that didn't stop them from congregating at every barrier. I might have been at the epicenter of this gargantuan calamity, but to them I remained a person unknown. A stranger among law enforcement, dressed in civilian clothes—grimy and disgusting jeans topped by a ripped and faded blue T-shirt. For the Fiend's benefit, my appearance was that of a man who had just murdered someone and dumped his body in the woods. Whoever I was, I must have looked to the media like a puzzle piece that didn't quite fit.

Gant came over to me, Kaminski too, both wanting to know how I was holding up.

"I'm hanging in there," I said, lying. In truth, besides being filthy, I was exhausted, sick, worried, sick with worry, and horrified by what was taking place. "I'm amazed at the size of this operation," I added, wanting them to know how much I appreciated all the effort.

"We don't know what's going to happen," Gant said. "All we know is that from this guy, you can expect anything."

Before I could respond, my cell phone rang.

It took a lot of hushing and gesturing to settle everyone down, but soon enough the only sound that could be heard was the helicopter rotors whipping above my head and the ringing of my phone. I answered the call.

"Hi ya, John. Glad you could make it." That voice—so familiar and still able to chill my soul.

"Where's Ruby?" I said, my voice cracking.

"She's inside. I'm not lying to you."

"Then let me come in and get her."

"Well, that's the problem. You see, the game isn't over yet. You've got one more task to perform. One more test of your criminal skills. Being criminal is not just about getting away with it. You have to be able to get in before you can get away. I should warn you, John, you can't keep your greatest fear locked up forever. The time has come to pick it open."

"Tell me! Tell me what you want!"

"I'm sorry, John, but I need to talk to the person in charge. Right now. Do it, now."

Reluctantly, I handed the phone to Higgins. He put the phone to his ear. It took about five seconds for Higgins to develop the look of a seasick mariner. Twenty seconds and I thought he might need oxygen. Forty and he nodded dully. Sixty and he handed the phone back to me, his color nearly gone. There was nobody on the line.

"What's going on?" I asked him. "What's happening?"

"Watch," Higgins said, pointing to the windows of apartment 7E.

The curtains blocking the view into the apartment parted. I saw a figure appear—a man, I believed, though sun and glare kept his identity a mystery.

Higgins picked up his bullhorn. "Hold your fire!" he shouted. "Do not, I repeat, do not open fire!"

Higgins's command must have been radioed around, because I didn't hear the click of a chamber being loaded. The window lifted, inch by grueling inch.

Who was opening the window? Where was Ruby? Why had Higgins ordered his task force not to fire? What the hell was going on?

The figure inside the apartment stooped to get low, as if preparing to climb out the window and onto the ledge. And then I realized that was exactly what he was doing. Slowly, methodically, the man slid out through the open window, one leg followed by another, hands next, spreading for leverage, torso bending to make room, head poking out to survey his terrifying surroundings. The ledge had to be no more than a foot and a half wide. The man wore something around his body—a vest of some sort with wires sticking out. Carefully the man unfurled his trembling body, rising slowly into a standing position, knees buckling, back pressed up tight against the brick wall.

Now I could see him clearly. Henry Dobson, shaking, stood on the ledge of the building, wearing a vest strapped with what had to be explosives of some sort. He looked like a suicide bomber.

Dobson tossed something from his hand. Keys, attached to a ring, dropped about seventy feet in a second and clattered on the pavement. Four officers pounced on the keys as if they might get up and run away. Higgins was looking through his binoculars when I heard him say to one of his lieutenants, "There's a lock on the vest. Just like he said."

That's when I knew what was coming next. I knew it without a doubt.

And it all made perfect sense to me.

CHAPTER 63

Chief Higgins pulled me over to Special Agent Brenner. I kept looking for Clegg but couldn't find him anywhere. I also kept looking up at Dobson, as did everyone else, judging by the collective gasps.

A breeze kicked up, hard enough to ruffle hair and launch tiny dervishes of dust and debris into the air. The gasps from the crowds grew louder when Dobson momentarily lost his balance. He quickly recovered, his arms pressed spread-eagle against the wall. Dobson's body moved in one giant quiver. Every part of him seemed to be shaking. I was amazed that he didn't shake himself right off the building's ledge. I didn't know what scared him more—the possibility that he could fall or the fact that he was wearing a bomb strapped around his chest.

"Here's the deal," Higgins said. "Our guy is watching this nightmare from someplace. He says he's not anywhere near here, but who knows if that's true. Says he's got a camera that can see the ledge and another one inside the apartment and that he's watching. Apparently, this guy Henry Dobson was taken hostage sometime last night."

"Anybody even remotely connected to me is a target," I said.

"What's Dobson wearing?" Brenner asked. "Do we know anything about the device?"

"I was told the bomb is fifty pounds of a homemade explosive mixed with iron shrapnel. It's enough to take off the top of the building, that's for sure. Agent Brenner, I want your people on it. See what you can make of it, and give us your analysis."

"Of course," Brenner said. "But did he say what he wants?"

"There's a switch to deactivate the bomb that's inaccessible because of a lock he put in front of it."

You can't keep your greatest fear locked up forever. It's time to pick it open, I thought.

My other thought: *Computer hackers love picking real locks.* It's all about figuring out how mechanics work, finding the weakness in the design, and exploiting every bit of that vulnerability for fun or for profit. That's the hacker creed. That was the game I started to play the moment I stole Uretsky's identity. So it was fitting in this Fiend's corrupted logic chain that it should be my final test as well.

But this was more than just about lock picking. He wanted me to do it standing on a ledge, looking down at the pavement, facing my greatest fear. This was his ultimate test of my ability and my will.

I was processing all of this when Higgins said to Brenner, "He wants John to go out onto the ledge and pick the lock, then hit the switch to deactivate the bomb. If anybody else goes up there, he says he'll trigger it remotely."

"That'll kill Ruby!" I shouted.

"I think that's the idea," Higgins said. "Ruby is tied up in the apartment, at least according to him. If anybody tries to untie her, he'll blow the bomb. Anybody else goes inside, he'll blow the bomb."

My phone buzzed. I lifted it up to read the text message.

Get the keys and get inside, John. You have sixty seconds to make your move.

CHAPTER 64

"Give me the keys!" I screamed to Higgins, showing him my phone. "Give me the keys, dammit. We don't have time! Now!"

Dobson's terrified screams rained down from above, mixing with my own. I broke away from Higgins when he nodded, and rushed the police officers that had taken the keys. I grabbed one of the big men by the shoulder, reaching frantically for the keys, trying to force them out of his hand. He knew who I was, but still he looked ready to toss me to the ground.

"Please," I said. "Please I need those keys."

Higgins whistled to get his attention.

"Give him the keys," he said.

Rushing to the front door, I forced my hands to stop shaking long enough to slip the key into the lock. Once inside, I took the stairs three at a time up five flights. I unlocked the door to apartment 7A, and in I went.

I saw Ruby right away. She was lying on the hardwood floor, the ball gag in her mouth secured around her head by leather straps, her arms pulled behind her back, bound with climbing rope. Her legs were tied together at the ankles. Then I saw the video camera attached to a computer—a live broadcast, I presumed. It was set up on the table, the only piece of furniture in an otherwise completely empty two-bedroom condo. I remembered the instructions. If I tried to untie her, the Fiend would see it, and boom would go the dynamite—or homemade explosive, in this case. There were no rules about kissing, though, so I pressed my lips to Ruby's forehead, overcome with relief that for the moment, she was alive.

No matter what it takes, or how far I have to go, I'm not going to let her die.

"I'll be right back, baby," I said. "He's watching us. If I try to untie you, he's going to blow the bomb Dobson is wearing. I just have to go out onto that ledge for a second." I pointed to the window. How nonchalantly I said that! Ah, just a quick little jaunt out on a narrow ledge five stories up, when I got sick to my stomach looking out a window.

Ruby rolled her head from side-to-side in a frenzied motion, screaming through the gag, twisting her body to get free. Of course she didn't want me to go. Of course she worried that I would fall. I worried the same.

"Trust me," I said. "I'm going to do it. I'll be all right." I kissed her forehead once more, rose from my crouch, and headed for that open window.

CHAPTER 65

M y fear hummed hard enough to shake my legs. I walked to the window as though crossing a tightrope, one foot in front of the other. A sense of dread redoubled with each slow and purposeful step. Before I knew it, I was standing in front of an open window. I forced myself to look all around and saw the scene from an entirely different vantage point. The police looked like specks from up here; the helicopters were distant planets. I heard Higgins call through the bullhorn.

"John! Are you all right?"

Where was Clegg?

I nodded and gave the thumbs-up sign, even though I couldn't speak. Glancing to my right, I saw Dobson plastered flat against the brick exterior. He had his eyes closed, nostrils flaring, while his cheeks puffed in and out like fireplace bellows. Sweat had darkened his light blue shirt to navy. Every muscle, every limb on his body was trembling wildly.

"Henry," I said. "It's me. It's John."

Dobson opened his eyes and moaned, "John. Help me. Please. Help me."

"Henry, I'm going to try."

The vest was made of a green canvas fabric secured to the body by Velcro straps at the sides. Canvas pockets on both the front and back of the vest held at least a dozen steel pipes with threaded caps at each end. Clear plastic pockets running across the front and back of the vest provided a window into a showcase of nails and ball bearings that would become deadly projectiles upon detonation. Red and white wires were connected to the top of each threaded cap and terminated inside an opaque plastic case, which I assumed hid a button or switch to arm the weapon.

I didn't know how powerful the blast would be or if the nails and ball bearings stuffed inside the plastic pockets would rip through the windows fast enough and accurately enough to kill Ruby. I didn't care to find out. The padlock securing access to the plastic case wasn't an expensive type, but rather something common in the locker room of a local YMCA. Nothing fancy. It should be easy enough to pick for somebody who knew how to pick a lock.

Unfortunately, that somebody wasn't me.

"Henry," I said. "I'm told I've got to get that lock open, but I don't have anything to open it with."

"It's in . . . my . . . pocket," Dobson said between uneven breaths.

A rattling gust of wind forced Dobson to claw at the brick for balance, his fingernails digging into the mortar until they came away gray.

I said, "I'm going to come out there, Henry."

I didn't know whether Dobson heard me. He answered a completely different question. It was as if he heard me ask "What happened?" but that wasn't what I said.

"He must have broken into my apartment," Dobson said, still breathless. "He drugged me. I don't know. All I know is that I woke up in this apartment here with Ruby, wearing this vest. He gave me a lock-pick kit, which I'm supposed to give to you."

"Did you see his face?" I asked.

"No," Dobson said, whimpering. Okay, so he heard me. "He kept a ski mask on all the time. Please, John, can you do it?"

I sucked in a breath and swallowed a jet of bile souring my throat. I blinked once, then twice, but it didn't change a damn thing. I was still up really, really high.

I can do this. . . . I can do this. . . .

But I couldn't do it. I was stuck. I had my body partway out the window, arms pressed up against the windowpane, ready to provide enough leverage to get my legs up and through, but I wasn't going anywhere. I looked down. Shouldn't have done that. The ground seemed to drop out like an elevator cut from a cable. Down it went, farther and farther, fading into infinity.

No matter what it takes . . .

I couldn't look up. The ground below me was spinning, a swirling vortex pulling me into its epicenter. So I closed my eyes, and with one leg out the window, I pushed until my other leg rested on the sill.

Or how far I have to go . . .

My legs were shaking like those of a newbie on ice skates. With my head poking out the window, the elements seemed exceptionally harsh to me—the wind blew fierce, and the sun blinded. The last time I felt wind this strong, I had cut a rope tethered to Brooks Hall. *No, it's not like that.* My mind was tricking me into thinking the wind up here matched the force on the mountain. But the mind can be a powerful deceiver. My body shivered with a cold that was imagined as well. I thought about those nails exploding outward and saw them buried into Ruby's arms, neck, and skull. I forced my head farther out the open window.

I'm not going . . .

My eyes stayed closed. My face felt on fire. I shuddered and shook and couldn't imagine how I was going to stand on a ledge without tumbling right off.

Brooks, please forgive me. Please give me strength.

That was when I saw him. It was just like the time I rode the glass elevator in the Wilhelm Genetics skyscraper. Back when I had faith I could find a way to get Ruby her medication. Before I became a criminal. Only this time, Brooks's eyes were blue and infinite, not black and dead. He was standing on the summit of a mountain, waving a flag in victory. His smile could melt the snow. He beckoned me to come.

To let her die . . .

A time warp, that's the only way I can describe it. One minute I was perched on the windowsill, body halfway in and halfway out. The next thing I knew, I was standing on the ledge, flush against the wall, feeling the scratch of rough brick rubbing against my back. The wind kicked up with startling power. Or maybe that was just how my brain perceived it. My muscles twitched and contracted with powerful spasms that threatened to expel me from the ledge. My knees were wobbling; my heart lodged in my throat. The world below me kept spinning and spinning and spinning.

"Look at me!" Dobson shouted. "Look at me, and don't look down!"

His voice sounded far off and distant, no more powerful than a fading echo. But he commanded my attention, so I looked at him.

"You've got to get closer," Dobson said. My hesitation, it seemed, gave him strength. His voice sounded less shaky. He needed me able-bodied so that we could both live.

I took shuffling side steps, inching my way closer to him, closer still. The sound of my feet scraping along the cement ledge pierced my eardrums. I could feel an invisible string pulling my head lower, trying to make me look down. My muscles tensed to the snapping point. Each breath brought in little air. One second the skin of my face was afire, and in the next it would turn frostbite cold. But somehow I took another shuffling side step toward Dobson, my toes dangling over the ledge. I got close enough that I could feel his hot breath bathe my face.

"You've got . . . to get . . . the lock-pick kit," Dobson said, stuttering. "It's in the front pocket of my pants. Can you reach it?"

I stretched, wishing my fingers were elastic. Keeping my back against the brick, I let my fingers become my eyes, and bit by bit they found the inside of the pocket. Slowly, carefully, I slid my hand in deeper, gripped something leather, and was able to remove a small black zippered case.

"He told me it's the easiest lock to pick," Dobson said.

Down below I heard horns blaring. Higgins's voice crackled up through the bullhorn. People were shouting. Helicopters whirled overhead. But I refused to look down. I kept my gaze locked on Dobson. I brought the case close to my chest, but to unzip it, I would have to let my arms come free of the wall. I would need to become more vulnerable than I already was. Determination overcame my momentary paralysis. I took out the tools, a tension wrench and a pick, and let the case fall from my hands. I didn't watch it drop, but I heard people cry out, as if I'd just let a baby fall.

"I don't know how to do this," I said.

"You can do it, John. I'll tell you how."

"You know how?"

"Just trust me. He told me the steps to follow."

I took a shuffled step toward the window. I couldn't do this. But then I worried that leaving the ledge would be a violation of the Fiend's rules.

Boom goes the dynamite.

It had to be done here, and it had to be done now. I swiveled my hips to the right, allowing me to use both hands, while keeping my feet glued to the cement. Dobson spoke clearly, his instructions both precise and methodical. I followed them as best I could.

I blocked out all distractions—the wind, the honking horns, the helicopter chop, the people, Dobson's erratic breathing. Everything. Getting myself centered and somehow calm, I steadied my hand enough to slip the tension wrench into the lower portion of the keyhole. Turning the wrench clockwise, I applied torque to the cylinder, feeling the give. Dobson's instructions were clear and easy to follow. They focused me, channeled my energy. Slipping the pick into the upper part of the keyhole, I could feel the tip of the pins with the tip of the pick. My teeth were chattering, and my hands were awkward and clumsy.

I kept working the pick. Some of the pins were harder to push up than others, just as Dobson said, so I applied more tension with the wrench to increase the torque. I did this several times, feeling around with the pick, pushing up on pins, and adjusting the torque, until I heard a satisfying click. My eyes went wide as the lock fell open.

Dobson squealed in delight. It was Dobson who pulled the lock from the hole that allowed the opaque case to pop open.

I searched the inside of the newly opened case, looking for a button, an off switch of some sort, but all I saw was a piece of paper taped to the inside cover. I took the paper in my hands, unfolding it. A note was written in the same handwriting the Fiend had showed me during our soundless chat.

LOOKING FOR SOMETHING? GET BACK INSIDE. WE'RE NOT DONE YET.

CHAPTER 66

I shook my head furiously from side to side, trying to send a signal to Higgins that the mission had failed, but I couldn't look to see if he understood. If Higgins sent in the cavalry, the Fiend might still detonate the bomb. Something had gone wrong. There wasn't a switch to deactivate the device, and I had no idea how to shut it off.

"What's going on? What's happening?" Dobson shouted at me. "What's that note?"

His shaking returned. The strength and resolve he'd shown earlier seemed to have abandoned him. His eyes betrayed his state of mind. I'd seen it on the mountain. Brooks had the look. Clegg did, too. "I'm going to die." That was what his eyes said. "This is it. Sayonara. Arrivederci. This is the end."

"Come on, Henry. Get inside with me. You can do it."

I shuffled to my left, one sliding step scraping across the concrete, followed by another. Dobson came along, shuffling in sync with me. I reached the window, slipping a leg inside, bending at the waist, and getting another leg in there. Awash with relief, I glanced behind me and saw Ruby still thrashing about on the floor.

"The bomb isn't deactivated," I said to her. "I don't know what to do. If I untie you, he might detonate the device. I'm going to get Dobson back in here. Stay patient, sweetie. Just hang in there."

She didn't like my words. Not one bit.

I poked my head back out the window, encouraging Dobson along. He got to within a foot of his portal to safety when a gust of wind slapped at his knees. Dobson lurched forward, arms flailing for balance. At the same instant, I leaned out the window and reached for him as he fell. My hand clasped his forearm just as the rest of his body vanished from my view.

The collective holler of the onlookers lifted skyward in a singular crescendo. I gripped his arm with my other hand and used the windowsill as a barrier of sorts to keep the pull of his body weight plus the added weight from the vest from dragging me out. He grabbed hold of me as well. I could feel him but couldn't see him.

Dobson swung pendulum-like against the outside of the building, scraping the side of the wall from left to right, then back the other way, the force of his grip crushing the bones of my wrists. My throbbing hands threatened to release the tenuous hold I had on his forearms. I leaned farther out the window, our eyes locked, Dobson's terror becoming my own. I had no idea what was happening on the street below us. Had the fire department set up any netting? One of those inflatable mattresses, perhaps? I didn't know the answer, so I pulled, feeling the snap and stretch of the muscles in my shoulders, arms, and legs as they exerted themselves against an unrelenting strain. They burned for relief as Dobson's terrified screams ripped through me. Here was my chance to make some amends for the sins of my past. The rope I had to cut. The life I had to take to save my own. Here was a piece of salvation.

Pressing my feet against the underneath of the windowsill, I pulled hard enough to dislocate Dobson's shoulders. I felt him inching upward, so I pulled even harder. There was Brooks on that mountaintop again. I saw him waving to me from somewhere, from that great beyond. Who knows? I pulled, my body shaking, teeth clenched, making savage grunts and groans.

No more death. No more dying.

Thrusting with my legs, I allowed the full force of my backward momentum to carry Dobson up the side of the building like he was hitched to a pulley system. Dobson came tumbling through the window and landed right on top of me. I felt the nails from the bomb vest poke against my chest. Dobson rolled off me, breathless and heaving.

I stood up first and then helped Dobson to his feet. Marimba chimes rang out. My phone. I answered.

It was Clegg. "What's going on, John?" he said. "Are we sending people in?"

"The bomb . . . is . . . still active," I told him, hands on my knees, body bent, heaving and struggling for breath. "I don't know what's happening."

"Should we come up there? You give the word," Clegg said.

"He might detonate it if you do."

"Let me talk to him," Dobson said, tapping me on the shoulder. "The kidnapper said something to me that might help."

I handed Dobson the phone. He turned his back to me. Ruby was screaming through her gag. My stomach threatened to rebel. It wanted me to untie her. But if I did . . . if that was the wrong choice . . .

I went to her, caressing her face, trying to calm her down. Smoothing her hair, I told her it would be all right, just stay patient, that sort of thing. I turned back around and saw Dobson standing in front of me. He held up the phone, offering to give it back, and I reached for it.

"Congratulations, Johnny. You're a real criminal now," Dobson said. His voice had shifted into a rasp familiar and chilling enough to set goose bumps on my skin.

I was confused, trying to process what I just heard. I was looking at the phone, still reaching for it, getting my brain around the strangeness of Dobson's voice, which was why I didn't see his other hand, the one holding a knife. As I took the phone, Dobson plunged a seven-inch blade into my stomach.

Again.

And again.

And again.

CHAPTER 67

I don't know how many times I got stabbed. Five? Six? Ten? It's hard to count when you're being murdered. I crumpled to the floor like I'd been unplugged, clutching my gut, feeling myself grow weaker by the second. Blood seeped through the makeshift dam of my fingers to collect on the floor beneath me. The world looked askew, everything tilted. Dobson's canvas sneakers—yes, those made the most sense for standing on a ledge—came shuffling toward me, but my eyesight was blurry and fading. I sensed Ruby near me, a beacon of sorts guiding my hands toward her, and yet everywhere I reached I couldn't seem to find her. Now I understood—too late, of course. She hadn't been begging for me to untie her. She'd been warning me about Dobson—the Fiend.

Dobson's footsteps spoke a language all their own. "I'm coming," they said. "I'm coming, and there's not a damn thing you can do about it." He bent down, getting close to me, and lifted me up by my shoulders. Not off the floor, entirely, just enough so he could slide the bomb underneath. I felt those nails and ball bearings pressing up against the knife wounds, a searing pain.

"Can't risk an autopsy showing that you were stabbed," Dobson said, again speaking in that raspy, guttural voice I recognized as belonging to the Fiend. "Oh, and by the way, thanks for saving my life out there," he said in his normal speaking voice. "That little slip and fall incident wasn't planned, I can tell you. Not at all. Whew!" He wiped the back of his hand across his brow to show his relief. "I thought you did amazing, by the way. I mean, talk about a true test of your criminality. You faced your greatest fear and picked that lock!

You're a master, John. You've won the game. Wow, what a rush! I knew this would be great, but I didn't know how great. I mean, my heart is really pumping. It never did that when I was choking the Uretskys.

"Anyway, the good news is you're going to die a hero, John. I'll tell them I took off the vest in a panic and tossed it to the floor. I ran out the door, quick as a bunny." Using two downward pointing fingers, he pantomimed the idea of legs moving fast. "Well, I guess I must have dropped the vest near Ruby. I saw you going for the bomb just as I was leaving. You wanted to save your wife, naturally. Makes perfect sense. And then, boom, it went off. Well, it didn't go off by itself. I've got the remote trigger, which I'll get rid of on my way out of here."

"They'll know," I said. "The police will figure out that you don't work for UniSol, and they'll hunt you down."

"I thought you'd know me better by now. I'm looking forward to having them try and find me. It's just another game to play. Sorry, buddy, but that's how it ends. You were so much fun to play with. I mean, I really, really loved playing with you. Guess I'll see you on the other side."

He smiled wickedly. I saw his feet turn. *Time to go.* Next, I heard those footsteps as they headed for the door. Slow moving. No need to rush. I listened to the sound of his footfalls on the hardwood floor. I listened. And I listened. And when I didn't hear footsteps anymore, I knew he'd gone out the door and into the carpeted hallway. I counted to ten, having no idea how long he'd wait to set off the bomb. Five seconds? Three? He'd want to get safely down the stairs. Maybe a flight. Maybe two. So I counted to ten, filling my lungs with resolve.

One . . . two . . . three . . .

I pushed myself off the floor onto my hands and knees.

Four . . . five . . .

I got to my feet, shaky and off balance, wincing in pain, with blood seeping from my body in a steady stream.

Six . . . seven . . .

I picked up Ruby, feeling my stab wounds ripping. The agony burning from within turned my vision black.

Eight . . . nine . . .

I carried Ruby over to the window—dragged her—my steps shuffling and off balance, but effective.

Ten.

I pushed her out the window.

Eleven . . .

The bomb went off.

CHAPTER 68

The blast waves hurled me out the window in rocket-propelled fashion. I was in free fall. Nails sliced through the air with the speed of missiles. Glass shattered and spread out in all directions. Bricks exploded outward, pelting me with debris, but my rate of descent pulled me down faster than the objects on a collision course with my body. Most of the debris lost thrust and posed more of a risk to the people down below than it did to me. For me, the real danger was falling. Oh, and my stab wounds.

Brooks. I thought about Brooks. The fall would last only a few seconds. My thoughts came and went quicker than a streaking star. This must be how he had felt. Now I knew. Dropping into the infinite. Not knowing what awaited him. The ground rising as fast as the sky fell away. A scream. A yell. One final cry. One last confirmation of life. Or was it?

I hit the inflatable mattress dead center. The *whoosh* of displaced air filled my ears. I savored the bounce as the mattress gave way to my weight, then rose up again. Ruby rolled into my body. The gag muted her sobs. I fought a tide of billowing fabric to get off the mattress. Bodies converged on us. Hands latched onto my arms and pulled me toward the edge, staining the mattress with long streaks of my blood. Clegg helped me down, propping me up with his arm. I hung on him, limp and useless.

"Don't move me. Don't move me," I said.

We were standing—well, he stood; I was propped—directly in front of the glass door entrance of 157 Beacon Street. Angry spurts of blood spilled my life force onto the street. My vision darkened. The world began to spin. Round and round. Quick like a bunny. I saw Dobson's fingers making that same gesture. Quick like a bunny. I remembered the coolness of his touch. How clammy his skin felt on mine. But I stayed on my feet, waiting . . . waiting.

The front door opened, and out stepped Dobson. He had the frantic look of someone who had panicked in the face of grave danger and had rushed to safety, leaving Ruby and me behind to die in an explosion. That look faded as soon as he saw me, replaced by one of total surprise.

"It's him," I wheezed loudly enough for Clegg to hear. "It's Dobson. . . . He's the bomber . . . the Fiend. . . . He's the Fiend."

Dobson gave me a wretched look. He glanced in all directions. Then he smiled a big, toothy grin. I saw him touch his fingers to his eyes. He walked toward me. Clegg didn't budge. He kept me propped upright.

"You need to see this," Clegg said to me. "I owe you this." Dobson came closer, his smile widening.

"Show me what?" I said, my voice weakening. "Aren't you going to arrest him or something?"

"He's not going down like that."

Dobson got closer.

"How's he going down?" I asked.

Dobson reached into his pocket and pulled out the knife, still stained red with my blood. He sliced the air with the knife, smiling, coming closer.

"This way," Clegg said. Then he shouted, "Police. Drop your weapon!"

Dobson was no more than ten feet from me, crazed, deranged beyond reason. He lunged forward, thrusting the knife out in front of him as though wielding a bayonet. He got to within an arm's reach of me when Clegg, in a singular motion, took out his gun and fired a shot. The bullet just barely nicked Dobson's ear as it zoomed past his head.

Dobson staggered backward but managed to stay on his feet, weapon still in hand. Blood spewed out sideways and down from the wound in Dobson's head.

Clegg kept his gun trained on Dobson. Dobson broadcast his intent by raising his knife overhead. Suicide by cop, that was how he was going down.

"I said drop your weapon!" Clegg shouted again.

Dobson still advanced. Clegg fired again, this time skimming the side of Dobson's mouth with his bullet. Dobson's splintered teeth sprayed like ceramic snowflakes, falling in all directions, the knife clattering to the ground.

As Dobson fell backward, blood sputtering from his shattered mouth in a thick river of red, Clegg fired a third time. The third bullet struck Dobson square in the right eye, sending blood, bone, and brains bursting from his body through a massive hole put in his skull.

"Game over," Clegg said.

I blacked out.

Epilogue

"Okay, we're live in five . . . four . . . three. . . ."
The producer conveyed the countdown on his fingers as well. After what I'd been through, I didn't think anything could scare me. But then I thought, *Millions of people watch* The Today Show. I pictured folks puttering about their homes, drinking coffee, getting ready for work, getting kids ready for school, with the TV on. I was about to enter many a household to share my story, and that thought put a lump in my throat and sweat on my palms.

Matt Lauer sat at the news desk with *The Today Show* logo projected numerous times on the blue screen behind him. I had whispered to Ruby, "Okay, I can see the attraction," when Lauer greeted us a few minutes before our *Today Show* exclusive interview was scheduled to air. The guy radiated magnetism, and his charm seemed homespun authentic. He made sure we had everything we needed—water, something to eat; all in all, he proved a very gracious host.

I winced as I settled myself onto the studio couch. Stab wounds like those I suffered don't heal completely in a month's time. I had spent two weeks recovering in a hospital and another two weeks at home on bed rest. My mom came out for much of that recovery period. Bless her! Nothing beats a mom when you're on the mend. I lost my spleen, and it took ten hours of surgery to stitch back all the inside parts Dobson—aka the Fiend—had punctured.

Ruby and I had gone from obscure to world famous within an ambulance ride. Meanwhile, Winnie surprised us all by taking a break from the booze to become our protector, safeguarding our privacy like a reinforced steel door. I figured Clegg would do that job, but he was off climbing somewhere. Higgins took his badge and gun pending the outcome of the internal affairs investigations, so he had plenty of time to kill. When the interview requests came—and come they did—Winnie, at our behest, declined them all. But when *The Today Show* called, I told Ruby we needed to take that one. The circle wouldn't be complete unless we did.

"You should get a suit like Matt's," Ruby had said to me before the producer's countdown began.

"So now he's Matt to you, is he?" I whispered.

Ruby smiled. "Jealous?"

I looked over at Lauer and shrugged. The light on top of camera one went red. We were live.

"And now to the story of John Bodine and Ruby Dawes, the young couple at the epicenter of the SHS Killer story, which gripped the country just four weeks ago. John and Ruby are here in studio to share their story exclusively with *The Today Show,* but first Natalie Morales reports on their harrowing ordeal."

They cut to Natalie, who gave a brief introduction, then cut to the prerecorded segment. A lot of what was filmed would be used for a *Dateline* special about the SHS Killer. The producers at NBC had done some hefty editing and in less than ninety seconds recounted for viewers Ruby's cancer, my desperate ploy to get her medication, Dobson's first contact with me, and my subsequent life of crime, which ended with me tossing Ruby out a window and Clegg killing the SHS Killer in front of hundreds of witnesses. Lauer joined us on the couch before the taped segment ended. Production people swarmed about, all frantic and fiddling, but Lauer ignored the commotion. He was too focused on us, settling our nerves and boosting our confidence. As the taped segment came to an end, a different producer did another countdown and once again we were live on air.

"John and Ruby are here in the studio now for an exclusive interview," Lauer said. "Welcome, and first of all, how are you doing?"

"Thanks, Matt," Ruby said. "We're doing much better now that John is out of the hospital."

Lauer looked at me.

"You suffered some pretty serious stab wounds," he said. "How is your recovery?"

We talked about my injuries long enough for Lauer to get squea-mish.

Lauer said, "Tell me, did you have any idea that when you were helping Henry Dobson off the ledge that he was the person respon-sible for everything that happened to you?"

"No," I said. "Absolutely not. In fact, there were a few times that I was with Dobson when the SHS Killer contacted me."

Lauer looked interested. "How is that possible? Can you tell us?" he asked.

By "us" I knew Lauer meant millions of viewers and not just the people in the studio, but somehow he made me forget about all the TV cameras.

"The first time Dobson showed up at our apartment, he was pre-tending to be an investigator from UniSol Health. He seemed official, and given what we'd done, Ruby and I weren't about to contact UniSol to verify his employment. On his way out the door, the phone rang. It was the SHS Killer, telling me that I was going to rob a liquor store next."

"But if Dobson was in the room with you, how did he make the call?" Lauer asked.

"It was a recorded voice," I said. "Dobson took out his phone, pre-tending to check a message, but he was really initiating a computer program that dialed my number and played a prerecorded message. He wanted me to think it couldn't be him. That was part of his game. He even sent me a text message while he was standing on the ledge. That was automated as well."

"So Henry Dobson was a computer expert?" Lauer asked. "Is that how he found out you stole the Uretskys' identities?"

"From what the police have told me, the real Henry Dobson was a Grade A computer hacker," I said. "He didn't work. He made his money scamming people online and spent most of his free time play-ing online games. Turns out the FBI was after him for a variety of cyber crimes, only they didn't know it was Henry Dobson commit-ting them. Dobson and Elliot Uretsky formed a friendship through a violent online game they both played, but Uretsky didn't know that Dobson wanted to live out his violent fantasies. Dobson took over the Uretskys' identities after he killed them. When I stole the Uret-skys' identities, UniSol sent an automatic e-mail to Uretsky's e-mail account, which Dobson was monitoring. That was how he found out somebody else was using the Uretskys' identities. He hacked his way into the computer systems of Post Boxes Unlimited and found out our real names and addresses."

We didn't talk about Carl Swain or Edwin Valdez. I was glad Lauer didn't ask about them. The police found their bodies cut up and stuffed into a large freezer in Dobson's basement. They also found another listening device planted in our Harvard Avenue apartment. Forensic guys later determined it was activated on the day Dobson paid us a visit after we learned of the Uretskys' murders. I had spoken to Clegg by phone about Swain and Valdez shortly after Dobson left, so that's how he knew I thought they were involved. He killed them so the police wouldn't be able to find them. He did it so that I would have more people to suspect. He did it because, in a way, they were connected to me.

"You've been through so much," Lauer said, "but I have to ask you—and I think a lot of our viewers who have been following your story have the same question—when you tossed Ruby out that fifth-story window, did you know the fire department had inflated safety mattresses? Or did you think, I'll take my chances that she'll somehow survive the fall?"

Ruby fixed me with a pointed stare. The question had been gnawing at her as well. "Yeah, sweetie, did you see the mattresses?" she asked, smiling a little.

"I had faith," I said, "faith that somebody did their job. I just believed that she'd land safely. When all this started, I didn't want to put my faith in anybody. Ruby wanted to come on *The Today Show* to plead our case, but I shot down the idea. Mountaineering taught me the virtue of self-sufficiency. But at that moment I had to put my trust, my faith, in the hands of somebody else. The biggest regret I have in all of this is that I didn't reach out to others when I needed help the most." My voice cracked a little. Ruby took hold of my hand and squeezed hard. "I'll spend my life living with that regret, and I'll do everything I can to help those who have been personally impacted by this ordeal."

Lauer gave me a moment to regain my composure.

"And how are things now?" he asked.

"Now," Ruby said, "Atrium has decided to fully fund my course of treatment. There was a huge push online to get them to change the policy once people learned of our story. I'm scheduled to have surgery next month, so hopefully between the drugs and the surgery, I'll be cancer free, and John and I can try and pick up the pieces of our lives and go from there. We want to start a family soon. We just want things to settle down first and get back to normal for us. We're hoping that will happen soon."

"Well, you're a remarkable couple with a bright future, and I wish you both the best of luck," Lauer said.

I looked over at Ruby and could tell by the look in her eyes what she was thinking.

Which songs have the phrase "best of luck" in the lyrics?

Acknowledgments

I owe a tremendous amount of a gratitude to a number of people who contributed their time, expertise, and talents to the creation of this work. Dave Trudo patiently answered my questions regarding health insurance. I could not have written John and Ruby's conundrum without his assistance. Lisa Adams not only lent her name to a character in this story, she also shared her very personal experiences that greatly influenced my portrayal of Ruby's illness. In addition, Dr. Anthony Zietman assisted with all the medical aspects of Ruby's cancer therapy. Any errors in depicting Ruby's course of treatment are exclusively my own. Lieutenant Rich Mello once again answered all my questions about police procedures. While Christopher Sloane, from Boston's Fire Investigation Unit, gave me insights I could not have gotten elsewhere.

I'm lucky to have my father, Michael Palmer, as a sounding board for my ideas. I'm equally fortunate to have wonderful readers, Judy Palmer, Clair Lamb, Phil Redman, and the team from the Jane Rotrosen Agency. This book is better from their efforts. Speaking of the Rotrosen Agency, my deepest thanks goes to Meg Ruley, agent extraordinaire who makes all of this possible. I'd also like to thank the team at Kensington, John, Laurie, Adeola, Lesleigh, and Steve. I couldn't ask for a better publisher. My friends Don and Erik deserve a shout out simply because they rock, for real.

I'm most deeply grateful to the love and support of my wife Jessica and my two children. You make every day special.